Ma'am,
Let me assure you that I ⟨...⟩ ⟨...⟩ ⟨...⟩ ⟨...⟩ ⟨...⟩ e
wiles into offering you another pe⟨...⟩ ⟨...⟩ed
piece of property.

—*Sebastian Cavenaugh*

After conventional means fail, Sebastian, Marquess of St. Just, takes reckless measures to secure that crumbling monstrosity known as Trembledown—a haven for local smugglers and moonlighting spies. He plans to scare, not seduce, its owner, but when a midnight encounter leaves them soaked, stranded, and possessing just one blanket for warmth, Sebastian, a.k.a. Robert the Brute, discovers that the widow Violet Treacher is not only willful and unafraid, she is maddeningly desirable . . .

My Lord,
Enclosed find your unsigned contract. Pray do consider your
offer as being rejected.

—*Mrs. Perceval Treacher*

Though the wilds of Cornwall hold no allure, Violet won't give the arrogant marquess the satisfaction of a sale, so here she shivers, in a wreck of a house, with lips still burning from the passion of a masked smuggler. She knows he's near—for her own bit of real estate is quite the magnet for secrets, danger, even treachery. But how will she recognize the gentleman by day . . . with only the memory of his kiss in the dark.

Praise for Alexadra Bassett's
HIS CHOSEN BRIDE

"A charming frolic of a book."—Teresa Medeiros

**"Absolutely delightful and completely charming.
I couldn't put it down."—Victoria Alexander**

Books by Alexandra Bassett

HIS CHOSEN BRIDE

MY FAVORITE MARQUESS

Published by Zebra Books

Alexandra Bassett

My Favorite Marquess

ZEBRA BOOKS
Kensington Publishing Corp.

www.kensingtonbooks.com

ZEBRA BOOKS are published by

Kensington Publishing Corp.
850 Third Avenue
New York, NY 10022

All Kensington titles, imprints, and distributed lines are available at special quantity discounts for bulk purchases for sales promotion, premiums, fund-raising, educational, or institutional use.

Special book excerpts or customized printings can also be created to fit specific needs. For details, write or phone the office of the Kensington Special Sales Manager: Attn. Special Sales Department. Kensington Publishing Corp., 850 Third Avenue, New York, NY 10022. Phone: 1-800-221-2647.

Zebra and the Z logo Reg. U. S. Pat. & TM Off.

ISBN 0-8217-7787-4

First Printing: July 2006
10 9 8 7 6 5 4 3 2 1

Printed in the United States of America

A Brief Correspondence Concerning the Sale of a Certain Property in Cornwall . . .

December 12, 1814

Mrs. Perceval Treacher
Peacock Hall
Yorkshire

My Dear Mrs. Treacher,

Pray do not think it presumptuous of me to write to you this way, with little in the way of introduction. I am the Marquess of St. Just, and I have the honor to reside at Montraffer Place, near Widgelyn Cross in Cornwall. Montraffer is a near neighbor to Trembledown, the estate that I understand came into your possession after the unfortunately premature demise of your late husband. Allow me, dear lady, to extend my belated condolences on that esteemed man's untimely parting from this life. Though I could claim no great intimacy with your husband, Percy Treacher was remarked by all who knew him to be a man possessing a sober and punctilious character as well as a remarkable kennel of hounds.

As you may or may not be aware, Mrs. Treacher, Trembledown only recently fell into the possession of your husband's family. Indeed, prior to a lamentable bet on a curricle race, the house and lands had been in the St. Just possession for many generations.

It has long been an ambition of mine to reunite the St. Just holdings of Trembledown and Montraffer. Therefore, I am pleased to inform you that I am willing to make a very generous offer for Trembledown, despite its lamentable state of deterioration.

With this intent, I have had my man of business draw up the necessary papers, which you will find enclosed. All that remains is for you to sign the sales agreement and return it to my direction. Upon its receipt, it will be my pleasure to release the funds to your man of affairs.

I trust you will believe me, madam, when I write that it gives me the utmost satisfaction to be of service to you.

Yours faithfully,
Sebastian Cavenaugh
The Marquess of St. Just

December 20, 1814

The Most Hon. the Marquess of St. Just
Montraffer Place
Cornwall

My Lord Marquess,

It was with the greatest interest and no small gratifi-
cation that I read your recent letter. Your kind words
about my late husband's character and hounds honor his
memory most fittingly.

I confess that I was wholly unaware of the history of
Trembledown and your estimable family's tenuous connection to it. That fact alone will make me appreciate my
dear Percy's legacy to me all the more.

For while I am gratified by your offer, I fear I must decline the honor you do me. In good conscience I could
not part from an estate left to me by my departed husband, at least not before viewing the property myself. I
am sure you can understand a widow's sensibilities regarding this matter. While there was—unhappily!—no
issue from our marriage to whom to pass Trembledown
as a legacy, my husband surely had my own security at
heart when he left the property to me. I am certain he
would not have wanted me parted from it for less than its
true value. A value which, despite whatever condition

your relations left it in before their unfortunate gambits with curricles, I have always heard is considerable.

I hope to visit Cornwall within the next twelvemonth. After viewing my property, I will be happy to consider negotiating a sales price with you or your representative.

I have the honor to be,

> *Your Lordship's obedient servant,*
> *Mrs. Perceval Treacher*

January 3, 1815

Mrs. Perceval Treacher
Peacock Hall
Yorkshire

Dear Mrs. Treacher,

Thank you for your swift reply to my letter of December. Alas, I must disbosom myself of a bit of confusion. It was my understanding that, to forfend an extended lawsuit, the Treacher family settled the unused property on you after your husband failed to provide for you to your satisfaction.

No doubt this was merely wicked rumor.

Nevertheless, while I am always sympathetic to a lady's sensibilities regarding her doubtless much lamented husband, I fail to see that these should still be a factor some three years after said husband's parting from this world. As for his providing for your security, you could do no better than to sell the property now, before it deteriorates further from its present condition—a state, I assure you, that has occurred since the property was acquired by the Treacher family.

Meaning no disrespect to yourself, I gleaned from your missive that perhaps your reluctance could more likely be ascribed to a desire for me to raise my offering price? If so, consider it done. I hereby raise the selling price to 10 percent over my original offer.

I am confident that this will soothe any widow's qualms you may still entertain and you will see that selling is the best choice for yourself.

> *Yours sincerely,*
> *Sebastian Cavenaugh*
> *The Marquess of St. Just*
> *Cavenaugh House*
> *London*

January 15, 1815

The Most Hon. the Marquess of St. Just
Cavenaugh House
London

Dear Lord St. Just,

I am all gratefulness at the kindness you have shown me in trying to take my estate off my hands. I only wonder why, if Trembledown is crumbling, you would want it at any price. You must have a remarkable desire to see the St. Just empire restored to its former glory.

Although I must again decline your offer, still not having seen the property with my own eyes, perhaps in the near future we may come to a mutually satisfactory arrangement regarding the estate? I notice that you are currently residing in London. I, too, shall be in town directly in order to assist in the presentation of my youngest sister. She is a very promising girl of lively temperament, and my family is naturally anxious to see her succeed. I, of course, know many esteemed personages in London, but I always believe that widening a young lady's circle of society, especially among the aristocracy, cannot but help but benefit a young lady.

Perhaps we could meet in person and discuss these matters?

Yours sincerely,
Mrs. Perceval Treacher

January 24, 1815

Mrs. Perceval Treacher
Peacock Hall
Yorkshire

Ma'am,

While I do not see the need for a personal meeting, I will agree to one if I must. However, let me assure you that I will not be manipulated by any feminine wiles into offering you another penny more for such a dilapidated piece of property. Nor have I any intention of becoming involved in any activities regarding your sister's come-out, which doubtless would benefit from the patronage of one of my station.

When you wish to proceed with the sale of Trembledown, please sign the enclosed sales agreement (that includes the very generous 10 percent mentioned in my previous epistle) and bring it with you to London. Upon your arrival, you may schedule an appointment with my secretary and we will finalize the sale at that time.

St. Just

January 28, 1815

The Most Hon. the Marquess of St. Just
Cavenaugh House
London

My Lord,

Enclosed find your unsigned contract. You may herewith consider your offer rejected.

I also regret to inform you that I no longer anticipate being in London in the near future. Your assurances of Trembledown's state of neglect, although belied by your eagerness to purchase this same shambles of an estate, lead me to believe that the house is in need of my attention. It is now my intent to travel into Cornwall immediately to view the buildings and grounds and personally see to any restoration work that might be necessary. Once any improvements have been accomplished, I will then evaluate whether I wish to sell the property or not, and to whom I wish to sell it.

> *Regards,*
> *Mrs. Perceval Treacher*
> *Peacock Hall*
> *Yorkshire*

Prologue

John Cuthbert's lips turned down grimly as he stared at Violet Treacher's latest letter, a communication which put certain plans in a bit of a coil. He picked up the missive, sending a shower of confetti spilling down on his desk blotter. "What is the mess in this last envelope? There are tiny bits of paper spilling everywhere."

Sebastian's lips flattened into a rueful expression. "I believe that is the 'enclosed contract'—she failed to mention that she had shredded it into a thousand bits before including it."

"You certainly have a shrewd way with the ladies, St. Just."

Sebastian, warming himself before the fire of Cuthbert's office, smiled in spite of this unfortunate turn of events. "That is quite a compliment, coming from you!"

Cuthbert shook his head. His stooped shoulders and perpetually funereal expression gave the impression of a man who had received a mortal blow from which he had never recovered. Happily, no such event had ever occurred.

Cuthbert was merely a sober man dedicated to his work . . . and nothing else. "It is true I give the ladies a wide berth, but that is because I have no business with them. I am fortunate in that regard."

"Life cannot be all toil."

"It can if one has the temperament for it, which I fortunately have. And because of this, and because I am a bachelor and likely to remain in the single condition for all my days, I am a happy man."

Sebastian laughed as he considered his companion's morose countenance. "A happy man? I would never have thought of you as that!"

Cuthbert lifted a long finger crooked from years of service maneuvering a pen for the Crown. "Ah, but that is where you are wrong. We eternal bachelors exist in perfect contentment because we know our lives shall never become disordered by the presence of a woman. We shall never be reduced to that state of fevered agitation known as love. Not for us the restless nights, the consuming distractions, or the clownish antics of the male in pursuit of a female. Our vocabularies will remain free of insipid words of endearment. We rest easily in the assurance that the words 'My little partridge' shall never issue from our lips."

"I, too, am a bachelor," Sebastian said, "yet I can enjoy the company of women. Some of them can be quite amusing." He cleared his throat. "In all sorts of ways."

Cuthbert regarded him sadly. "Then you are putting yourself at great risk, my friend. A man may dedicate his life to whatever he chooses—service, his family, work, God—but all women are designed to seek out husbands. It is their natural avocation, and some of them pursue it with the cunning and gusto of a Wellington."

"Ah, but they are not all successful," Sebastian rejoined. "That is the sport of it."

"But look at the ones who are." Cuthbert tapped the letter on the desk blotter before him. "Even this Treacher termagant charmed a poor fellow to taking up the harness."

Sebastian scoffed. "Percy Treacher was a fool whose only requirement for finding a wife was that she be rich, and Mrs. Treacher's father is Sir Harlan Wingate, who made a fortune in trade."

Cuthbert drummed his fingers in thought; his musings on marriage were at an end and he was back to business again. "It would seem that Montraffer and Trembledown are doomed to remain un-reunited, then. And now not only do we not have unfettered access to the Trembledown property, we shall soon have to maneuver around Mrs. Treacher's troublesome presence there."

Sebastian shook his head. "I told you that it was better to let sleeping dogs lie, John. No doubt if I had not instigated negotiations—upon your urgent request, I remind you—Mrs. Treacher would be snugly ensconced in London for the Season instead of now winging her way to Cornwall."

Cuthbert sighed. "Well, it can't be helped now."

"Do not feel too bad, John. If Mrs. Treacher does take possession of Trembledown, she will not be in residence long. I did not exaggerate when I described the dilapidated condition of the place. And from what I have heard of Mrs. Treacher, she is not the type to endure hardship for any length of time—these merchant cits are deplorably dependent upon modern comforts in their abodes. She will doubtless flee the place at the first sign of hardship."

"And if she doesn't?"

Sebastian gave his companion a rather devilish smile. "Then I will have to ensure that during her brief visit to Cornwall she encounters plenty of trouble."

"More trouble is all we need."

Both men sobered as their thoughts turned to the current political scene. For a while it had seemed that with Napoleon exiled on Elba, Europe's problems would soon be over. But here it was, almost a year later, and negotiations at the Congress were still ongoing. Not to mention, rumors abounded that in France the tide was turning against the King and antiforeigner sentiment was running high.

Now Sebastian would have to waste valuable time ensuring that Violet Treacher did not interfere with the smuggler's network operating near, and sometimes actually on, her property so that they could continue to receive such reports from France. His contact in Cornwall, Jem, would have to be alerted that Trembledown was about to be inhabited.

Cuthbert looked soberly at the stack of papers on his desk, including an intercepted letter that hinted of an existence of a spy loose in the country, code-named Nero.

Nero had made himself odious to Cuthbert during many years of the war with France. More than one of Cuthbert's men's lives had been lost as a result of this traitor. But Nero's activities had stopped with the sudden suicide of a certain nobleman whose uncle was in a position of some authority in the government. It had been assumed that said nobleman was Nero himself. Now, Cuthbert and Sebastian were wondering if they had been mistaken and Nero had only coincidentally stopped operations at the time of Lord Waring's death. After all, it had only been a short while after the disappearance of Nero that Napoleon had surrendered.

"The situation on the continent is very precarious, Sebastian. It's more important now than ever that we have an ear to the ground and that we find out who this Nero is and what he could be up to now—you'll remember he had an uncanny knack of nosing out vital information during the war. According to my sources, Nero has been instructed to head to your area and keep an eye out for a certain famed Cornish smuggler—one Robert the Brute!"

"That is quite interesting. I believe I can safely say that if Nero comes anywhere near Montraffer, I shall be there, waiting for him." Sebastian grinned. "Or rather, that blaggard Robert the Brute will be waiting."

Cuthbert shook his head. He and Sebastian did not always see eye to eye on the necessity of Sebastian's traveling about in the disguise of a smuggler—not to mention cultivating such a reputation as a cutthroat—but he had to admit that Sebastian and his connections had garnered results for the country back in the days of the war. They had also garnered a cabinet well stocked with smuggled French brandy for both of them.

"I wish you would inform the local authorities of what you are doing."

Sebastian shook his head. "What if Nero *is* one of the local authorities? There's no knowing for sure that Nero isn't already ensconced in the area. A man in uniform can turn traitor as easily as anyone else. More easily, sometimes."

"And what if one of these local constables finally takes it in his head to catch Robert the Brute?"

"That is a risk I take," Sebastian declared. "But I only take it knowing the inefficacy of the local constabulary as well as I do."

"Be careful there, Sebastian, and mind you don't get sidetracked by the Treacher woman."

Sebastian laughed. "That is unlikely."

"Temptations abound in this work," Cuthbert said, sounding decidedly curatelike. "Remember Lord Hawthorne? He was supposed to be gathering information in Paris and instead ended up besotted with an opera singer!"

"You needn't worry about anything of the kind happening

to *me*." Sebastian chuckled. "There are no opera singers in Widgelyn Cross."

Not to mention, Sebastian was nearly as averse to romantic entanglement as Cuthbert was. Especially to the type of woman—Mrs. Percy Treacher and the like—who would marry a man for his title, as his own mother had done. His parents had endured twenty gloomy years of unaffectionate matrimony before both had succumbed to rheumatic fever one winter while Sebastian was at university. Watching his father's conjugal misery had made him determined never to marry himself. There were several St. Just cousins to assume the title when Sebastian's time was up.

He kept his relations with women strictly on a business level and managed to enjoy himself in his own reserved way. Sebastian was known to be dedicated to a life among the highest *ton*. He enjoyed a well-cut coat, a spectacular piece of horseflesh, and other amusements of society. He took inordinate pride in his homes, his privileges, and his duties as a peer. No one understood custom and *noblesse oblige* better than Sebastian Cavenaugh. He was well aware of his reputation as rather cold and standoffish. In fact, he cultivated it. It made it that much easier to enjoy the double life he had made for himself, which was not only stimulating work but of great use to his country.

"A woman doesn't have to be an opera singer to be a nuisance," Cuthbert said.

"Never fear, John. By the time I am through with her, Mrs. Treacher will be happy if she never sees Cornwall, smugglers, or a marquess ever again!"

Chapter One

As the carriage and four trundled through inky darkness over the rutted moors of Cornwall, Violet thought, and not for the first time, that this journey had stretched on too long. Far too long. Agonizingly long. They were to have reached Trembledown by nightfall, but the driver, Hal, seemed to have misjudged the distance. Now the inhabitants of the carriage—herself, her manservant Peabody, and her cousin Henrietta Halsop—were all cold, hungry, and on edge.

Violet, of course, was managing to control her own travel fatigue in an exemplary fashion. (True, she had brought Hennie to tears by calling her a tiresome magpie, but that had been a full hour ago.) Peabody and Hennie, unfortunately, were showing no such restraint.

"It's so frightfully dark out!" cried Henrietta, releasing one of the dramatic moans that now seemed to come out of her with the regularity of the cuckooing of a Swiss clock. "Woe betide us all if we should be overtaken by Robert the Brute on this black night!"

Exhibiting heroic courtesy, Violet turned toward the curtain of the carriage's window so her cousin would not witness the extravagant rolling of her eyes. Hennie had been prattling on about this Robert the Brute character since they had left the last posting inn, a horrid little hole with no private parlors. There Hennie had tended to linger whilst eavesdropping on the conversation of the uncouth characters milling about. No doubt tales of this smuggler were greatly exaggerated for the benefit of an impressionable spinster. But such was the gullibility of her cousin.

Yes, it was as dark as pitch, and the fact that the road was riddled with pits and stones did nothing to soothe anyone's nerves inside the carriage. But *smugglers*? Really! Violet feared the only thing in danger of being overtaken this evening was what was left of Hennie's feeble brain.

Until recently, Hennie had resided with her great-aunt Matilda, a querulous woman who had been the greatest nipcheese of Yorkshire. When the old lady died shortly before Christmas, the family discovered that she had amassed a sizable fortune in the funds. While the house that they occupied had been entailed to her husband's great-nephew, the majority of the money went to Hennie. Some said that Matilda had only so favored Hennie to spite the nephew who, having no notion that a fortune was in the offing, had failed to ever once visit or even so much as write Matilda since her husband's death.

Thus it was that the heretofore penniless spinster, who was fast approaching forty, while currently homeless, need never worry about finances again if she was careful. Hennie was so pathetically grateful that she had ordered an extensive mourning wardrobe and planned to spend the entire year in unrelieved black—half-mourning was not good enough for such a benefactress, Hennie was fond of claiming.

As the coach hit another pothole, Peabody braced himself on the edge of the seat. Even in the darkness, Violet could make out his bulging eyes. "Did you hear that?" he quavered.

"What?" Hennie went rigid. "Was that a gunshot?"

"No—a different sound . . . more horrible . . . like that of *breaking china.*" Peabody's voice cracked. "Yes, I'm sure of it. The Limoges will be all in shatters by the time we arrive at Trembledown!"

Since the china had been scrupulously wrapped by Peabody himself, crated, and securely lashed on top of the carriage, it stretched credulity to think that one could have actually heard it breaking from where they were sitting. Violet pointed this out.

"But the road is so ill kept!" Peabody said.

"And so dark!" Hennie echoed.

Hennie and Peabody were united in their disgust with the conditions of their ride through Cornwall. From their complaints, you would think that Violet was hauling them across England by donkey cart rather than in the relative comfort of her father's well-sprung traveling coach.

"I had not reckoned on what punishment the china would have to withstand," Peabody lamented.

"Or what dangers *we* might have to withstand at the dread hands of Robert the Brute!"

Just then, Peabody gasped.

"What is it?" Henrietta cried, startled.

The manservant collapsed, clasping his hands to his head as if he were suffering the agonies of the damned.

Violet feared he was having an attack of apoplexy. "What *is* the matter?"

"The soup tureen!" he wailed.

Violet stared at the agonized figure with waning

forbearance. "Surely you cannot tell exactly what piece of china you imagine to be broken. Really, Peabody!"

"No, it is not broken." He lifted his head up with resignation, like a schoolboy ready to receive his punishment. "I—" He released a shuddering breath before confessing, "I *forgot* to pack it!"

Violet absorbed this information with astonishing equanimity. Perhaps at some point in her life such news would have thrown her into peevish displeasure. (In fact, at *any* point in her life before she had begun this wearisome voyage it would have.) But now she rated such a triviality as unimportant.

The only important thing was getting out of this blasted carriage.

"No matter," she said, trying to reassure Peabody.

Peabody mistook her indifference for remonstrance. "You see, it wasn't in the display cabinet, but in the cupboard. Things were at such sixes and sevens when all the packing was occurring . . . It was all so hurried, with your making the hasty plan for this trip . . . Please forgive me . . . There was so much to tend to . . . And then at the last minute we were forced to make room for the harp."

Hennie, who was sensitive on this issue, looked as if she were under attack. "I'm sure I never *forced* anyone to allow me to bring my harp. That I would never do. I merely pointed out that since I do feel that I am being of service by accompanying Violet on her little adventure and since my pleasures are so few . . ." She swallowed. "But of course I know I am lucky to have been asked. After all, I am nothing but a homeless spinster. I thought that if my harp could provide a few moments of enjoyment for us, it would be a partial repayment of the debt I owe Violet for the honor she does me by consenting to let me join her household."

Violet gritted her teeth—after all, Hennie could now afford an establishment of her own, but Hennie had expressed horror at the idea of herself, an unmarried lady, living alone. "It is I who am grateful to you for accompanying me, Hen. And as to your harp"—which, when plucked by Hennie, was as effective an instrument of torture as anything Torquemada had to work with—"it was no bother at all to bring it."

Actually, it had caused a great deal of trouble, and explained the presence of Peabody, who would normally be riding in the baggage coach with Violet's maid, Lettie. Hennie had objected as vociferously as she was able to the harp's being secured to the top of the carriage. Something about its tone being ruined. Violet had never been present when anything approaching a pleasing tone had ever escaped that wretched instrument, so she was skeptical of this claim. Nevertheless, Hennie was adamant, and there had been nothing for it but to place the harp inside the baggage carriage, which barely left room for Lettie. That Peabody would suffer to ride in such discomfort was out of the question.

Violet secretly hoped that the evil lyre would meet with an unfortunate accident as it was being unloaded from the baggage carriage, which, due to a broken wheel, was now almost a day behind them.

"*Nevertheless*," Peabody said, "the harp did rather confuse matters at the last minute. And that is how the soup tureen came to be left in the cabinet."

"I said it does not matter, Peabody."

"But, madame, what shall we do?"

"Do?" she snapped, finally reaching the frayed end of her last nerve. "We shall drink soup directly from the pot if we have to! Who cares? At this rate I shall count ourselves lucky if we ever get close enough to a hearth to have soup served to us in any container!"

"Indeed!" Hennie couldn't help injecting fretfully. "Especially with Robert the Brute about. They say he has waylaid carriages such as this one before!"

"*Enough.*" Violet clapped her hands like one of her tiresome old governesses. "I will hear no more of crockery and cutthroats."

Hennie nearly fainted. "Do you think he *would* cut our throats?"

Violet attempted to stifle her cousin's growing hysteria with a glare that could have cut through stone.

Difficult as it was for Violet to believe now, when she had embarked on this trip a week ago, she had been grateful to have these two accompanying her. Especially Peabody, who was her father's butler at their home, Peacock Hall, in Yorkshire. Normally the butler would be considered indispensable to her father, but this spring Sir Harlan had decided to travel to Italy. He explained his newfound mania for travel by saying that he had secretly longed to go to the continent for years, a desire now made possible because Napoleon was confined to Elba. But Violet suspected that his sudden wanderlust had more to do with his youngest daughter Sophy's first Season.

Sophy, a man-mad youth, was now loose in London— a town brimming with Corinthians, dandies, rakes, and all manner of other males, both suitable and unsuitable. Violet feared her sister would naturally lean toward the latter. No doubt contemplating the potential havoc his youngest was likely to wreak on the capital accounted for their father's sudden yearning for foreign soil.

Violet only hoped (though rather doubted) that their aunt Augusta was up to the demanding task of chaperoning such a minx.

In fact, she feared that the two of them together would just result in twice the mischief. That was one of the reasons she had so easily relinquished her plan to accompany Sophy to London and share the chaperone duties with Aunt Augusta. Chief among the other reasons was the fact that she was not quite prepared to be seen as a chaperone, the older sister (emphasis on *old*). She was not yet twenty-eight, and while that could no longer be considered the first bloom of youth, she hadn't been able to contemplate with indifference the experience of being set to the side at Almack's like that institution's notoriously stale cakes.

Then had come her correspondence with the Marquess of St. Just.

That top-lofty toad's snide remarks angered her so, nothing would have induced her to come within fifty miles of London while the insufferable creature was there. Treating her as if she were some sort of social barnacle! Indeed, it had made her want to hurry her departure to Cornwall to take care of business while she had reason to believe he was not in this area.

If she were of a charitable mind, and less cold and fatigued, she might have thanked the irritating marquess. His correspondence had started a plan spinning in her brain. After being cast out by the Treachers, she had been at loose ends, unsure of her future, wasting away her life on her father's estate in Yorkshire.

This had been especially brought home to her last summer when her other sister, Abigail, had managed to make a happier marriage than Violet had ever supposed was possible for the rather plain, reclusive, bookish spinster. But it turned out Abby hadn't been wasting her time under their father's roof. Instead she had secretly been penning successful gothic novels under the pseudonym

Georgina Harcourt. Violet had never seen their father so impressed as when he had discovered the secret. And on top of that, Abby had managed to win the heart of the only semi-eligible bachelor in the area. Not that Violet herself would have considered marrying Nathan Cantrell for one moment, but she had to admit that it looked to be a very good match for Abby, and the couple obviously doted on each other. Quite bourgeois, but rather sweet.

The whole episode made Violet realize that since Percy's death she had been frittering away her best years instead of making a new life of her own choosing. Now, thanks in part to the odious marquess, she saw a path to self-sufficiency. She would see to Trembledown's repairs, have the estate appraised by a reputable third party, and then offer it for sale. With the proceeds she could set up her own household in a more pleasant part of the world.

Once she would have set her sights on London, but not now. She had finished with attempting to break into the *haute ton* of London. Perhaps she would try Bath. If she shared a household with the newly well-off Hennie, they should be able to acquire a very nice accommodation in that quaint town.

Hennie was already eager to go there because Imogene Philbrick, an old school friend, lived in that city. Violet shuddered to think what that woman—who had been described by Hennie as "Not quite as outgoing as I"—could possibly be like. Violet had no intention of joining a tiresome band of tea-drinking, needle-working women; yet there was no reason that they could not share expenses and largely go their separate social ways. With the sale of the house in Cornwall, she would have enough money to create an impression of lavish gentility that she rated necessary for success in Bath.

As she eyed her cousin's ensemble, she noticed that

her cousin's petticoats were showing. Typical of the rather untidy Henrietta, Violet thought. Then, narrowing her eyes, she squinted to make out the color. Good heavens! Hennie had even procured black undergarments!

"I was just remembering some more of the conversation I overheard at the inn," Hennie informed them. "It's said that Robert the Brute is horribly disfigured! That's why he wears a mask."

Clearly, the smuggler had lodged in her brain.

Peabody, always interested in fashion, was unwillingly drawn in. "Always?"

"Yes, and no one, not even his most trusted associates, knows his identity. For no one who looks on his visage is allowed to live, they say!"

"Has he killed many men?" Peabody asked.

"Oh my, yes! Hundreds, according to the innkeeper at the last stop. That kind man was most concerned that we make it to Trembledown before nightfall, lest we fall into the blackguard's hands!" Hennie gazed anxiously out the window, though by now there was nothing to be seen but blackness. Clearly, they had failed to follow the innkeeper's advice and were, therefore, doomed.

"We must trust Hal hasn't taken a wrong turn and gotten us hopelessly lost. I am sure it would be easy to do so on these terrible roads," Peabody said, bringing the conversation back to *his* favorite lament.

"I can't see that the state of the roads has anything to do with the direction we are heading," Violet said.

All the same, she was annoyed that they were wandering in the dark down an unknown road, well past dinnertime. She was famished, and heaven only knew what awaited them at Trembledown. She had written the caretaker, a man by the name of Barnabas Monk, in advance of their arrival, but from his terse, barely literate reply, it sounded as if the house was not properly staffed.

"That's just my point, my dear," Hennie said. "Who can tell where we are headed in this darkness? There is no moon at all tonight. Which is when the smugglers are most active, as anyone knows!"

"I had no idea you had become the authority on Cornish smuggling."

Violet's ribbing was lost on Hennie. "I felt it my duty to listen with courtesy to the innkeeper after you had administered such a snub."

"I would hardly call it a snub to demand some service," Violet said. "That is his business, after all. If he wants to spend his days spreading tales, let him become a town crier instead of innkeeper."

What Hennie's response to this might have been was cut off by the sound of a loud boom and the whinnying of horses as the carriage came to a jarring halt. Violet was thrown from the seat and landed on the floor with her skirts around her waist, revealing a shocking amount of leg that she was helpless at first to wrestle back under her garments.

Just as Hennie and Peabody were reaching down to assist her, the door to the carriage was thrown open.

Expecting to see her coachman, Violet began remonstrating. "Really, Hal, what is the problem? I am going to be black and blue tomorrow and I have torn a new pair of stockings!"

"I regret the damage, milady."

The gruff, sarcastic voice, barely intelligible through a thick Cornish accent and attended by a mocking bow, *was not* that of the faithful old Wingate groom. Violet looked up and felt her jaw go slack. The carriage's exterior lamps clearly showed the person leaning into the carriage to be a giant beast of a man—tall and unkempt—with a fiendish leer on his horrid mouth.

"Seldom 'ave I seen a more worthy set of gams encased by France's finest silk." He ogled the leg once more and then looked into Violet's face.

Another moan fluttered out of Hennie, and Peabody's audible gulp very nearly shook the carriage. Violet managed to remain silent, though she felt herself drawing back against the seat and a deep trembling begin in the marrow of her bones. Their intruder's scruffy boots, dirty buckskins, and lamentable coat alone would have been enough to cause her to recoil. Likewise, the shining black barrel of the pistol that was pointed at her would have excused the swooning sensation in her head. But, amazingly, these things she noted only with the briefest horror. Indeed, they seemed trivial next to the mask that was covering some half of the stranger's face.

Good heavens! *Could it be . . . ?*

"Robert the Brute." Hennie and Peabody breathed together.

The man swept off his hat and treated them all to another mocking bow. His disguise gave him the appearance of a sinister masquerader. "At your service." He stepped into the carriage and slammed the door closed after he had bellowed at the driver to get moving.

"Remember!" he shouted. "My pistol is trained on your charges!"

He grasped a gaping Violet and yanked her onto the seat next to him. Across from them, Hennie and Peabody were clinging to each other, quaking.

The jolt she received on hitting the seat shook Violet out of her momentary stupor. What was going on here? "Just what do you think you are doing in my carriage? Get out at once!" She leaned to the window to shout for

Old Hal to pull over but felt her arm wrenched by the intruder. She winced.

When he spoke, his horrible growl had an acid edge of formality. "Sorry to trouble you, Highness, but recent events have made it necessary for me to depart this vicinity in a bloody hurry."

Hennie, who had had practice deciphering both the Cornish accent and the ways of smugglers at the inn, assessed the situation more quickly than the rest of them. "Excise men?" she asked breathlessly, flaunting her newly acquired expertise.

The man smiled at the older woman's knowledgeable guess. "Just so, ma'am. I am afraid I parted ways from my horse, and the tidesmen were closing in on me. Imagine my relief to see your carriage lumbering over the hill!"

"Oh yes! That was very fortunate indeed." In response to Violet's dagger stare, Hennie added quickly, "Fortunate for you, that is."

But Violet could tell she was inordinately pleased to have guessed right about the excise men.

"Fine," Violet said. "We have traveled some way now, so perhaps you wouldn't mind removing your person from my carriage?"

He shook his head, his wolfish teeth glinting in the dark. "Not so fast, Highness. Unless I miss my guess, this coach is liable to be stopped at any minute by people searching for me. Naturally, I expect you to deny seeing me."

"Of course we will," Peabody assured him. "Anything you say, Mr. . . . Brute."

"Yes, it would never occur to us to do our civic duty by revealing your dastardly whereabouts to the rightful authorities," Hennie added.

Just then the carriage began to slow speed and the three hostages exchanged fearful glances. "Remember, not a word about my presence, or the consequences could be unpleasant." The Brute snatched Peabody's lap rug and threw it over himself as he placed himself on the floor at Violet's feet. His head rested on her lap and his arms came around her waist.

"Get your filthy hands off me!" Violet exclaimed. She pushed ineffectually against the distressingly muscular arm encircling her waist, but she desisted the moment the muzzle of his gun pressed into her right rib cage. Her heart, which in the first shocking moments of the carriage being overtaken had seemed to stop beating altogether, now raced uncontrollably. Was he just holding them captive to hide from the government men? Surely. If they did as he said, he would have to let them go.

Wouldn't he?

"Now remember, I have no desire to hurt the lady, but I will if necessary," the man growled from his hiding place. Feeling his hot breath against her leg made nausea rise up in Violet's throat.

How could this be happening? Would he really kill her?

"Oh, Violet! You are certain to be Robert the Brute's latest victim!" Hennie whispered in a horror-stricken voice.

"*Shh!*" Violet hissed, annoyed that her cousin's words had exactly mirrored her own thoughts.

The carriage was at a complete standstill, and they could hear voices consulting with Hal. Then there was a knock on the door, and a young man in uniform appeared. The lantern he shined inside the carriage made them squint like mice whose nest had been disturbed. God knew how they must have appeared to the man. Violet could hardly stand to look at the pale, stricken faces of her companions for fear of breaking down herself.

The officer, however, seemed to sense nothing amiss. He sent them a genial bow. "I am Captain Smythe, ma'am. I am sorry to bother you ladies, but a rather serious criminal has been spotted in the area. I was wondering if you had noticed anything outside your window that struck you as unusual this evening."

"No, sir!" they all chimed together.

"We certainly have not seen Robert the Brute!" Hennie assured him loudly.

The gun pressed more tightly into Violet's flesh. In response, she gave her cousin a swift kick.

Hennie bleated.

Captain Smythe frowned. "Robert the Brute?"

Nervous laughter burbled out of Hennie. "Did I say that name? Oh, well . . . I-I just assumed that anyone depraved enough to stop our coach would be a master criminal." She squeaked, "Not that anyone *did* stop our coach, of course. And not that I ever have personally laid eyes on the man. Heavens, no!"

The captain eyed her steadily. "You might thank your stars for that, miss. There's no greater villain about on these moors than the Brute."

A keening moan caught in Hennie's throat.

Feeling the hard iron pressing against her ribs, Violet hastened to add, perhaps too brightly, "My cousin was given an earful of your local lore at the last posting house. She has quite an active imagination."

"I see," the captain said slowly.

"Yes, indeed," Hennie assured him. "Naturally I have no *personal* knowledge of what that half mask he wears looks like . . . or the way his eyes gleam evilly from it."

Violet hitched her throat in warning.

"Not but that he mightn't be *perfectly charming* if he were dressed properly and not so terribly disfigured," Hennie went on. "I always think tall men look so distinguished, don't you, Captain?"

The captain actually seemed to be pondering the question. "As to that . . ."

"Not that any of us have personal knowledge of the man's height," Peabody interrupted, giving Hennie a pinch.

"No!" Hennie agreed. "Or anything else about him, for that matter."

"As my cousin says, Officer," Violet said, cutting her cousin off before she got them all killed, "we have seen nothing this evening, and we are anxious to reach home."

The soldier turned from looking mistrustfully at Hennie and held up his lantern a little higher as he focused on Violet. She responded by smiling brightly, hoping she did not appear half as petrified as she felt.

The officer returned her smile and leaned toward her with just the slightest hint of flirtation. "Where have you come from?"

"Yorkshire."

She felt the arms around her waist tighten and prayed that the officer could not see the trickle of sweat gathering on her brow.

Smythe seemed impressed. "That is a long way. I'm sorry you are not able to see our countryside at its best at the moment." He laughed. "I daresay you can't see it at all!"

The three of them chimed in with nervous laughter.

"It *is* a dreadful evening, is it not?" she asked him. "So cold and damp! I don't know how you brave men endure it night after night."

The officer positively glowed.

Violet batted her eyes at the man and asked breathlessly, "Would it be all right for us to proceed now? I am sure you understand our desire to seek the fires of home."

"Of course, no trouble at all, miss. I am only sorry that I

have had to delay you this evening. If you will just provide me with your name and direction you can be on your way."

"I am Violet Treacher. This is my cousin Henrietta Halsop, and we are on our way to my late husband's estate of Trembledown."

The villain's grasp on her tightened, and she had to work hard not to let panic show in her face. Was she not supposed to tell the officer *her* name, either? If only Smythe would leave!

But at the same time, the thought of his leaving caused another panic to sweep through her. What if he left and the smuggler killed them all? There was no telling . . .

"I heard that the new mistress was expected any day now," Smythe replied with agonizing casualness. "Everyone in Widgelyn Cross is looking forward to meeting you. Trembledown has been uninhabited a long time. Stirred quite a bit of interest when it came out 'twas a lady was to take over the property, as you might imagine. Rather unusual, that."

Violet smiled tightly. Couldn't the fool man see that this was not a time for discussion of freehold property?

"But I dare say the place could use a lady's touch after all these years. You'll be very welcome in Widgelyn Cross, I'm sure."

"It is nice of you to say so," she said, her heart in her throat. "My cousin and I are looking forward to making the acquaintance of local society." Could she really be sitting with a gun trained on her person as she made such ladylike, and such inane, small talk?

"I only hope that we shall actually be in the position to meet local society!" Hennie worried aloud.

Fortunately, Captain Smythe was no longer paying much attention to Hennie. He only had eyes for Violet . . . but could he not see the desperation in her face?

"Oh, there's not a doubt of it, ma'am," he said. "Everyone is very friendly here. I myself am stationed in the village quite nearby. "He looked at Violet hopefully. "I hope that I shall have the pleasure of seeing you again soon."

The cold steel bit harder into her skin.

"Th-that would be lovely." Violet chirped. "But now, I am sure you will understand my hurry . . ."

"Certainly." The man looked disappointed to have their *tête-à-tête* brought to a conclusion, but he finally stood back and slammed the door of the carriage shut.

Old Hal immediately whipped the horses, and they were off.

Gun or no gun, Violet grabbed the smuggler's hand, which had come to rest just under her bosom (not by accident, she would wager), and gave him a shove. She yanked the lap robe away from him. "There, you are safe. Now kindly get away from me, you cretin!"

The man laughed and gave her waist a last, lingering squeeze before getting up and settling on the seat next to her. His gun, she could not help noticing, remained trained on her.

"Put that thing away before you hurt someone. There is surely no need for it now that you have escaped the dreaded excise men."

The man grinned and, quite surprisingly, did as she asked, tucking the weapon back into his jacket. "I must congratulate you on ridding us of that pesky ass, *Mrs. Treacher."* He seemed to take great amusement in her name.

"Yes, indeed, Violet," Hennie piped up. "You behaved wonderfully. You may not have noticed, but *I* was just the teensiest bit nervous."

Robert the Brute sneered. "Were you now?"

Hennie nodded. "At one point I was almost afraid that I had said too much!"

"Impossible!" the Brute said with broad sarcasm. "The soul of discretion, you were."

Violet asked sweetly, "And now, sir, where may we drop you?"

"Oh, just a few miles up the road. "The Brute winked at her. At least it looked like a wink; it was hard to be sure with that mask.

Those few miles seemed to take a lifetime. For the first time in over a week of travel, Peabody and Hennie were both blessedly silent. *I should have picked up a fugitive days ago*, Violet told herself with rising hysteria.

The Brute continued to stare at her as the carriage rattled along, until Violet thought she might scream. Those eyes, that leer, that mask! Not to mention the sheer bulk of him. It was affecting her strangely, making her flush. It had been so long since she had . . . well, bodily contact . . . with a man. And never had any person of the opposite sex looked at her with such frank interest.

Finally, when Violet thought she could take the smuggler's grinning presence not a moment longer, the man banged on the roof for Old Hal to halt.

After he descended from the carriage, he took Violet's hand as if to kiss it good-bye. Violet was so relieved at this sign of his departure that she made no protest, but then he tugged strongly on her arm and had her to her feet. When she resisted, he reached over and lifted her bodily from the carriage. A sharp cry escaped her lips, and the carriage's other inhabitants squawked in protest. Peabody lunged and grabbed her sleeve, so that for a moment there was the briefest tug-of-war between the two men, with Violet playing the role of rope.

The Brute won, and held her before him like a cumbersome trophy.

"Just what do you think you are doing?" Violet demanded.

"Taking you with me as insurance, you might say."

As the words sank in, Violet went cold with fear. "Y-you can't seriously be planning to abduct me?"

"Can I not, Mrs. Treacher?" He then dumped her to the ground and barked at Peabody. "You there, grab that hat with the black veiling and come here."

Peabody appealed to Violet. At her nod, he reluctantly approached them.

"Tear the veil off the hat and tie it around your mistress's hands. I don't want any trouble from her."

"I am so sorry, ma'am," Peabody said as he ripped at the hat. At the rending sound, Hennie began to weep—she had been quite proud of this particular bonnet. Peabody then tied Violet's hands together—much too tightly, Violet thought crossly. But then, Peabody had always been a stickler for following directions to the letter.

"Now get back into the carriage," the Brute barked at Peabody. "If you want to see your mistress again alive, you will head directly for Trembledown and await her there. *Without* notifying the authorities. If all goes well this evening, she will be returned to you in a few hours."

Hours? Just the past thirty minutes seemed to have crawled by like months. How was she ever to survive *hours* with this ruffian?

Then again, what choice did she have?

Peabody and Old Hal looked mutinous at these strictures and Violet feared that they would head straight back toward the government men. She had no doubt that in that case the man would be as good as his word and kill her.

Robert the Brute yanked her arm.

"Do as he says, Peabody," she blurted out. "If I am not home by tomorrow morning, you have my permission to call in the authorities. But don't worry, I am sure I will see you there long before then." Violet gave them all a wobbly smile.

The heroic effect of this speech was spoiled when the smuggler grabbed her elbow and she tripped as he jerked her off the road. Violet threw several longing glances back toward the carriage, the confines of which she had been so eager to escape not so long ago. She squinted in the darkness, eager to keep her eye on the last connection to her life.

She felt a pang of remorse mixed with the numb fear and awful uncertainty churning inside her. What she wouldn't do now to be back in the carriage, listening to Hennie and Peabody's tedious prattle! But within moments she lost sight of both the carriage and her companions as the heavy paw of her captor dragged her along in the direction of the sea, and her uncertain fate.

Only Hennie's voice drifted out through the darkness to her, carried on the wind. "Whatever you do, Violet dearest, do not disturb his mask! Remember, to look upon Robert the Brute's face is certain death!"

Chapter Two

Her captor's gloved claw shackled Violet's arm as he tugged her over the rough terrain. The smell of the sea grew sharper by the moment, and yet it felt to her as if they would never reach the water. Instead, the vast ocean seemed to send a stinging wind as its surrogate. The damp cold cut right through her cape and dress, and the salty air pierced each of the thousand little scrapes she had already accumulated since being dragged away from the carriage.

Exhaustion and fear raged in her. She could not say if she had been stumbling along for twenty minutes or two hours. It seemed like an eternity to her already. Her legs were numb, her feet hurt, and the crazy pounding of her heart would not abate.

Where was the Brute taking her? Worse, what did he intend to do with her when they got there?

Perhaps it was just as well that she had only been half listening to Hennie's yammering about the notorious smuggler. No doubt ignorance was bliss, given her current situation. Still, she couldn't help recalling that *death* had featured prominently in her cousin's tales of terror.

And in the back of her mind, she wondered what other atrocities the man was capable of.

Certainly the fact that he was nicknamed *the Brute* did not speak comfortingly for his character or bode well for her own prospects.

She cursed as a sharp stone—not the first—penetrated the sole of her left shoe. When she had dressed that morning, she could not have anticipated that her footwear would need to stand up to jagged rock and this-tles. It felt as if she had set out on a breathless country hike in dancing slippers. A persistent throb had taken up residence in her left big toe.

If she did not remove her shoe, she would spend the rest of her life hobbling about like an old gouty man. Up until the last few minutes she had been too paralyzed with fear to protest the pace he set, but fatigue and pain were starting to surpass fright. She was so tired that a reckless part of her no longer cared what Robert the Brute thought.

When they came across a largish boulder, she dug in her sore heels, bringing them to a dead stop. The Brute swung around, nearly yanking her arm out of its socket. She winced but managed to suppress the squeal of pain that was in her throat.

"What do you think you're about?" he growled at her, pronouncing the word *you* with such a thick Cornish accent that it sounded like "yow." Really, the man was barely intelligible at times. "We're not out here to enjoy a night stroll, Highness. There's nae time to rest."

She lifted her chin and glared at him. Murderous rep-utation be damned. She was not going to cower before this bully. "I am taking off my shoe to remove a stone."

"You'll stop when I say."

"Oh, really?" she barked back at him. "That's fascinating—because it appears to me that we *are* stopped, and I don't recall asking *yowr* permission."

The man's mouth dropped open at her audacity and then quickly clamped shut. For a moment Violet feared that he would deliver a blow to her. Instead, he muttered a curse at her and then roared, "Be quick!"

Hopping on one sore foot, she sank against the boulder and wrestled her shoe off her foot, a task that would have been easier had her hands not been tied. She shook a small quarry of stones onto the ground as her captor sighed and fidgeted. Her toe felt immense relief to be free of its torment, though she of course would have to put the shoe on again. There was no way she could scrabble about this countryside with bare feet.

She reluctantly bent to secure her shoe once more.

"Quickly, damn you!"

She narrowed her eyes on the savage. "If I do not buckle my shoe, I will stumble all the more, thereby slowing you down even further in the long run." When the tilt of his head let her know he didn't give a jot for her reasoning, she said hotly, "If you're in such a hurry, you should not have dragged a lady with you!"

"Would that I hadn't!" he shot back.

Her sentiments exactly. He could have as easily taken Old Hal or Peabody, but no, he had taken *her*, and she was not some big lummox who could walk for miles and miles without rest.

Not to say that Peabody was a lummox. And indeed, she wouldn't wish this misfortune on Peabody or Hal. But she was so tired, and hungry, and she felt so unlucky, a little self-pity was difficult to resist. Why did things never seem to go right for her?

"Be done, now!" the ogre yelled at her over the wind whipping around them.

That wasn't helping things, either. The biting wind caused her eyes to squint shut at times. If she died on this night, she decided it would almost be a mercy, because she shuddered to think what result all this cold salt air would have on her complexion. Small wonder all the locals at the last carriage stop had appeared so leathery!

"Get up now, Highness," the man said, grabbing her arm once again.

She attempted to shrug him off. "If you're in that much of a hurry, you can always leave me here. Just point the way to Trembledown and I'll be happy to continue on without your escort!"

"Thank you for your consideration, but I'm not as yet ready for us to part." The man shook his head. "Haven't you finished yet?"

"I have to do my other shoe. It's not such an easy task when my hands are literally tied. If you would care to untie me, I could make faster work of the job."

A smirk touched the man's lips, and he made a show of kneeling at her feet. "Allow me, Highness!" He yanked her shoe off and shook the pebbles out of it. Then he shoved the shoe back on her foot so fast the whole exercise seemed to have been executed in one economical, uninterrupted motion.

Yet when it came to fastening the shoe, he suddenly started to linger about the task, taking an excessive amount of time to see that it was on her foot securely. After buckling it, his hand closed around her ankle. Sensation shot up her leg; Violet was breathless. Despite the coolness of the evening and the sharp wind, she felt too warm. As she looked into the face of her captor, his eyes glinted. She could not discern their color, exactly, because they were obscured by the mask and the dark. Yet the leather mask itself, which had seemed so grotesque by the light of the carriage lamps, now gave him a rather roguish appearance.

Good heavens, what an odd feeling this gave her, alone in the dark with this strange beast's hand about her leg. How long had it been since anyone had touched her there . . . or had anyone ever? When was the last time she had even been alone with a man?

When he spoke, it was in a gravelly purr. "What a neat ankle you have, Highness."

He moved his hand slowly up to her calf and was continuing toward her knee when Violet came to her senses. Disgust—with him, with herself—welled in her, and she delivered a swift kick to his chest. To her delight, the man toppled backward. She was tempted to make a mad dash for freedom, but no sooner had she stood than Robert the Brute jumped up and clamped his hand about her.

"I should tear you apart for that!"

"I would have done the same to any gentleman who manhandled me so!" she fired back.

"Aye, but *I'm* not a gentleman," he said, tightening his grip on her.

Something in his tone, and the threat of his bulk looming over her, caused fear to quiver through her once again. Perhaps she had been a tad bit rash in kicking the man. She swallowed against the dry lump of fright in her throat. "Let us just forget about it, shall we? The sooner we get to where you want to be, the sooner I can make my way back home. As you promised."

To her immense relief, the man seemed to retreat a step from her. He shook his head. "Sure you really wish to return to home, are you now? Perhaps you're of a mind to go adventuring wi' me. I'm always on the lookout for a sassy wench with pretty ankles."

"You disgust me!" Violet exclaimed.

Her tormentor gave out an exaggerated sigh of regret. "So be it. You don't know what you're missing, Your Highness."

"Then I shall just have to muddle along the best I can in ignorance," she sniped, though the thunderous look he sent her made her regret answering back at all.

After another fifteen minutes of rough terrain, the ground suddenly began to dip sharply, and the air was thick with the sound of waves slapping the not-too-far-away shore. Violet glanced up from the rocky terrain at her feet for a moment and suddenly there it was—a vast plain of water with caps of white illuminated by the stars on this moonless night. It should have been beautiful, yet now its dark expanse seemed frightening.

The angle of the descent didn't make her walk any easier—and her shoes were now filled with both pebbles and sand. A new torment. Every time she stumbled in the dark, she could sense Robert the Brute's amusement. When she fell to her knees and let out one of her father's favorite oaths, she actually heard him snicker. His laughter infuriated her. Was that why he'd taken her hostage, so he could humiliate her?

The sound of that laughter made bile rise in her throat. Why her? What had she ever done to deserve this? Had she not endured enough abuse in her life; did she have to stand for a dirty smuggler's derision as well?

Back in school she had been laughed at because her father was in trade and had purchased his knighthood after becoming rich. During her Seasons in London, she had also sensed the sneers. Everyone assumed that any man interested in a woman of such undistinguished birth would simply be looking to scare up a fortune for himself. And when Violet discovered after her marriage that those whispers had proved 100 percent correct, she had sworn she would comport herself in such a way that no man would dare look down on her.

And yet here was a ruffian beast, laughing at her!

She was so consumed with her thoughts that she failed at first to notice that her tormentor had led them onto a rise of land that sloped gently down to a cove. The damp sand beneath her feet made walking more difficult. Pulling her by her elbow, the Brute steered her to a boulder.

"If you care a farthing for your life, you'll stay quiet," he warned, pushing her down to a seated position.

"What are we doing here?" she asked.

His lips turned up in a sneer. "Don't follow directions very well, do you?"

"I only wanted to know."

"We're waiting on . . . friends. And they aren't such gentle folk as I, Highness, so you'd best do as I say and keep your pretty lips buttoned."

As she placed her tied hands to her right side in order to steady herself, she noticed that the rock she perched on was covered in some sort of slime. So much for this, her favorite carriage dress. Though maybe it was just as well, since the matching shoes were undoubtedly ruined as well.

"Perhaps it would be best if you let me go now," she suggested after a moment. "After all, I'm only apt to get in your way."

"Not a chance," he sneered.

"But—"

He swooped down till he was inches from her. "I said *quiet!*"

The ferocity of his hot breath on her face shut her up.

As the minutes dragged by with the smuggler staring distractedly out to the sea and not speaking, Violet began to grow yet more anxious. What, and who, were they waiting for? Was there a more sinister reason why he hadn't let her go before now?

As she scanned the beach around her, it occurred to her how alone they were. He could do anything to her, and who was to intervene on her behalf? Of course, she'd known this as they had trudged along, had in fact spent the first minutes in blind terror, but somehow when they were moving she had been focused on her discomfort and was able to not think about what might lie at the end of this trek.

The smuggler took a few steps toward the shoreline, and Violet glimpsed a light being flashed—like some sort of signal. There was a boat out there.

She began trying to piece the situation together and was dismayed by the picture she came up with. Robert the Brute must be meeting up with the rest of his gang of smugglers—his friends, as he had called them. The ones that weren't as nice as he was.

She shuddered. Why didn't the Brute want to be rid of her already? It would take her a long time to find her way to Trembledown. He and his smuggler friends would be miles from here by the time she could locate a constable.

Then a terrible, startling thought occurred to her— what if the Brute had no intention of letting her go? What if he was planning on taking her along to meet up with his merry band?

"I am always on the lookout for a sassy wench with pretty ankles," he had said.

She shivered as she remembered his hand on her leg— she thought he had been joking about not wanting to let her go, but what if he wasn't? What if he was some sort of flesh peddler? She had read accounts of women being abducted and taken to far-flung reaches of the earth, never to be heard from again!

Or perhaps—a thought that turned her blood cold—he would just allow his band of outlaws to use her for their own pleasure!

Good Lord, she grumbled to herself, *I'm beginning to have thoughts as lurid and melodramatic as Hennie's.*

It was past time that she took control of this situation. She had no intention of going quietly to a fate commonly referred to as worse than death at the hands of a bunch of criminals. She scanned the area desperately. The hills they had just stumbled down would take her forever to climb back up. Catching her would be as easy as chasing a lame sheep. The sea, of course, would be certain death, since she could not swim well at all. The cliffs farther along the shoreline looked impossible to scale.

Then, lo and behold, she spotted a dark opening in the rocks . . . a cave!

And so near! It was not more than ten yards away and looked to have a wide entrance. Perhaps it was deep enough that she could hide herself until Robert the Brute sailed away with his cohorts.

Violet was careful to make as little noise as possible, though with the sounds from the ocean, she doubted that the Brute would hear her—if he would only keep his back turned for five minutes! The cave had seemed close, a mere dash, but her feet sank into the sand, making for slower going than she anticipated. And yet she made it— and her captor was so involved in the message blinking from out at sea that she managed to elude him.

Once she stepped foot inside the mouth of the cave, a rank odor stopped her cold. If she had thought the rock she was sitting on had been slimy, this place was positively grotesque with ooze! Still, it was either the cave . . . or the

Brute. Violet willed herself to not think about bats, spiders, or whatever else might be lurking and slipped farther inside.

The darkness was complete. She literally couldn't see her hands in front of her face—and she was wearing what had once been white gloves! She picked her way inside gingerly, her bound arms probing ahead of her in the blackness. As the floor seemed relatively level, she began to move more quickly. After about ten feet, the chamber broke off into two directions. Violet veered right and promptly hit a wall. She retraced her steps and went the other way until she made it back to the fork.

It seemed to her that the cave's pathway was leading her up, as if it might eventually stop toward the top of the hill. She had read that some of the caves in Cornwall were intricate—had been made so by years of smugglers. As she came to another fork, she thought she might have stumbled upon such a one. With any luck, Robert the Brute would never find her in here . . . even if he did notice that she was no longer sitting obediently on his slimy rock.

She huddled in the darkness, working at the bonds that tied her hands. Who would have guessed tulle could be so strong! Finally, she edged toward the wall, which she had been trying to avoid, since it was the walls that no doubt housed spiders and other undesirable creatures. She felt along it for a moment, and when she hit a sharp rock jutting out, she began to work the knot Peabody had tied against it. Lord, he had done an expert job. If she ever saw Peabody again . . .

If. A heavy lump formed in her throat. She couldn't let herself think that way. She *would* see him again. Soon. And when she did, she would be kind and understanding and listen uncomplainingly to his worries about soup tureens . . .

After she gave him a piece of her mind for tying this infernal knot so tightly!

It took her some time, but finally the material was rent and her hands were free. Free! She would never take the use of her arms for granted again. Indeed, she swore to herself that if she ever got away from Robert the Brute, she would dedicate herself to making the most of each precious moment of freedom.

She heard something behind her and tensed. The noise wasn't footsteps, exactly, so much as the sound of some- one splashing toward her. She took a step herself and suddenly realized that water had seeped into the cave and now covered the floor. The bottom of her skirt was soaked. She had been so preoccupied with freeing her hands . . .

Just then, she hit another wall. Blast! She would have to backtrack again.

But what if she backtracked right into her pursuer? It was so dark, she would not know if he was inches from her.

She thought she had carefully noted each turn she had taken on the way in, but now the cave began to seem like a hopeless maze. Her head felt muddled, and the rising tide, presently hitting her at midcalf, made movement all the more difficult. There was no way to get her bearings, and she worried that going back the way she had come would simply lead her back to Robert the Brute.

And she was right.

"Stop at once!" His voice echoed through the darkness at her. "We've got to get out of this cave before the tide comes all the way in!"

Ha! Like she was such a fool as to believe *him*. Al- though the water *was* getting higher, she noticed. But the cave was also leading to higher ground, so hopefully she would make it to a chamber that was above the tide mark. As she heard her pursuer's foot splashes growing closer, she quickly chose to veer off to her left.

Fortunately, it sounded as if the Brute had continued on past this tunnel. She increased her pace. The water was to her knees here, which was cause for worry. What if she *did* become trapped?

As if in mocking reply to that question, she hit another wall. She would have to make her way out to the main passage and hope that she could avoid the smuggler in the dark. For all she knew, he was as turned around as she was by now, or had even passed her. She just might be able to return to the beach and make good her escape.

But as she took two steps back toward the mouth of the cave and fell into hip-deep water, she knew she would never make the beach. She had to turn in the direction taken by Robert the Brute and hope that he wouldn't notice her in the dark.

She scooted as close as she could to the side of the passage and started to move cautiously forward.

Sebastian detected the slight swishing of water as Violet crept closer to him, though he could not judge for certain how close. So, like a cat waiting to pounce, he held his breath and stood perfectly still.

He couldn't believe she had fled to this cave, a disgusting place, in order to escape him! His disguise as Robert the Brute must be more fearsome than he'd imagined. Which was ironic, considering that he feared he had given himself away as a gentleman countless times. At any rate, he doubted a real smuggler would have been able to resist the urge to club Violet on her pretty head.

He had only achieved that feat by summoning a wellspring of forbearance he had never dreamed he had inside himself. It also helped to be able to yell at her.

And to think he had found her merely irritating in those letters!

He still wasn't sure what had prompted him to kidnap the woman. It was only desperation that had made him stop her vehicle. He had been playing decoy this evening, leading the excise man as far away from Jem and his boat as was possible when he had suddenly lost his horse and become cut off. It had seemed providential when he'd spotted a carriage foolishly lumbering along the quiet road after dark. It was true that he didn't want the carriage turning around and going to the authorities before he had a time to meet up with the boat from France; he hadn't been entirely certain how he was going to manage that without taking a hostage. But it was only when he realized that the carriage he had blundered into belonged to none other than Violet Treacher, his letter-writing nemesis, that his decision had been made. What could be a better introduction to her new neighborhood than being kidnapped by a smuggler?

Maybe it would make her appreciate the benefit of selling him that wretched property of hers.

But Mrs. Treacher was proving to be troublesome in more than just her unwillingness to part with her late husband's estate. In fact, she had fouled things up completely. Thanks to her, he was now chasing after her instead of making contact with the boat from France. Instead of trying to glean from Jem any information that had slipped across the Channel recently, he was hip deep in mucky water hoping to catch a foolish woman.

Consequently, he had never felt more of a chucklehead himself. Or more angry. So far his dealings with Violet

Treacher always seemed to end with his feeling the fool. He wondered briefly whether *she* was somehow doing this on purpose to task him. Maybe she had guessed his true identity and was acting like an exasperating twit on purpose. Could she be that deceitful?

At last he heard the sounds of Violet's breathing, and he knew she was close. The water was so high now it was going to be a near thing for them to make it to the safe room before they drowned, he realized. This thought steeled his determination. At the precise moment that she came abreast of him, he reached out and hauled her to him.

She let out a bloodcurdling scream—Sebastian was unsure of whether he would ever hear in his left ear again—and began flailing her arms at him. Landing some significant blows, moreover. How the hell had she managed to get her hands free?

"Let me go, you-you-you *brute*!"

He tried to keep her at arm's length as he bowed his head mockingly. "Robert the Brute, at your service."

"The only service you could render me is to drown or have your brains blown out by your fiendish cutthroat friends!"

He gritted his teeth. After all, she did have some right to be angry. "We will both drown if you don't come with me."

"I'd rather die than follow you a step!"

"Fine." Taking a breath, he dipped his knees quickly and positioned his shoulder at her waist. Then he lifted up again, hoisting her like a sack of potatoes. He managed the lift easily, though soaking wet she seemed twice as heavy as she had on dry land. She let out an astonished shriek.

"Sorry, Highness, but there be no time to waste." He waded hurriedly toward a cavern that he knew would be above the tide level. After her initial screaming, Violet was surprisingly quiet. No doubt she was plotting her next move. He wondered if he should confess his identity to her and explain the situation as rationally as he could.

But that would be placing a great deal of trust in a woman who, all things considered, he trusted not one whit. And only Jem and Cuthbert knew the identity of the Brute. His disguise was essential to him now, essential perhaps even to the security of England. He was not sure a woman like Violet would be able to grasp this.

The last few feet towards the safe chamber were steep and he was worn out by the time he crossed the threshold. He dumped his load to the ground quite unceremoniously.

As Violet's posterior made sudden and jarring impact with the cold rock of the floor, she quickly found her voice again.

"Oaf! I think you've broken my back!"

"That's not your 'back' I tossed you down on. If anything, you've busted your a—"

"I'll thank you to keep a civil tongue in your head!"

Sebastian laughed, then made his way to a corner, where he went about striking flint to light the candle stored there. Within moments, the small flame illuminated the chamber.

Judging from Violet's expression, the lady would have preferred to remain in darkness. The chamber was not appealing. It was about eight feet square. In the corner stood the table that contained the candlestick he'd lit, along with a small keg. Sebastian shook it and was relieved to find that it was not empty. At least they wouldn't go thirsty.

He reached inside his coat and pulled out a flask that he proceeded to fill from the keg. Unable to resist, he took a long sip before setting it down on the table. God, that tasted good. He had needed a good slug of something after the day he'd had. He started to unfasten his shirt.

His companion had remained quiet during the first part of his activities, but as he began to unbutton his shirt she squawked, "What are you doing?"

"Undressing. I advise you to do the same."

"*What?*"

"Unless you want to catch your death of a cold. There's a blanket in the corner over there."

She gaped at him in astonishment mixed with more than a little trepidation. "If you think I am going to remove my clothes in your presence, you must have bats in your head!"

Given what such a lady must think of the intentions of a blackguard like Robert the Brute, he could not help but be startled by, and not a little admiring of, her fire. "God knows this whole enterprise makes me doubt my own wisdom, Highness. I might be crazy, but I feel bound to share the one blanket with you, though you've been naught but a nuisance. But I have no intention of letting you get the blanket soaked, so if you don't remove that sodden gown, I will personally strip it from your pretty backside."

"You wouldn't dare!"

"On the contrary, it would be my pleasure to undress you." He aimed a leering grin at her. "Is that what you wish, perhaps?"

Her mouth opened and closed, giving her the appearance of an outraged, beached fish.

He chuckled. "I know that for certain gentlewomen this could be a fantasy come true. Alone with a dashing stranger . . ."

"You flatter yourself!"

"Do I?" He rubbed thoughtfully at the beard stubbling his chin. "I noticed that you were quite unable to take your eyes off me during our journey."

"How would you know *where* I was looking? You were racing ahead of me so that I could hardly keep up."

"And yet whenever I glanced back at you, you were looking at me."

"You are not only an evil rogue, but a vain buffoon as well. Where else was I supposed to look when you glared at me through that mask?" She snorted. "And while we are on the subject, why wear a mask at all if you are so certain of your irresistible appeal to the female sex? Are you a coward?"

He crossed his arms. "You have about thirty seconds to begin removing that rag you are wearing, Highness."

"It wasn't a rag until you got hold of it. It was brand new, as a matter of fact, and I'll have you know, it was all the crack!"

"Ten seconds, Your Highness."

Violet threw one final look of disgust at him and began to undo the buttons down the front of her dress. When she was ready to remove it, she insisted that he turn toward the wall while she scrambled for the blanket. He took the opportunity to take another sip from his flask. As the brandy burned down his throat he began to feel somewhat human again.

His admiration of her tart tongue only went so far, especially since he was growing chilled standing out in the cold without his shirt. Damn. They would need each other's warmth as well as the blanket before the night was over.

Surprisingly, she said not a word as he approached. Her back was to him and she held herself rigidly aloof as he slipped under the other half of the blanket. He noticed that she had left him as much of it as possible while still keeping herself decently covered.

But her restraint didn't help. They were still touching, and her shapely body could not help but have an unfortunate effect on him. She was so soft! She had kept on her silk shift, but it was almost dry. Some devilish part of him wanted to order her to remove that, too . . . though he supposed he should be grateful for her leaving that much of a barrier between them.

She shifted uncomfortably and brushed his leg with hers. He gritted his teeth.

Somehow he hadn't thought it was going to be this hard to lie with her on the floor of an uncomfortable cave. Of course, he was only just now, in the flickering candlelight, beginning to realize the depth of beauty possessed by this woman. She had hair like spun gold, beautiful fair skin, and the bluest eyes he had ever seen. It was as if some Italian portraitist had dreamed her out of whole cloth—until she opened her mouth. Then it struck him anew that looks and demeanor did not always make a perfect match.

Perhaps if he could keep her talking, he would be completely cured of this blasted attraction he was feeling.

"Feeling cozy, Highness?"

Her only answer was a *tsk* and more shattering movement. She was shivering from cold or fear, he wasn't sure which. He pulled out his flask and took another, longer tug from it.

Then he got a bright idea. He reached over and poked her in the back. "Here, you better have some of this."

She turned, and her nose wrinkled. "No, thank you."

"It will warm you up." Perhaps it would put her to sleep, too.

She sniffed. "Ladies do not imbibe strong spirits."

"Bosh! 'Tis no different than wine."

"You *would* say that!"

He let out a chortle. "I haven't noticed many of the fairer sex avoiding the wine bottle at dinner."

Her brow arched. "Do you attend many dinner parties, Mr. Brute?"

He had to stop himself from clapping his hand on his skull. He would have to take care. "Nay, but I know *real* women. The kind who aren't afraid of doing what's necessary to survive."

In her irritation she sat up and faced him. "What are you saying? That just because one is a gentlewoman, one lacks the ability to take care of oneself?"

"A smart woman would drink to ward off the cold."

As she looked at the flask, she shrugged her shoulders (causing one creamy breast to almost spill over the top of her shift, he noted with unwilling interest). "Fine, give it to me. I always did want to know what men found so irresistible in hard drink." She took a long draught. As the brandy reached her gullet, the color completely leeched from her. Then, just as suddenly, she turned scarlet. For a moment, tears stood in her eyes, and when she spoke, her nonchalance was belied by her strangled voice. "As I always suspected, nothing special."

He forced himself to bite back a laugh at her bravado. "Go ahead—have another sip."

She choked as she took another mouthful, then sat still for a moment as the fiery liquid worked its magic. "It *does* give one a warming sensation, doesn't it?"

He nodded.

She blinked at him and laughed a little. "I feel flushed."

After her third sip, which was more of a *glug*, Sebastian reached for his flask. "I think that's enough for you, Your Highness."

She held it from his grasp. "Not so fast. For your information, I have decided to start living my life the way I see fit. And right now I'm still thirsty!" She took another drink and quietly hiccupped.

Uh-oh, Sebastian thought. He wasn't sure he wanted her to get tipsy. "You don't want to be selfish, though, do you?" he asked, trying to pry the flask out of her hand.

As a compromise, she tipped the bottle to his lips and allowed him a short sip and then went back to drinking down the contents herself.

Maybe if I can get her talking, he thought. Maybe she would forget about the flask.

"You said you would *start* living life as you see fit," he said. "Has your life previously been out of your own control or such a trial?" He couldn't imagine that this was so. And yet, beneath her pampered, icy exterior there seemed to be a hint of vulnerability.

She thought for a moment. "No, I had a very happy childhood, very free, but that all ended when I was twelve and sent off to school. My second day there I overheard the other girls laughing at me because my father was in trade. After that, I vowed to become the most perfect lady that Mrs. Pargeter's Academy for Young Ladies ever turned out. And I was, too!" Her head wobbled a bit. "Till now."

"It seems to me that you chose that path for yourself," Sebastian pointed out. "You didn't have to give in to the prejudice of a bunch of silly girls."

"Oh, you think so?" Violet answered angrily. "Well, let me tell you that Mrs. Pargeter's rules of propriety were nothing compared to those that governed me during my first Season in London! Once again, as the daughter of a merchant I was examined twice as closely as other girls."

"And were you as great a success as you had been at your school?" he asked leadingly.

"No, not really," Violet admitted, deflating slightly. "I was there under the auspices of my aunt Augusta, who is considered very good *ton*, but somehow, I just didn't seem to take. The only interest I received that first spring was from fortune hunters. Aunt Augusta kept telling me to show more vivacity, but it's hard to be ladylike and sparkling at the same time. At least it is for me."

"So where does your lamented husband fall into this scenario?"

Belatedly, he remembered that the Brute would know nothing of her bereaved state.

Luckily Violet was in no condition to notice the lapse. She seemed off in a world of her own now. "I didn't meet Percy until my second Season. He had missed my come-out year because of a case of the mumps. Percy was always of delicate health."

"He sounds like the answer to a young maiden's prayer, if only he hadn't been a mere mister!"

"Oh, I know you mean it sarcastically, but to me, at that time he was a hero! And he was the heir to his uncle, a marquess." Violet took another sip of brandy and looked a bit tearful. "I met him at the first dance at Almack's that second Season. He was the perfect suitor from that moment until he asked for my hand during the waltz at the closing dance where we had first met. I thought it was terribly romantic."

"And did life with Percy live up to this romantic view?"

She shook her head sadly. "No, Percy didn't believe in romance. He said it was shabby-genteel. He was quite concerned that I dismiss such notions in order that I might overcome my rather unfortunate family connections. He told me on our honeymoon that he had suffered doubts about offering for me but that my cool demeanor and ladylike behavior convinced him I would one day make a tolerable marchioness."

"He sounds like a first rate jackass to me!" Sebastian growled.

"Yes, I am beginning to think you are right," Violet agreed absently. Then she shook her head, "That is . . . how dare you."

"It seems to me that you have spent your life socializing with a bunch of stuffed shirts. I can't believe this husband you married wasn't interested in love and passion with you."

She bit her lip in a thoughtful pout. "But don't you see? It's *me*. I don't seem to be a passion-invoking person. Back at school, it was constantly being drummed into our heads that we had to watch out with men, that they were always on the lookout for an opportunity to take advantage. But no man has ever tried anything the least improper with me. "Violet hiccupped and continued, with a hysterical note to her voice, "I probably couldn't get a man to offer me a slip on the shoulder if my life depended on it!"

He shook his head. "That's ridiculous, I'm sure all sorts of men have lustful thoughts about you." Sebastian patted her shoulder and joked, "How could they not, with your neat ankles?"

Her lips parted, and color rose in her cheeks. "Do you really think so?"

"You can depend on it, Highness."

She smiled almost coquettishly at him and slurred, "You don' shound like a Brute, do you know that?" She hiccupped softly.

"You don't sound much like a lady at the moment, either."

She laughed and continued to stare up at him with

eyes large and luminous in the glow of the single candle. Then she leaned over to him and whispered, "Kiss me, Brute."

Maybe he was tipsy himself. Or maybe boredom got the best of him. (What else was there to do in this blasted cave?) Or maybe he was just one of those opportunistic men Mrs. Pargeter had tried to warn Violet about. Whatever the reason, he didn't spend much time resisting her request.

No time at all, as a matter of fact. He bent down and pressed his lips against hers, fully expecting that their embrace would go no further.

But the soft warmth of those lips was very alluring, as was the taste of liquor and hint of perfume that swirled about her. Even after all she had been through today, her hair still smelled of some sweet scent, like roses. It seemed to go straight to his senses.

He wrapped his arms around her, and her mouth opened to his. He couldn't resist deepening the kiss, she was so responsive . . .

She put her hands in his hair and lightly kneaded him. He never knew that the whisper-soft touch of fingertips could affect him so. He couldn't resist running his hand up and down the satiny skin of her arm. She moved her hands languorously from his hair to his shoulders.

He tore his lips away from her mouth and then trailed kisses down her neck to her shoulder. When he reached her breast, her hands suddenly stopped their kneading motion and she clutched his shoulders and moaned.

Without thought, Sebastian laved one breast through her chemise while palming the other with his free hand. Her breasts felt perfectly shaped and he marveled at their youthful firmness. Her nipples hardened at his first touch. And she had thought she was lacking in passion!

In fact, she was so *not lacking* in passion that he

feared if he did not stop them now it would lead to madness. Though he enjoyed playing the blackguard Robert the Brute, he was certainly not one in actuality. Quite the opposite! No one would ever accuse Sebastian Cavenaugh of being a rogue.

He whispered in her ear, "You see, it is not at all difficult for a man to wish to take advantage of you, sweet Violet."

Her lips formed a kittenish smile. She seemed wholly unwilling to end her first foray into passion, and his position left her room to place her hands on his chest and conduct her own investigations of his person. As her fingers firmly explored his chest muscles, he felt a fierce swell of desire.

Violet felt it, too. She rubbed herself against his obvious arousal in a most enticing manner. Then, shocking him with her boldness, she leaned over and took one of his nipples in her mouth and sucked hard. An intense burning sensation shot straight to his groin.

All rational thought fled him. His only aim now was to satisfy their mutual desire for each other. He turned her onto her back and pinned her lower half with his own body. *Now to make a more thorough inspection of those charming breasts*, he thought to himself and pulled her chemise down to her waist. He didn't think he'd ever seen such a perfectly formed woman—the pale skin that covered her chest was flawless. As he ran his palms across the warm flesh, he marveled at the satiny softness. He leaned down and kissed one orb, then he flicked his tongue over its surface. Violet was straining her upper body toward his mouth. She had fisted her hands in his hair and was pulling his head more firmly against her breast. Finally he gave in to her demand and opened his mouth over a tightly puckered nipple and pulled strongly.

While sucking her breast, he smoothed a hand over her abdomen and down toward the apex of her thighs. As his hand neared her warm center, Violet began rocking rhythmically against him. He wasn't sure how much longer he could go on without exploding, but he continued to stroke her in time to her enticing movements.

Within a few minutes, she was straining against him and making low crooning noises. He knew that she was very near now, and he nipped one of her earlobes and whispered, "That's it, Highness . . ."

Violet suddenly arched against him and gave a shouting moan that reverberated in the tiny chamber. Her delicate figure convulsed for a few moments before she lay completely relaxed in his arms.

He was grateful that he had been able to stave off his own desires until she had reached satisfaction—it had been a close thing. The need for release was nearly driving him mad. He adjusted his breeches, pushed her legs apart and positioned himself over her.

Violet was making deep, breathy noises, and he leaned down to kiss her one last time before joining them together. He lowered his lips to hers.

In response, Violet put her hand to his face and shoved it away.

He pulled back from her in astonishment. She took the opportunity to flip over onto her side beneath him. A loud, satisfied snore echoed through the cave.

Astounded, Sebastian rolled away from her. He couldn't believe it—his ardor had put her to sleep!

Or more likely, the brandy had put her into a drunken stupor.

Although this might not surprise anyone back at his

London club, where he was rated to be a rather cold sort, it would not do Robert the Brute's dashing reputation with the ladies any good!

He took a last longing look at her slumbering form, then regretfully covered her with the blanket.

As Violet's snoring continued (though more softly now, he noted with relief), Sebastian arose and went to the corner to refill his flask. He couldn't help laughing, despite himself. He had vowed to provide Mrs. Treacher with plenty of trouble when she came to Cornwall, but it seemed that she was reciprocating more than in kind.

Chapter Three

When Violet awoke, the world had been turned upside down and shaken. Her head ached horribly, as if some fiend had sneaked a tin drum in there and was beating it ceaselessly. The inside of her mouth felt like cotton wool, and her stomach rumbled with ominous threats. Her misery exceeded anything in her previous experience; she suspected it might have surpassed anything in the history of mankind, as well.

And yet to reach this hellish state of being she had the sensation of having swum out of a deep, pleasurable sleep. In her dreams she had been so happy, so mindless of care. Percy had been making love to her.

Her wince of pain became a puzzled frown. That couldn't actually have been Percy in her dream, could it? Percy's lovemaking had never been so passionate. Her husband had never left her breathless and panting. She had never moaned in ecstasy at his touch.

Unable to make sense of it all, she clutched a hand to her throbbing temple. Maybe she had contracted the influenza? The dream could have been a result of fever.

She certainly ached all over. It felt as if she were resting in a bed of rocks.

Attempting not to upset the delicate equilibrium of aches and pains that was her unfortunate present state of being, she shifted.

Her eyes flew wide open. She *was* lying on rock—and that realization caused her plight to roar back into her memory. Robert the Brute! She must still be in the cave with him. Odd that she couldn't recall falling asleep . . . or too much else, for that matter. The last she remembered was drinking some of his brandy. *What could have happened after that?*

His hateful voice boomed out through the darkness. "Good—you're awake!"

She shook her head, trying to clear it, but only succeeded in agitating the demon with the drum. She felt as if she were weaving, even lying down.

The candle was just a dying glow from a nub of wax, but she had no trouble making out her captor's mocking grin. Or his eyes shining through his mask. He probably slept in the thing! "I was beginning to think I'd have to kiss you awake, Highness."

Kiss me?

Something about that phrase made her bolt up to sitting. A fatal mistake. Her head roared in protest. Then, as the blanket fell off her shoulders, exposing her bare breasts to the ruffian, she nearly swooned with mortification. How had her shift come undone?

She gazed in panic about the cave. *That dream.* It *had* just been a dream, hadn't it?

"How long have we been here?" she asked frantically. *And how, exactly, did we pass the time?* That last question she left unspoken.

"A sight longer than I intended," he said, sneering.

"'Course, I could nae have known you would suck my brandy jug dry and fall into a stupor now, could I?"

"I've never been drunk in my life!" she declared.

He snorted. "Aye, till now."

The blood drained out of her face. Oh, heavens! *That's* what was wrong! Brandy. But she just remembered having a tiny sip. Or maybe two.

"You got me drunk!"

And again, she wondered about her state of undress. More than wondered, in fact. A horrible suspicion scratched at the back of her mind. Those passionate moans . . . had they been real? Had she been crying out in ecstasy in the arms of this beast, this criminal?

"I got you drunk." He cackled unpleasantly. "I like that!"

What a horrible creature he was. She shuddered at the idea that he might have . . . well, she didn't even want to think what he could have done.

And yet it was impossible to think about anything else.

She lifted her head and proceeded to do what had stood her in good stead all her life when she was in trouble. Issue denials. "I *never* overindulge."

"If you'll remember, Highness, I warned you against drinking too much. I'd no idea such a high-quarter lady could put so much away."

"Just because I may have been led into overimbibing doesn't give you an excuse to take advantage of a poor defenseless widow!"

His eyebrows darted up above the line of his mask. "And that poor defenseless widow is supposed to be you?" He practically bent over double with mirth.

She immediately wished she had held her tongue. It was beneath her to even broach the subject of his boorish behavior. Now she had inadvertently given him another line of teasing to torment her with.

"I'm thinkin' you've got that wrong, Highness. Or don't you remember begging me to kiss you?"

Her cheeks felt fiery. "I would never!"

Would she?

"Listen, Highness, there don't be time enough to waste arguing o'er your wanton ways." He chuckled snidely. "The tide's out again and 'tis time for us to be gone. Now get yourself dressed quickly."

Anything was better than more of this man's idea of conversation. Violet scrambled to dress, and then winced at the pain this caused her head. How could men regularly drink too much? They must be bigger fools than she had always taken them for.

Yet her physical pain was as nothing compared to her mental anguish when she saw that her chemise wasn't just off her shoulders but tangled about her waist. What, oh what, had gone on here? Had she completely taken leave of her senses? Had they actually—she gulped at the thought—performed the act?

Impossible! She had certainly not missed conjugal intimacies with Percy since his death. Her husband's nocturnal attentions to her person had at first seemed repellent to her, but later had just dwindled over time into another chore to be performed. To think she would let this barbarian touch her, much less violate her, was laughable to contemplate. She would have fought the man tooth and claw before letting him lay a paw on her. Tooth and claw.

Yet he appeared to be none the worse for wear. In fact, he was irritatingly composed . . . and fully dressed. No visible scratches from this tooth-and-claw effort of hers to ward him off. His imposing figure seemed to consume most of the space in their small cave, and she felt unaccountably angry at him for being so tall, for having such a deep, resonant voice and such a wicked grin. Whoever knew that a criminal could have such dark, penetrating eyes and such white, even teeth?

She blushed at the complimentary turn her thoughts had taken. *I must still be tipsy*, she decided in her own defense.

Anyway, there was no use asking him what had happened during the night. Not unless she wanted to endure more of his taunting. He would probably only make up some wild tale about her throwing herself at his person— just as he had accused of her of practically wrestling the flask out of his hands. An accusation which was so preposterous it didn't even bear argument.

Except . . . now that she had a moment to think back, she *did* remember tipping the bottle to her lips a few times. The drink had given her a sort of giddy, light-headed feeling. She had giggled. And she *never* giggled. *Oh, Lord.*

To think that she, Violet Wingate Treacher, could have arrived at such a state! She, who had been married to a man who might have been a marquess, had everyone died in the proper order. Not even her sister Sophy had ever gotten herself caught in such an incriminating escapade—and Sophy had been disgracing the family on a weekly basis since she had escaped from the nursery. But Sophy had never approached this level of disgrace. Swilling brandy in a smuggler's cave? With Cornwall's most notorious smuggler, Robert the Brute?

And heaven knew what else had happened!

It was that *what else* that plagued her. As she struggled into her clothing, Violet tried to discern whether she had been violated. She didn't think she had shared relations with a criminal, but how did one know for certain? He could have done anything to her while she was in a state of drunken unconsciousness. That thought made her even more ill.

What if she *had* been befouled by this low character? How would she possibly be able to hold her head up again?

"Ready?" he barked at her.

Her head snapped up. "You might give me a moment!"

"Takes you a damn sight longer to dress than it did for you to strip," he said, laughing.

She glared at him. "Did I take my clothes off, or did you tear them off?"

Those dark eyes shone at her through the mask. "Don't you remember?"

She bit her lip.

"Blacked it out, 'ave you now?" He clucked his tongue at her. "Highness, you hurt my feelings!"

She set her jaw. "I hardly see why *you* should be offended!"

"Naturally a man doesn't want to feel that his efforts to please a lady have been forgotten."

Please her! It was all she could do not to spit.

And yet she had to admit that there was something in that deep voice of his that seemed to resonate through her today. She could almost imagine that voice purring at her through a sea of brandy, calling her Highness, making her tremble . . . and not with fright, either.

She trembled now.

It had not been a dream.

Oh God. To have sunk to such unspeakable depravity!

But of course, she *hadn't*. She couldn't have. He was just toying with her, making her worry that something had happened when it hadn't.

But if it didn't happen, a little voice asked, *what was your chemise doing puddled around your waist?*

That was a question only Robert the Brute could answer. And she would die before asking it.

She hurriedly fastened the final buttons on her dress, picked up her sodden cape, and stood as quickly as her delicate physical condition would allow. So help her, if she ever got out of this filthy cave, she would never touch a drop of drink again. Or touch a man again, either, even to dance. She would become one of those ascetic gentle-women who sat around cataloguing flora and translating religious passages from their original Greek. Not that she knew Greek . . . although she had always loved her garden. So she would cloister herself away from society. All she needed were a few servants, an accomplished cook, and access to fashion periodicals.

"Enough now," the smuggler said gruffly. "Get going."

He poked her on the shoulder and she stiffened an-grily. What had him in such an ill humor?

A hopeful thought stirred in her. Perhaps she *had* fought him off. Her thwarting him would have pricked his male pride.

She cut a glance over to him. "I suppose I was quite restless in my sleep last night," she remarked, attempting to strike a casual tone.

That chuckle rumbled through the corridors. "Restless—aye."

Hmm. That wasn't much of an answer.

"I notice that I seemed to have exclusive use of the blanket. Such a pity that you were left out in the cold," she taunted.

"Oh, I wasn't cold." His voice was practically a leer.

Her heart sank into the heels of her shoes. But maybe he wasn't really implying what she thought he was.

"I'll take a wench's passion over a blanket any day," he said, dousing her last hope.

So much for thwarting him! She could almost remember now. And the horrible part was that she couldn't recall being at all revolted by the experience. Just the opposite, in fact. She remembered warmth, and a pleasant thrill at his touch, and the realization that she hadn't kissed a man since Percy. But Percy had been cold and mechanical, whereas when the Brute had taken her into his arms, it was like the stranger had put a flame to tinder and she had gone up in smoke.

But just how far up? she worried.

What if she was with child? That thought nearly caused her legs to collapse beneath her, and yet she managed to keep going. Her mind raced at the horror of it, and she imagined bleak scenarios for hiding possible evidence of her shame from the world . . . Hiding herself away for nine months on the continent. Or hurling herself off a cliff.

It was still dark when they reached the mouth of the cave, although it looked like the dawn was not far away. The sound of the sea was less menacing than it had seemed before, and just the beautiful sight of open space after her night in the confines of that dark cave made her want to weep with relief.

"Now what?" she asked.

"Now we say good-bye, Highness."

She nearly whooped for joy, but stopped short. If she seemed too happy he might keep her just for spite. "What a pity!"

His lips turned up in a caustic smile. "Aye, a great pity."

"And yet I suppose you have your work to get back to."

"That I do, and I advise you to head for home."

"Home," she repeated. But where was her home? She had no idea. Was he going to abandon her here to fend for herself?

"Unless you would care to accompany me?" he asked, mirthfully noting her hesitation. "I think you know my sentiments on your ankles, and after last night, I am certain ours could be what you might call a mutually enjoyable partnership."

"What do you mean, *after last night*?" she blurted out, unable to stop herself. She knew it wasn't ladylike to delve into such matters. But how could she live not knowing whether she was still a respectable lady or— heaven help her!—a smuggler's strumpet?

He gave her arm a playful squeeze, and the eyes beneath that mask glinted once more, sending a wave of heat through her. "What I meant was, it was not at all unpleasurable sharing a blanket with you, Highness."

"Not too pleasurable, either, I hope," she said.

He grinned.

Damn! Why didn't he just come out and say it?

He sent her an exaggerated bow. "And now, I bid you farewell, Highness." The Brute turned to go.

"Wait!" she cried out.

She could hardly believe her ears, yet she couldn't help calling him back. How could he just leave her? If she never saw him again, how would she know if the passion she had flashes of was just a dream or a true memory of the night they had shared?

"Something wrong?" he asked.

"Yes!" But even as the question formed in her mind, her lips seemed incapable of voicing it. She crossed her arms and asked instead, "How am I to head for home from this godforsaken spot?"

He looked surprised. "Didn't I mention it? All you have to do is climb to the top of that rise over there." He pointed to a steep hill. "'Tis Trembledown over there.

The coming dawn should provide a most picturesque view of your new home."

Her lips parted—and not just to hear the word *picturesque* fall trippingly from the smuggler's tongue, either. "So near?"

He grinned. "I was about to tell you afore you made your daffish dash into the caves. However, I shouldn't begrudge you the night's adventure. It was not without its highlights."

Violet shivered, and not just from the bone-chilling cold. She turned to make good her escape, but he grabbed her arm once more. "You said I could go," she snapped.

"Aye, but no kiss good-bye?"

She snorted. "Not likely!"

"Then good-bye to you, and good riddance. It's always good riddance to a woman, I say."

"And what do you imagine me doing in the coming weeks," she shot back, "pining after your criminal person?"

He was laughing at her again, but Violet no longer cared. Sanctuary lay just over the hill, and she was already speeding toward it. She didn't look back to see the boat that came to shore or to see her captor turn and wave her a last farewell before it put back out to sea. She didn't care. She hoped she never saw the wretch ever again.

She lumbered up the hill faster than she could have ever thought possible, given her sore feet, fatigue, pounding temples, and tortured psyche. Home—she was almost home!

She was already trying to put the whole terrible episode behind her. Now that she knew she would reach the comfortable sanctuary of her new home, images of hurling herself off a cliff in shame already began to recede. After all, she did not know what had happened, so she felt reasonable in assuming nothing had. Yes, they had kissed—perhaps more—but whose fault had that been? Not hers, surely. There was no doubt in her pounding head that, in the unlikely event that something more dreadful than a mere kiss *had* taken place, the ruffian had forced himself on her.

She had confused memories of pleasurable sensations. But passions stoked in a moment of unintentional drunkenness surely could not be considered a blot on her character. She would not have *chosen* to be abducted, plied with liquor, and made love to by a smuggler. Far from it!

How often had her sisters accused her of being a snob? And there was, she had to admit, a bit of truth to the charge. But would a *snob* engage in such wanton behavior with an unwashed, uncouth criminal? Absolutely not!

"Kiss me, Brute."

The memory of those words, spoken in a slurred voice that was at once unfamiliar and undeniably her own, stopped her in her tracks. Oh, heavens! She *had* asked him to kiss her. He hadn't been lying about that.

But that didn't mean that she had voluntarily drunk from that flask. That was the true culprit in her crime of passion. Demon rum.

Never again, she thought.

Violet pressed on again, and when she crested the hill she got her first glimpse of her new home. At least, she assumed it was hers. For, unfortunately, there were no other houses on the horizon.

She gawped for a moment, trying to restart her breathing mechanism. The sight was almost enough to send her running back down to the cave. Her head began to pound with renewed vigor.

This was Trembledown?

Although it was still dark, she could easily make out the place because all the windows had lights in them. Every one. It was startling, and oddly dispiriting. For while her heart should have been gladdened that Peabody and Hennie were holding a vigil through the night for her and had lit her path home, so to speak, the home they had lit might have been more favorably approached in total darkness.

Trembledown was like something out of a gothic novel . . . or a nightmare. Nothing about the edifice seemed at all secure. The house was set back from a cliff, but was still close enough to give the illusion of the house just waiting for a few centuries to work the landscape and wash it out to the sea. The building even tilted seaward—actually sagged to one side. Shutters, where they were not missing entirely, hung askew. Windows were boarded where glass had been broken. Rhododendron bushes, overgrown and leafless—probably dead—stood like skeleton sentries in front of the house. Around the perimeter was an old stone wall, moss covered and in various stages of collapse.

The name Trembledown was certainly perfect for the place—it looked as if one stiff storm could send it trembling into a pile of rubble.

Questions reeled through her mind, one after another. *This* was the place her in-laws had seen fit to buy her off with? (They must despise her more than she'd ever suspected!) More puzzling still . . . could *this* truly be the ancestral home the haughty Marquess of St. Just was dying to get his hands on? Was the man a lunatic? She herself had turned her back on a Season in London helping present Sophy so that she could try to bring some order to this disaster? She had staked her hopes for the future on *this*?

She stumbled down the thistle-strewn path that led to the door. There was no sweeping drive, no courtyard. Near the wall, a few crocuses, now past their prime, made a sad attempt at adornment. Violet couldn't even make out a road leading nearby. The worn stone steps leading up to the door were slippery with moss. She almost fell.

Suddenly the door was thrown open, and there stood Peabody in his snowy white nightgown, robe, and cap. Though it was almost daylight, he held a candle in his hand and blinked at her as if she were crawling toward him out of pitch darkness.

"Oh, ma'am!" he exclaimed, rushing forward.

They fell on each other like long-lost friends, and it was all Violet could do to bite back tears. "Peabody!" she said, her voice quavering. It was so good to see him, words failed her. Gone was all thought of scolding him for tying her hands so tightly. Look how upset he was— and the frantic relief in his eyes to see her! Loyal, wonderful Peabody. Her champion. Her rock!

"I have been worried almost beyond reason!" he exclaimed. "Why, I—"

Suddenly, his words came to a dead stop, and the color drained out of his face.

"What is it?" she asked.

The improbable worry that leapt to her mind was that he could tell what had happened just by looking at her. She feared she had *the Brute's moll* written all over her.

And yet, when he did speak, his words had nothing to do with the smuggler. "Is that your blue dress?" he asked.

As she looked down at it now, it seemed to have faded overnight to gray. Not to mention, it was ripped and smudged with black in several places. The skirt was still wet and had dragged in the dirt all the way home. The hem looked as if it had been trimmed in mud.

Her skin burned with mortification. "I had to spend the night hidden in a cave, on the rocks."

He gasped. "With Robert the Brute?"

She hesitated only a moment before a lie slipped easily from her. "Hiding from him, Peabody."

It sounded good, and she was about to embroider her story further when she realized that Peabody wasn't listening to her anymore. In fact, in the next moment—just after his searching glance took in the spectacle of her completely ruined shoes—her champion and rock nearly fainted dead away.

"Henrietta, if you don't stop crying I shall send you packing back to Yorkshire."

Henrietta, who was perched on the edge of a badly stained brocade chair, sniffed in an effort to bring her emotions under control. Her nonstop snufflings were wearing on Violet's nerves. In the cave Violet had thought that if she could just escape Robert the Brute, she would embrace the world and her companions in it in the true spirit of love and kinship. She had anticipated the milk of human kindness flowing through her veins. Her conversion to saintliness was entirely premature, obviously. The only thing circulating through her veins at the moment was irritation.

Was it any wonder? She was so tired! Tomorrow, no doubt, she would feel more kindly toward the world, after she had had a good night's sleep in a real bed. If there was a real bed to be had in this ghastly house. What she had seen so far did not make her hopeful on that score.

The very couch she lay on was a good example of the

problem. One leg of the mildewed piece of furniture was shorter than the other, so that every time she moved, it jarred both her and the scraggly cats that draped themselves on the cushions and across the back. She had shooed the cats away—they were three of a seemingly innumerable feral herd that had taken over the house—but the moment she had closed her eyes they were back. One, an orange long-haired beast with only one eye, stared at her menacingly.

The house, besides having been taken over by a pack of frightening felines, was a shambles. Walls, cracked and water stained, seemed to trap the cold air rather than any sort of warmth. Of course, warmth was hard to come by, since the chimney was clogged and smoke had filled the room when Peabody had attempted to light it. Dust and soot stood everywhere, except where four-legged creatures had left tracks—and that was to say nothing of the smell!

The caretaker, Barnabas, apparently had never laid rag to surface area. Nor swept. She was hard pressed to think what the old man *had* been doing all these years, save leeching a living off the Treachers. Not that she had a problem with that. Leeching a living off *her*, however, was another matter entirely.

Peabody picked his way through the room, all the while hunching slightly as he looked up at the ceiling, as if he feared it would collapse around his ears at any moment. And she had to admit that the timbers crisscrossing over their heads did seem rather threatening.

"Perhaps the best thing to do would be to retreat," he suggested as he laid a very neat tea tray on the wobbly table next to her. He had evidently found time during the traumatic night to unpack the Limoges. "Back to Yorkshire, I mean."

"Or to Bath!" Hennie said, apparently still eager to join up with her friend Imogene Philbrick and start indulging in an orgy of tea drinking and tatting. "I am sure they have no difficulty with smugglers in Bath. Or if they have, my friend Imogene has never mentioned it."

"How could we leave when we've only just arrived?" Violet leaned back against the dusty velvet pillows of the sofa and tried to think. But it was impossible to consider how she would deal with the house. Other things weighed rather heavily on her mind.

Taking in Violet's worn expression, Peabody poured the tea himself. "I am sure after the horses have rested for another day, they would be ready for the journey."

"A day!" Hennie blew her nose noisily. "Who knows what could befall us in another day here! What with Robert the Brute still out and about!"

At the name, Violet stiffened.

"He might still be searching for you, Violet! He might come murder us all in our beds!"

Violet had told them that she had run away from Robert the Brute and spent the night in a cave—alone. Having evaded her captor made her a sort of heroine in their eyes, so she could not set their minds at ease and tell them that the Brute's parting words were that he was well rid of her.

A curious sinking feeling nagged her. She would probably never see him again. For all she knew, he was in a boat bound for France as they spoke.

Her eyes suddenly focused on a mound in a corner. She hadn't paid attention to it before, but she had assumed it was a pile of blankets such as what must have been covering the furniture before they arrived. Then the pile moved.

Violet screamed.

Hennie followed her lead and actually jumped out of her chair, shrieking. "What is the matter?"

Violet pointed. "That mass of filth!" she cried. "What is it?"

Peabody followed her gaze and some of the tension went out of his body. "That's Barnabas's sheepdog, Rufus."

Violet sank back again, her heart still drumming hard. A dog. That was all they needed—and not even a self-respecting dog that would have rid them of all these cats, but a mangy, ineffective creature. Much like Barnabas himself, she thought.

"What are you going to do?" Hennie asked.

"What can I do?" Violet said.

Hennie scooted to the edge of her chair. "I spent the whole night wondering about this myself." She shook her head and admitted, "Well, in those few moments when I wasn't wondering what could become of you at the hands of Robert the Brute, and what would become of us if something ill befell you. It would have been too awful."

"Yes, you would have suffered greatly," Violet said, biting her lip.

Hennie nodded. "And so soon after Aunt Matilda's tragedy, too! How should I have mourned for you both at once?"

This was indeed a puzzle, Violet had to allow. Once you had donned black underwear, as Hennie had, one would assume you had reached mourning's limits.

"But then I remembered—actually, Peabody reminded me—that the Marquess of St. Just had offered you money for the house. Isn't that right?"

The Marquess! The horror of the house's interior had knocked all thought of that person from her mind. But now . . .

Now her mind seized on his name like a lifeline. Yes!

He had offered her money for the house. A very generous sum, too. Laughably generous, now that she saw the place with her own eyes. Oh, why hadn't she accepted his offer?

Vague dreams of fixing up Trembledown and selling it for an outrageous amount came back to her. As did her foolish aspirations for making enough money off the sale to return to society in a blaze of glory. Now she wanted to weep at how foolish she had been. If she could just hear from the Marquess of St. Just again, she would beg him to give her even a quarter of what he had originally offered her for this pile of rubble. She would grovel, if she had to.

Why not start groveling now?

"Quick, Peabody," she said, sitting up. "My writing paper."

Peabody gasped. "Are you going to write to the marquess, ma'am?"

"Just so," she said.

Peabody clapped his hands together. "But I have not unpacked all your things," he said. "I'm not sure where your stationery is."

"That's all right," she said. "Any paper and quill will do."

Although he looked as if he would argue with that statement, nevertheless Peabody hopped eagerly to follow her instructions, nearly crushing a cat in his hurry. The scraggly animal released an outraged yowl but gave no ground. At the door, Peabody pivoted back to Violet. "I knew you would deliver us from this place," he said worshipfully, as if she were Moses about to lead his people out of Egypt.

As Peabody was scuttling to find paper and pen, there came a loud knock at the door that made Hennie jump ten feet.

Violet scolded her. "Really, Hen—smugglers will not come knocking, you know."

"Nothing would surprise me in this strange place!" Hennie exclaimed.

It wasn't a smuggler, however, but the constable whom Peabody had sent Barnabas into Widgelyn Cross to fetch earlier that morning. Constable Farkas stomped into the room in his muddy boots, and after brief introductions were made and an offer of tea was refused, he swatted two cats out of the way and sank down onto the couch with Violet.

Violet tensed at such an ill-mannered intrusion. Also, at the prospect of questions the man was certain to ask her. She had lied to Hennie and Peabody, but could she lie to the law?

"Now you say you were abducted by one Robert the Brute."

Hennie gasped. "But Constable, it was undoubtedly he. I saw him with my own eyes!"

The constable, who was unfashionably furry of face, turned his attention to Hennie. "And had you seen the man before?"

"No—but the proprietor of the Frog and Cock Inn told me all about him!"

Constable Farkas laughed. "Did he, now? So you're an expert."

Hennie preened modestly. "I wouldn't go so far as to say that . . ."

With a roll of his eyes with which Violet was in complete sympathy, the man turned back to Violet. "He was wearing a mask, you say?"

"Oh yes! He's never without it."

Throughout Hennie's reply, the man kept his eyes trained on Violet. "And you, Mrs. Treacher?"

"I never saw him without it." Though she had to steel herself not to blush at remembering that, though she had not seen his face, she had seen quite a bit of the rest of him. His chest, for instance, which had been so hard and lightly dusted with hair.

Percy had certainly not been so fine a specimen as the Brute . . .

"Mrs. Treacher?"

Her chin snapped up. Had she really been daydreaming about the chest of a villain? "Yes?"

"I asked did you meet any of his accomplices?"

"Oh, no." Violet proceeded to tell the man the whole story of her ordeal . . . up to the point of making a run for the cave. "After that, I have no idea what happened to him. I never saw him again. Indeed, I was in fear for my life because the cave I took shelter in was overwhelmed by the tide."

Hennie released a moan. "Oh, think of drowning in such a way! You might have been safer with the Brute!"

"Not likely." The constable stared at Violet, scrutinizing her, until she was forced to look away. And yet his next words gave her cause to think he believed her.

"Well, then. There's not much you can do to help us, then."

Violet felt her face go red. "Help *you*? I would think that you would be concerned, rather, at saving the citizens in your charge from being terrorized by such a ruffian."

"The government is also concerned with the smuggling, ma'am."

"So there are a few bottles of brandy hidden away in caves," Violet argued. "Is that the end of the world?"

The constable's gray eyes remained pinned on her. "Was there brandy in your cave, then?"

Violet's jaw hung slack for a moment as she attempted

to form a reply. Naturally she did not want word getting out that she had been swilling liquor in a cave all night. Though of course that was better than having them know she was frolicking under a blanket with the Brute . . .

"I saw a half-empty cask," she said, swallowing. "Barely worth mentioning."

"And yet you did mention it."

She bristled. "I simply don't understand how the law can care more for smuggled goods than for the safety of people."

"Hear, hear." Hennie agreed. "She could have been killed."

The constable raised a furry brow. "Aye? I'm more apt to think the Brute had met his match." He wheezed out a laugh at his own joke.

Violet took a bracing sip of tea. Horrid man.

He finally stood. "Then you canna tell me where the Brute got off to?"

"No," she said.

"Or what the boat looked like that you saw in the cove?"

"I'm sorry. I only saw a light."

"Perhaps you could show us this cave."

Her heart beat frantically. The cave! What if they went to the cave and they found evidence of the possible debauchery of her night with Robert the Brute? The blanket, the brandy, the candle . . . there might have been other evidence of the Brute's presence there that she hadn't noticed. What could she answer to all the questions that would surely be put to her?

Then again, what if they found information there that actually led to the Brute's capture?

Her first thought at that possibility was entirely selfish. What tales the man could tell on her! Her reputation would be in tatters.

Also, if he was caught, they would hang him.

To her surprise, the thought of her abductor swinging from a yardarm did not bring her the slightest pleasure. Indeed, her heart leapt in panic at the very thought. They could not catch him.

What madness! Of course she did not care what became of such a one as he. They could hang the man twenty times before she would shed a tear for him. But she did care about her good name, and she could not risk letting it be sullied by the Brute if he were to be captured. Because if he found out that her information led to his capture, he would surely avenge himself by reciting the worst possible version of events of their night together.

Or he might manage to escape and avenge himself on her in a more horrific way! Hennie had said the man had cut people's throats.

"Mrs. Treacher?" the constable said, giving her a verbal nudge.

She gulped. "I-I'm sorry . . . it was so dark . . . even this morning."

"Then you don't think you could find the cave?"

She lifted her shoulders. "It would be doubtful. Aren't there many caves along the coast?"

The constable released a heavy sigh. "Aye."

She sagged a little in relief. "Then I'm sure I would be of little help to you. Though certainly I shall notify you first thing if I can remember any particulars."

The constable took a step toward the door and walked through a puddle of water. "What's this?"

"The roof leaks," Violet said.

The man looked incredulous. "But there is a floor above this one, is there not?"

Violet's mouth set in a grim line. "The ceiling leaks, too." The house could have served well as a potato strainer.

"You should get that fixed!"

"Oh, yes. I intend to see to it first thing," Violet said.

Another lie. She wouldn't be here long enough to fix anything. Not if she could help it. Now more than ever, she was determined to unload this godforsaken wreck of a house—cats, the caretaker Barnabas, leaks and all—on that pompous gasbag, the Marquess of St. Just. She needed to move quickly, too, before he had the opportunity to see what a wreck the place truly was.

After Peabody showed the constable to the door he returned to the salon to collect the tea tray. There was another knock at the door.

"See who it is, Peabody," Violet said, "and tell them not to knock so hard next time, or else the whole house will tumble about our ears."

She sank against the sofa, depressed. No matter how she looked at the situation, her Cornwall gambit had been a disaster. It was hard to imagine things getting any worse.

And then Peabody, looking extremely rattled, announced their latest visitor.

"The Marquess of St. Just, ma'am."

Chapter Four

What was *he* doing here? The marquess was supposed to be in London!

Or at least she had assumed that he was safely tucked away there for the moment; obviously she was wrong. There was no time to prepare, to put the best face on what was obviously going to be her disadvantageous situation. All Violet could do was sit tall on her mildewed sofa and square her shoulders regally as their guest approached. Her guest, the marquess.

How she would have relished that phrase in another time, another place! To have a marquess come calling would have been a coup she and Peabody would have savored in better days. But now! The churning in her stomach had absolutely nothing to do with the amount of spirits she had imbibed during the previous night, and everything to do with the dismay she felt to be seen under these conditions, especially by the Marquess of St. Just.

Worried that her own expression mirrored Peabody's utter mortification, Violet was careful to make her face a mask of pleasantry, no different than if she were greeting him in a London ballroom.

The marquess seemed to be doing the same. The man at Peabody's side was handsome, with fine thick blond hair arranged in a careful improvisation of the windswept. His figure was tall and angular, but even through his impeccably tailored morning coat and breeches she detected a whipcord strength at odds with his light complexion and long elegant nose. His gait as he crossed the room to greet her was graceful, and the deft way he maneuvered around the damp patches and cat tails hinted at a natural athleticism.

Violet disliked him on sight. In fact, she thought that she would have felt an aversion to him even had it not been for their prior correspondence—even if she hadn't been greeting him from the unfortunate vantage of the wreck of a home she had refused to sell to him for what in hindsight seemed a princely sum. Despite the surprising pleasantness of the man's individual parts, his face radiated haughtiness, especially as he stopped to peer at her through his monocle.

Violet felt an instant antipathy to anyone wearing a monocle. Her husband had adopted the new mode after discovering it during a trip through Vienna. Percy had been fond of making a production of putting in his eye ring and training it on her whenever she had displeased him. She had grown to hate the sight of his left eye, made hideous through the single lens looking disapprovingly at her across the dinner table.

The marquess was bestowing such a look now through his eyepiece. Though the glance was directed at a cat and not herself, Violet still found herself shifting uncomfortably.

If the marquess hadn't come for the specific purpose of enjoying the sight of her installed in squalor after rejecting his previous offers, he was certainly gloating now. Oh, he was making a show of being a gracious noble greeting the newly arrived gentry, but his air of smug politeness didn't fool her. She'd used it once too often herself—say, when she would heap compliments on the homely girls sidelined near the punchbowl at Almack's as she was being escorted by Percy, a future marquess. Lord St. Just's full lips were practically quivering with mirth. He had her at a disadvantage and could hardly contain his glee.

"Mrs. Treacher," he said, sidestepping a bit of moldy rug before bowing extravagantly. Doing it much too brown, in her opinion. "We meet at last!"

She smiled frostily at him, not bothering to extend her hand, which was ungloved and an unsightly mess after scrambling around the dunes and caves of Cornwall. The skin was blistered, the nails ragged. "My lord, you do us a great honor visiting so soon. We have scarcely had time to catch our breath."

She considered making a comment about how the house was not yet ready for company but decided that fact was self-evident. Instead, she introduced Hennie, who was visibly impressed by the fake charm oozing out of the marquess.

"Do forgive me if I have descended on you too abruptly." St. Just flipped his coattails and sank down on the couch next to her, sending up a plume of dust, as well as a yowl from the one-eyed cat that had been in residence where his lordship's posterior now rested. "I *beg* pardon!" cried the marquess, startled.

Violet shuddered with the effort it took not to laugh at the man being goosed by her cat. At the same time she felt as if she were dying inside. It was difficult to maintain a fiction of unflappability. Besides the humiliation of having the man see her in the rattletrap that was her new home, she felt her chances of selling the property to him dwindling apace. Of all the luck! The galling man would have to intrude on them now. If she'd had more time, she might have . . .

Actually, it was hard to think what she might have done to make Trembledown present a better impression, short of burning it down and starting from scratch. But in her present frame of mind she wanted to blame the Marquess of St. Just for something, and premature visitation seemed as good a sin as any to pin on the man.

A look of effusive concern overcame the nobleman. "After hearing of your terrible ordeal, Mrs. Treacher, I could not help paying a call."

Oh Lord. How on earth had news of her *ordeal* traveled so quickly? Had he had his ear to the ground for the first stirring of misfortune to befall her?

As if being Trembledown's owner weren't all the misfortune any person could require.

"Let me say, madam, that hearing of such a calamity befalling you cut me to the quick."

"You, sir?"

"Well, naturally. You seemed determined to come to Cornwall only after I had offered you money for it, an offer you . . ."

You so foolishly refused was the silent implication.

How right he was!

Though of course she would rather eat mud than admit as much to the egotistical creature. "Do not concern yourself, my lord. I had long been planning my trip to Cornwall, even before your very obliging offer."

"You had?" Hennie blurted out.

Violet glared at her cousin.

The corners of the marquess's lips jumped into a smirk. "I never meant to imply that it was your own obstinate foolishness that brought about your own downfall."

"Of course not." She returned his smirk with a frosty

smile. What gossips these natives must be! Probably no sooner than Peabody had sent for the constable than word of her *downfall* had spread. "And I assure you, though last night's miserable experience was trying for me, I in no way consider that I experienced any kind of *downfall*."

Heavens, how she hoped not!

"A thousand pardons. I never meant to insinuate that . . . Oh dear, no!" He leaned forward. "Though of course I did hear that you were gone all the night."

"Indeed she was!" Hennie interjected. "She spent the night in a cave, eluding both Robert the Brute and high tide."

The marquess's eyes widened so that his monocle fell out and dangled from a buttonhole in his waistcoat. "Remarkable! You spent the entire night in a cave . . . *alone*?"

Violet had repeated this tale often enough that she was able not only to lie, but make a jest of it. "My abductor did not allow me to bring a chaperone, alas."

"Naturally he would not," St. Just replied humorlessly. "And yet I wonder that he would allow you to escape."

"I did not give him a say in the matter."

The marquess sat back and ogled her with profuse admiration. "Brave creature! I am all astonishment at your fortitude. One would not have expected the Brute to be so careless as to allow his victim to escape without giving determined chase."

Violet fixed a modest expression on her face. "Perhaps I was lucky."

Hennie, warming to her favorite subject, released a pleasurable shudder of dread. "Lucky not to suffer a fate worse than death!"

"Indeed!" The marquess lifted a gloved hand. "Although, to be fair to the Brute, he does not have the reputation of violence against virtuous women."

Violet stared down at her hands, praying that no one noticed them quaking. She shuddered to think what the marquess's assertion said about *her* virtue.

"Do you mean to say, my lord, that he is a brute of honor?" Hennie asked.

Violet could barely cover a snort. That just showed how much the Marquess of St. Just knew of Robert the Brute!

The marquess appeared to consider his words carefully. "I am not certain if it is morality or a lack of necessity. It is said that one needn't steal what is given freely. The Brute is rumored not to lack in female attention."

"Where did you hear this?" Violet asked, too sharply. Blushing, she added quickly, "He seemed quite repulsive to me."

"Naturally," the marquess said. "No lady of your impeccable character would find anything at all to admire in such a man. But some silly women hear tales of outlaws and then see a dashing figure in a mask and practically fall at his feet."

"Imagine!" Hennie exclaimed.

"Not I," Violet said.

Hennie considered for a moment and then added, "Though he did seem quite tall—and remarkably strong. Why, he lifted Violet as if she were no heavier than a feather pillow!"

The marquess's brows raised in alarm. "Then the blackguard *did* lay a hand on you?"

Violet bridled. "Of course. I was abducted."

St. Just shuddered. "How terrible. I feel that all of us in the neighborhood bear a collective responsibility for not doing more to eradicate this human stain from our midst."

"I absolve you of responsibility, my lord."

"Courageous lady!" he exclaimed. "I shall have my man Griggs send you a ham."

"That will not be necessary," Violet said.

The marquess would not hear of rescinding his generous offer. "But you must tell me more. Unburden yourself, if it would help."

"It sounds like you had heard quite a bit before you arrived."

He drew back. "Only because there was overwhelming concern for your welfare."

Overwhelming desire to gossip was more like it. "There is no more to tell," Violet said. "As I explained to the constable, I could barely describe the man. Indeed, I doubt I could even find the cave . . . it was quite a distance away."

The marquess's eyes darted up, as if he had discovered her telling a falsehood. For a moment, Violet's heart jumped at the idea that she had been caught. Yet how would he know? This preening popinjay had probably come no closer to a smuggler's lair than she herself had before last night.

"You must have spent a good portion of the night finding your way home," he observed.

She cleared her throat. If only she had spent the night stumbling in the dark, instead of wrapped in a blanket with a smuggler. "Yes . . . yes, I did."

"And to think of the state you must have been in! Nothing to eat, or drink . . ."

Fuzzy memories of tippling brandy caused her to fight a blush. She turned a cool glance on her visitor. "I'm sure you will understand why I would prefer not to relive the ordeal, sir."

"Of course, of course!" He looked down at his gloved hands and shook his head for a moment before replacing his monocle and giving her a long, piercing once-over. "You seem remarkably well for a woman who must have had no sleep."

Her lips flattened. "Thank you."

He honored her with another bow of his impeccably coiffed head. "I must declare my admiration for the way you are so calmly comporting yourself, ma'am, and yet you must hate that Brute fellow."

"He's horrible!" Hennie cried. "Even if he is strangely fascinating . . ."

St. Just continued to stare at Violet through that awful eyepiece, which made his right eye seem startling and all-seeing. "Did *you* find him fascinating?"

"Me?" Violet shuddered at the memory of ogling the man's broad chest. "No! Not at all."

"Of course, if you were not long in his presence . . ."

He seemed to imply that if she had simply spent more time alone with the man, she would have gone swooning into his arms.

Which, of course, was precisely what she had done. Shame burned in her so hotly that it seemed the only way to smother it was to vigorously deny what had happened. "Were I with the man for days on end," she declared hotly, "indeed, if we were the only two humans on the planet—I would not succumb to such a one as he."

Violet comforted herself by vowing that if she was ever with him *again,* she would abide by these words. After all, the next time she would be prepared for that broad chest, that animal growl of a voice, the disarming glint of those eyes through that mysterious mask . . .

"Well said, Mrs. Treacher!" the marquess complimented her. "My feeling is that men of that sort—ruffians, no better—should be hunted down and shot on sight. A trial would be too good for the likes of Robert the Brute."

Hennie straightened primly. "But as an Englishman, my lord, you surely would want the laws of our great land obeyed."

"Men like the Brute have put themselves outside the law. I should like to hunt that rascal down myself. Believe me, if I ever had the blackguard in my sights, he would not live to molest another good woman."

The marquess's braggadocio rubbed Violet the wrong way. "Why don't you, then?"

His monocled eye stared at her unblinkingly. "Why don't I what?"

"Hunt the man down. He seems to enjoy using this area as a base of operation. If your feelings against the man are so strong, I would think you would have hunted him down before now."

"Well, he is hard to catch. Deuced hard!" he sputtered ineffectually. "The king's army hasn't managed it."

As if this fop had even tried! Violet bit back a laugh. "Still, my lord, I would think it would be easier to simply shoot him than go about handing out hams to all of his victims."

Hennie gasped, and the marquess's face reddened slightly.

Violet sincerely regretted having blurted out her rejoinder to the marquess. Belatedly, she remembered he was her best hope (her only hope, really) for unloading Trembledown and fleeing this godforsaken country. She kicked herself for getting carried away and blamed his monocle, his manner, and his unceasing talk about Robert the Brute for making her forget where her best interests lay.

The three sat stonily for a moment, each person straining to think of something to break the silence. Hennie once cleared her throat, giving an indication that she might be on the verge of making one of her priceless observations—

which for once Violet would have welcomed—but then at the last moment her mouth closed firmly, and she emitted only a sigh.

Violet tried, unsuccessfully, to bring the conversation around to a friendlier topic. She asked after Montraffer, his opinions on the weather, and the best carriages, to drive in Cornwall. In her experience, most men enjoyed nothing better than talking of carriages, but in the marquess's case the conversation remained moribund despite her best efforts.

Finally, Peabody came sweeping in with a fresh tea tray, relieving them of their futile struggle for conversation. He tottered over to the side table next to Violet and looked beseechingly at his mistress as he placed the tray for her to serve. His glance reminded Violet of what was at stake during this man's visit. That no matter how rude his questioning and insinuations about her night with Robert the Brute had been, the marquess remained Trembledown's most likely potential buyer.

She wished there were some way for Peabody to inconspicuously scrape the moss off the half timbers on his way back to the kitchen.

St. Just cleared his throat. "So, Mrs. Treacher, how do you like Cornwall?"

"I am afraid I haven't been here long enough to make an informed opinion," she replied, glad he was making the effort to restore civility. "It is quite wild, of course . . ."

"And such foul weather!" Hennie said. "It will be good when we are able to lea—"

"My cousin is susceptible to chills," Violet broke in.

The marquess smiled with what Violet felt sure was spurious concern. "Then the situation of this house must be very troubling to you. Breezes from the ocean whip right across the moor here."

Right through the house, too, Violet nearly added, suppressing a shiver. She forced the corners of her lips up. "A bracing wind is refreshing, I always feel."

"Violet, not an hour ago you just said it felt like we might all be blown to blazes!" Hennie scolded.

When Violet turned away from glaring at Hennie, the marquess was hiding a smirk. "And how do you like the house?" he asked.

"It's more than I ever dreamed!" Violet said.

More awful, she meant.

"Did you know it is one of the oldest houses in the district?"

"No, but I might have guessed. It has such a-a-a"— she searched for a word that was even remotely complimentary—"*mature* feel to it."

"It predates Elizabeth."

"Does it indeed?" she asked politely.

By the condition of the place, Violet would not have been surprised to hear that it dated back all the way to Ethelred the Unready.

As if to confirm the house's antiquity, a small avalanche of plaster pieces cascaded to the floor near the dog. The dog did not notice. Presumably he was used to having bits of ceiling raining on him.

The marquess's brow arched. "Yes, I believe it was an inn before it came into the hands of my family. But of course that was centuries ago."

"I wonder that your family could bear to part with it," Violet said, not wanting the marquess to think that she was too eager to unload her property. "Now that I have seen it, I doubt *I* ever could."

Hennie choked so that her teacup rattled violently on its saucer.

"Naturally," Violet continued, "I have just arrived, but I find Trembledown has such . . . such . . . rustic charm."

Hennie's eyes looked both startled and perplexed. "But, Violet!"

Violet poured another cup of tea from the service and gazed meaningfully at her cousin. "Have some more tea, Henrietta. The hot liquid might soothe your throat. Also, it might help if you *keep quiet.*"

"Oh—oh yes!" Hennie, finally understanding, took a huge gulp from the cup handed to her.

Violet leaned back and tried to assume the air of a lady in a palace. The task really wasn't that hard. All her life she had suffered because she wasn't living quite in the manner which she felt to be her natural milieu. She had grown accustomed to rising above her circumstances.

The marquess looked at her admiringly. "I am so glad you see the value in your new home. So many ladies might see only a few superficial flaws."

A sharp, unexpected laugh escaped Violet, which she attempted to cover by taking a quick sip of tea. The whole house was one giant flaw! And now she simply had to keep up the pretense of liking it until she could foist it off on her guest. If he was still willing to offer.

Oh, how she prayed he was still willing!

"It is good to hear that Montraffer will have a permanent neighbor," the marquess said.

Violet felt her brows pinching. She did not want him to think that she was overly reluctant to sell, either. "Naturally, I have yet to make any *firm* decisions," she said. "I have only just arrived."

"Of course! Most likely you will probably feel like resting here for a month before making any plans at all."

A month! Did he intend to wait that long to renew his offer? She would go mad . . . and poor Peabody might take it in his head to decamp back to Peacock Hall, even if it meant taking the public stage. There was no guessing what desperate acts they all might be driven to in the event of such a delay.

"Of course, if you are still interested in making me an offer on the place, I would be happy to entertain it," she blurted out. Then, fearing that the specter of her butler riding public transportation might have made her sound overeager, she hastened to add, "Not that I make you any promises, mind you. Now that I see this historic place, I am glad I did not act hastily."

St. Just coughed. "Yes, undoubtedly."

Violet felt a stab of irritation. Was the man going to play cat and mouse with her all morning? "I know you were eager to regain Trembledown, my lord."

"Yes, I was." He took a sip of tea and smiled wistfully. And remained stubbornly silent.

"You were *most generous* in your offer."

He trained his monocle around the room, where his gaze, unhappily, lingered first on the mossy timbers, then the cats. "I confess I had not been in the house for a while."

Violet gnashed her teeth in frustration. She felt like a starving man waiting for a fish to nibble his line. Her fish was not cooperating at all. "Of course, the house might be altered soon."

"You still intend to do work on it?"

"Naturally." She chuckled lightly. "It's been let go shockingly! But my man Barnabas and I have spoken together, and we are seeing eye to eye on what needs to be done. He seems quite a competent jack-of-all-trades."

He narrowed his cool gaze on her. "Rummy Barney, you mean?"

Oh Lord. Was that what they called him? That explained quite a bit. "People can be so cruel with their name calling."

"You intend to have *him* do work here?" he asked, aghast.

In his eyes, she could see the offering price sinking. "Oh no!" she said quickly. "I was only planning on consulting with him for advice on local tradesmen. I will of course supervise all work personally."

This last seemed to stagger the marquess even more than putting Rummy Barney in charge. "You? Supervising the renovation of Trembledown?" He gestured around the room. "My dear lady, you must know that it would be a Herculean endeavor. Certainly not for a woman such as yourself to oversee."

She stiffened. "And why not?"

"From what little I know of your history, Mrs. Treacher, it does not make me inclined to believe that this is a task you would be up to. No, indeed."

Her mouth dropped. What did he know of her? "Why would I not be?"

"That would be a task better left to a gentleman of taste."

Such as himself, no doubt! She fumed silently, barely holding herself back from braining the man with her teacup. He looked so lofty and disdainful in that moment. No doubt the *history* he alluded to was the fact that her father was in trade, and therefore not up to the discriminating standards of St. Just!

"No, no," he continued, oblivious to the great glob of rage clogging her throat, "It would not do for you to take on such a project. Especially now that you know the dangers hereabouts."

"Dangers?"

He looked surprised. "Why, the Brute, of course."

"I will not be run out of my home by a criminal."

"But, Violet—" Hennie interjected.

"Indeed, I will not," Violet insisted. "Nor will I be forced to listen to implied insults against my family, my taste, or my abilities."

The marquess appeared taken aback. "My good lady, I beg a thousand pardons if you feel I have done anything of the kind."

At that moment, Peabody swooped into the room. From the worried look on his face, he had been listening at the door again and decided to intervene before the situation with the marquess deteriorated further. He shot Violet a look as he proceeded to whisk away the tea things, no doubt hoping to keep her from braining the marquess with a teapot.

Violet decided her servant's stepping in at this critical juncture was a good thing. Perhaps now the Marquess of St. Just would get the idea that it was time to pack up his monocle and hie himself back to Montraffer. To give the man another nudge, she herself stood, which in turn made the marquess rise.

"Thank you so much for coming, my lord," she said. "Believe me when I say that I hope we shall be good neighbors for many years to come."

"*Years?*" the marquess asked.

"Yes," Violet said rashly, too angry for rational thought. "I have just made up my mind. I believe I will stay here at Trembledown."

Nearby, just beyond the hallway door leading to the kitchen, where Peabody had just disappeared, there was an audible moan, followed by a crash and then the sound of shattering.

"What was that?" the marquess exclaimed.

Violet pursed her lips. "Merely the sound of a hundred-year-old Limoges tea service smashing to bits."

Poor Mrs. Treacher! Sebastian thought. What a miserable time she was having!

What a delight it was to see.

Sebastian was never one to gloat. Oh no, not he. Or he had not been, heretofore. Yet as he reclined in front of his cozy fire, slippered feet propped, hot toddy in hand, he could not help glancing about his well-appointed country home with a certain satisfaction. Nay, smugness.

Who would have thought the day would come when he would appreciate the absence of a draft in his salon? Or be forced to acknowledge that a lack of crumbling plaster and peeling paper was a joyful state of affairs? That which he had heretofore taken for granted he could overlook no more. He beheld the dry, un-moth-eaten carpet beneath his furniture with an appreciative smile and took in the complete deficit of cats—or any animal life whatsoever—crawling about the place with positive glee.

He mentally sifted through his visit to Trembledown the way a sporting enthusiast might relive a particularly pleasing match, smiling as he remembered the horror on the woman's face when he had sat on a cat, and couldn't help chuckling. And her obvious attempts to make him renew his offer! Not to mention her utterly forlorn look when he thwarted her . . . That alone had been worth the visit to that drafty, filthy house of hers.

Poor Violet!

He chuckled, recalling her discomfort in discussing her ordeal of the night before. Her insistence that she had spent the night alone had nearly caused him to drop his disguise.

What a fiction she had told her companions, and apparently the constable, too! Of how she had bravely eluded her abductor and spent the night alone in the cave. The credulity of her companions stunned him. Had no one noticed the brandy on her breath upon her return? The spark of guilt in her eyes?

Why, one look into that maddeningly beautiful face this morning would have told him the whole story at once, even had he not already known it from firsthand experience. She looked guilt stricken and fearful. Somehow that companion of hers and the household staff mistook Violet's flustered air for fatigue and distress, but he knew better. He knew she was thinking almost exclusively of the time she had spent in the arms of the Brute and trying to recall exactly what had occurred between them. And wondering whether there was any chance of any of her new neighbors discovering the truth of her less-than-ladylike conduct.

He sank more comfortably into his leather chair and sighed. That woman had occupied quite a few of his thoughts this morning. The softness of her skin, the bewitching blue of her eyes, the warmth of those lips . . .

Obviously, it was time for him to set up a new mistress. His last one had abandoned him some months ago for the respectable state of matrimony to a haberdasher. Because of the state of world affairs and a brief trip to Vienna last fall, he had been rather neglecting her for the past months. Small wonder she had found the time to seek out more congenial company.

But in truth he had never been much of a lady's man. Although he knew himself to be reasonably attractive, it was useful to him to cultivate a more distanced persona, albeit one who enjoyed society. He was the kind of man around whom women and men could talk freely—too freely. He tried to be as formal and yet as curious as an old spinet in the drawing rooms he visited; to be ubiquitous, but not a subject of conversation himself.

Now he sometimes wondered where the character he was impersonating—that monocled marquess—ended and Sebastian Cavenaugh began.

His lovers had often seemed to be playing an elaborate game, too. They regarded him as the marquess, a man of riches and influence in society—a prime *partis,* in fact. All their practiced responses to his physical attentions rarely seemed like anything other than what they felt they owed him as their provider. After a time, the elaborate dance became a bore, and he found that the periods between his mistresses grew longer and longer.

Sometimes he despaired of ever knowing true passion. The closest he had come to it was last night, in that cave.

He frowned into the embers of the fire. No doubt his recent sexual abstinence had left him susceptible to the charms of the first woman with whom he happened to find himself alone. Even one he was predisposed to dislike.

Violet was just as he had imagined she would be—only more so. He couldn't remember the last time he had met a woman so full of airs, so prickly about her status, so beautifully raw in her anxiety to come out on top of the heap.

And yet there was something about that kiss that she had shared with the Brute. There had been no guile in it . . . it had not felt rehearsed. He had sensed nothing besides her pure need. In fact, he had never experienced such raw desire before. He would never forget it.

The troubling part was that she obviously had. She had forgotten the details of their encounter. More disturbingly, she had forgotten *him.*

That was what truly stunned him. Walking into her

parlor this morning had been a brazen act. A part of him expected her to recognize him right away, to point her finger at him and cry out, "Call back the constable! *That* is the man who abducted me!" But she had not. She had apparently seen nothing in him to remind her of the man who had moved her to reveal so much of herself mere hours before.

This was an entirely new wrinkle in his romantic history. He had had rather rote encounters with women. But to his knowledge, he had never been completely forgotten before.

Sebastian was no longer chuckling.

He downed the rest of his drink and clasped his hands in his lap. Not that it bothered him that the lady did not remember that he was her kidnapper. Indeed, it was far, far better for him that her mind had erased the details of his person. This way he would be able to continue his persona as the Brute.

Of course, his antics with Violet the night before had brought him no closer to discovering who Nero was. He had missed contact with Jem and the boat entirely; he hoped he hadn't let important information slip by as well. Unless . . .

Sebastian laughed.

But shortly, his lips turned down in a frown. Could it be?

He crossed to his writing desk and took out a sheet of paper. On it he quickly scribbled a note to Cuthbert.

Old fish,
Is there any reason to believe our Nero could not
be a woman?
Missing your smiles,
St. Just

Suspecting Violet might seem laughable. Yet he could not deny that the circumstances of her visit to Cornwall, and her newfound determination to stay, seemed suspicious on the surface. The timing was uncanny.

Still . . . could a woman like Violet Treacher, who was so transparent in the matter of a house transaction, have a penchant for espionage? Perhaps it was as well that he had held off from renewing his offer to buy her house.

It could be that posing as a widow fretting over selling her family estate was part of her game. Could she be cleverer than he gave her credit for?

Now *that* was a puzzle. He had thought he was playing Violet for a fool this morning. But what if it was she who was leading the dance?

Chapter Five

She was back in the cavern tunnels again, though this time as she raced through the maze, she was not running away, but searching. With increasing frustration, she hit another dead end and had to retrace her tracks. Finally, she spied a glow ahead and she sped toward it, her heart pounding madly.

At the mouth of the room, she paused to grab her breath and cast her gaze about the gloam.

A masked figure stood in the corner near a flickering candle. He beckoned her, holding out a silver flask. All at once her mouth was parched and she rushed toward him until her skirts brushed his legs. Wordlessly she leaned over and put her mouth over the opening of the flask as he tenderly cradled her head with his other hand and fed her as if she were a babe. When she had finished drinking, he thrust the flask aside and bent his head over hers and savored a few drops of brandy that pooled on her lips.

Violet reached her arms around his shoulders and sighed. "Kiss me, Brute!"

With feverish intensity his mouth plundered hers. Her knees grew weak; she felt as if she were drowning in the kiss. The Brute allowed the heaviness of her boneless cleaving to him to drag them both to the ground. They rested on a rather lumpy and scratchy blanket, but oh, his arms felt so heavenly, they might have been lying on the softest feather mattress. As his lips brushed across her neck and toward her breasts, she arched toward him like a budding flower stretching toward sunlight. Her throat purred at his sensual ministrations. The purring grew louder as the Brute unbuttoned the bodice of her gown and she felt the heat of his breath against her bare flesh.

The moment he put his tongue out and licked at the perspiration in the valley between her breasts, she felt a burning that was almost a pain. Nay, a pain that was like a scratch.

And now the purring was growing quite loud . . . In fact, it seemed something quite apart from her. What was causing it?

She curled her hand around the Brute's shoulder— which now, shockingly, seemed to have sprouted fur—and suddenly felt burning pain as something ripped through her flesh!

Violet lurched to wakefulness with a startled cry and sat up, gasping in confusion and considerable pain. As soon as her eyes could focus, her gaze came to rest on a menacing presence on her chest—that dreadful one-eyed cat. Violet swatted him off her bed, only to look down and discover that her entire bed was a writhing sea of cat fur. Half of the animals hadn't even bestirred themselves after her yelp of terror, though the few that had merely looked at her in sleepy annoyance.

She had never cared for cats . . . though she had to admit the fat one at her feet made a passable bed warmer. Too weary for a large-scale feline evacuation, Violet sank down, shivering, and looked around the room in the dim light of the guttering candle that she had been too weary to snuff when she collapsed for the evening. Trembledown's master suite, which must have been quite magnificent in the time of the Tudors, now resembled nothing so much as one of the attic rooms at her father's estate of Peacock Hall. Most of the furniture in the room was still under dusty covers. When her maid, Lettie, had arrived with the baggage coach, she had little time to do more than air out the bed, put on linens, and sweep the immediate area between the bed and the largest clothes press, which held her current wardrobe.

It would take work . . . but her exhausted mind protested thinking about that now. Heavens, how she wished she were back in her warm, catless bed at Peacock Hall—or better yet, back in her dream! It was terrible, shameful, but for a moment she closed her eyes, willing herself back into that cave, into those strong arms.

She couldn't allow herself to think about that, either.

Speaking of arms, her own itched like the devil. She scratched and then felt a strange crawly sensation on her scalp. Her fingers reached up as a terrible thought occurred to her. She opened her eyes and squinted at the bed linen.

Fleas! Her bed and nightclothes were covered in them! She released a bloodcurdling shriek and streaked out of bed, as if she could escape the infestation that way.

Poor Lettie was the first to arrive to find out what was the matter; she was quite alarmed to see her normally poised mistress hopping up and down. "Is something wrong, ma'am?"

"Fleas!" Violet cried, flapping her arms as if she could dislodge them from her person. "My room has been invaded by felines and their attendant vermin!"

"Oh, ma'am, I'm so sorry! I thought for sure that I

latched the door when I left you this evening, but it must have come ajar and then the beasties let themselves in while you slept."

Lettie looked duly upset but nothing near as horrified as Peabody, who skidded into the room in his nightcap and slippers, armed with a fireplace poker. Clearly he was expecting the Brute. "What has happened?"

His bravery was touching, even though Violet was still too revolted by bugs to appreciate it. "My bed has fleas," she announced angrily as Hennie appeared at the door.

"It probably has to do with these cats," her cousin supplied helpfully. "You really shouldn't sleep with them in your bed."

"I *know* that!" Violet stormed.

Peabody put his poker aside and beseeched her, "Madam, let us leave this place at once! This is no country for a refined lady such as yourself."

Of course he did not mention her refined butler, but he did not have to. Violet's mind latched onto the idea of flight with zeal. She stopped flapping and started listening.

"We could be gone tomorrow—to London!" Peabody said, noting the look in her eye.

"Or Bath!" Hennie interjected.

"*Anywhere,*" Peabody agreed, "so long as it as far from this place with its moldy furnishings, rummy caretaker, and brutes as four wheels may carry us."

Their enthusiasm for the escape was infectious. *Flee* had such a better ring to it than *flea.* "We could leave," Violet repeated. Yes. It had all just been a terrible mistake— one of those doomed projects that happen from time to time in life. After a few months she would have forgotten all of it—the fleas, the house, the Brute . . .

She would be able to get the night in the cave out of her mind. It would be as if it never happened!

She clasped her itchy hands together and wrung them, plotting it all out. If they woke Hal now and had him begin to prepare the horses, how soon could they be ready?

She looked back into the eyes of the others. Lettie seemed reluctant to take on another rickety carriage ride but ready to follow orders, Peabody's eyes were brimming with hope, and Hennie was as close to ecstatic as Violet had ever seen her.

"Shall I write Imogene and tell her we shall be passing through Bath shortly?"

Now even spending the London Season in Bath with two old spinster school friends had appeal heretofore unappreciated by Violet.

"Oh!" Hennie added, remembering. "And shall I pen a note to the Marquess of St. Just, thanking him for his call but informing him that we will no longer be in a position to accept his ham?"

At the mention of that name, Violet's planning crashed to a halt. Her jaw tightened. *The marquess!* Her hands fisted at her sides as she remembered him sitting in her decrepit parlor telling her that she wasn't up to the task of fixing Trembledown! Implying that she was somehow deficient in the qualities needed to refurbish a fine old manor like this one. He probably worried that with her merchant's daughter's taste, she would turn the place into a blight on his neighborhood.

Oh! But the shabby state of neglect from its former noble owners was perfectly acceptable!

"Madam?"

When her anger had abated enough for her to focus on something other than her loathing of the marquess, she saw that Peabody was peering anxiously at her.

"What shall we do?" he asked. "We are awaiting a word from you—just a word."

How she would have loved to leave! But the furious beating of her heart made her realize that she could not abandon Trembledown now, after she had told the marquess that she would be renovating it. There was a matter of pride at stake, and if she gave up and fled now, she would not forget it. Not in a few months, or possibly ever.

"Go back to your rooms," she said.

Her companions' faces tensed. "Go to our rooms . . . and do what?" Hennie asked.

"Whatever you were doing before. . . sleeping. We are not leaving Trembledown."

Poor Peabody looked like he might break down. "But the household, madam!"

"And the Brute!" Hennie cried.

"And those cats," Lettie reminded her.

The house and the Brute were too much for her mind to tackle now. But looking over at the bed, she took in the cats and felt spurred to action. "Help me get rid of these creatures," she instructed the others. "Then Lettie and I will change the bedding and we can all go back to sleep!"

Crushed, Peabody listlessly picked a squawking cat off the coverlet. Hennie followed suit, holding a kitten by the scruff with her fingertips as she minced out of the room.

Lettie, who—thank heavens!—was made of sterner stuff, started stacking cats in her arms like firewood. "Cats'll come back, madam. And what about the fleas?"

Violet had little experience with pests. "I don't know."

"I know what my ma would do," Lettie suggested helpfully. "She'd tie the whole furry lot into a sack with a few rocks and toss it into the river."

"Good heavens!" Violet exclaimed. "That's very pragmatic, but too gruesome for my taste."

Lettie looked a little embarrassed. "I was just sayin'."

"Yes, well, perhaps we needn't resort to a massacre quite yet. Maybe if I asked Mr. Monk . . . " Her own bitter laugh cut that thought short. Going to her caretaker Barnabas Monk for vermin control would be like going to the candy maker for tips on figure reduction. For all she knew, he was the wellspring of the flea population. "I think we should try baths first."

Lettie squinted at her. "*Baths*?"

"Of course. A good scrubbing in soap and water!"

"Have you ever bathed a cat, ma'am?"

"Me? Of course not!"

There were all sorts of things she had never done. On the whole, her life had not exposed her to the problems of day-to-day shifting. But that was about to change. From now on, she would transform herself into one of those practical people who got things done. Tomorrow, she would begin the task of turning Trembledown into a place that even a nobleman would envy.

The cornerstone of her plan to right all that was wrong with Trembledown occurred to her sometime during the night and by morning had fixed itself in her mind. She needed to let Barnabas Monk go. If she was going to make a success of her work here—and she was determined to—she did not need an old rumpot at the helm.

Peabody was made ecstatic by this plan—if he had to stay at Trembledown, he preferred it to be Monk-free. He even insisted on being present when she spoke to Monk. He seemed to harbor the odd idea that without his protective presence, Barnabas would fly into a rage and do no telling what kind of violence to her.

Violet could not imagine the man who had let a house rot around him bestirring himself to any task requiring physical exertion even out of anger, but she nevertheless welcomed Peabody's presence at the meeting. She had never been in the position of firing anyone before. Her father had taken care of the staff difficulties at Peacock Hall, and while she was living with the Treachers . . . well, the Treachers never trusted her to manage anything.

And now look. The task ahead of her would be made all the harder because of the Treachers' incompetence and neglect. (Things were ever thus, it seemed to Violet.) She did not relish letting Barnabas go; in all decency she was forced to pension the man off with money she could ill afford.

She was doubly happy to have Peabody there when he brought in a steaming pot of tea and placed the tray on the desk in front of her. No one made a better pot of tea than Peabody. As they waited for the old retainer to answer Violet's summons, Peabody stood formally and made free with advice.

"Be firm, madam. No doubt the man will not give up the reins easily."

"You could be right."

Peabody harrumphed. "No doubt he will want to continue on until the whole place falls about our ears!"

"Undoubtedly," Violet said, growing unnerved.

"I am sure you are making the right decision. He would fight your every change."

"Yes, most likely."

Growing bolder, Peabody suggested, "Of course the best idea would be to simply sell Trembledown as it is and let the future owner deal with Mr. Monk."

She shot him a look. They had been through this already.

Peabody shrugged. "Not that I mean to overstep my bounds, madam."

"Heavens, no." He had merely been galloping over those selfsame bounds all morning, begging her to sell. She did not hold his sudden outspokenness against him. There was almost as much pity for Peabody in her heart as there was for herself. They neither of them belonged in the rough-and-tumble, yet here they were. She had always considered her father's estate in Yorkshire a backwater, but this. This was beyond anything she had ever endured.

At last Barnabas lumbered in bashfully with his hat in his hands. This shambling was the fastest she had yet seen him move; usually he was about as active and alert as his sheepdog. The man's shoes might have something to do with that, she thought, taking a measure of the man. His boots were so shoddy they seemed to be held together with rags and glue. His clothes, which hadn't seen a good washing this decade, looked filthy to the point of being themselves organic; she wouldn't have been surprised to find weeds sprouting from his pockets and vine tendrils snaking out from the holes where there were once buttons.

He was not a large man, but he seemed to take up quite a bit of space, or perhaps it was just that she would prefer to give him a wide berth. A thinning orange-red thatch sprouted from the top of his head that clashed with the startling red hue of his nose, a bulbous protuberance that was so porous and rosy it resembled a large strawberry. By contrast, the rest of his face was pocked and pale beneath the burnt orange stubble of his jaw.

"Ma'am," he mumbled, stopping before Violet's desk. (Happily, not too close.) Though, to be fair, the mumbling might not have been his fault. Missing so many teeth would naturally make it difficult to be understood.

"Thank you, Barnabas, for coming to see me."

"I didna hev no choice. You told me to, didn't you?"

Violet had to focus all her attention to understand what Monk was saying to her. The man pronounced *you* as *yow,* just as the Brute had. In fact, this man made the Brute seem articulate and urbane by comparison.

Violet cleared her throat. "Yes. Yes, I did." She took a deep breath. The poor man really did resemble a sheepdog himself, a little. His eyes seemed to disappear beneath the droopy folds of his skin. "I called you in today, Barnabas, to discuss how we shall go on now that my cousin and I have decided to set up household here. Obviously, the house has been allowed to deteriorate to a deplorable degree."

"And wonderful it is to hear that you plan on gussying the place up, 'tis. She's a wonderful old house. It's gone to my heart to see the place fall into such decay." Barnabas pulled out a red handkerchief and honked his nose into it as if to emphasize his distress.

Violet glanced uncomfortably at Peabody, who seemed unmoved by pity.

"No doubt that would be why you have allowed the place to become overrun with cats and dogs," he declared with a sniff.

"I would just point out to you, Mr. Peasbaldly, that there is only one dog on these premises, and I didna see the harm in letting the cats in—they keep the rats out! A fine thing it would be to have had all the paneling in this place gnawed to bits."

"Instead our mistress has been gnawed to bits by the

fleas from the cure for these hypothetical rodents!"
Peabody scolded.

Violet didn't think it was at all proper to be discussing
such intimacies as her insect bites with Rummy Barney.
"This is all rather beside the point. I am not interested in
how Trembledown came to its present state, but rather in
how to most efficiently make repairs."

"The roof will be where you start, ma'am," Monk leapt
in to tell her. "Happens that a cousin of mine is in the trade."

"Oh?" True, Violet had told the marquess that she
thought Barnabas Monk would be able to help her in
dealing with tradesmen, but she hadn't actually thought
that would be the case. Not that she wanted to add another Monk to her payroll.

"Aye, he'll do a dandy job for you and for a most reasonable fee, most reasonable, I think I can promise."

Of course, she could not allow herself to be swayed by
simple talk. If the man had a cousin in the roof trade,
why had he allowed the roof of Trembledown to become
a sieve? No, she must remain firm.

"From the moment I saw you walking up from the
ocean, ma'am, I said, *there be a game lass.*" He snorted,
then added, "If you'll pardon. I said to myself, *she'll not let
the old place slide to the sea, like these other Treachers.*"

Violet was shaken, but not from having been called a
game lass. (She rather fancied that.) It was from what
Monk said about seeing her walking up from the ocean.
He had spied her coming back from the cave?

What else had he seen?

She could not let this pass. "Mr. Monk, excuse me.
You said you saw me yesterday morning?"

"I spied you a-trudging up from the ocean. First thing.
It were I who told your manservant here 'o your safe
return."

"Did you see . . ." She cast an anxious glance at Peabody. "That is . . . was anyone following me?"

For a moment, Monk's eyes narrowed until they had disappeared completely and he tilted his head back so she wondered that he could see her at all. This was his way of assessing her, and it was unnerving in the extreme. All at once, she felt certain that he knew more than he would say. Maybe he had witnessed her with the Brute that morning and knew it was not what she had told Constable Farkas.

"Nay, ma'am," he said at last. "You be alone that morning, as I could attest, if need be." Then one of his slitted eyes opened and closed quickly—good heavens, Rummy Barney had just winked at her!

Violet had felt a moment of relief, but that was before Barney had winked at her. The cave was close. The Brute had been with her on the beach. If Barnabas had been at the top of the cliff, on the path . . .

Maybe he was just waiting for a moment—perhaps a moment when Peabody was not with her—when he could blackmail her with his knowledge.

"Well!" she said. "Never mind that now. Let's see . . . where were we?"

"The roof," Peabody said, looking a little disturbed at the way she had been diverted. "But first, oughtn't you to take care of the matter of the household staff, madam?"

"Ah! Yes." Violet swallowed. The point of this entire meeting was to let Barnabas Monk go. If only Monk wouldn't stare at her so inscrutably . . . This was harder than she had expected it would be. "You see, Mr. Monk—the, uh, house is rather . . . well, it is quite a bit of work, naturally. For instance, we shall have to do something for the cook, who seems *quite* elderly."

Violet hadn't even known there was a cook on the

property until she stumbled upon the old woman sleeping on a cot in the larder.

Barnabas drew back. "Why, Ma would never think of leaving the place—she's worked here since she was a lass in the scullery!"

Violet's heart sank. It was his mother? "I hadn't realized the relationship there." Although now that she thought of the old woman's rather protuberant red nose she saw the resemblance. She could only assume that Mrs. Monk's scraggly gray locks had once been carrot red.

"You don't mean to set Ma loose, do you, ma'am?" Monk asked her. "That'd be bad luck—for you, too."

Violet tilted her head, startled by the prediction. Bad luck? What was he saying? It was hard to tell, because she couldn't exactly look into his eyes. But it seemed rather like a threat. Perhaps he was intimating that if she fired his mother, he would retaliate in some way. Perhaps by spreading gossip that would destroy her reputation completely . . .

Not that she would allow herself to be blackmailed for one minute. No indeed.

And yet, Mrs. Monk *had* managed to produce a very passable porridge that morning.

"If it's more help in the kitchen you're needin', ma'am, I've a niece who'd suit."

A niece. "You seem to be fortunate in being one of a large family."

"That I am, ma'am. Why, the Monks is famous in these parts!"

"Well . . ." Violet could feel waves of dismay coming from Peabody. Yes, she had determined to let Monk go. But look how helpful the man was being. Perhaps he only needed a guiding hand. "What I actually called you in for, Mr. Monk . . ."

The room was silent as she hesitated. And in that silence, all she could think of was Monk watching her and the Brute near the lapping waves of the ocean.

". . . was that I want you to get a new suit of clothes. New boots, too. And we must do the same for your mother."

"Thank you, ma'am. Should I give my cousin a shout, then?"

She was astonished. "Do you have a cousin who is a tailor, too?"

The man shook his head in confusion. "Nay—my cousin about the roof."

"Oh!" Violet hesitated, then she released a sigh. Why not? She knew no roofers herself, and the job had to be done before the next rainstorm drowned them all in their beds. "Yes, do."

Monk nodded and put his hat on his head. He appeared ready to go, but then stopped. "Though I do 'ave a sister what sews."

Violet nodded. She might have known. "Tell her to see me, by all means. And your niece, too, about kitchen work."

She stood up, eager to escape before she ended up responsible for the livelihoods of every Monk in Cornwall.

Peabody looked horrified at the turn the encounter had taken. "But, madam."

"Come, Peabody," she interrupted. "It's time to bathe the cats."

In that moment, she thought she had never seen her manservant look more demoralized.

At the church at Widgelyn Cross, the Trembledown pew was directly across from the St. Just's, which gave Sebastian ample opportunity for observing his new neighbor.

Granted, church was not a setting where he expected the spy Nero to show up and appear abjectly guilty for his or her crimes; still, Violet gave him much to wonder about. Most obviously, she looked as if she had been mauled. The peek of skin visible between her glove and her sleeve was notably lashed with red. There were similar markings on her neck, and even an angry little gash on her chin.

What had the lady been up to? It was hard to imagine any genteel activity that could result in such bodily harm, unless Violet had flung herself from her roof onto a rosebush. God knew if he had to live in that rundown barn of a house, he would be driven to similar acts of madness.

Not for the first time, she caught him staring at her and shot him a glance of annoyance that sent his face forward again. But there was little in Mr. Cheswyn's sermon to hold his attention. The vicar, a bachelor, was wheezing on in his normal way about the duty of God's children to appreciate the natural beauty around them. Mr. Cheswyn, an amateur naturalist whose enthusiasm for exercise had resulted in his being distressingly long-winded, fancied himself a sort of Martin Luther by way of Wordsworth. Once the man got started on daisies and the wonder of birds winging through the air, there was no guessing when the congregation would be released.

And now the vicar seemed to be distracted by another of the earth's beautiful creatures—his new parishioner, Mrs. Treacher. His calflike eyes fastened on her as he asked his audience to consider the blessings available to them from the humble duck, and more than once he lost his place and had to return to the beginning of his passage on the great gift of feathers to humanity.

Oh, Sebastian understood that feeling well. Those blue

eyes had caused him to lose his concentration more than once, to be carried away more than he ever dreamed. Which was why it was so easy for him to suspect that Mrs. Treacher was something other than what she presented herself as. Those blue eyes could be a very powerful tool in the hands of the enemy.

After the service, Mr. Cheswyn was quick to put himself forward to speak to Violet. Indeed, he and his sister, who kept house for him, fell over themselves to see how quickly they could invite Mrs. Treacher and Miss Halsop to dinner. These negotiations went on for a while before Mr. Cheswyn went on to detail for Violet the physical and moral benefits of taking brisk exercise in the brisk air. Which, if the color blooming in the cleric's cheeks was any indication, was the man's idea of a flirtation.

Henrietta was all smiles for Sebastian. She dropped a curtsy.

"It is wonderful to see you here, Miss Halsop," he told her. "I had great hopes that the Trembledown party would be a constant addition to our congregation here."

"We are honored that you think of us at all, I'm sure. I myself was astonished that Violet wanted to attend services this morning, but she said she would go mad if she did not get away from that house at least for an hour."

Sebastian smiled. "Understandable after the great stress of her move, I'm sure."

"Oh yes. And when I told her that *I* always enjoy services because they give me an opportunity to be thankful for all the good things that have happened to me, even though I have had rather unfortunate luck—much worse than hers, on the whole, I believe—Violet told me that she preferred to go to lodge her complaints."

He coughed to cover a laugh, which drew the attention

of the others. Violet caught him smiling and flashed a look at him. "Is something amusing, my lord?"

"Indeed no. Why do you ask?"

"Because you seem to have been watching me rather closely throughout the service. At one point you were staring at me so strangely I worried I must be giving the wrong responses."

"I was merely concerned about the gashes on your arms and chin."

"Oh that!" Henrietta said as Violet blushed. "Those are just from the cats. Violet insisted on bathing them after she woke up one night with fleas."

Mr. Cheswyn's eyes goggled. Fleas, apparently, were a part of the natural world he did not lovingly embrace.

"*Bathing cats?*" Sebastian asked, barely holding back a laugh. How he would have loved to have seen *that*!

"Oh, my dear Mrs. Treacher. I wish that you had consulted me first. The only remedy for such an infestation is Dr. Loftus's Vermin Powder. It is most effective."

Violet, who appeared uncomfortable talking about her fleas and their remedy, clenched her jaw. "I have never heard of it."

"It is absolutely the only manner to get rid of the pests. I shall have my man drive a tin over to your home."

"Oh, how kind!" Henrietta exclaimed. "Isn't the marquess kind, Violet?"

Violet's mouth stretched to accommodate a meager smile. "Too kind." She looked as if she were about to make a quick scurry toward her carriage when another of the Trembledown neighbors swooped down on her. "Mrs. Treacher!" she exclaimed, practically swatting the cleric and his sister aside. Those two moved on to speak with other parishioners. "I am so pleased to make your acquaintance!"

Sebastian stepped in to introduce them. "Mrs. Treacher, may I present Mrs. Blatchford." He also presented Miss Halsop, but Mrs. Blatchford barely spared her a glance and a nod. "How wonderful it is to have a new neighbor!"

Violet dropped a quick curtsy.

"Or didn't you know that my house is just a hop from yours? Just a hop!" The older woman, a rather stout widow more formally attired perhaps than was normal for the country, had taken Violet unawares and did not appear ready to give up the advantage the element of surprise afforded her. "It seems I have been waiting an age to meet you!"

"But I have only been here a week," Violet pointed out.

The other woman chuckled. "Well, one doesn't want to impose on newcomers *too* quickly."

Violet shot Sebastian a meaningful look. "That is not a deterrent to some people."

"Naturally, since we live so close, I hope we shall be great friends. *Les amis pour la vie!*" Mrs. Blatchford touched her new *amie* on the arm. "Excuse me for tossing about bits of *le francais,* my dear, but I do so adore Paris! I am hoping now that all the awfulness is over, I shall be able to see my dear city *encore une fois*! In fact, my dearest hope is to take Binkley."

Violet shook her head in confusion. "Binkley?"

"My nephew! Such a wonderful young man." She drew back as if an astonishing thought had just occurred to her. "Why, *you* must meet him. How you should hit it off—I am sure you would adore him. Everyone does, don't they, my lord?"

Sebastian could remember this paragon of a nephew only vaguely, but he nodded nevertheless.

"Binkley is almost as eager to make your acquaintance as I was!"

"But how would he know of me?" Violet asked.

Mrs. Blatchford waved hands gloved in lavender silk. "Oh, *everyone* knows about you, Mrs. Treacher. Your imminent arrival has been the talk for weeks—and then your daring escape from the Brute!" She gasped at the memory as Violet's face remained a flat, unsmiling mask. "Oh my heavens, what an ordeal! Why, you're the most exciting thing to happen in these parts since Guinevere fought off the Huns."

The company around Mrs. Blatchford frowned. Henrietta attempted to bust into the conversation with a correction. "But I thought Guinevere was the wife of—"

The older woman shooed away historical accuracy before it could even be voiced. "Oh yes, perhaps she was something-or-other, but no one doubts she was *extraordinaire.* And I'm sure that is what you must be, my dear Mrs. Treacher. *Extraordinaire!* A hundred years hence, your exploits will be legend."

Sebastian looked at Violet, who appeared perplexed yet flattered. "You exaggerate, I'm sure, but you are very kind."

The other lady beamed. "Yes, you and Binkley must meet. You simply must. He is modest, just like you. Of course he is in a position of some importance in the government and probably should not leave London, but now I shall have an extra enticement in my quiver—for I am sure that when he discovers that the beautiful Mrs. Treacher is finally established at Trembledown, he will be all eagerness for a visit to his auntie."

"What is his business, exactly?" Sebastian asked. If the man held a position of some importance, as Mrs. Blatchford said, it was odd indeed that he had never crossed paths with him in London.

"Oh, I wouldn't know about that, my lord," Mrs. Blatchford said, frowning slightly. "He is very high up in some office or another—Binkley is always busy. But if you ask me, a young man's most important task is to know his way around a ballroom and a whist table. I hope you do not mind if I call on you very soon now, Mrs. Treacher."

"Of course, I should be honored," Violet said.

Mrs. Blatchford chuckled. "*Au revoir*, my dear. I must fly home and pen a note to Binkley!"

The others blinked in astonishment as the older woman hastened away. Sebastian had to admit he was a little amazed by the woman's behavior himself. He had always known Mrs. Blatchford to be a kind, sociable woman, but this morning her behavior toward Violet bordered on manic. She seemed to have designs on bringing her nephew together with Violet, which was understandable, Sebastian supposed, considering that Violet was known to be from a wealthy family. And now she was a woman with property.

And what property! he sniggered to himself.

He adjusted his monocle and peered at Violet. She and her cousin were still staring in some astonishment at the retreating figure of Mrs. Blatchford.

"How fortunate it is that you decided to stay in Cornwall, Mrs. Treacher. It seems that you will not only enliven our society, but also our local legends as well. Thank heavens! Those King Arthur tales *are* getting rather tired." She darted a withering glance at him, but he couldn't resist adding, "And what shall the remains of the castle Tintagel be next to the ruins of Trembledown?"

"Trembledown shall not be a ruin," she said.

"Ah—still soldiering on with your plans, I take it?"

She lifted her chin. "Of course. I have recently hired more workmen."

He nodded. "More Monks, I heard."

She tossed up her hands in exasperation. "Well, who *else* is there to hire here?"

"You are quite right," he said. "Do not take offense. I myself employ a few Monks about Montraffer—distant cousins, I believe. Slightly less bulbous of nose."

"You have them imported, no doubt," Violet shot back, "while the local variety suit my requirements nicely."

Hennie nodded. "You would not recognize Rummie Bar . . . er, that is, Barnabas Monk, in the new suit of clothes Violet provided for him. He practically looks like a squire."

Knowing the local gentry's weakness for smuggled brandy, this statement was probably truer than Miss Halsop could have possibly known.

"Excellent," he said approvingly. "You are making great progress, no doubt. And once you have Dr. Loftus's Vermin Powder at your disposal, I have no doubt Trembledown will soon seem like a bit of heaven set down on earth."

Violet's lips twisted. "You are all generosity, my lord."

"Oh yes!" Hennie agreed, having filtered out the sarcasm in his tone.

"Though I must say I think you very intrepid for having stayed in a flea-ridden house this long. You must want to remain at Trembledown for a very particular reason."

She eyed him with barely masked hostility. "For the reason that the property was my husband's and now is mine, and is therefore my responsibility."

"Duty, then," he said.

"I think it could also be a very beautiful house. Barnabas Monk's cousin said it has strong bones."

"How very fortunate," he went on, smiling into her beautiful glower. "And how fortunate for us that you are a lady of such determination and spirit. I shall be watching with interest to see what your next move will be."

"I am sure you have more important things to tend to than nosing into my affairs, my lord."

"More important, perhaps," Sebastian said with a bow, "but none so enjoyable. Good day, ladies."

"Good day!" Henrietta called after him.

Violet, he noted, remained silent.

When he arrived home, he went straight to his desk, intending to scribble a note to Cuthbert. Yet the page before him remained blank. On one hand, there was a beautiful, pampered young widow living in a flea-infested house. That certainly seemed suspect to him. But what of Mrs. Blatchford's erratic behavior? And her love of all things French? Could her foolishness be masking something more sinister?

Could either lady be capable of treason?

His mind alit on the other woman he had spoken with outside the church. Then, unconsciously, he blurted out a laugh that startled both himself and the hound that was stretched out before the fire. The dog lifted its head in questioning concern.

"If Henrietta Halsop is Nero, God help the French!" Sebastian muttered.

Chapter Six

As Violet walked back to Trembledown from shopping in Widgelyn Cross, her gaze was drawn again and again to the coastline below the path—the waves lapping up against the rocks. The little coves. She told herself that these things were beautiful and would draw the eye of anyone who cared about the picturesque . . . and yet in the back of her mind she had to admit that she looked occasionally for a glimpse—just a glimpse—of a smuggler's boat.

Oh, it was terrible, she knew. The Brute was a criminal, a villain . . . and yet there was something about him. The way he spoke to her, both mocking and admiring. The spark of challenge in those mysterious dark eyes. The dangerous strength of his arms about her . . .

These were all girlish fancies, of course, and she was no girl. So why could she not get that smuggler out of her brain? In moments of repose, as she was drifting off to sleep on her pillow at night, say, she would think again of how unforgettably strong the Brute was, how masterful yet warm his touch, his kiss. At such times, when she caught herself pining after the embraces of one who would cause most good women to shudder in revulsion, she feared she might be losing her senses entirely.

She stopped, gathering her cape about her for warmth. For a moment she thought she spied a boat. But no, it was just a shadow caused by the sun passing over a cloud.

Someone called her name, and she turned to see Hennie running toward her in wind-flapped skirts, a paper in her hand and a trill in her voice. "Violet! Here you are." She had to pause a moment to catch her breath. "I just got a letter from my friend Imogene! She says Bath is *quite affordable* this time of year."

Hennie was forever thinking of Bath. Especially since a few days before, when she had discovered a rather large-sized mouse in her bedroom. (It had actually been a rat, though the servants had been instructed to say *mouse* to soothe Hennie's hysteria.) Bath day had convinced many of the more enterprising cats to seek dryer pastures, and the marquess's miracle powder *had* rid the remaining cats of fleas, as promised. But now that the cat population had diminished, the mouse population was growing bolder.

"Imogene said the town is quite empty."

"Then why should we want to go?"

Hennie, who had to hold the paper taut between her hands to keep it from blowing away, looked up. "Because Imogene is there."

"I thought that you would like it better here now that we have started meeting people. Didn't you enjoy dining with the Cheswyns?"

"Oh, of course, but I don't fool myself that the Cheswyns were interested in *me*."

"Of course they were."

"Mr. Cheswyn barely paid me the least attention, and

Miss Cheswyn just asked me a few questions about playing harp."

A question that had led to an hour's explanation from Hennie, by the by.

"And then Miss Cheswyn loaned you that novel by Mr. Richardson, which I am sure you had no interest in," Hennie said. "She made no such offer to me."

It was true. Indeed, Violet had just returned the volume mostly unread. She had longed for any excuse to get away from the house and the noise of the men working on the roof.

"I don't mean to sulk," Hennie said. "Sulking is not in my nature—but I felt that I was only there because they wanted your company."

"There is Mrs. Blatchford. She has promised a visit."

"But she was even worse! Not that I usually even notice such things, but she only addressed me once the whole while she was speaking to us outside the church. Indeed, the only person I felt the slightest bit welcomed by was the marquess."

At the mention of that man's name, Violet stiffened. She felt just the opposite about the man—he seemed forever to be smirking and peering down at her through that monocle. "I would not call his manner at all welcoming," she said.

"I think you are wrong about him, Violet. He has been very kind. Did he not send us the ham and Dr. Loftus's Vermin Powder?"

"Both gifts smacked of condescension, if you ask me."

"But of course. The Marquess of St. Just is a man of some account. And yet when we met outside the church, he greeted me in a most friendly manner. I was flattered."

"That is probably how he wanted you to feel," Violet said.

Hennie let out a long sigh. "I know this will sound odd, Violet, but when he speaks to me I feel rather special. Almost as I did when I was speaking to the Brute."

To hear the one man—her erstwhile disreputable lover and something of a legend in her mind—compared with the other made Violet draw back almost as if her cousin had committed a sacrilege. "They are nothing alike!" she said too forcefully.

Hennie was quick to assure her, "Of course not. Nothing at all. And yet when Robert the Brute spoke to me in the carriage, he seemed to listen quite politely to what I had to say, especially when I guessed that he was running from excise men. Do you remember?"

Violet's lips flattened. "I don't like to think about it."

"No, naturally!" Hennie said, anguished. "Do forgive me. I did not mean that the Brute was in any way an equal to the marquess or any less a villain for his actions—it was only that it seemed he was kind to *me*." At this point her brow beetled slightly. "But of course he did not kidnap *me*." She looked at Violet. "Should I feel slighted?"

"Sometimes you say the most preposterous things," Violet said. "You make it sound as if the Brute snubbed you at a dance. Maybe you wish that he would pay us a social call—perhaps to bring us some of the latest fashion journals from Paris."

"Oh no," Hennie said. "I should never expect that. He would kidnap us out of our beds, I should think, before he knocked on our door."

"He will do neither. The man is no fool." Hennie shot her one of those glances that made Violet wonder if her cousin suspected more went on while she was the Brute's captive than she had admitted. "That is, I don't know if he is a fool or not, but he must be somewhat canny to have evaded the authorities for so long."

Hennie thought for a moment and nodded. "I suppose that is true. And perhaps having men like the marquess in the area keeps his action in check, also."

The marquess again! "I would trust Barnabas's sheepdog more than the marquess to keep predators at bay."

"I think you underestimate him, Violet. There is more there than meets the eye, I daresay."

Violet grunted. "Less, I would say. But since he has obviously captured your heart, I shall say no more against him. For now."

Hennie blushed. "Nonsense—you know I am not inclined to have foolish feelings for the opposite sex."

Utter rubbish. Hennie went atwitter at practically any man's attention—from marquesses to smugglers to curates to fishmongers. Violet was beginning to believe that beneath that black shift beat a heart as man-crazed as that of her own sister, Sophy. And heaven knew that would be a difficult mark to reach.

"Just last week you were rhapsodizing over the shape of the paper hanger's leg," Violet reminded her.

Hennie blushed. "Well, he was on a ladder, and anyone could see his calf muscles bulging against his trousers."

Violet bit her cheek to keep from laughing. "Men's bulges are so hard to ignore."

"Yes," Hennie agreed. Then, seeing the mirth in Violet's eyes, she went beet red. "That is—oh, heavens!"

Violet couldn't help it—she knew she was behaving like her youngest sister, but she yanked playfully on Hennie's sleeve and whooped with laughter. And to her surprise, Hennie doubled over, and the two of them hurried, covering laughter, the rest of the way back to their noisy, moldering house.

St. Just:

The ravishing Widow Treacher could be just the one we are searching for. Your French-loving neighbor is likewise suspect. I asked after her nephew, and his "very important position" is a minor secretarial post with the Horse Guards. However, that would allow him dangerous access to government matters.

Under the circumstances, perhaps your credo should be trust no one. *Except, of course, your kindly smuggler associates.*

John Cuthbert

Just as he was chuckling to himself over this latest message of dire warning from John, Sebastian came upon Mr. Cheswyn walking along the sea path. They hailed each other from afar and then greeted each other again after they had closed the distance. In shaking hands, Mr. Cheswyn was forced to move the spyglass he carried with him from his right hand to his left.

"Good day to you, my lord," the vicar said.

Sebastian's gaze snagged on the small telescope, which was raising an alarm in his mind. Cheswyn was known to all as an advocate of walking as exercise, and yet Sebastian could never remember seeing him carrying an instrument such as this about with him.

Trust no one, Cuthbert had written. But, by heaven—the vicar? Surely his profession was grounds for eliminating that man from suspicion.

"Looking for something?" Sebastian asked him.

The vicar looked down at his spyglass and chuckled. "Oh! This is just something I often carry about to make my walks more interesting. It's very useful in watching and identifying birds." He offered the instrument to Sebastian. "Would you like to take a peek through it?"

Sebastian gratefully accepted the offer and exclaimed over the utility of the item. "I can see that it *would* be useful in examining nature." It would also be handy in other areas; say, watching for small ships coming in from the continent at night.

He handed the instrument back to the vicar. "Very interesting. And it is quite beautiful, as well. The grain of that wood is very fine."

"I bought it at a very good shop in Portsmouth when I was there last. Florence chided me about the expense—she is always going on about my spending too lavishly."

Sebastian had never given much thought to a vicar's salary, though he had noted on one occasion after dining at the vicarage that Cheswyn had served a particularly fine burgundy. Yet aside from his sister, he had no family to support, so surely the man could be forgiven a few excesses?

Unless, of course, his excesses exceeded his income and he was forced to find remuneration by other, less righteous activities than his avowed profession . . .

"A thing of beauty is a pleasure in itself," Sebastian said.

"Oh yes," Mr. Cheswyn agreed. "And the owner of the shop in Portsmouth said that it would last forever."

"Well then, it was worth the expense, I'm sure."

The vicar chuckled again. "Yes, but you know how women can be."

"Precisely why I live alone," Sebastian replied. "But do not let me keep you from your exercise, Mr. Cheswyn."

They bade each other good-bye and continued on in opposite directions. Sebastian could not shake the puzzle of the spyglass out of his mind. Was it really just a little toy the vicar had bought himself for observing birds? Was Cuthbert's note causing him to see sinister motive where there was only innocent enjoyment?

He was still meandering along the sea path pondering these questions when, from a distance, he spotted Violet standing at a point where the drop to the sea was especially precipitous. He stopped, awestruck by his fair nemesis. Her slender silhouette against the rocky sea cliff made his breath catch. A graceful cape accentuated her height and long, slender neck, and as the garment whipped about her, she seemed much like a young tree buffeted by the elements. Such delicacy in such a wild atmosphere!

He stood for a moment longer in a foolish stupor, watching her silently and against his will remembering the feel of her in his arms. If he had known then that he might suspect her of being Nero, he never would have allowed himself to behave so foolishly. And still, as he looked at her, he found it hard to believe that she could be harboring traitorous thoughts. Even under the influence of brandy, she had only spoken of life's disappointments and of womanly concerns.

But of course, Sebastian thought, pulling himself out of the fugue of memory, that night in the cave had shown him multiple sides of Violet Treacher. This was no delicate creature, no wilting flower. Not only could she put away the brandy, she also had a perversely stubborn streak in her. And why was she scanning the shoreline so intently? What did those cornflower blue eyes expect to see as they stared out at the sea?

He stepped forward quietly, hoping to get a peek of what she was looking at before she noticed him.

When he was almost next to her, he could see that there was nothing remotely odd along the shore. And yet she did seem so absorbed in her study of the landscape that she was almost leaning over the cliff.

He was unable to suppress a slight smirk. He had a fairly strong idea who she was looking for. The question was, did she look out at sea with anticipation or dread of meeting with her masked kidnapper?

"Looking for someone?" he asked.

Violet whirled, her lips rounded in a started *O* of surprise, and then slipped on the damp ground, losing her footing. For a moment she tottered just at the edge of the precipice, her long, graceful arms windmilling frantically. Her woolen muff was flung to the ground.

Sebastian reached forward, grabbing her about the waist, and pulled her to him. She landed against his chest and gasped in shock and relief. His heart was thumping with unnatural speed. Her lithe body felt so vulnerable in his arms. Again he felt that strange dichotomy of strength emanating from such ethereal beauty.

He looked into her face expecting some reflection of the mixture of his own feelings, yet found that her lips were twisting in a most unpleasant fashion and those blue eyes were hardening on him like crystals. "Unhand me!" she said.

Stunned, he did so, and yet as she hopped away from him, she slipped again and he reached out instinctively to grab her hand. She took it, righted herself, and then flapped it away from her as if it were a slimy object she had unwittingly picked up. "Would you let me go!" she said, jumping yet farther away and trying to gather herself.

"That's a fine way to address someone who just saved your life," he said, laughing at her antics.

Her eyes flew open. "*Saved* it?" she repeated. "You very nearly killed me! I could have ended up dashed to pieces on the rocks below!"

"Yes, I meant to warn you that you should not stand so close to the edge."

She rolled her eyes. "Had I known that someone might creep up on me, I certainly would not have done so!"

"My apologies if I startled you. I certainly did not mean to *creep*." A slight lie, he knew. But he preferred the term *approach stealthily*. It had a more professional, less lurid quality to it. "I could not help but notice that you seemed very interested in whatever it was you were looking at. Were you perhaps hoping to catch a glimpse of your romantic kidnapper, the Brute?"

Her mouth dropped open. "That is ridiculous! Why would I be looking for him?"

He took out his monocle and polished it with a handkerchief. "For *auld lang syne*?" he joked.

Her mouth turned down at his little jest, but she asked with a look of unease, "Surely smugglers are not active in the daytime?"

"No, I believe their usual work schedule is at night, although you can never be sure which boats at sea are actually being used for fishing or as cover for the gentlemen." Sebastian added, "But whether you are in more in danger from smugglers or from your own uncertain footing, you should be more careful."

"I was only enjoying the scenery," she said.

"Yes, you seemed quite absorbed in it. I just passed Mr. Cheswyn—no doubt you saw him, too."

"No, I did not."

"Ah—he must have been slightly ahead of you, then.

That is unfortunate, because he had a most beautiful spyglass with him that would have allowed you to enjoy the scenery much more effectively." His eyes narrowed. "You might even have been able to spot boats out on the sea."

Two blotches of red appeared high in her fair cheeks. He wondered what that meant.

"Was it to tell me of Mr. Cheswyn's spyglass that you sneaked up on me unawares?"

He smiled. "Your assumption that I was sneaking would seem to indicate some suspicion of your behavior on my part. And what on earth would I have to suspect you of?"

"What indeed!" she shot back at him. She took that moment to bend to the ground and recover her muff.

"Perhaps your great love of the outdoors explains why you seemed almost as if you were looking for something as you scanned the shore."

Straightening again, she stared at him icily. "I have lived most of my life landlocked in Yorkshire or in London. I have not often traveled to the sea. Isn't it natural that I should find myself drawn to it now? Besides, Trembledown is at sixes and sevens at the moment. The workmen have started—they are retiling the roof and papering the salon as we speak."

"Ah, then your redecorating scheme for the house has already begun."

"Not just the house, my lord. I also have great plans of making something quite beautiful out of the grounds." Violet then added, "And at least the building will not crumble in the first strong wind, which I had feared when I first laid eyes on the place."

Sebastian chuckled. "You led me to believe that you considered it a jewel only to be parted with at the highest price!"

"And so it is, it turns out," she said, flashing him a

saucy smile. "And by the time I finish polishing it up, the price will be considerably higher."

"Then you were very right not to sell the property to me, I suppose, when I offered for it. Just take care you do not overdo," he said, "or you will have difficulty finding a buyer. As you might have noticed, the society in this area is not particularly lively."

"I would beware of disparaging the society too harshly, my lord," she said, a tight smile on her lips. "You seem to be the grand personage at its center."

He bit back a laugh. "Rather like the dog looking down on all the hounds, is that what you mean?"

"You are much cleverer with words than I am," Violet said, casting her eyes down with assumed demureness.

He couldn't help chuckling in spite of himself. "With the addition of two so charming and illustrious ladies to the neighborhood, I can see the tenor of local society is on the rise."

Red flooded back into her cheeks; this time, however, instead of playful antagonism there was something forbidding in her expression that he could not quite read.

"Did I say something wrong?"

She drew herself up even taller. "Do you not think I know a sneer when I see one, my lord? That *illustrious* allusion was doing it too brown! Perhaps you believe, then, that my antecedents do not add to the quality of local society."

The words shocked him. "I didn't mean that!"

"My father, as I am certain you knew only too well, was in trade."

"What possible difference could that make?" he asked. "Why, I never—"

Then, remembering that he *had* said something rather disparaging about Violet's merchant background to Cuthbert, he could not help feeling angrier still. At himself, and at Violet for flying off the handle and putting him in such an untenable position. To defend oneself against being a snob by saying one was not outright inevitably sounded insincere.

He should have known better than to have fallen into this trap. During their night in the cave, Violet had revealed her insecurity on this matter, just before he had taken her in his arms. His anger lost steam as he was once again reminded of their encounter in the smuggler's hole.

Her brow wrinkled slightly as she stared at him. And no wonder, since he had dropped off in midargument. "My lord?"

That blasted cave! He should not think of it. And yet, how could he avoid it? She seemed to have bewitched him in those few hours. Like now. Even though he had only an interest in finding out *why* she had been looking out to sea, here he was thinking of how like the sea her brilliant blue eyes were.

Foolish nonsense, of course. And yet, the history of man's downfall was full of such instances of foolishness. Sebastian had never been susceptible to the whims and wiles of females. *A trifle stodgy,* he had heard someone once mutter of him at his club.

Not that Sebastian had cared one whit—it was this reputation that made it all the easier to manage his double life. No one suspected that he secretly carried on as an unofficial government spy.

And yet, he wondered when the time came for him to give up the Brute and he no longer had an outlet for more adventurous impulses, would he really notice the difference? His natural inclination was toward the phlegmatic. His brother—one of the rare, flamboyant St. Justs of history—had often goosed him for his lack of flair.

On this melancholy memory, a shudder went through

him and Violet reached out to his elbow, her expression worried. "Are you quite all right?"

Sebastian felt an electric thrill where her hand grasped his coat—it seemed to burn through the wool. Now it was his turn nearly to go over a cliff. He gave himself a mental slap and braced his lips into something resembling a smile. "I'm sorry, I was thinking of someone I used to know."

She eyed him doubtfully for a moment, and then forced a smile. "It is not flattering to tell a woman you are thinking of another woman when you are looking at her, you know."

"This was not another woman."

"All the worse!" she said. "To be ignored in favor of a man's carousing companions is hardly better."

Had he and Phineas caroused? Not often enough, Sebastian thought regretfully. "I was thinking of my brother."

"I was not aware . . ." She frowned. "Does he also reside in the area?"

"No. Phineas was killed three years ago, on a battle-field in Spain."

Violet's face fell slack. "I am sorry, my lord. It must be dreadful to lose a sibling. Mine frequently drive me to distraction, but I can't imagine life without them."

"I felt much the same way about Phin. We were not alike in character or demeanor, but still he was my closest friend."

"How were you not alike?"

"Phin was all laughter and bonhomie. He was always getting into scrapes. Of course, he was allowed this freedom, not being the oldest son and heir. To me fell the responsibility of keeping up the good name of the St. Justs."

"I think I know a little of how you feel. I was the first to go off to school and into the world and learn that there was prejudice against us out there. I tried to avert disaster for my siblings by earning a sterling reputation and preaching propriety to my two sisters. I am afraid the lessons didn't take very well."

Sebastian laughed. "I can see how they might not. Phin only laughed when I tried to lecture him on the errors of his ways. Now I wish I had spent less time lecturing and more time laughing with him."

As a strong gust of wind blew strands of hair across Violet's face, she shivered.

The wind seemed to break his spell of melancholy. He smiled politely at her. "No doubt you are wishful of returning home. I will bid you good day."

For a moment she looked almost regretful, which made it even clearer to him that he should take his leave of her before he made a complete ass out of himself.

"Good-bye, then," she said. "Take care."

"Yes, I will be careful to tread noisily so as not to scare any further unsuspecting damsels."

On the way back to Montraffer, two different trails of thoughts kept crossing in his mind. First, that on the face of things, Violet seemed very suspicious indeed. She had arrived in Cornwall at the exact time the message had warned of Nero's appearance. She had stubbornly decided to stay, although she could not be happy living at Trembledown. And what *had* she been doing on that cliff, really?

But then another series of questions seemed just as compelling. Had not he himself been the catalyst for her coming to Trembledown?

What if she *was* merely admiring the beauty of the coastline?

More troubling yet, what if he had developed a fatal weakness for the woman he was supposed to suspect of a wicked crime?

Chapter Seven

The parlor at Trembledown was finally habitable. It was so improved, in fact, that Violet no longer wanted to leave it. Whereas a few days before she had hardly been able to force herself to stay away from the cliffs overlooking the sea to watch for a sign of the Brute, now she simply wanted to collapse in her chaise and dwell on her accomplishment.

Part of what drove her indoors was the experience of nearly being tossed off a cliff by the marquess. Also, she had caught Barnabas Monk watching her suspiciously as she came back from a walk and feared she would fall prey to more of his silent, subtle blackmail. God knew there seemed no end of Monk relatives for her to hire; most recently she had acquired one Clarence Monk, gardener, although that elderly gentleman seemed more fond of naps than nasturtiums.

For all these problems, she might still be outdoors were it not for the weather. A storm had blown in, driving all sensible creatures inside (including the cats, who had only just been convinced to embrace the great outdoors by threats of regular dousing in Dr. Loftus's powder). Not only was the driving rain accompanied by an incessant howling wind, the incessant downpour seemed to play tricks on everyone's minds. Hennie was more fretful; Peabody more morose.

Violet had even experienced her own senses becoming disturbed. One night, as the storm had blown in, she had actually thought she had heard the Brute calling out to her and had run out the door in her gown and cape. The wild moment—and the fact that she had ended up drenched and chilled and feeling foolish—had put an end to her obsessing about the Brute. He had said he would bother her no more, and finally she believed him. To do otherwise likely would result in pneumonia.

And so now she was happily housebound, which was fortunate given the inclement weather. Her parlor was a pleasure to her. The plaster had been patched, the timbers fixed and oiled. Rotten boards in the floor had been replaced, and the chimney was cleaned so that a roaring fire now kept the room cozy. She had picked paper for the room that was just the perfect shade of robin's egg blue. The sofa had been reupholstered in a midnight velvet that, now that her maid Lettie was on constant guard for cats, bore pleasurably few signs of fur.

One cat, stubbornly, remained in the salon—the scraggly one-eyed cat Violet had unofficially christened Sebastian for his habit of showing up where he was least wanted. That and the fact that with his bad eye permanently closed, the other large blue one reminded her of her noble foe with his monocle.

Sebastian, the nonfeline incarnation, she had not seen, though his man had brought over a leg of lamb the Saturday after she had run into Sebastian on her walk. The cut of meat apparently was reparation for nearly sending her over the cliff.

Violet had to admit that for all his irritating qualities—his sneakiness, his smirking through his monocle at her, his endless questions—there had been something about his manner when they had been walking along the cliff that had made her feel a surprising sympathy toward the man. The way he had seemed so melancholy when he had spoken of his brother dying had left her in no doubt that he was capable of feeling. Her prior conversations with Sebastian, and certainly their correspondence, had made her assume him a very cold character. And yet he had not seemed at all cold on that day.

At least not all of the time. And yet he could be so infuriating.

Hennie, sitting on her usual chair, let out a sigh. She had been doing this with increasing regularity throughout the day.

"What is it?"

"Oh, nothing," Hennie replied, "nothing at all."

Violet waited. When Hennie said nothing, it usually meant something.

"Except this inclement weather does wear on one's nerves," Hennie said. "Does the wind not howl most frightfully? I keep thinking the sound is meant as a warning. *'To Bath . . .'* it seems to say. Do you not hear it say so?"

Violet bit her lip. She knew too well the dangers of hearing in the wind what one wanted to hear. "Not exactly that. To me it seems to be saying, *Repair the shutters . . .*"

Hennie looked astounded, then she laughed as she recognized Violet's attempt at humor. "And yet I *do* think we should go to Bath."

Violet never would have guessed life at Widgelyn Cross would be such a hardship for a woman who had spent most of her life shut up with her invalid aunt outside a similarly tiny town in Yorkshire. Or maybe it was just that reason that made Hennie so restless and intent on enjoying the fleshpots now. She was a like a bird escaped from her cage who wanted to try every branch.

Violet had once thought they should leave as soon as possible, too. Yet her triumph with the parlor and then the main hallway had made her think she wanted to make a success of the entire renovation. The workmen were currently at work on the dining room, and she had hopes of starting on the little ballroom on the second floor soon, too. Now that the roof was nearly rainproof, she felt secure in redecorating the upper floors of the house.

At the doorway, Peabody cleared his throat. "A letter came for you, madam."

"Who is it from?"

"Mrs. Blatchford."

If Hennie seemed unhappy that they had not retreated to Bath, Peabody was practically inconsolable. He sulked about Trembledown like a thwarted child, rolling his eyes at the exploits and inefficiencies of the Monk family. Though Violet had once considered him as one of her closest confidants, he now fell into sullen silence more often than not. Occasionally she had wondered if he had been hitting the bottle. Simple communications like this one had become a chore.

"Could I read it, please?"

Peabody handed her the note. Violet cut him a sidewise glance as she broke the seal and unfolded the letter.

My Dear Mrs. Treacher,

Forgive me for not paying you a call as I had promised. Alas, the rain has kept me indoors. I did

*so want to see your progress on Trembledown, and
also to extend an invitation to have tea here Thursday afternoon. I do so hope you can make it, and
your friend Miss Halsop, too! The Cheswyns will be
here, and the Marquess of St. Just has just popped
by unannounced and promised to grace us with his
presence. He dropped so many hints of being fond
of Cook's Dundee cake that I felt compelled to
invite him. In all my years in Widgelyn Cross, I have
never known the man to be so sociable.*

    *Best of all, my nephew, Binkley Jacobs, whom I
may have mentioned to you when first we met, is to
arrive tomorrow and will most certainly be here to
make your acquaintance on Thursday. At long last!
I know you shall get along famously. I have a sense
for these things.*

    À bientôt!

    Yours very sincerely,

    Hortense Blatchford

Violet read the missive aloud for Hennie, adding many
explanations about the nerve of the marquess. "Practically *forcing* poor Mrs. Blatchford to extend an
invitation!"

"I wonder if this nephew of hers realizes how his arrival has been built up," Hennie mused when she was
done. "Or what competition he shall have."

Violet blinked at Hennie. "What are you talking about?"

"Why, the marquess, of course."

"Don't be a goose!" Violet chided her cousin. "It is not
as if I am looking for a husband. It is enough that I have
a house to take care of. And as for the marquess!" She
let out an unladylike snort. "Binkley Jacobs has little to

worry about on that account, I assure you. I am leery of any man who tries to kill me."

"You said you slipped on a rock."

"Yes, but in retrospect I am not sure that isn't like the chicken declaring he ended up in the soup pot because his neck got stuck in the wrong pair of hands."

"Oh, Violet! You know you slipped. The marquess is a perfect gentleman."

"Far from perfect, in my opinion," grumbled Violet as she perused the letter again. "This comment about his wanting Dundee cake! Clearly even Mrs. Blatchford saw that he was using the cake as a ploy. The question is what motive he could have for wheedling an invitation."

"Perhaps he just wants an excuse to see you again."

"I cannot see why he would bother," Violet scoffed.

Hennie shot her a knowing look. "I can."

Hennie was suggesting some sort of romantic hankerings, which was utter nonsense. To Violet it seemed as if the marquess was actually antagonistic toward her. She could not forget the way he was staring at her in church. And why had he been sneaking up to her when she was standing next to that cliff? He had never answered that question to her satisfaction.

The idea of his having a fondness for her was absurd on its face. Men didn't go around pushing the women they loved off precipices. Not in her experience, anyway.

Hennie looked at her thoughtfully. "Before we left Yorkshire, I'm sure you would have savored a marquess's company above all others. Except perhaps a duke's."

"Really, Hen, how vulgar."

"How often did I hear you lament the fact that your husband died before he could assume his rightful place as a marquess?" her cousin reminded her.

Violet shifted uncomfortably. Perhaps she *had* been rather vocal on that unfortunate point. "I was grief stricken."

"Of course. But after all, just as soon as you tossed off your mourning you were willing—nay, eager! —to settle for an earl. And the Earl of Clatsop was twice as old as Sebastian, and there is simply no comparing their physical attractions. Not even the most charitable woman would have described the earl as handsome."

Violet frowned as she mulled this over. She had been quite determined in her pursuit of that old coot Clatsop and his title. Happily, she had discovered that the earl possessed a decrepit castle that made Trembledown look like a palace in a fairy tale. Thank heavens she had come to her senses before she had snared him.

Of course, she must admit he had become happily engaged to someone else before she had managed to snag him!

"I am beginning to think I have undervalued men like Binkley Jacobs," Violet told Hennie. "Certainly he is bound to be a refreshing change from the marquess."

"Oh, madam, *don't!*"

Peabody let out such a cry of anguish that both Violet and Hennie looked up, startled. Violet had almost forgotten that he was still standing there. "What's wrong?"

"If you knew how it pains me to hear you saying such things!" he exclaimed. "Have you forgotten where you are or the horrors that have befallen you here? Have all our ambitions to lift ourselves to a higher station in life completely deserted you? I have heard that the marquess owns a copper mine large enough to supply pots for all of Europe. Now is not the time to turn democratic!"

Peabody, sensing he had said too much, lifted his hand to his face and fled from the room.

"What has come over him?" Violet asked.

Hennie shook her head in sympathy for the man. "It is

the wind and rain of this place, no doubt. It shall be all of our undoing."

Violet stood quickly. Perhaps Hennie's wind theory was correct, or maybe they were all just too much in each other's company. In which case, tea at Mrs. Blatchford's would be a welcome change.

"Are you going to write Mrs. Blatchford a note of acceptance?" Hennie asked her.

"Yes, of course. But first I must assure Peabody that I am not about to elope with a commoner before he starts to make inroads into Mrs. Monk's cooking sherry."

"What a lovely day we have!" Mrs. Blatchford trilled out to Violet and Hennie as she greeted them from a sunroom done in startling shades of yellow and red. In a moment she was on her feet and galloping toward the newcomers full speed. "I worried and worried that terrible old rain wouldn't stop, but Binkley was all the night assuring me that the day would be fair. *Et voilà!* Binkley is so smart about the weather."

Not only was Violet dazzled by the flaming wall color all around her, which she had not expected as she'd entered the little gray stone cottage, she was also a bit dumbstruck by Mrs. Blatchford herself, who, by the pungent smell of jasmine that accompanied her, had bathed this morning in cologne. She was dressed in a black satin underskirt with a robe of gray watered silk; on her head was an Armenian turban of silver and black satin. On her short, round bulk the ensemble made quite an amazing impression. "Welcome to my *salon!*"

Violet and Hennie shot each other assessing glances; from their muslin and bonnets, they had obviously not expected such an exotic affair in Widgelyn Cross.

As Violet stammered a reply about being glad their carriage did not get stuck in the mud, she peeked around her hostess's shoulder. Mr. and Miss Cheswyn (in muslin, too—thank heavens!) were sitting on a sofa, while the marquess, monocle in place, held court in a chair nearby, cup and saucer in hand, a plate of cake perched on his knee. It was quite a feat of balance.

Mrs. Blatchford wrenched her guest's attention from the marquess by volubly calling for her nephew. "Binkley! Come greet my newest neighbor, Mrs. Treacher." She stood aside to let a young man scoot by her in the doorway and added, almost as an afterthought, "Oh, and this is Miss Halsop."

Violet could see at once why Mrs. Blatchford was inordinately proud of her nephew. Binkley Jacobs was a young man of average height, but he carried himself very well and greeted Violet with an open, friendly smile. She was caught by the contrast of his golden hair and his darker brows and brown eyes, which were practically the color of rich honey.

Binkley made a deep bow to both ladies. "I am so pleased to meet you, Mrs. Treacher, Miss Halsop. I cannot tell you how glad I am that my aunt will have someone new to visit here in Widgelyn Cross."

Mrs. Blatchford laughed. "Listen to the boy! He worries I lack for society, when I keep telling him that I am as happy here as I would be in Mayfair."

"I am sure one would not find better society there than you have assembled here today, auntie."

That was overstating the case a bit, Violet thought as her hostess finally ushered her two newest guests into the sunroom.

As they exchanged greetings with the Cheswyns, the marquess rearranged his various plates and saucers on a small side table, secured his monocle, and stood. "Wasn't it charming of Mrs. Cheswyn to have us all?" he asked. "And she seemed to know instinctively of my fondness for Dundee cake!"

Violet bit her lip. "Perhaps she possesses clairvoyant powers."

"Oh no," Hennie reminded her. "Remember the letter? He told Mrs. Blatchford he liked it during his visit."

The marquess smiled, not the least ashamed to be caught in a little fib. "Yes, no doubt I did. And it was so kind of her to go to the trouble." He smiled at Violet. "And I am so glad you and your cousin could join us."

"It is good to see you, too, my lord. Especially since there are no cliff faces in the vicinity," she said, harking back to their last encounter. To the bewildered stares of the others, she explained, "Several days ago the marquess startled me so that I was nearly flung off the sea path onto the rocks below."

The others in the room seemed astonished into silence by this accusation, while Hennie cast a ludicrous look of gratitude at Sebastian. "My cousin told me you had saved her from her clumsiness."

"That is not exactly how I put it, Hen." Violet shot an amused glance at her cousin. "I was pushed; I have no doubt of it."

The marquess laughed. "Ah, but how else could I contrive to rush to your rescue?"

Violet took a teacup offered her by her hostess. "I see. Supplied with a damsel, you create your own distress."

"You have to admit, there is logic to my method," he said.

Binkley's dark brows beetled gravely. "It sounds very dangerous to me. I am amazed you can jest about such things, Mrs. Treacher."

Mr. Cheswyn nodded his agreement and hastened to

add a few words to exonerate the marquess, who, after all, he was dependent on for his living at the vicarage. "I blame your shoes, Mrs. Treacher. I am sure you were wearing a pair unsuitable for walking. Ladies are forever gadding about in foot coverings that are bound to allow them to slip—why, they even call them slippers!" He took a few moments to chuckle at his own joke before admonishing, "Boots, Mrs. Treacher! What you need is a sturdy, snug pair of boots such as I wear."

Rather shockingly, the cleric lifted his trousers to better model a pair of square-toed black boots, polished to a high gloss.

The ladies were rendered speechless by the demonstration, but the marquess moved closer to inspect the footgear through his monocle. "Very fine quality," he observed. "Are they from a local bootmaker?"

"London," Mr. Cheswyn replied.

"Then they likely cost you a great deal," the marquess observed.

"One of my brother's little extravagances," Florence Cheswyn said, with a chuckle to hide what seemed to be embarrassment. "I am forever scolding him about expenditures."

"And yet fine things last longer, I have discovered," Binkley said. He smiled affably at Mr. Cheswyn. "And you obviously take great care. One could almost use those boot tips as mirrors! Does your man polish them for you every day?"

Mr. Cheswyn seemed taken aback by the question. "I have no valet."

"Then I congratulate you, sir! I am sure my man Quimby could not polish a pair of boots half so well, and he is renowned for his skill."

At the mention of the name Quimby, Mrs. Blatchford

rolled her eyes. "Mr. Quimby is my nephew's valet, and such a stir he caused this morning! *Quel horreur!* Finch was convinced that half the silver service had gone missing and positively insisted that all rooms be searched for the missing cutlery. Several of the maids raised a breeze and Cook almost walked out. But the greatest uproar came from Binkley's new valet, Quimby, who was quite top-lofty, insisting that *his* room not be searched. Quite as if he were one of the family!"

"And how I wish you had heeded him, auntie," Binkley said, breaking into her tale of domestic woe. "Quimby, whose services I only recently acquired, almost turned in his notice. I was quite lucky to get a valet of his training. Why, he once worked for a viscount!" He looked around at the others with a smile. "Anyway, it turned out that old Finch had forgotten that he had moved the silver into one of the cellars for safekeeping, so it was all much ado about nothing."

Mrs. Blatchford sniffed. "I still don't think your Quimby had any right to complain when all the servants' rooms were searched. Even my Nellie's—and she has been my maid since before I married your uncle!"

"But really, aunt, Quimby is simply irreplaceable. I was fortunate to get the man—all the finest bucks in London vied for his services. I was quite afraid that he would balk at coming to Cornwall during the Season, but he took it very well. But to then arrive and instantly be suspected of pinching the silver—I was mortified, I can tell you!"

Violet silently clucked in shared exasperation over this tale. The man sounded as dictatorial as Peabody.

"In the end, I had to give Quimby the day off," Binkley said. "I sent him into town to cool his head. If I hadn't done, I fear he might have tendered his resignation, leaving me without a valet in Widgelyn Cross for heaven knows how long!"

"Then your visit is to be a long one?" Violet asked Binkley.

"I hope so. Now that I am here, I would like to stop a while."

"And I shall want him to stay even longer than he can, Mrs. Treacher!" his aunt interjected.

"Dear aunt!" Binkley said, fondly.

Violet could not help noticing that although the marquess was listening politely to some remarks exchanged between Hennie and Miss Cheswyn, his ear seemed bent toward her and Binkley.

"Do you get to Cornwall often to visit her?" she asked.

"Not as often as I would like. I am afraid it is a case of when my work permits me to get away, which is infrequently."

"I am surprised your work permitted you now," the marquess said.

Binkley jumped a little in surprise. He apparently had believed he was having a confidential exchange with Violet. "Actually, sir, things are rather slow at the moment. Napoleon is tucked asleep on Elba; our troops on the continent are dwindled in number and stationary . . ." He shrugged. "It seemed a good time to ask leave to visit Auntie. She is the closest relative I have."

Well. That seemed to answer the marquess's prying question thoroughly, Violet could not help thinking with a smirk.

"And of course," Binkley added, looking at her warmly, "this area has other enticements as well."

Oh dear. Such open flirtation was not at all called for, or desired. Violet took a quick sip of tea and looked away; unfortunately, her flustered gaze collided with the marquess's keen stare. Having that large eye peering through the glass at her got her back up, and yet she couldn't forget Hennie's insinuating that the marquess was interested in her. Indeed, by the sharp way he looked at Binkley, one would almost think the man jealous.

Simply preposterous.

"But that is enough about me," Binkley said, taking no heed of the marquess. "I am more interested in hearing about you, Mrs. Treacher. How do you like Trembledown?"

"Very much."

"Trembledown is one of the oldest houses in the area. Auntie said there was quite a bit of talk when it was heard that the Treachers had bestowed it on you. I would imagine it makes you a lady of some standing in Widgelyn Cross?"

Violet did not deem it appropriate to answer to her standing—substantial or otherwise—and so changed the subject. "I am also quite taken with Widgelyn Cross and the seaside generally. I have always been landlocked, and so I find the ocean views quite lovely."

As the subject had turned to nature, Mr. Cheswyn's head came up. "If it is views you love, Mrs. Treacher, then by all means we should take a stroll after tea. Mrs. Blatchford's property possesses one of the best vistas in all of Cornwall—the sight across a cove to the property on which sits Montraffer, the marquess's estate."

The marquess bowed smugly from his chair. "The house *is* very well situated," he agreed without hesitation.

"It is one of the most beautiful homes in all of England," Mr. Cheswyn waxed on, "and exquisitely well kept. The landscape is the loveliest I have ever laid eyes on. I say that not only because his lordship is my patron, but as an inveterate admirer of beauty in the natural world."

Not to mention an inveterate windbag, a demon in Violet's brain remarked caustically. She smiled.

"I am sure the ground is very damp," Mrs. Blatchford said, apparently anxious lest the breathtaking views of the marquess's house outshine the more personable attributes of her nephew. "I would not like to see anyone slipping off a cliff here."

"Do not worry, Mrs. Blatchford, I will endeavor to stay more than arm's length from Mrs. Treacher," the marquess said, to general laughter.

"Walking is the best thing for one after consuming rich cake," Mr. Cheswyn pressed on, oblivious to the fact that, with the exception of the marquess, no one seemed enthusiastic for his plan.

Or so it appeared, until Hennie piped up, "I should enjoy a walk myself. Ever since I heard Mr. Cheswyn's sermon, it has occurred to me that I ought to see more of the countryside here."

"Then you must allow me, Miss Halsop," Mrs. Blatchford said politely, "to loan you a lovely book I have detailing the history of our area. It details some magnificent local walks, and talks about all the buildings of significance." Perhaps she thought the bestowing of literature could avert the need for a walk.

Hennie smiled gratefully. "Thank you. I am sure I would enjoy reading that very much."

"I believe Montraffer is featured in that book," the marquess said. Immodestly.

"And Trembledown?" Binkley asked.

"Doubtful," came a chorus from the room.

Binkley looked offended for Violet's sake. "I'm sure it deserves to be. Whenever I've seen it in the distance, I've always exclaimed over what a remarkable edifice it is. Have I not, aunt?"

Mrs. Blatchford blinked at him. "Why yes, I think you have."

"I am attempting to remedy the unfortunate state it has fallen into," Violet said.

"You seem to be a woman of spirit," Binkley said, smiling frankly at her.

"Oh, watch out, Mrs. Treacher," Mrs. Blatchford teased with a matronly wink. "My nephew does not flatter many women, but when he does, he can make himself quite a pest."

Violet laughed somewhat nervously. It did feel as if Binkley was dumping the butter boat on her head.

Happily—or unhappily, in the opinion of Mrs. Blatchford—the little party soon decided that it was time to see for themselves the magnificent vistas Mr. Cheswyn was telling them about. The French doors from the sunroom led out to a nicely laid stone path to the sea walk.

All was as Mr. Cheswyn had said. The cottage was situated near a part of the road where there was a much gentler sloping hill that led down to a small cove. There was no danger of anyone toppling off a cliff here. It was a lovely day, chilly yet clear, with the almost-still cerulean waters lapping gently against the shore. And across the cove, up a hill in the distance, stood Montraffer, which was, as the vicar had predicted, a house like no other.

"Oh, how lovely!" Hennie rhapsodized, staring off at Montraffer. "What an extremely elegant home, my lord. You must be so proud of it!"

As Violet peered up to Montraffer, she was chagrined to admit that it would have been difficult to overstate the beauty of the place. The house was constructed in stone similar to that used at Trembledown, but the architectural style was of a more modern vintage. It was a magnificent house—palatial in size and its stately aspect, with the one ornamental flourish of a turret jutting up through the right side.

Violet could not look at that turret without a pang of envy. She loved turrets! She did not normally consider herself a fanciful person, and yet how easy it was to imagine oneself a princess in such a place—a medieval princess pacing in her turret awaiting the arrival of a loyal knight! Or better yet, one's princely husband, who would arrive back from faraway lands bearing jewels. She would be able to keep an eye out to sea and await the return of her lover.

Utter nonsense. And yet that was the power of good architecture—like a work of art, it had the power to transport one out of the humdrum everydayness of life.

No end of exclamations over the appearance of the house and the beauty of the day followed from the other guests. Violet was surprised to find even Binkley rather obsequious in his praise. Of course, it was difficult not to exclaim over such a place, not to mention the land-scape. Fat rhododendron bushes covered the grounds, nearly breaking Violet's heart. In another month there would be a riot of blooms on those bushes, to follow the beds of spring bulbs pillowing the ground with their blooms now and early wildflowers in white and blue skimming up the hill. How she would love to have brilliant color like that around Trembledown!

"What lovely shrubs!" she said, almost against her will.

She caught the marquess looking at her—no doubt awaiting for more offerings of praise from her. She sent him a tight smile and turned her gaze back to the sea, feeling rather foolish for her outburst. Before she settled at Trembledown, she never would have taken notice of a man's shrubbery.

As the rest of the party milled about, letting the sun warm their faces, Violet found Binkley at her side once more.

"I can see why the marquess was eager to join our party today," he whispered to her.

"Why?" Violet asked idly.

He pointed to the view of Montraffer. "Who wouldn't want to spend the afternoon forcing one's neighbors to admire all one's riches?"

"Do you not appreciate architecture, Mr. Jacobs?"

"I do. But I believe my lord's house is rather . . . gaudy, don't you think?"

Actually, she thought it was wonderful. "Well, it is his family's home. It is not as if he built it himself."

"And yet by his smug complacency, you would never guess the fact."

Finally! Someone else who found the marquess smug and irritating. She leaned in toward Binkley. "And yet when we first saw it, you were praising the house to the skies."

"Do you find me insincere?"

"I was merely pointing out a contradiction, Mr. Jacobs."

He snorted. "A roundabout way of pointing out that you think I am a humbug. Well, I am a humbug. He is an important man, and I was flattering him."

She chuckled. "Never have I seen a man wear his insincerity more honestly."

He sent her a mock bow. "I am not one of those men who does not admit to being a toady. I accept that life requires a man of my station to flatter and fawn. And with all other things, I find that if one must perform an unpleasant task, one should perform it with zeal."

"How then can one know whether your words are true

or simply spoken with an eye on personal gain?" Violet asked him.

He touched her hand with meaningful pressure. "In your case, Mrs. Treacher, you have my word that I am perfectly sincere."

She felt color rise in her cheeks that caused her to express a sudden desire to speak with the Cheswyns. She was not unhappy when Binkley joined her, either. She appreciated his honest humor, his good looks, and the fact that he seemed to see through the marquess's pomposity, as she herself had. And though she had surprised herself today by enjoying a few moments of banter with the marquess, it was Mr. Jacobs, she decided, who was her preferred companion in this company.

One glance at Hennie, who had strolled a few paces away from the others with the marquess and was now staring worshipfully into his lordship's eyes, told Violet that her cousin had reached the opposite conclusion.

Although Miss Halsop seemed unaware that she was being watched by her cousin, Sebastian was not. He had been conducting a subtle investigation of Violet all afternoon, noting how she comported herself around the others in general and especially her reactions to the unsubtle overtures of Mr. Jacobs. (She enjoyed them too well, in his opinion.) That man had raised his suspicions, too. According to Cuthbert, Jacobs held a minor post in the Horse Guards, yet he traveled like a gentleman with his own valet. A gift of gab and a fondness for his old aunt had to be added in his favor, yet these qualities did not preclude his being a spy.

Sebastian began to wonder if a more sinister purpose than romance made Jacobs so desire to establish a fast friendship with Mrs. Treacher. Or perhaps they knew one another already and were disguising that fact. Could they be in league together?

He hoped to get information out of Henrietta, who seemed to be looser of tongue than her cousin. Less tart of tongue, as well.

Right now she was still in raptures over the view. "I do not think I have truly appreciated the beauty of Cornwall until now. My, but how it does make me itch to be at my easel again. I wonder if I could ever do justice to such a prospect!"

Surprised, Sebastian observed, "I didn't realize that we had an artist in our midst. Do you specialize in portraits or landscapes?"

She folded her hands modestly. "As to being an artist, I am the merest dabbler, you must know. In fact, some years ago my aunt became so ill that she could no longer abide the smell of paint in the house, so I was forced to give up my hobby. But I begin to think that it is time that I took it up again."

"You should. Any time you feel the need to recapture this moment of inspiration, I hope you will feel free to come to Montraffer. Indeed, I would feel honored if you would do so."

"Oh, my lord. That is a very kind offer. I have no paint with me, but I suppose I could sketch . . ."

"It is a pity you have no paints. Perhaps you could send for some? I imagine you and your cousin are in communication with your relatives in London?"

"Yes, Violet's sister and aunt are there." Her brows knit. "Her sister Sophy might be able to procure some paints and canvases for me."

"I wouldn't doubt it. Does Violet . . . er, Mrs. Treacher

. . . have a great deal of correspondence to tend to each morning, as most ladies seem to?"

"Just a few notes from family."

That was good.

"Her father is on the continent at the moment, in Italy. So she gets letters from quite far-off places, too."

That was not good.

Henrietta looked at him keenly. "It is very kind of you to take an interest in our postal situation, my lord."

She obviously thought he feared a rival; perhaps that could be useful to him as well. "No mysterious notes, then, that might indicate a dashing lover?"

Miss Halsop giggled. "No, indeed."

"I have been accused more than once in having too much curiosity. Forgive me."

"Do not apologize, my lord. Indeed, I think it very fortunate that you have graced us with such marked attention. I admit I was quite worried about Violet when we first arrived."

"Why?"

"I had never seen her so restless."

Ah. "Naturally, with so much amiss at Trembledown, she would have a lot on her mind. I worried that a lady would wear herself out taking charge of a vast project on what is, after all, a rather negligible piece of property."

Hennie frowned. "No . . . I don't think her troubled state of mind had to do with Trembledown. Not entirely, that is. Violet was always very good at taking charge of practical things."

"Then perhaps her ordeal with the Brute—"

"Those were my thoughts exactly!" Henrietta broke in. "There has been something disturbing in her behavior these past weeks. She has told me more than once that we have nothing more to fear from Robert the Brute, and yet for a while I think she *did* fear he would return. Nay, it almost seemed as if she was watching for him."

"Why did you think this?"

He halfway expected Henrietta to relate tales of nighttime disappearances and rough men at the back stairs. Indeed, she looked so anguished for a moment that he expected only the direst revelations from her.

She wrung her hands. "I should not gossip, my lord."

"Please," he said. "You can trust me, surely. Anything you tell me will be treated with the utmost discretion."

"Yes, I know. And you have been so kind." Still, she paused, as if leery of revealing information too confidential or damning.

Which, of course, was precisely what Sebastian most wanted to hear.

And most dreaded.

"Go on, Miss Halsop. What was it that you noticed? You can tell me."

Henrietta bit her lip, then blurted out, "She took walks!"

Sebastian could feel the tension drain out of his face. *Is that all?*

"I have seen her take walks myself."

"I thought perhaps she was just interested in physical activity of the type Mr. Cheswyn advocates," Henrietta said. "But the other night, during the terrible rain, I looked out my window and I was never so shocked! There she was, her cloak flapping around her, looking out to the sea."

Sebastian crossed his arms. Now *this* was interesting.

"I didn't dare confess that I had seen her, of course," Henrietta said. "But I fear the Brute has taken hold of her imagination. It can happen—as I know only too well. When first I saw the Brute, I myself felt that terrible mix of revulsion and attraction! It shames me to confess it now, but it was so. Though naturally I was able to put such thoughts aside. But Violet . . ." She shuddered. "Well!"

Sebastian was puzzled. He had guessed Violet might have a lingering inquisitiveness about the Brute. But was that all it was?

Keep an eye out for a smuggler named Robert the Brute, the intercepted message for Nero had said.

Or perhaps Henrietta was wrong.

"Don't misunderstand, my lord. The Brute has a hold on all he encounters, I am sure! Even I, sometimes, as I am dropping off to sleep, still envision that terrible masked face, that broad chest . . ." She let out another anguished breath. "That is another reason I tried to convince my cousin to go to Bath."

"But she did not want to go?"

"No, she was decidedly against it."

Interesting.

"But of course, now even I am growing to like this place." She smiled fondly at Sebastian. "And I feel better for having unburdened myself to you."

"I am honored that you confided in me."

"Well, after all, you have been so kind."

As they joined the others, Sebastian kept his eye on Violet until she caught him staring and glared at him again. What a puzzle she was! Did the lady love a smuggler, or did she merely wish to use a smuggler for her own ends?

Perhaps, he decided at last, it was time to reunite Violet and the Brute and find out.

Chapter Eight

John Cuthbert hovered over his desk blotter, frowning at the letter he had just received. Like the many from Sebastian that had come before it, it was penned in a breezy, impudent manner.

Greetings, O Solemn One! the message began. (Thus far, at least, all seemed quite normal.)

Events plod on in the same fashion here at the Cross, where our fiddling Roman friend has yet to make himself known. Binkley Jacobs has appeared. Could you start an investigation to see if B. J. might have had reason to leave London in haste? I cannot believe that love for his aunt alone brought him here this time of year.

Also, I need to know the cost of a rather fine spyglass. Our vicar has a taste for selective luxury and a mania for exercise. (This fellow might not even require a smuggler contact to get his message to the enemy. He could swim it to France himself.)

Regarding the ladies, Mrs. B.'s cook makes a ghastly Dundee cake that could double as a weapon of war, and the widow Treacher's beautiful blue eyes have already bewitched our newcomer. I have plans for her myself, however!

Your humble slavey,
St. Just

Something in those few short paragraphs made Cuthbert uneasy. First, it seemed that, the marquess's protestations aside, something *was* brewing in Widgelyn Cross. Mrs. Blatchford, Binkley Jacobs, and this vicar seemed highly suspect, even from the maddeningly circumspect descriptions Sebastian had provided in this note and his few others.

But what most disturbed him, he had to admit, was that last bit about the widow. What sort of plans did Sebastian have for her?

Cuthbert wondered if Binkley Jacobs was not the only man falling under that woman's spell. Sebastian did not ask for information about *her*, he noticed. Nor did he posit the theory that occurred immediately to Cuthbert: Mrs. Treacher and Mr. Jacobs could be working in tandem.

It was not that Cuthbert did not trust Sebastian. On the contrary. But throw a woman with bewitching eyes into the equation and nothing was certain. Why, just this morning he'd overheard colleagues telling the tragic tale of Lord Feddleston, the most honest man who ever walked. And yet Lord Feddleston had gotten involved with an actress who had cooked up a scheme for Feddleston to rob a *lady's* coach and share the proceeds with her. Feddleston was caught, but not before the jewels and the actress could escape to her native Ireland.

Cuthbert did not believe Feddleston's case was in any respect rare. Was not the history of humankind riddled with such stories?

Not that he was overly worried that the widow Treacher's blue eyes would be the downfall of the British Empire. Not yet, at least.

But these plans Sebastian spoke of . . . those Cuthbert found at least as ominous sounding as a vicar with an expensive spyglass.

The post, subject to the vagaries of the weather and the mood of the dour driver who made the rounds, arrived at Trembledown for once in a timely fashion the morning after the tea party at Mrs. Blatchford's.

Peabody came into the breakfast room bearing the letters on a salver. Violet, who was involved with her egg cup, did not spare him a glance until he was placing the small silver tray in front of her. She assumed the slight trepidation in his step could be explained by his fear of treading on a stray cat tail, though Lettie swept the room for stray felines each morning. When Violet did look at him, however, she understood his hesitance at once. She swallowed back a cry of alarm.

"Peabody!" she exclaimed.

She had to say *something*. Peabody had been experimenting with pomade, and now all the hairs from the sides of his head were defying gravity to form a curious peak on his mostly bald dome. It was too startling a change in appearance to ignore.

Even Hennie let out a small gasp at the sight of that small eruption of glistening hair run.

Violet swallowed. She did not dare laugh; Peabody could be so sensitive. "You have changed your hair."

Peabody straightened self-consciously. "Thank you, madam," he said, as if she had paid him a compliment. "During my day off yesterday, I took the opportunity to visit Widgelyn Cross. While taking a bit of refreshment at an establishment called the Pied Hare, I chanced to meet a former acquaintance, one James Quimby, who by happy coincidence has recently come to the area."

"Quimby?" Hennie's brows knit together. "Wasn't it he who Mrs. Blatchford was speaking of, Violet?"

"Mr. Jacobs's new valet," Violet said, remembering.

"Mr. Jacobs is very fortunate," Peabody said. "Mr. Quimby is a man of impeccable taste and exacting standards. I was rather shocked to see him at the Pied Hare, for I found the beef there rather tough. But Quimby said that he enjoys brief stays in the country and that Cornwall is among his favorite rural idylls."

He spoke of his friend with a reverence he usually reserved for the well titled. "When did you know him?" Violet asked.

"In London, madam, before I went to work for the Treachers. We are both Dromios."

"Dromios?" Hennie asked.

"The Dromio Society for gentleman in the service of gentleman," Peabody explained. "It is quite selective. At that time, Quimby was already quite famous for developing the Cumbrian cravat knot—though he has scaled greater heights since. Naturally, when he told me I should style my hair in a more modern fashion, I took his advice."

Violet hazarded another glance up at that head and swallowed. "It is . . . striking."

Peabody allowed himself a rare swagger. "It is called the Olympian."

"I am glad you have found friends in the area," Violet said, deciding it was best to let the whole matter of his new coiffure drop.

"Yes, it is gratifying," Peabody said. Then, on the

brink of turning to leave, he stopped. "May I say one more word, madam?"

"Yes, of course."

He wrung his hands. "I feel I must apologize for perhaps not giving life here at Trembledown its due. If Quimby sees nothing amiss with Cornwall, then Cornwall must be more estimable than I had reckoned."

"Well, we have all been rather uneasy with the transition we have been forced to make," Violet said diplomatically.

He bowed and then handed a package that he had been holding under his arm out to Hennie. "This bundle was left for Miss Halsop."

"Oh, thank you!" Hennie said, as excitedly as if he were presenting her with a gift. She undid the twine around the paper and pulled out a large book. There was a note attached, which she scanned quickly. "It is the history of the Widgelyn Cross area promised me by Mrs. Blatchford. *A Short History on the Lands and Edifices of Cornwall.* She said she had to tear the house apart and finally found it under a chair!"

"That is a peculiar place to store books," Violet remarked absently, examining her post. She had disappointingly few letters, although the one addressed in Sophy's hand was two pages thick. She unfolded it and read a few lines before she noticed that Hennie was not even looking at the letter Peabody had left for her on the salver. Nor did she seem to be particularly interested in perusing the book from Mrs. Blatchford. Instead, she was jotting notes on a sheet of a paper. Making a list of some sort.

Curiosity got the best of Violet. She had never known Hennie not to be eager for letters, especially since this one was addressed in the small, eye-straining hand that could only mean another letter from Imogene singing the praises of Bath. "What are you doing?" she asked.

"I am making a list of things I might need from Penzance."

"Penzance!" Violet exclaimed. "What for?"

"I thought Hal might drive me there this afternoon. I need a sketchbook."

Good heavens. Violet had heard Hennie nattering on about the marquess telling her she should go to Montraffer and draw, but she had not thought Hennie would take the man seriously.

"And pencils," Hennie added, looking critically at her list. "And naturally, if there is a store that sells oils, I will purchase those, too. I shall have to see what's available. I did enjoy painting, until Aunt Matilda said she could no longer abide the smell of paint and I was forced to give up my hobby. Do you remember?"

Violet did. One spring Hennie had decorated their aunt's salon in strikingly odd studies of heather fields that had followed Hennie's acquiring a new shade of purple paint. It couldn't be entirely chance that their aunt's intolerance for paint fumes coincided with those undulant heather depictions appearing on her walls.

Hennie sighed. "The marquess was quite inspiring when he encouraged me to take up artistic pursuits again. I think he must be the nicest of men, don't you?"

"Emphatically not. I found his manner yesterday most objectionable. All that preening about his house was embarrassing. I don't like the way he looks at people, either, and always questions them. It's very unnerving. Why, did you hear him interrogating Mr. Cheswyn on the cost of his boots? It was most unseemly of him."

"But I never saw him looking at *me*," Hennie pointed out. "That is, not unless he was speaking to me particularly. If he was looking at you, it is perhaps that he feels an inclination there that you do not wish to acknowledge."

"Indeed I do not! And I do not believe such an inclination exists, except in your imagination."

Violet turned her attention back to the letters in front of her. The first was a brief one from her sister Abigail relating the glad tidings that she and Nathan were expecting their first child to be born in the fall. This was very good news, she supposed. It was hard to imagine Abigail a mother, but she rather thought that Nathan and Abigail would do quite well with a little one. And imagine, she herself was soon to be an aunt!

Not liking the sound of that so much, Violet turned to a note from Sophy. Her little sister was all enthusiasm about the start of her first Season and seemed to think every gentleman she danced with was top of the trees.

They were going to have trouble there, Violet thought ominously. And not for the first time. Back at home, Sophy's history had been spotted with embarrassing episodes, usually involving those in the household and stable employ. In the end their father had resigned himself to having Peacock Hall staffed entirely by the female, the aged, or the unsightly.

After she went on at some length about her delight in the news of Abigail's *interesting condition* (this letter was quite like Sophy's conversation—both overly exuberant and too long), Violet paused upon an unsettling passage.

Hennie tells me there is a devastatingly handsome marquess living down the road from you. Dear Violet, what luck! I will understand now if you fail to write back promptly, since you doubtless have more important schemes afoot. Oh, I am so glad for you! You always did want to marry a marquess, or some

*such titled gentleman—and this one sounds ever so
much better than that wheezy old earl you were chasing last summer. I am sure you will be betrothed in
no time. I have great hopes in that direction myself—
but hush! I mustn't speak of it now.*

*Love to you, Hennie, and of course Peabody!
Lucky, lucky Peabody! To finally contemplate restoration to the service of the aristocracy. He must be in
alt to contemplate butlering at a marquess's estate.
(Isn't there a name for that?)*

Yours,
Sophy

Violet read over this part of the letter again with growing exasperation. The picture her sister painted of her!
Here was another reminder of Violet's brief infatuation
with the earl of Clatsop. The man *had* been on the
wheezy side, she had to allow, but that had been all over
last year. For Sophy to extrapolate from that one measly
episode that Violet would be conniving to maneuver the
marquess into matrimony was highly insulting.

She hoped Sophy didn't speak of her in these terms to
others of her acquaintance in London.

Violet was still mulling over these disturbing thoughts
as she tore into another letter. The paper it was written
on was rather dirty, though she did not notice this until
she unfolded the single sheet and a sprinkling of sand
dropped into her lap. She flapped her napkin as her eyes
scanned the scratchily penned lines. Within moments,
her face felt as if it had caught fire.

Highness,
I have not forgotten you, or our passion-filled

*night. Word is about that you've taken to walking
along the sea path. Looking for someone?*

*Mayhap one moonless night we shall meet
again!*

Yours,
Robert the Brute

The message startled her so, the paper slipped from
her grasp and fluttered to the carpet like a leaf shaken
from a tree. Hennie glanced down and shifted in her
chair, as if about to retrieve the paper herself. In a panic,
Violet leapt off her seat and pounced on the note.

Hennie's eyes widened. "Are you all right?"

Violet, who prided herself on ladylike languid movements, could understand why her cousin might be
surprised to see her hopping about on the rug with the
quickness of a flea.

"Yes! Just fine!" Despite her words, she was unable to
regain composure as soon as she would have liked.

"Not bad news, I trust?"

Violet climbed back onto her chair, the letter clamped
in her profusely sweating palms. "N-no!"

She felt a dizzy wave and took a long sip of lukewarm
tea. Oh Lord! She was in a fever. She itched to read those
few lines again, but she didn't dare. And why should
she? The words were burned across her brain.

Who had told him of her walks? Barnabas Monk?

Or had he seen her himself?

Did he really mean that they would meet again, or was
he mocking her?

For a moment she feared she might faint dead away,
and yet she could not. At least not until she had condemned this dreadful missive to the fire. Until then, it
simply could not fall into anyone else's hands.

But wasn't there a threat implied in the message? An implicit acknowledgement that the Brute was stalking her? She should go to the constable, and straightaway. She needed to ask for protection.

And yet . . . there was his reference to their passion-filled night. How could she explain that? Everyone would know she had lied about the night she had been kidnapped. It would be a scandal.

She stared at her half-eaten breakfast with a queasy stomach. What was she going to do?

Hennie eyed her with concern. "Violet, you look ill. I am sure you are keeping something from me. Is it news from home or London? Something to do with Sophy's debut?" (Violet apparently was not the only one anticipating trouble in that quarter.)

Violet bit her lip and tucked the Brute's letter beneath the one she had received from her sister. That gave her an idea. Hennie would never stop pestering her if she didn't give her an excuse for her change in demeanor. "If you must know, I received a letter from Sophy and I am quite put out. She was full of talk of the marquess, who I am sure *I* never mentioned. And yet Sophy practically has us betrothed already."

In a telltale sign of guilt, Hennie's face went pale. "Oh dear."

"I wish you hadn't gossiped about him, Hennie. You know what a fanciful head my sister has. She will probably be spreading faradiddles about me all across London."

Poor Hennie's face turned white. "Oh my! I am sure I never meant any harm."

"Of course you didn't—but you know Sophy."

"But naturally when we first arrived I had to write about something—one cannot always be writing about the weather, you know. I had already filled several letters with descriptions of the howling wind. And to complain about the noise and dust from the workmen is something I didn't like to do—you know I cannot abide whiners. And the marquess *is* such a strikingly handsome man, and was so generous with his meats . . ."

Violet grunted, cutting short this new round of huzzahs to the marquess. "She assumes I would be chasing after the man just because he has a title."

Hennie hesitated for a moment before plowing on bravely, "But you know, you always did say that it is a woman's duty to marry well—preferably into the aristocracy—if she has the opportunity."

"Yes, and where has that philosophy gotten me? To a rundown shambles at the end of the earth, a place of brigands and other unsavory souls! And look at my sisters—when have they ever considered duty? Abigail married a penniless neighbor who is sinking all his, and a good part of Aunt Augusta's, money into a mill scheme—and she is foolishly, sickeningly happy! She writes that she and Nathan are going to have a child."

Hennie was ecstatic. "Oh, how wonderful, Violet. You shall be an aunt!"

Violet moved along. "And then there's Sophy! She simply swoons at anything in breeches. She will never bring home position or fortune. Why should I be the only Wingate who looks to better our position in society? I can't carry an entire family on my shoulders. I, too, desire happiness."

Hennie looked contrite and patted her hand. "Indeed you do. But in this case might not your ambitions and your natural inclinations merge into one romantic object?"

"Never," she swore. "The marquess and I would not suit. The man is a worse snob than Percy Treacher ever dreamed of being."

Hennie sighed. "And yet he was very kind to me. He all but offered me the run of his property for my sketching."

Violet grunted. She wondered why, exactly, the marquess had done that. But she was too distracted by the missive in her hand to give voice to her curiosity.

"I do think you're wrong about him, Violet. He seemed quite concerned about you."

"About me?" Violet asked. "What did he say?"

Infuriatingly, Hennie chose that moment to be circumspect. "Nothing in particular. He just seemed interested in you and how things were coming along here."

"No doubt he still has hopes that I will fold up and leave him to snatch Trembledown for a song."

"I doubt that," Hennie said. "At least, that is not what he indicated to me."

Violet's head snapped to attention. "What did he say to you?"

Hennie bit her lip, remembering. "Something about how he regretted your troubling yourself over Trembledown, because it was rather a small, negligible house."

"Negligible!" Violet howled in outrage. "I hope you set him straight as to its charms!"

Her cousin eyed her in confusion. "I wasn't aware of any." Before Violet could sputter any more at her, Hennie defended herself by insisting, "You just called it a rundown shambles, Violet."

Violet's jaw jutted stubbornly. "It is one thing for us to speak so among ourselves . . ."

Hennie shook her head. "And to hear Peabody talk about this place—"

"Peabody!" Violet snorted. "We'll leave Peabody out of this, if you please. He won't be happy until he's living at the Royal Pavilion at Brighton. But his lordship has no right to judge. It was his family who built this bloody place."

"Violet!"

Violet grumbled unapologetically, "Well, they did."

So the marquess was now of the mind that she was wasting her time and money. Well! She would show him. She stood resolutely. One good thing she could say for the marquess—her annoyance with him often served to make her forget her other troubles.

"I am going out," she announced.

"Shall I carry your letters up to your room for you?" Hennie asked, noting at the short pile next to Violet's forsaken breakfast plate. She reached out and almost touched the Brute's letter.

"No!" Violet practically threw herself on the letter. How could she have allowed it to leave her grasp for even a second? "I shall take them—I want to reread Sophy's letter."

If Hennie noticed anything amiss in her behavior she did not show it. Indeed, she seemed to accept this bizarre behavior from Violet as a matter of course.

Thinking that over, Violet felt a pang of irritation. From Hennie's reaction, one would think her cousin considered Violet one of those people of erratic temperament who were so trying to be around.

Violet had never held a spade in her hands before— never intended to—and yet on this morning she found herself in the curious position of having to dig a hole. She had acquired a rose to plant in the sun next to the front gate but discovered to her frustration that Clarence's gout had flared up, rendering him helpless for tasks such as this. And Barnabas was nowhere to be found.

In the end she decided a little physical exertion might help rid her of the mental torment brought on by receiving first the Brute's note and then news that the marquess had called Trembledown negligible!

"We shall see how negligible it is when I am through with it!" she vowed, chipping away at the hard ground with ill humor.

The activity was much less satisfying than she had anticipated. Despite the nip in the air, sweat beaded on her brow—a ghastly feeling. In the days of her marriage, she had considered herself quite an adept gardener; she had been famous for her rose arrangements, and she had often clipped the blooms herself. Now, however, she realized that there was a vast difference between issuing instructions to her husband's head gardener about her wishes for planting and actually doing the physical labor on her own.

As she was attempting to drag her hair out of her eyes, she heard horses' hooves approaching. She whirled, half expecting to see the Brute himself charging toward her. Instead, it was just the marquess and his groom trotting up in his phaeton.

In bygone days, she had thought a phaeton was the most dashing of all conveyances. In fact, the sight of one had never failed to raise her admiration . . . until now. Of course, it was very difficult to think of the cold and haughty marquess and the word *dash* in the same breath. And how very impractical of Sebastian to drive such a thing in the country!

He reined his horses in precisely and drew alongside her. Throwing the reins to his groom, he descended and tipped her his hat. He then fixed the hated monocle in place and observed, "What a pleasure to find you out and about this morning."

Would that she had truly been *out* as in away from home, Violet thought ruefully.

"And looking so fresh, too! Why, you practically glow."

Because she was perspiring. She self-consciously dashed a bead of sweat from her brow.

"I did not know you were such a gardening enthusiast—one rarely sees a lady sporting a spade."

"I am simply mad for outdoor work." She was too proud to tell him of her gouty gardener.

"Wonderful!" he exclaimed. "Because, by coincidence, one of the reasons I came this way was specifically to give you this." His groom dutifully stepped forward with a rhododendron with its roots bound in canvas. The plant was swollen with buds. "It is called a Montraffer Red."

"Thank you. It was kind of you to think of me."

"You were most vocal the other afternoon in your admiration of my shrubs," the marquess observed.

She bit her lip. The smug glint in his eye suggested that he suspected her of admiring him for other reasons as well. She would have been exasperated with him had her attention not been drawn to the plant. It was true—she had coveted his rhododendrons. That was before. Now all she could think of was that she had to dig another hole. Damn.

"Thank you," she said through gritted teeth.

He bowed. "I have several more in my greenhouse I shall send over. I did not want to overwhelm your man all at once if you weren't appreciative." He chuckled with artificial sheepishness at her lack of help. "Now I see it was only you I should have considered overwhelming."

"Do not worry, my lord," she said, smiling. "I cannot imagine you overwhelming anyone."

"Still, one does strive to be neighborly."

"You have gone quite beyond the call of duty already. You have won my cousin over entirely."

"Alas," he decried facetiously. *"Only* your cousin?"

His flirtatious manner was so arch she could not take him seriously. Nor could she resist answering in kind. "Does one-half of a household not satisfy you, my lord? Must you triumph over all?"

"I admit that nothing would make me happier."

"Then you will be ecstatic to learn that you are one step closer to obtaining perfect joy." She waited a moment before finishing, "My butler is quite overcome with admiration as well."

"A sensible man, obviously."

There was simply no battering down this man's wall of self-love. Violet doubted it was even worth the effort to try. "Well . . . thank you for the plant. It will set off the house beautifully." She decided to let him know that he was entirely wrong to think of her house as *negligible.* "Perhaps when I have finished my plans for Trembledown, Hennie and I will have a special party. Everything should be finished soon—the plasterers are working in the ballroom now."

He frowned. "Ballroom?"

"On the second floor. Naturally, it has been quite neglected—but I expect it will be charming when I am done. A perfect place for a party."

"I had entirely forgotten it, as a matter of fact. But you're quite right." The marquess brightened. "How generous of you! No one has thrown a ball locally in simply an age."

"A ball?" *Who said anything about throwing a ball?*

His lordship was all eagerness. "When shall you have it? You will want to leave yourself plenty of time for organization, but I shouldn't wait too long—soon everyone who is anyone will have left for London. Late in the month should be a perfect time, I think."

How could she possibly have a ball? An affair on that scale would cost her a fortune in refreshments alone. "Oh, but—"

"Yes, later in the month would suit me very well. Just before April. Only do make it a masquerade. Those are always the jolliest, and I have been bemoaning the fact that I will be missing Minerva Plimpton's masquerade ball this year. I do adore Minerva! She is so good about sending notes and keeping me abreast of all town goings-on while I am in Cornwall. And her masquerade balls are renowned. Doubtless you will remember."

Her head was spinning, although she was somewhat mollified by his correct assumption that she was familiar enough with society to recognize the name of Minerva Plimpton, the ale heiress and darling of the *ton*. In fact they had made their come-out together. They had been somewhat in competition, both being heiresses of less than blue blood. But while Minerva had never seemed to mind some of the sneers and had behaved in a truly original manner, Violet had tried to cover her antecedents behind an icy mask of propriety. For the first time, she questioned whether she would not have done better to have taken a page from Minerva's book.

"Who shall you come as?" Sebastian asked, bringing her back to the present. He obviously considered the matter of a ball settled.

"It is difficult to say—scant minutes ago my hostessing plans were entirely unknown to me."

A deep chuckle rumbled out of him, and he looked at her as if she were being coy. "I know you ladies like to be secretive about your costumes."

Her lips managed to pull into a semblance of a smile.

"If we were not secretive, the masquerade would be rather pointless, would it not?"

"I suppose you are right," he conceded. "You should be careful which day you choose. The evening should coincide with the full moon, of course."

"Full moon?" She was a bit bewildered that they were suddenly negotiating specifics for a party that moments before had been merely hypothetical.

"During the light of the full moon we need not be overly concerned with the Brute. I know he can never be far from your mind."

Those words made her jump. "Why? What do you mean?" Before he could answer, she asserted, "I never give that vile person a thought."

"Very wise—and, if I might add, very brave of you as well." Sebastian leaned close to her and whispered so that the groom would not hear, "You need not pretend with me that the incident with that low fellow did not touch you in ways you dare not confess to others."

She rounded on him, heart hammering. What was he insinuating? "I'm sure I don't know what you mean. I told the constable what happened."

"Naturally—and your word is as good as gold, I'm sure. And yet you could not in so short a narrative have provided *all* the details of such an ordeal."

The knowing glint in his eyes, that smug smirk on his lips, made her want to fly at him. If only his words were not true! And if only she were a man and could just land her clenched fist against that strong, jutting jaw.

"I assure you, my lord, the Brute is so far from my thoughts I would never take him into consideration in anything I do."

"Good! Now let me see . . ." He did some calculating. "I think the twenty-eighth of March would be the best night possible for the ball, all things considered. That is a Saturday."

"You seem to have all the plans in train." She was stunned that he would go so far as to name a date. Of all the high-handed—

He bowed. "I am delighted to be of assistance and look forward to attending. We have been a trifle dull this spring, and this will ease my missing Minerva's party. In fact, I had already made up my costume, and now it will not have to go to waste."

"How convenient for you, my lord. Perhaps you would be happier altogether if you hied yourself back to London."

"Yes, but I would never do that now, of course. I have no doubt your soirée will be as memorable as any meeting of the *ton*."

She frowned. How on earth would she ever be in any condition to have a formal ball in that short amount of time?

Another carriage approached—a gig that looked like a farm cart next to the marquess's phaeton. At the reins was Binkley, very striking in his morning coat and breeches. His ever-present smile turned to a scowl when he noted the marquess standing next to her.

"I was going to see if you wanted to go riding with me," he said after curt nods were exchanged between him and Sebastian. "Though naturally if you are busy . . ."

"Oh no!" Violet said hurriedly. She was not terribly enthusiastic about riding with Binkley in his decrepit gig. And yet, she did not want to return to digging, and she saw by the look in the marquess's eye that accepting Binkley's invitation would rile Sebastian. For some reason all the two men seemed to share was a mutual antipathy.

Binkley would appreciate this latest turn of events. "The marquess just decided that I should have a ball at the end of the month," she told him.

Binkley looked at her with surprised mirth. "Did he?"

"Yes, I hope you will be able to attend. His lordship has decreed it should be a masquerade."

"I shall be delighted."

Sebastian shot a sharp look at Binkley. "You don't intend to return to London before then?"

"No, I am resting with my aunt a while." He beamed at Violet. "Indefinitely, actually."

This news was a little disturbing to her for some reason. She hoped he was not staying on her account, as his expression seemed to imply. She did not intend to encourage the man. Still, she could not help smiling at Sebastian. "Mr. Jacobs seems to have fallen in love with Cornwall as much as I have."

"Indeed I have—more than ever. There has never been so much here to intrigue me."

She flushed, feeling almost guilty for accepting this kind of insinuated compliment without protest. Yet she would not allow the marquess the satisfaction of hearing her rebuff Binkley. In fact, she was quite enjoying the bemusement on his face. He had fallen silent and was watching them with genuine curiosity.

Her heart did a strange flutter as she fell victim to the keen, piercing intensity of that dark eye magnified by his eyepiece. Why was he staring at them so strangely? Was he actually jealous?

Binkley took her hand, jolting her out of her thoughts. "So, shall we take that ride?"

"Oh, yes." she said, though part of her feared it was ill advised. Yet what harm could a short drive do her? "I'd love to."

She also would have loved to see the look on Sebastian's face when Binkley handed her up onto the cart. But when she turned to say her good-byes, the marquess had already climbed into his phaeton and seemed lost in thought.

He really was handsome, she realized. When he wasn't smirking at her.

He saw her on the hill, her head shaded by a wide-brimmed hat, her thin frame swathed in a flowing dress that caught the breeze. It was black, of course. Hennie always wore black.

He approached her from behind, so that for a moment he was able to admire her artwork from over her shoulder. What was she sketching? He believed it was the house, albeit a very free interpretation of that building. The turret was there, but outsized, like a cannon shooting out of the building. Entire wings appeared as just that, appendages that appeared about to fly off into the sky. It was an amazing piece of work. Who would have guessed such an ordinary little bird of a woman possessed such an imagination?

He cleared his throat and she nearly leapt out of her boots.

"I saw you standing and could not pass by," he explained.

"But you shouldn't have peeked at my drawing," she scolded him even as she blushed furiously. "It is only a first effort."

"It seems very . . . expressive."

She smiled. "Do you think so?"

"Without a doubt—it is the most imaginative rendering of Montraffer I have ever seen."

"Oh!" She clasped the sketchbook to her bosom. "Thank you so much for allowing me to come here. Your encouragement means a good deal." A laugh trilled out of her. "Who knows, I may end up giving Madame Le Brun a run for her money!"

"They say with practice all things are possible." He looked around. "But did you come here alone?"

"Oh yes—Violet was so kind. She allowed me to take the cart."

He stared at an old nag hitched to a very primitive-looking wagon. "You should have brought your cousin with you."

"She never would have come," Hennie blurted out before she could think better of the remark. Two patches of red rose in her cheeks. "Oh, not that she would not be thrilled to see the grounds of Montraffer . . ."

"But antagonism toward its owner would hold her back?" he asked, repressing a laugh.

Hennie looked uncomfortable. "Oh no! That is . . . well, she perhaps is not so great a nature lover as you and I are, my lord."

"And yet you said she enjoys walking along the cliffs."

She frowned. "No more. She has been staying closer to home of late."

Now why would that be? Perhaps his note had something to do with it; if so, then his ploy was paying off. "I see." He chuckled to himself but was careful to keep a solemn expression.

Poor Hennie writhed in anguish, sure she had offended her patron of the canvas. "It is simply that she is so consumed in fixing Trembledown just now, my lord. The rhododendrons you sent will be magnificent. Violet is always pottering about in the yard now. She has even commandeered a little shed near the garden for her exclusive use. She won't allow anyone near it. She says she wants all her things organized just so."

"Very interesting."

"Violet was always most particular, you know."

"I wish she were more particular about the company she keeps," he could not help confiding.

His listener's eyes widened. "Do you mean Mr. Jacobs?"

He said nothing more. Though if Binkley Jacobs was involved in what he suspected him of, perhaps he *should* say more. He did not think that Violet and the man were in cahoots; yet it was disturbing that Jacobs always seemed to be hanging around Violet. Sebastian could not help fearing that he was using her in some way.

Of course, without proof . . .

"I believe Violet is simply trying to be kind to him, on account of Mrs. Blatchford," Hennie said. "I am certain she has no particular preference for him."

"Perhaps I will be reassured on that score when I see them together at your masquerade ball."

"I am so looking forward to it!" Hennie said.

"As am I," he agreed with a bow. He frowned again at the cart. "I do feel anxious that you drove yourself over—you must be careful to leave well before dark."

"It was a pleasure. I enjoy driving."

"But it is dangerous after nightfall."

Hennie's eyes grew big again. "Do you think so?"

"My good lady, have you forgotten the Brute?"

She gulped. "But Violet assured me that the Brute was gone! She called me a goose the last time I mentioned him. She said that he had obviously moved on or we should have heard from him again."

He bit back a smile. "She did?"

"Oh yes."

No doubt she was horrified to think anyone might sus-

Take A Trip Into A Timeless World of Passion and Adventure with Kensington Choice Historical Romances!
—Absolutely FREE!

Enjoy the passion and adventure of another time with Kensington Choice Historical Romances. They are the finest novels of their kind, written by today's best-selling romance authors. Each Kensington Choice Historical Romance transports you to distant lands in a bygone age. Experience the adventure and share the delight as proud men and spirited women discover the wonder and passion of true love.

Get 4 FREE Books!

We created our convenient Home Subscription Service so you'll be sure to have the hottest new romances delivered each month right to your doorstep—usually before they are available in book stores. Just to show you how convenient the Zebra Home Subscription Service is, we would like to send you 4 FREE Kensington Choice Historical Romances. The books are worth up to $24.96, but you only pay $1.99 for shipping and handling. There's no obligation to buy additional books—ever!

 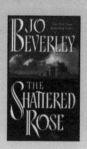  

Save Up To 30% With Home Delivery!

Accept your FREE books and each month we'll deliver 4 brand new titles as soon as they are published. They'll be yours to examine FREE for 10 days. Then if you decide to keep the books, you'll pay the preferred subscriber's price (up to 30% off the cover price!), plus shipping and handling. Remember, you are under no obligation to buy any of these books at any time! If you are not delighted with them, simply return them and owe nothing. But if you enjoy Kensington Choice Historical Romances as much as we think you will, pay the special preferred subscriber rate and save over $8.00 off the cover price!

We have 4 FREE BOOKS for you as your introduction to
KENSINGTON CHOICE!
To get your FREE BOOKS, worth up to $24.96, mail
the card below or call TOLL-FREE 1-800-770-1963.
Visit our website at www.kensingtonbooks.com.

Get 4 FREE Kensington Choice Historical Romances!

▶ **YES!** Please send me my 4 FREE KENSINGTON CHOICE HISTORICAL ROMANCES (without obligation to purchase other books). I only pay $1.99 for shipping and handling. Unless you hear from me after I receive my 4 FREE BOOKS, you may send me 4 new novels—as soon as they are published—to preview each month FREE for 10 days. If I am not satisfied, I may return them and owe nothing. Otherwise, I will pay the money-saving preferred subscriber's price (over $8.00 off the cover price), plus shipping and handling. I may return any shipment within 10 days and owe nothing, and I may cancel any time I wish. In any case, the 4 FREE books will be mine to keep.

KN076A

NAME _____

ADDRESS _____ APT. _____

CITY _____ STATE _____ ZIP _____

TELEPHONE (____) _____

E-MAIL (OPTIONAL) _____

SIGNATURE _____

(If under 18, parent or guardian must sign)

○ Offer limited to one per household and not to current subscribers. Terms, offer and prices subject to change. Orders subject to acceptance by Kensington Choice Book Club.
Offer Valid in the U.S. only.

ll..l..lll....ll.l.l.l.l.l.l.ll.l.l.l..l.ll...l

KENSINGTON CHOICE
Zebra Home Subscription Service, Inc.
P.O. Box 5214
Clifton NJ 07015-5214

pect her of communicating with her lover-smuggler, even if the smuggler had initiated the correspondence.

"It would put my mind at ease if you would return home in my carriage. It is already quite late. I will see that the cart is returned to Trembledown tomorrow first thing."

Hennie gazed at him worshipfully. "You are too kind for words, my lord."

He shook his head and sniffed. "Believe me, I would rather die than meet up on the road with the Brute myself. I am sure I would be grieved should some ill befall you on my lands."

The look in Hennie's eyes told him that if she were kidnapped by murderous smugglers, she would never be able to forgive herself for the trouble she had caused him.

Sebastian did feel a qualm of conscience when he looked in Hennie's admiring expression. His kindness was so shamefully self-serving. He needed an excuse to go to Trembledown . . . and leave a communiqué from his alter ego.

Chapter Nine

Mrs. Blatchford, hearing through Binkley of the marquess's horticultural largesse, came up with a gift of her own days later. Pots of blooming narcissi, tulips on the brink, and two substantial-sized lilacs were delivered to Violet by Binkley himself with his aunt's compliments.

Violet eyed him with mock reproof. "I think you had a hand in this."

He grinned. "A mere housewarming gift, weeks overdue."

She hoped he wasn't trying to set up in competition with the marquess. She would have disabused him of the need, but she feared that would sound like encouragement. Binkley possessed an attractive, bright manner—far preferable to the marquess's cold, smirking superiority—but she had to admit that she felt no attraction to him other than as a friend. The drive she had taken with him, mainly to annoy Sebastian, had probably been a tactical error. She saw a gleam in his eye now that made her very uncomfortable.

"Please thank your aunt for me," Violet said in a tone that she hoped was properly formal. "It was most generous of her."

"Shall I give your head gardener instructions on where to plant the lilacs?"

She fought a cough. "No, thank you." Head gardener! What a luxurious sound those words now had to her ears.

Even Clarence and his gout seemed like a luxury to her. She was spending all she could afford on the workmen inside Trembledown; the marquess's ball had caused her to take on two more Monks. The repairs were costing her a small fortune. Yet it was often said that sometimes you had to spend a fortune to make one. She felt the same gambling spirit that had made her father, Sir Harlan Wingate, a rich man thirty years earlier.

That last thought gave her pause. Violet had always considered herself more refined than her father, but perhaps the urge to turn a profit was a trait that bound them.

Binkley pressed on. "Are you sure? Servants often respond more readily to a man's instructions than a woman's."

Really, this bordered on impudence! The man seemed to think a bumpy carriage ride gave him rights of ownership. She wasted no time in correcting that misperception. "That may be true, if the man is actually their employer."

"Such independence is admirable," he said.

"In my case, it is also a necessity."

"But surely you will wish to marry again?"

"Someday, perhaps," she clarified. "If the right man were to come along."

He grinned. He had a winning smile; she had to give him that. A trifle puppyish and overeager, perhaps, yet a woman would have to be laid out for burial not to respond to it. "Perhaps he already has, and you simply haven't realized it."

"Do you think me suffering from amnesia that I don't remember meeting a paragon?" she asked, crossing her arms. "Or perhaps it is your belief that women simply do not know their own minds?"

"No, indeed," he protested. "But, excuse me, both sexes often fail to be thoroughly acquainted with their own hearts."

"That is not my difficulty," she assured him. "I consider myself acquainted with my own heart's every thump and murmur. If I am struck by Cupid's arrow, I assure you, I will be the first to know."

Binkley looked uncomfortable and obviously decided a change of subject was in order. "I am looking forward to dancing with you at your ball. What costume are you planning to wear?" He did not wait for an answer. "No, don't tell me, Nor will I tell you what mine will be. But I have something most unusual in the works, I assure you."

She couldn't help laughing at his childlike enthusiasm, even though the reminder of the ball caused her to quake a bit. She was afraid the house would never be ready in time. "I never knew men were so wild for masquerade parties."

"Who else?" he asked.

"The marquess."

Binkley's good humor seemed to mute a bit at the gentleman's name. "Oh, him."

"His lordship assures me that he loves a masquerade above all things."

"No doubt—it allows him to pretend he is not himself."

Violet lifted her hand to her mouth to cover a smile. "That is a very wicked thing to say."

"Forgive me, but I have to wonder at his intentions sometimes."

"His intentions?" Violet asked.

"You are too modest, of course, to realize that you

are a widow, obviously without means, and he is loitering with intent to take advantage of you."

"Fiddlesticks!" She laughed. "He is a marquess! There are many worthier people he could take advantage of than me."

"You said yourself his family lost Trembledown," he observed. "And why else would he be tarrying in Cornwall at this time of year?"

She had asked herself the same question once or twice. Then again, she had wondered the same thing about Binkley. "A very interesting theory," she said, her lips turning up in a skeptical smile.

"He does seem to hang about quite often, pestering you."

She tilted her head. "Not so often that you haven't been able to match him visit for visit."

Binkley sputtered. "Yes—but—well, that is an entirely different matter! You have to admit, he thinks very highly of himself."

"Oh yes. And yet I've never met a man lacking a healthy dose of self-reverence."

"I hope you do not lump me into that generalization."

She whooped. "Why, Mr. Jacobs, I would place you right on the top of the heap."

By this time his laughter had dissolved into a confused pout. "I must be going. Auntie will be expecting me home for luncheon."

"Then you should not be late," she said, dismissing him. "Please do not fail to thank your aunt for the kind gift."

When he was gone, she breathed a sigh of relief and another of exasperation. Those lilacs were large—to move them would require use of the wheelbarrow, a heavy, rickety contraption. Clarence was nowhere in sight and she knew that Peabody and the footmen were extremely busy this morning in the ballroom. The foyer had been deserted this morning when Binkley had arrived; she had opened the door to him herself.

Peabody was growing so unpredictable! Just the night before, after another misspent night at the Pied Hare, he had asked her for a ridiculous sum for new staff livery designed by Binkley's valet, Quimby. He had been quite miffed when she had vetoed his proposal; her morning tea had been distinctly tepid that morning. Asking him to wield the wheelbarrow for her might result in downright mutiny.

She supposed it was up to her to move the pots out of the front drive, but she refused to dig any more holes—she would simply wait until Clarence recuperated or Barnabas could put himself to use.

She trudged back to her gardening shed for the first time this morning, pondering how it was always left to her to put things right. She tugged open the sticky shed door with an unladylike curse, then stared about the dark room with arms akimbo, as if she could intimidate the spiders she knew were waiting for the opportunity to hop upon her person.

Next quarter, when she received her allowance, she would set aside money for an experienced gardener. It still galled her to remember that she had been cheated out of so much of her cash dowry—having to accept Trembledown in lieu of almost half the cash her father had forked over to the Treachers. She had her father to thank for the cash that she had; he had insisted that half her dowry be settled on her outright before consenting to the marriage. At the time she had been mortified that her father was so crass as to not trust the Treachers to take care of her when they were such an illustrious family, but she was certainly grateful to him now. She would never have been able to refurbish Trembledown without those funds.

As she glanced around the shed that had become her domain, her eyes alit on a sight that chilled her.

A letter!

Her stomach churned as she recognized the stained, yellowed paper that had been fastened to the opposite wall with a small knife. The missive looked as if it had been stabbed, as indeed it had.

And now her chest felt stabbing pains too. Her hands shook so that she could hardly work up the coordination to pull the knife out. She did so, however, and the letter dropped to the dirt floor.

She stooped to retrieve it and quickly ripped it open.

Highness:
I will wait for you Monday night. Tell no one.
R the B

Violet felt distinctly faint and was actually surprised to find herself still drawing breath and standing upright after reading the communication a second time.

Her mind, however, was frantic, and far from rational. Monday . . . that was *today*! How could he possibly come this very evening? Or any evening, for that matter? Weren't evenings when he did . . . well, whatever nefarious smuggling deeds he was up to?

Although she guessed even a smuggler was entitled to an occasional night off.

But, oh Lord, what was she thinking? She could never meet him! Why did he continue to pester her? Could he find no other women to meet with illicitly? Certainly, she could never meet him. She would rather die.

She had finally stopped thinking about the man, blast

him. She did not want to return to those days of him annoyingly invading her every dream.

And yet . . . Why was her heart beating so, almost as if she *did* want to meet with him? And what did it mean that he had written so briefly, so assured that she would see his note and *want* to meet him? She even stared for a moment at his signature, the abbreviated *R the B.* Was that an endearing informality . . . or mere laziness?

In the midst of this reverie she gasped as an alarming thought occurred to her. This was no mailed missive, like the last one. Robert the Brute—or an emissary—had actually been here. When? Was he nearby now?

Perhaps he was spying on her at this very moment!

She peered outside the shed and scanned the area around her. She saw no one, nothing at all on the horizon. He must have sneaked in under the cover of night. Just as he would sneak in tonight.

A Hennie-like moan escaped her. What did he intend—an assignation? Or was he considering abducting her again?

Her mind stopped its onward rush. The hopeful scenario of seeking protection from the constable—bumbling and ineffective as he was—disintegrated into a million pieces until there were only three words. *Tell no one.*

Indeed, what would she tell? *My secret smuggler lover, who I am not entirely sure is my lover, intends to be in my gardening shed tonight?* Of course, she could always leave out the prior physical entanglement and just do her duty as a British subject to see that the notorious outlaw was brought to justice.

But that could mean death to the Brute. Violet despised the man—how could she not?—and yet she could not rest easy at the idea of sending him to the gallows. She seemed to be stymied in the contradiction of hating the man, fearing him and the feelings he aroused in her . . . and yet not quite prepared to seal his doom.

But if she did not go to the constable and the Brute arrived tonight, looking for her . . .

She shuddered.

Of course, there was always the possibility that, if the man were to see her cousin sitting up with her, he would leave her alone. But how could she expect Robert the Brute to respect civilities when he hadn't hesitated to abduct her from under Hennie's nose before? Not but that dragging her out of her own parlor wouldn't be a great leap forward in boldness . . .

And it would be just like him to attempt it.

Oh Lord! She was in trouble.

Forgetting the wheelbarrow and the lilacs, she stumbled back into the house to find Hennie twittering about in her artist's smock.

"I did not think you were here," Violet said as she tottered toward the sofa. She needed to sit before her legs collapsed from under her.

"I am going this afternoon. It is so nice of—" Her words stopped before she could declare again what a paragon the marquess was. "Why, Violet, what is wrong?"

Violet forced herself to look Hennie in the eye, though she wasn't at all sure she actually managed a smile. "Nothing. Why do you ask?"

"You're positively green."

"Nonsense. I am just a trifle windblown and maybe a touch overheated," she said. "I have been in the garden again."

Hennie had the decency to look stricken. "Oh dear coz! How selfish I've been—thinking only of my own artistic pursuits and pleasure while you have been working so hard."

Hennie was completely off the mark, of course, but her words made Violet sound so self-sacrificing that she couldn't hold back a satisfying martyrlike sniff. "Well, someone must stay and see that the work gets done."

"But you have been so kind to me!" Hennie said chastened. "I feel I owe you so much."

"I wouldn't want you to help out of a sense of guilt, Hen. Of course, I've hours of work to put in still . . ." Violet began to wonder how much work she could squeeze out of Hennie while her conscience was smiting her.

Hennie's face was a mask of contrition. "I will not go to the marquess's today, Violet." Before Violet could raise a peep of protest (which, frankly, she had no intention of doing; there were those lilac bushes, after all), Hennie raised her hands to shush her. "No, don't try to talk me out of it. I am quite settled on this. I have a duty to stay here and help you."

"That is very kind."

"Not a bit! I will fix us some tea and then after we have refreshed ourselves, we will go back outside and work, work, work."

We?

Violet straightened. When she had envisioned having Hennie labor for her, she had imagined Hennie laboring alone.

"I'll not leave your side for an instant," her cousin promised.

Violet leaned back with a moan, shading her eyes with her arm. "Really . . . I am feeling so weak."

"Then I will stay in and nurse you until you are better."

Violet's lips pursed. Damn. Was there no getting the upper hand here? "Perhaps you should go painting after all, Hennie. I think I will simply take a short, refreshing nap."

"Would you like me to read to you as you fall asleep?

I have been reading your sister's latest novel, *The Pirate of St. Syr*."

Oh heavens—the last thing her mind needed now was any of Abigail's fanciful ramblings about pirates. Pirates were altogether too close to smugglers for her taste. She would never be able to put Robert the Brute out of her mind. Though, come to think of it, she probably would not be able to expel him from her thoughts in any event.

"No, you should go. We can work some other time."

"But—"

"St. Just would be disappointed if you failed to take advantage of the opportunity he has presented you."

"Oh yes! He's been too kind."

With all the encouragement she had received from the marquess, Hennie now considered herself a late-blooming Leonardo. She had not let Violet have so much as a peek at her masterpieces, yet Hennie insisted that Sebastian believed she had a decided talent, so obviously *he* was allowed to see her work. Violet could not believe that Hennie could have improved much since the days of the waving heather. What was the marquess about, ladling out such flattery?

"He made a point of seeking me out last time I was there."

So Hennie had said many times. "What do you talk about with our fascinating neighbor?"

Hennie bit her lip. "You, primarily."

"Me?" This got Violet to straighten up and pay attention. News of herself always did. "What about me?"

Her cousin shrugged her shoulders. "He seems concerned that he stay in your good esteem."

Violet snorted.

"He does, Violet."

It was beyond the limits of Violet's vanity not to be

pleased by this news. Anyone who appreciated her could not be entirely bad, she had to allow. The marquess had his good points—tops among them being his rhododendrons and the fact that he was a marquess. She would also allow that he was physically not unattractive. Still, he seemed so cold and passionless, so lacking in dash and daring, so unlike . . .

She blushed and then fell back against the sofa cushions. She had almost managed to forget about the Brute!

"Are you relapsing?" Hennie's puckered brow and worried eyes loomed over Violet. "Should I stay after all?"

"No, no, I am only resting. Do go on—I shan't be able to rest easily until I know that my troubles haven't ruined your pleasure."

That last statement came out more long-suffering than Violet had intended, and yet Hennie didn't seem to notice. She was already skipping toward the door. "All right. Feel better, my dear!"

When the door had shut, Violet found worry once more engulfing her just as the couch cushions were. How could she possibly hope to feel better when hanging over her head was the prospect of the unknown fate that awaited her this evening?

Sebastian was never as surprised as when his study door opened and Griggs announced a visitor. And not just any visitor.

"Mr. John Cuthbert to see you, my lord."

"My word!" Sebastian shouted, jumping up. Griggs hopped back a little in surprise—and Griggs had probably never hopped before during the four decades of his employ at Montraffer. At his servant's reproachful glance, Sebastian smiled. "Show him in, Griggs."

In all the years he had known John Cuthbert, Sebastian had never seen him outside of London. Indeed, he only visited with the man at his office or his club. Of course, one assumed Cuthbert had a home, too—but probably only for the sake of propriety. It had always seemed that the man could have happily turned his musty government office into his permanent dwelling.

This made Cuthbert's sudden decision to leave his beloved surroundings and appear in Cornwall all the more startling. This could be no pleasure visit, and very few people merely passed through the neighborhood this far south in Cornwall.

When the older man appeared, his normally dour countenance looked even gloomier than was customary. As he shook Sebastian's hand, Cuthbert's head was shaking too. He did not keep the marquess in suspense. Say what you will about Cuthbert, he was never coy.

"Bad news," he said tersely. "Napoleon has escaped."

The news was so terrible, so unbelievable, at first Sebastian could only repeat it, in hopes that it would sink in. "Escaped!"

"He escaped from Elba at the end of February. God only knows what this will mean if he is not recaptured."

"Good Lord." But why would Cuthbert not have written him this news?

As if he could read Sebastian's mind, Cuthbert explained, "I wanted to tell you in person. Also . . ." His countenance darkened further.

"What?" Sebastian prompted him.

Cuthbert continued, looking even more morose, "There's a rather serious memorandum that has unfortunately gone missing. It details the location and strength of England's and her likely allies' troops on the continent. I don't have to remind you that this is exactly the sort of information that Nero delighted in trading in. Naturally we hope that Napoleon will be recaptured quickly, but just in case it is imperative that Nero not be allowed to escape with this information to France."

"That is serious. Do we know when the report was stolen?"

"Alas, no. It could have been missing for weeks. It had been filed rather routinely away—its significance was small until the news about Boney being on the loose."

Sebastian shook his head in commiseration. "What a mess! I'm still surprised that you journeyed all this way to deliver this news in person. Is there something more you have to tell me?"

Cuthbert was obviously reluctant, but he squared his shoulders and continued, "Judging from your last letter, I thought it might be best if I inspected the situation here."

"Why?"

"Well . . . because of Mrs. Treacher."

Sebastian laughed. "So you think I am going the way of the poor fellow who fell for the opera singer, do you?"

"You seemed to have dismissed your suspicions of her."

"Nothing of the kind." Sebastian shrugged. "True, she is passably well off, not at all political, and if I may say so, rather too absorbed in her own problems to care much for those of the greater world. But even so, I have devised a scheme that I hope will let me learn for certain her guilt or innocence."

"Part of the plans you wrote of?" Cuthbert's face remained twisted into a concerned scowl. "You were rather vague about those."

"Where I have failed to learn the truth from Mrs. Treacher, Robert the Brute might succeed."

"Did it occur to you that Jacobs and Mrs. Treacher might be partners?" Cuthbert asked.

For some reason, Sebastian heard himself rising to Violet's defense. "I considered it, but she didn't even know the man until a few weeks ago."

"Are we sure?"

"No, but my gut tells me they are not conspirators."

It was the first time he had voiced the thought, even to himself. But after all, it was one thing for him to hold suspicions; he had no official authority. One word from Cuthbert, however, and a person could find himself clapped in irons. Much as Sebastian would have liked to clobber Violet from time to time, he was not so certain her shortcomings warranted an extended stay in the stocks. "If you could but see her . . ."

"And so I hope to," Cuthbert said. "If you could arrange it?"

"Of course," Sebastian said. "There is to be a ball at Trembledown this weekend."

Cuthbert's gray brows knit together. "That is longer than I could possibly stay."

"That's too bad. Then perhaps something else could be arranged. I suppose we could drop in on our neighbors." He had planned to drop in on Violet this very night, in fact. He laughed to himself. This might be difficult to stage-manage. He couldn't very well be two people at once. "Maybe at the dinner hour."

"Yes, and the sooner the better. Tonight, if possible," Cuthbert said. "I will need to get back to London."

"But you must stop a little while," Sebastian said. "A few days, at least. Now that you are here, you owe it to yourself to reap all the advantages of a sojourn in the country."

Cuthbert's eyes clouded even more gloomily, so that

Sebastian felt the need to give him a bracing slap on the back. "Besides, you could be instrumental in helping me identify and capture Nero. Wouldn't you like to be here for that?"

Oddly enough, *this* prospect seemed to cheer Cuthbert a little. No doubt making this a working holiday would probably make him fell less like an idler.

"You could take this afternoon to roam about a little, get to know the country."

"Roam?" Cuthbert asked, his nose scrunching in distaste. The man had probably not taken the air—even in the royal parks—since he was a lad. If then, even.

"Walk about," Sebastian explained, feeling a bit like Mr. Cheswyn. "You should, you know. It's good for you—my vicar is forever preaching the benefits of nature. Meantime, I will go into town and try to make contact with Jem. We haven't spoken in a few days."

And at some point, he needed to ready himself for his moonlight assignation with Violet.

Cuthbert hesitated. "Perhaps I will. It would be beneficial to get the lay of the land, so to speak." His brow beetled. "Although I did bring several reports to review . . ."

Sebastian laughed. "Never mind that! I shall instruct Griggs to remove the papers from your bags until you have taken a bracing constitutional."

Cuthbert let out a long-suffering sigh. "This is what comes of leaving London."

He had been half joking, but by the time Cuthbert had crested his first hill, he was convinced that perhaps his words were truer than he first suspected. He was not used to scrambling up hillsides over uneven ground (terrain more suitable for goats than people, he thought). He had only just arrived, but already he missed the comforts of his club and his office and felt bereft of his routine.

On the other hand, coming here gave him a unique perspective on why this area should be such a haven for the criminal element. The shore, pocked with cove towns, caves, and unapproachable stretches of coastline, was probably irresistible to such characters.

He also felt glad he would meet Mrs. Treacher for himself. He was still not entirely reassured on that score. St. Just would not be the first man to be taken in by a pretty face. (Of course, Sebastian had not described her beauty in so many words; Cuthbert was reading between the lines.) Cuthbert, though, had never been susceptible to a batting eyelash or a flash of ankle. If anyone would be able to dispassionately assess a woman's character, it was undoubtedly he.

Lost in thought, he strolled on until he started down the other side of a hill and stumbled upon a woman sitting on a blanket sketching—he had only just missed treading on her skirt spread out on the blanket.

"I beg your pardon!"

The woman, naturally startled, jumped up. She had been drawing a particularly picturesque strip of seashore—though her rather exaggerated style made it seem even more untamed than perhaps it was.

"My, how you startled me!" she said breathlessly.

The lady, for she was unmistakably such, had clear gray eyes, pale skin with a bloom of color to the cheeks, and a small, neat figure regrettably disguised by her mourning dress. Even her artist's smock was black. In spite of all this funereal garb—or perhaps because of it—she made quite an arresting picture, peering up at him from under a rather lamentable floppy bonnet of black straw that had faded to a purplish hue from exposure to sun and sea air.

Cuthbert could not drag his gaze away from those eyes. Not blue exactly, he pondered. Too light for that. Yet he had never seen gray eyes so vivid and lively.

She noted his unresponsiveness. "But perhaps I startled you as much as you did me," she said. As he continued to stare at her, her color pinkened even more.

He felt as if he were in a trance—one he finally made a mighty effort to shake himself free of. "I thought I was alone here. My host did not warn me that there were artists dotting the hillsides."

Her laughter was a bright, lively sound that almost caused him to smile. "There is only me." She tilted her head at him. "Are you a guest of the Marquess of St. Just?"

"Yes, I have just arrived, rather unexpectedly, from London."

"Oh! You have had a long journey." She leaned toward him. "I trust you met with no unpleasant incident on the road?"

"No."

"Good! You are lucky—my own carriage was stopped by Robert the Brute just a few short weeks ago."

Cuthbert gulped. "*Your* carriage?" He knew only that Sebastian had overtaken Mrs. Treacher's carriage a few weeks earlier; surely Sebastian did not make a habit of kidnapping women out of carriages. In which case . . .

This could not be.

"Oh yes. It gave me such a fright!"

"I have no doubt of it!" Cuthbert exclaimed, feeling a stone in the pit of his stomach.

This was the widow Treacher?

Cuthbert let that possibility—nay, probability—sink

in. Poor St. Just! Devising schemes and assuming a smuggler's identity to entrap or exonerate the woman, when here she was, on Sebastian's very own property, sketching the coastline in her widow's weeds! She might be making maps, or watching the comings and goings of boats, or even engaging in some elaborate signaling.

He angled a look at the drawing she was making and then closed his eyes briefly. There was all the proof he needed that something was afoot. The seascape she was working on was like no drawing he had ever laid eyes on. It had to either be the work of a madwoman or a woman creating a code of some sort.

And what had his own reaction been to the woman? A fanciful digression on the shade of her eyes! He paused briefly to ponder the treachery of beauty. No wonder Sebastian was so taken in; her seeming simplicity and kind good humor only made her that much more bewitching.

He was a bit surprised to find that she was rather more mature in years than he had supposed. She must be several years Sebastian's senior.

Oh, but what did age matter to a woman determined to deceive a man?

He shook his head.

"Are you quite all right, sir?" she asked, peering into his face with concern. "I am beginning to believe this salt air can affect some people strangely if they are not accustomed to it. My companion is frequently subject to bouts of light-headedness whenever she is outside."

Ah yes, that must be the spinster cousin he had heard some talk about—some foolish woman. Trust these old maids to always be going into spasms, Cuthbert thought.

The lady continued to smile at him and said, "I live at Trembledown, just down the road."

"Yes, I know."

She looked rather surprised. "You do? Then perhaps, the marquess has mentioned—"

"Indeed he has. He informed me that we would be paying a visit to Trembledown. Perhaps this very night."

She clapped her gloved hands together as if she were genuinely pleased and guileless enough to show her enthusiasm. But perhaps guilelessness was just another facet of her wily nature. "I'm so glad. You must come for dinner. Do. We dine at seven."

His curt bow seemed to set off some alarm in her. "Th-that is," she sputtered, "if you think it would be convenient for his lordship. I would not want to impose our schedule on him, or you, either, of course. The marquess has been so kind, so—"

Easily taken in, Cuthbert could have finished for her. But he himself felt his brain screaming the same conclusion as his friend had reached. This lady was surely no spy!

And yet . . . what evidence they had, circumstantial though it was, pointed to her.

Cuthbert cut her off with a raised hand, suddenly desperate to return to the house. How he wished he had never gone walking, had never seen those eyes. "And now, I must bid you good day, ma'am."

The eyes in question widened at his sudden decision to depart, but she was mistress of herself enough to drop him a curtsy as he turned.

Cuthbert stumbled back in the direction he had come from. He did not stop until he was sure he was out of her sight. He was out of breath, but not from fatigue. His heart was beating out of control from that first, devastating glance into those celestial gray eyes.

He felt appalled by his reaction, and yes, rather shattered. To have met such a delicate, alluring creature—only to discover that she might be a duplicitous traitor. It felt heartbreaking, especially since he had only that moment discovered that he might have a heart to break.

Chapter Ten

Though Violet had been eager for Hennie to follow her artistic pursuits at the marquess's estate, she nevertheless became a little perturbed when her cousin did not return for hours and hours. Time alone, as it happened, left her imagination unbridled, so that Hennie's absence had been spent entirely in conjecture about Robert the Brute. Would he really come this evening . . . and when? Would he try to sneak upon her unawares, or would he appear in the house and snatch her away again right under the noses of Hennie and Peabody?

Or perhaps he did not mean to snatch her away at all. Perhaps he harbored plans altogether more nefarious. She was far from understanding the workings of the criminal mind, but maybe he thought, erroneously, that she knew too much of his illegal doings. In that case . . . Well! She would be done for.

It was in the middle of such a gruesome reverie that Hennie appeared, humming a song best suited for dancing around Maypoles. With bright cheeks and sprightliness astonishing to behold, she practically pirouetted across the room. Her arms were weighted down by a preposterous armload of March flowers.

Violet, who had been lying in a semiswoon on the sofa—the best position for brooding about her violent demise at the hands of the Brute—sat up straighter. The floral bounty Hennie was hauling around in her arms was enough to distract her. Her cousin must have denuded every plant in her path. "Where did you get those?"

Her cousin stopped and smiled distractedly at her. "Oh, hello!" It was as if she had not even noticed Violet sitting there. "Are you feeling better?"

"Aside from a headache and my nerves, I am fine," Violet said.

Any sarcasm that might have seeped into that answer sailed cleanly over her cousin's head. "Wonderful!"

"Where did you get those flowers?" Violet asked again.

"Oh . . . here and there . . ."

"Not from our yard, I hope."

"Perhaps a few of them . . ." Hennie didn't even bother to look guilty, though it was obvious by the sheer volume of that bouquet that "just a few" flowers would have left Violet's garden decimated. But of course, Hennie meant well. Violet could not resent anyone thoughtful enough to bring flowers to cheer her.

She lifted a hand listlessly but appreciatively. "I think there is enough there for a vase for here and in my room."

Hennie's face registered alarm. "Oh dear! I had meant these for the dining room."

Then the flowers were not meant for her at all. The grateful smile faded from Violet's lips.

Her cousin jumped in, "Though of course you might take some for your own use . . . if you insist."

Violet's lips tightened. "I don't see that they would

do us much service in the dining room. We are there so rarely."

"I picked them expressly for our company." That faraway look returned to her expression.

What was the matter with her?

"Company?" Violet repeated.

"Our dinner party. The marquess and his guest."

For a moment Violet wondered whether her cousin was entirely right in the head. Evidently she was imagining dinner guests when there was nothing but another dull, solitary evening ahead, to be followed by a ghastly, possibly grisly, crime.

Violet wondered if she ought to send Hennie to Bath after all. Very possibly this house was driving her mad.

Yet Hennie seemed very insistent on the point of their having company. "I ran into him just hours ago, at Montraffer."

"The marquess?"

"No, his friend."

"What friend?" Violet asked impatiently.

"The gentleman from London," Hennie responded in kind, as if Violet were being purposefully obtuse.

"Hennie, I have no idea who you mean."

"But you must. They are coming here to dine tonight."

"*Tonight*!" She shot to her feet. Impossible! She was expecting the Brute tonight!

"Of course," Hennie said. "That is why I picked the flowers."

Violet put a hand to her temple, which really did feel as if it were throbbing now. So now, according to Hennie, she was expecting a smuggler *and* two gentlemen? How could this be? "But I have invited no one."

Hennie paused, tilting her head. "Really? Are you quite certain?"

"Of course!" Violet said. "I had no idea the marquess had any friends, much less one staying with him. Who is this grand personage?"

Nervous laughter fluttered out of Hennie. "As to that, I do not know whether he is grand, exactly. I am sure he is a gentleman."

Violet could not quite hold back a skeptical grunt. During one of her unsuccessful Seasons, Hennie had famously mistaken a footman for a viscount, a misperception that she had steadfastly refused to acknowledge until she saw the alleged viscount she had been flirting with in a hallway serving punch to guests in the ballroom. "What is his name?"

Hennie's dreamy smile faltered. "I do not know."

"Then you were not introduced."

"Not exactly, no. But I know he is staying at Montraffer."

"For how long?"

Hennie had the good sense to look abashed. "I . . . well, I don't know that, either."

"You seem to know next to nothing about this man." Hopefully she didn't know about his dinner plans, either. "How did you ascertain that this person was the marquess's guest?"

"I saw him on the grounds there."

Violet laughed. "Then he could be anyone. He could have been a poacher!"

"Oh no!" Hennie declared vehemently. "He had an honest face. And he said that he and the marquess were coming to dine with us."

Violet rolled her eyes. "An honest gentleman who invents invitations for himself and his host! How shall I ever straighten this out?"

Hennie drew back in alarm. "You don't mean to disinvite them, surely?"

"Well, yes, if I can locate this person. So far all we really know is that a man roaming the countryside believes he has been invited to our house for dinner."

"But Violet, I told you—"

"Hennie," she said, cutting her off. "We are not prepared to entertain. Surely it is far better to rescind an invitation than to turn someone away at the doors . . . or frighten them away with cold meats for supper."

"Oh, but I will do all I can! We must have them. It would be entirely uncordial of us to rescind the invitation."

"But the invitation was never extended to begin with."

"Well . . ." Hennie blushed as if a realization suddenly occurred to her. "Oh dear!"

"What?"

"Perhaps *I* extended the invitation by mistake."

Violet groaned. "Oh, Hen!"

"But only because I thought *you* had invited them first, coz."

Violet made Hennie backtrack and recount the entire conversation she had had with the mysterious guest of Montraffer. After listening to the strangely uneventful encounter, Violet sensed that the man *had* been invited, if in a rather indirect way. It was a rather underhanded affair, she had to say. Despite Hennie's claiming all culpability in the matter, Violet suspected that the marquess had a hand in setting the whole misunderstanding into motion.

Sebastian usually did seem to be at the bottom of all her troubles.

"But after all," Hennie continued on, "there is no reason why we should not have guests tonight."

Violet could think of a hundred reasons. What would they serve? The house was not ready. The short notice would put Peabody completely out of sorts . . .

And then the most startling objection of all came rushing back to her. *The Brute!* What was she going to do?

"Violet?" Hennie peered into her face. "Are you all right?"

"Oh . . ." Violet sank back down on the sofa.

"You've gone green again."

How could she hostess a dinner party? It was impossible to imagine herself caring about her guests' comfort or whether the wine decanters were full when she would be risking violent death or abduction at any moment. What if the Brute burst into the dinner party and snatched her away in front of all her unwanted guests? Would she be able to fight him off, or would she succumb to his superior strength?

For a frenzied moment she seized on the idea of Sebastian fending off the notorious intruder. But then she remembered who the marquess was. More likely he would shove her into the Brute's arm to secure his own safety.

"Violet?"

Violet looked up into Hennie's concerned gaze. *Stop thinking these things!*

Or rather, perhaps she should think of them in a different light. This gathering tonight might be her salvation. After all, it was possible that having company would scare the Brute away entirely. There would be safety in numbers. She pounced on that thought like a drowning woman grasping at flotsam.

The idea even made her feel more kindly toward her uninvited guests. "Did you say this man was a young man?" If so, he might be helpful . . . just in case.

"Not young, but not too old." Concentration tensed her expression, as if this were a subject that had been much in her thoughts. "I would say not a day over forty-five."

Violet's hopes sank. Forty-five was not a promising age in terms of exerting brute force against smugglers. "Perhaps he is a youngish forty-five."

"He's very handsome." Hennie blushed, which of course meant very little in itself. Hennie was always turning red over something or another.

And yet . . . was Violet wrong, or did this blush have a hint of something else in it? Something she had never detected before in her cousin. It was a blush she was more accustomed to seeing in her young man-mad sister Sophy—the blush of a lovesick girl.

Violet's interest was piqued. "Handsome, you say?"

Hennie immediately began to stammer. "That is . . . I-I'm sure I did not notice any of his features in particular . . . though he was staring at me so curiously . . ."

Could it be that this stranger had a *passion* for Hennie? "You seem to have made a conquest."

"Oh no. Quite possibly he was only interested in my drawing. He stared at it long enough."

That, Violet doubted. Despite her other worries, an intense curiosity to meet this man overcame her. "Very well. I shall send a card to St. Just to confirm the time. I hope Cook has prepared enough for dinner. We cannot have marquesses and friends of marquesses going hungry at Trembledown. Peabody would be mortified."

The words transformed Hennie back into the humming, light-footed creature who had entered the room minutes before. "Oh, I think that would be the hospitable thing to do, Violet. Certainly. You always manage these matters in just the right way."

Violet couldn't help being gratified by this acknowledgement of her social prowess, though naturally she never would have remarked upon it herself. Of course, it was that very modesty that accounted for the fact that so many of her talents went entirely unappreciated.

Perhaps by putting her hostessing talents to work she could forfend—or at least temporarily forget—the terrible fate that might await her this evening at the hands of the Brute.

"It is a strange coincidence."

When his comment received no reply, Sebastian looked across the carriage at Cuthbert. The man seemed to be lost in thought, as he had been all evening. In fact, Sebastian was giving up hope of ever hearing his friend's voice again. One walk in the Cornwall countryside seemed to have rendered the man mute.

"John!"

Cuthbert jumped. "Good heavens, man. Why are you shouting at me?"

"That is generally what one does when someone is some distance away, which you seemed to be." He drew a deep breath and tapped his stick impatiently. "I was going to say that it seemed quite a coincidence that on the very night we were going to drop in on the ladies at Trembledown, an invitation arrived."

"Mmm."

"And how odd that Mrs. Treacher knew I had a guest. One who I had, until just this afternoon, no knowledge of myself."

John looked uncomfortable, then confessed, "I did not tell you before, but I believe I might have been the catalyst for our neighbor's hospitality. You see . . ." His brow darkened. "I happened upon Mrs. Treacher during my walk."

Sebastian sat up straighter. Damn! Why was Violet

wandering near Montraffer? Could it have something to do with the note he'd left her? Yet she couldn't have been on the lookout for the Brute, surely. She already had a rendezvous planned with him for that evening.

That last thought made him pat the small case on the seat next to him. It contained his Brute clothes, for later.

"Are you sure it was she?" he asked John.

Cuthbert nodded, and his usual glum look was back full force. "The widow of Trembledown herself."

"What did you think of her?"

"Oh . . . She was all that you said . . ." He looked up suddenly, and his gaze sharp, almost accusatory. "And yet your description did not fit her at all."

"Did I not tell you she was beautiful?"

"Yes, yes," Cuthbert said dismissively. "But you did not mention her eyes. Or perhaps you did, but you did not do so properly."

Sebastian leaned forward. The catch in John's voice was unfamiliar to him. "Her eyes? What are you going on about?"

"No matter!" Cuthbert shook his head violently, giving the appearance of a man at war with himself. "I'm sure they are quite immaterial to us. Of course they are. And yet . . . one can tell so much by looking into eyes."

Sebastian's brows rose. He had never heard Cuthbert talk this way. It was rather astonishing. Looking into someone's eyes was not solid proof of character, was not a rational analysis of anything. John Cuthbert was nothing if not a cool, rational human being.

"Mrs. Treacher does have lovely eyes," he admitted, biting back a smile as a peculiar suspicion took root in his mind. "Did she strike you as a guilty woman?"

"Heavens, no!" Cuthbert said. "That is, not at first. Her eyes were as innocent as a babe's."

"And what else did you see in those fascinating orbs?"

The man looked down at his gloved hands. "Oh . . ."

For a moment, Sebastian could hardly speak himself. *Zounds!* Violet Treacher had even managed to crack the cool marble edifice that was John Cuthbert's heart. A feat no woman before her had ever managed—or as far as Sebastian knew, had ever thought to attempt!

After a moment of pure shock, his mind shifted uncomfortably. Had Violet done this on purpose . . . or was there actually a genuine attraction between the two?

Amazingly, he felt a moment of jealousy. First that troublesome Jacobs fellow—and now a new rival from a quarter he never would have anticipated!

Not that what he felt toward Violet in any way would have justified thinking of anyone as a rival. He did not feel real affection for the woman. Attraction? Of course. He was not blind. And he admitted to a sort of reluctant admiration of her spirit. Also, she had a dry sense of humor that appealed him. She saw his posturing, but not knowing that it was purely that—a posture—she enjoyed poking fun at him.

And yes, he had to admit he had been as giddy as a schoolboy all day about the little prank he had planned for this evening—he really did enjoy a masquerade. He wondered what would happen. Would Violet nibble at the bait he cast for her? He hoped not. Much as she exasperated him, he did not want to think the worst of Violet.

Would he kiss her again?

Oh yes, came the immediate answer. He could hardly imagine passing up the opportunity to take her in his arms again and reacquaint himself with those sweet lips.

And yet, even gathered together, what did all those stray feelings amount to? Certainly not the lovesickness he had detected—he could still hardly believe it—in poor Cuthbert's face.

"I know what you are thinking," his friend said.

Sebastian stilled. *Good heavens, I hope not!*

Cuthbert looked anguished, almost shamed. "Do not be concerned, my lord. I have not forgotten why I am here . . . No, I have not forgotten what is practically my purpose on this earth—my solemn duty to my government. Naturally it has been humbling to realize that I am not immune to the wiles of the female. Many a man since Samson has accomplished his own destruction through such weakness as I felt this afternoon."

That must have been some meeting, Sebastian thought, astounded. And once again that green devil jealousy seemed to take up residence in his heart. *Cuthbert?* She had flashed those impossibly blue eyes of hers at *Cuthbert?*

"But you will not find me forgetting my duty," the man said. "You will find that I am able to put my feelings aside quite easily tonight."

"Of course."

"I shall ignore her entirely—as much as one can ignore one's hostess—and devote myself . . . well, perhaps to the spinster cousin you told me about."

"Very wise of you, John."

"Let no man ever say John Cuthbert did not do his duty."

He spoke with such a tone of self-denial and noble sacrifice that Sebastian almost felt sorry for the man. And he couldn't hold back a little irritation. What was Violet about, toying with the man's affections this way?

What was she up to now?

They rode the rest of the way in silence, and when they did arrive at Trembledown, Cuthbert climbed out of the carriage and marched to the house with a grim determination. The butler, Peabody, showed them in, and within moments, they were greeted in the hallway by Violet and her cousin.

Sebastian popped his monocle in place. "I suppose you know Mr. Cuthbert," he told Violet.

She looked confused at first—had she thought she could keep meeting his guest a secret from him?—but then dropped a curtsy to Cuthbert. Not that Cuthbert was looking at her. His eyes were fixed on Henrietta. Cuthbert had said that he would devote all his attention to Miss Halsop this evening; apparently he was wasting no time.

"My cousin, Miss Henrietta Halsop."

Cuthbert bowed deeply. "Miss Halsop! You have no idea what a pleasure it is to formally make your acquaintance!"

Two dark stains appeared in Henrietta's cheeks, and her eyes seemed not to know where to look. Sebastian felt likewise confused by his friend's behavior . . . but then John Cuthbert had done nothing but surprise him all day long.

John was true to his word. Sebastian watched him closely; all through dinner he barely spared Violet a glance. He absolutely devoted himself to Henrietta, treating that woman with more deference in two hours than she had probably heretofore received in a lifetime. Under his unexpected attentions the older woman was glowing, and it suddenly occurred to Sebastian that, though she naturally paled next to the undeniable beauty of Violet, Hennie was not unattractive. Not at all.

Hennie was obviously flattered by all the attention, yet Sebastian wondered if John wasn't doing it a bit too brown. For one thing, his lavish attentions on the cousin were having unforeseen consequences, because Hennie grew so flustered that within an hour she had tipped her wineglass over twice, caused a small conflagration by catching her handkerchief in the flame of a candle, and then soiled Cuthbert's pants when she inadvertently whacked her wrist against his soup bowl.

Sebastian had never seen his friend in any other state besides immaculately clean. He was a bit taken aback that Cuthbert did not seem to mind having his gray trousers doused in broth. He must have been concentrating very hard indeed on not drawing the attention of his hostess.

If he had looked at Violet, however, some of the attraction he felt for that woman might have dissipated in the face of her indifference.

Violet Treacher was a woman distracted. Sebastian, though he did his best to keep up conversation in the face of the tête-à-tête going on between Cuthbert and Hennie, found himself struggling to hold Violet's attention. She did not eat, and she did not seem to listen. Every so often Sebastian would notice that her eyes were fixed on the windows of the dining room (those that weren't obscured by an extravagant bouquet of flowers). She was, he was sure, looking out for the Brute.

That fact filled him with an almost foolish satisfaction. And relief. Perhaps John was mistaken—or the attraction had been all one-sided. Whatever the case, Violet's thoughts were now undeniably all focused on Sebastian. Or rather, Sebastian in his incarnation as the Brute.

Being entirely shut out from the quiet conversation between Hennie and John at one end of the table, Sebastian turned to his hostess. Unlike John, he could hardly keep his eyes off her. She was dressed in a green velvet gown that gave her an especially regal bearing. It also made the usual dinner chatter harder than usual for him to think of.

Not that she was listening. Sebastian had to repeat a remark three times before it got her attention.

When Violet finally heard him, she appeared almost dumbfounded to find herself seated at a tableful of guests. "I'm sorry?"

Sebastian sniffed. "I was going to compliment you on your cook's preparation of the asparagus."

"Asparagus," she repeated.

"Yet you do not seem to have touched yours," he noted. "A grave show of self-denial."

"I am simply not hungry, my lord."

"My dear Mrs. Treacher, to appreciate asparagus this fine one need not be hungry at all, any more than one must hunger for art to appreciate Michelangelo. What texture—and what a wonderful sauce! Not to sample such perfection would be a crime."

"Then you should call at once for Constable Farkas, because I have no appetite."

To her obvious astonishment, he cut a piece on her own plate and held it up to her mouth.

Her lips fixed themselves in a stubborn line. "I have not been spoon-fed since I was a babe, my lord."

"But you must try it."

Rather than argue, Violet took a reluctant nibble and chewed with a lack of gusto; she might as well have been eating stale bread. "Mmm, yes," she said dutifully. "Very good."

"I beg your pardon, but I'm not sure you tasted it at all. You seemed a million miles away." His lips twisted in a smile. "It is a condition that appears to be catching."

"Hmm?" She was already looking out the window again. "Oh yes."

And so the evening passed through two more courses. If Sebastian hadn't known he himself was the reason for Violet's distraction, he might have been insulted. It helped that in the competition for her attention, he was only losing to himself.

After custard had been served and virtually ignored by all but Sebastian (he took advantage of his position by eating his hostess's portion, as well), Violet stood. "Hennie, perhaps we should leave the men to enjoy their port."

She was halfway to the pull that would summon Peabody when Cuthbert stopped her. "Oh, but we require no spirits tonight, do we, St. Just?"

Sebastian was taken aback by the question. He certainly would have liked a glass—not to mention the opportunity to tell Cuthbert that he need not avoid their hostess quite so studiously. If Violet weren't so preoccupied, she might have found the man's behavior suspicious. John Cuthbert usually sought to be unobtrusive above all else.

Until tonight. "I see no reason to separate ourselves from these lovely ladies for so much as ten minutes, do you, St. Just?"

The words set Hennie into a spontaneous bloom. In the face of her reaction, Sebastian could hardly contradict his friend.

"Oh, all right," he grumbled. "Though perhaps we should go into the parlor. I seem to recall seeing Peabody lighting a fire there."

"Excellent!" Cuthbert said. "And perhaps Miss Halsop will play harp for us. She is very modest about her talents, but I am sure I would enjoy nothing more than music right now."

Sebastian noted a subtle shuddering of Violet's shoulders. "Very well," she said leadenly, escorting them out with little enthusiasm.

Within ten minutes, Cuthbert and Hennie were planted side by side on a bench behind a large harp. Hennie's nervous hands slipped erratically over the strings, creating sounds that seemed neither rhythmic nor particularly musical. And yet neither seemed to notice anything the least atonal afoot.

As the recital progressed, Violet and Sebastian migrated farther and farther away from the harp. He joined her next to the glass doors at the end of the long room, which looked out to a crumbling stone terrace. Weeds grew in the cracks of the floor, and a stiff wind from the sea rattled at loose panes of glass in the door.

"You seem fascinated by the outdoors tonight," he observed.

She looked up sharply, as if he had startled her. "It is very dark."

He sniffed. "Yes, I shall have to instruct my driver to be very careful going home. There is simply no telling who might be lurking about on a night like this."

Her eyes shuttered for a moment. "Yes!"

He coughed to conceal a laugh. "I should have brought some outriders with me this evening."

Her lips twisted and she folded her arms. "Surely you are not so scared, my lord. A smuggler would have to be a fool indeed to attack a carriage as fine as yours."

He drew back. "My dear lady, that is precisely who those unsavory characters want to attack. I heard of a gentleman in Hampshire who was killed fighting them off."

"And would you fight to the death, my lord?"

"Dear heavens, no!" He performed a horrified shiver for her benefit. "What purpose would that serve? Should I lose my life in a vain attempt to rid the world of one troublesome fellow?"

"I believe the point would be to make the attempt not be in vain."

"I don't care for the odds, myself." He leaned against

the door and found it pushing open. "Mrs. Treacher, this is a very flimsy catch on this door!"

She squinted at it. "Yes."

"Why, any kind of brigand could push it right open. Perhaps even Robert the Brute himself!"

Her body went stiff, her face pale. "The Brute!" After a moment she caught him studying her and laughed nervously. "But why should he?"

"Why indeed! Why should he attack my carriage? Why should he be a criminal at all? Because he is a villain."

Hennie's playing increased in volume as she segued into what might have been meant to be a waltz. It was difficult to say with any certainty. Yet she and Cuthbert were as close to dancing as two people could be sitting side by side on a bench. They seemed not to notice that their audience had drawn away, and they certainly did not notice the alarm in Violet's eyes.

"I am sorry if I have frightened you," Sebastian said. "If it would make you feel better, I shall have a word with Barnabas about setting up watch."

"*No!*" Violet blushed at her outburst. "That is . . . I'm sure that will not be necessary."

"But if you are scared . . ."

She lifted her sharp chin. "I am not scared. You forget, I have met the Brute before and survived. I am not a jot frightened of that creature."

"Brave woman!"

"I have barely given the beast a thought in the past weeks, until you put him into my head."

"Would that I could take him out again." He oozed forward in an extravagant bow. "My apologies. I only worried . . ."

She looked up at him. "What?"

"Well, that the man might have developed an obsession with you."

She blinked in surprise. "Why would you say that?"

He leaned closer to her. "Well! If you do not mind my forwardness in saying so, you are quite an attractive woman. Of course it would not have occurred to you that a man—even a lowborn one such as the Brute—would notice your beauty. Such is the modesty of woman! Why, with just one encounter you have quite won over my friend Cuthbert."

Her brow creased with doubt as she looked over at the piano bench. "He seems won over by someone else."

"Yes, that is how it would appear. And yet, how often is indifference a sign of hidden affection?"

Her brows arched. "And how often is indifference merely indifference?"

He wanted to laugh. She really did not seem to think much of her encounter with John that afternoon. Impulsively, he reached for her hand and bent his lips over it quickly. "And yet I cannot imagine any man being quite indifferent to you, Violet."

Her cheeks stained red and she tugged her hand away. "My lord, I can only assume that you are trying to hum me again with this type of behavior. I cannot guess why you should do so, but I do not enjoy being the end of a joke."

"Indeed, I meant nothing humorous by my impulsive action. Yet I cannot help noticing by your reaction that my attentions are perhaps not to be greeted with overt enthusiasm. Pardon me. I naturally assumed . . ."

Her shoulders squared, and two little dots of red appeared in her cheeks. "Assumed what?"

He took a deep breath and plunged forward, mentally preparing himself for fireworks. "Well! No one denies that titles usually carry a certain allure."

He had to hold back a belly laugh as Violet's countenance changed from confusion to thunderous rage in the span of a heartbeat. Her slender frame shook, making him wonder momentarily if the earth wasn't about to witness an eruption to rival Vesuvius.

He decided that it was best to retreat while the good lady was still able to swallow her spleen. He turned quickly, leaving her quietly choking back anger.

"Well, Cuthbert!" he called across the room. "Perhaps we should be returning to chez Montraffer. I feel quite knocked up all of a sudden."

"So early?" Cuthbert asked, reluctance dripping from his words.

Hennie boldly touched his arm. "You are welcome here any time, Mr. Cuthbert. Indeed, we would be disappointed if we did not see more of you while you are in Cornwall. Wouldn't we, Violet?"

Violet, still stewing, barely spared the man a glance. Her chest was heaving as she glared at Sebastian. "Oh yes. You must come, by all means. Indeed, you must come alone if his lordship is not available."

Sebastian understood from her expression that the last option was actually preferable to her.

He and Cuthbert made their exit as soon as the carriage could be brought around. Once inside, Cuthbert sank back against the cushions. "Such an excellent woman!"

Sebastian regarded him with surprise. "Your strategy of avoiding our hostess seemed quite successful, John."

Cuthbert looked down at his hands. "Well . . . ahem!" He coughed uncomfortably. "You see, I discovered when we arrived at Trembledown and were introduced to our charming hostesses that a slight misunderstanding had taken place. The woman I had assumed was the widow . . ."

"Hennie!" Sebastian exclaimed.

"Precisely! But you see, she was dressed in mourning and said she was from Trembledown."

Sebastian laughed. "And yet you saw no reason to avoid her as you would have Violet."

Cuthbert blinked at him. "But no suspicion has ever fallen on Miss Halsop."

"You are wrong there," Sebastian said gravely. "I still find her a highly suspicious character."

"*What?*" His friend looked outraged. "Why, anyone looking into those eyes would know they were not those of a traitor, a spy."

Sebastian bit his lip to keep from laughing. "And yet, she *also* arrived just as we started looking for Nero in earnest."

"Good heavens!" He looked stunned for a moment, then admitted, pained, "You are right!"

"I am?" Sebastian asked, surprised.

"I had forgotten . . . I saw Miss Halsop drawing a map of the coastline."

"A map?"

He nodded mournfully. "In her sketchbook. Right on your property, St. Just."

Sebastian could not keep that joke up for long. Not only did Cuthbert look too pained, it was just not possible for Sebastian to contemplate the world's least subtle female as a master spy without laughing. "Those 'maps' you saw were more likely renderings of my house, or fruit bowls. Your lady love is no spy, Cuthbert, but she is a rather deplorable artist."

He tapped his stick on the carriage ceiling for the coachman to stop.

"Why are we stopping?" Cuthbert asked.

Sebastian grabbed the handle of the case he had left on the carriage seat during dinner. He was glad that he had included a brandy flask in his Brute kit. He could certainly do with a short dip in the bottle before facing Violet again. "Business. While you may toddle off and have sweet dreams of your charming Miss Halsop, a spy's work is never done."

"Oh, I see. I had quite forgotten your very secretive plan."

"Let us hope that by the time I return to Montraffer we will be able to rule out Mrs. Treacher, at least."

Cuthbert's brow clouded. "Perhaps I should accompany you . . . on whatever it is you are doing."

Sebastian laughed. "Why? Do you think that Miss Halsop might fancy you as a smuggler's aide?"

Cuthbert's jaw dropped. "No, indeed! I would not— that is, Miss Halsop would not—" His words broke off.

"Never mind," Sebastian said, deciding his friend had been teased enough. "There are some jobs, Cuthbert, that must be done alone."

Chapter Eleven

As the clock struck eleven, not ten minutes after their guests left, Hennie yawned extravagantly and stood. "I think I shall retire now. Good night, Violet."

Violet, more aware of the ominous darkness outside now that the men were gone, jumped out of her chair. "But it's so early! Wouldn't you like to stay up a bit? We could chat!"

"I'm exhausted. It must have been all that walking I did today."

"B-but we could play cards." Hennie always enjoyed playing cards, though Violet rarely wanted to play. Granted, cards with Hennie wouldn't be much of a distraction from the fears plaguing her, but it was something.

"I don't think so, Violet. You know how I annoy you during a game. I always forget the cards I've played."

Perhaps if the Brute saw that there were two of them . . . Violet cast about for something else to tempt Hennie. "Don't you want to talk about Mr. Cuthbert? He seemed very taken with you, Hen."

Hennie's face lit in a fiery blush. "Oh, I am past thinking about romantic nonsense."

"No one is too old for romance."

"I'm sure you never will be, Violet. You will always retain your bloom. Whereas I . . ." She let out a long breath. "Well, I know that springtime has passed me by. No doubt Mr. Cuthbert was simply being nice to me to curry favor with you."

"That is absurd!"

"I really am frightfully tired, Violet." Despite her words, her eyes seemed bright. Talking about Mr. Cuthbert only seemed to make her more determined to retire, however. Violet could only guess that Hennie was eager to go upstairs and scribble in her diary or pen a note to her friend Imogene.

"All right, then," Violet said, relenting. "I won't keep you."

"Good night."

The moment Hennie headed for the stairs, Violet followed. Closely. "If I am to be left on my own, I may as well go to bed too," she grumbled.

She shut herself in her room (checking to make sure there were no smugglers hiding in her wardrobe, and securing the latches on her windows) and washed her face. It was utterly ridiculous to be so nervous! Why, she was trembling like a child who was afraid of the dark. She was in her own home; nothing could happen to her here.

She was slipping into her nightgown when she heard a sound downstairs. At least she thought it was from downstairs. In this drafty old stone house it was hard to tell. She thought she could hear rattling. Perhaps it was a branch scraping a windowpane in the wind.

Or perhaps it wasn't.

Her conversation with the marquess came back to her. A blackguard could push her door right open, he had said.

She was tempted to jump in bed and pull the covers over her head. But she could not. The memory of that flimsy door would not leave her. She should go down and secure it. If she pushed a table in front of it, for instance . . .

Of course, in the morning she would have to explain to Peabody why she had been rearranging furniture in the middle of the night, but better safe than sorry.

She pulled on a robe and pushed her feet into a pair of slippers, then crept down the stairs. Strange how much more sinister everything seemed at night. The scant light coming through the windows cast long shadows, making perfectly innocent chairs hulk menacingly before her. As she made her way to the glass doors, she tripped on a carpet and let out a shriek. She froze, expecting Peabody and Hennie to come running out of their rooms to see what the commotion was about, but after a half a minute of standing statue still in the middle of the room, she realized that her cry had been unheard.

A fine thing! She could be killed down here and probably no one would even bother to poke their heads out of their doors.

She continued on her way in a more pragmatic frame of mind. This was probably all foolishness. The Brute, if he had any intention of coming here at all, had probably seen that she had company and left. More likely still, his notes were left just to tease her; men were often all bluster.

She would push something in front of the door just to set her mind at ease, and then she would go to bed like a sensible person.

She was inspecting the furniture in the room for what would be the best and most manageable piece to move in front of the double doors when suddenly a cold breeze blasted through the room; a hand shot around her waist, and before she could so much as cry out, she was yanked outside through the very entrance she had meant to barricade.

Violet's heart slammed against her ribs. *The Brute!* He

had come, and now she was in his clutches, staring up into those disarming dark eyes through that mask. Before she could utter a peep of protest, his mouth covered hers. Hard. Hungrily.

Oh heavens!

The first thing she noticed was that he smelled of brandy and old leather . . . and that these things were familiar from her memory of their time in the cave, memories that she had gone over and over so often that they were almost comforting in their familiarity. His kisses lit the same spark in her, too. Forgetting herself, she sank against his chest.

The ruffian took terrible liberties with her, running his hands over her body like it was his very own possession. And indeed, he knew so well just where to touch her that she began to wonder if she did belong to him in some primal way.

Had his hands been so forceful, so knowing, so roughly tender before? She could not remember. She only knew that his handling of her suggested a disturbing mastery of her person.

Then it was true! She had been his . . . his . . . moll.

She stiffened against him.

The Brute pulled back. The wind whipped at her robe and the skirts of her nightgown, making her feel as if she were in a tangle around him. "What's this? Do you tire of my kisses so quickly, Highness?"

"Please let me go," she whispered. After an entire day of worrying over this encounter, it was all she could think to say.

"Does his lor'ship kiss you better?"

Her brow creased and she stared up into his face, uncomprehending. "What do you mean?"

His lips broke into that broad grin, but there was a bitter cast to it. "Aye, I saw you with him, at the window tonight."

Oh, Lord! He had been watching all this time . . . just waiting to pounce. And now he had pounced, and all she could do was melt in his arms. It was shameful. She truly was a lost soul.

"You didn't seem to mind his pawing at you."

"He didn't paw at me, as you say. That is more your style."

"Aye, you females love those hand-kissing, toadying fellows. As long as they have enough blunt in their coffers."

"You're wrong. The marquess is nothing to me but a nuisance."

Only after the words were out did she wonder why she was arguing with him over this matter. Her feelings about Sebastian were hardly any of the Brute's business.

"A rich man is never a nuisance to a lady. Especially when he's a handsome devil like that fellow."

Violet sniffed. "Handsome? Ha!"

"Aye, and don't tell me you hadn't noticed," he rasped.

Of all the . . . !

But yes, the marquess *was* handsome. In fact, she was taken aback by this fact when he had leaned over her hand and brushed his lips against her skin. She hadn't known what to say. She had been so distracted by the thought of the Brute bursting in on her dinner party that the marquess's kissing her hand had taken her utterly by surprise. But she remembered now that she had distinctively felt a shiver when his lips had touched her.

Perhaps she was just going through some terrible change and turning into a true wanton. She would have to be, to be responding in a like manner to all the male attentions she had received this evening. Both the marquess's gentlemanly salutation and the Brute's more passionate embrace had heated her blood.

There was no need to admit this, however. "Believe me, the Marquess of St. Just should give you no cause for jealousy. He is a pompous ass." Just remembering him telling her she should welcome his affections because of his title made her quiver in indignation all over again.

The Brute tilted his head. "Aye? He seemed quite taken with yow, he did."

The man had seen a lot through that window, apparently. "The only person he is taken with is himself, believe me. For that matter, I could never imagine any woman losing her head over that man. He is as overly civilized as you are overly crude."

That grin hit her full force. "Then your pref'rence be for crude?"

She pushed farther away, turning so that he could not see her face. "It is not a question of preference—I could live without the attentions of either of you."

"You didn't seem to mind just five minutes ago."

"You took me by surprise."

"You mean you weren't expecting me?" he asked, disbelief in his gruff voice. "And here I thought you'd come to open the door for me."

"Actually, I was coming to bar it against you."

"Ah, so that's why when I pulled you into my arms you sank against me like you'd been waiting a lifetime for my kiss!"

She blushed all the way down to the toes in her slippers. "I was in shock, that is all."

His deep chuckle rumbled right through her. "I see. You prefer I should pay calls on you with flowers, like that other foolish popinjay who pays court to you."

Then he knew about Binkley, too! She felt suddenly as

if she had been stripped bare. What else had he witnessed as he had been spying on her? "Don't you have anything better to do than watch me?"

"Better, perhaps—but more entertaining? Nay!"

She tightened her hands into fists. "Well, if you were truly being attentive you would know that Binkley Jacobs is most truly the gentleman and—unlike some cretins— has no base designs on my person."

"Then what is he doing?"

"He is simply being a good neighbor."

"I don't like him."

"I see," Violet said, forcing a laugh. "In future I should bring all potential friends to you for approval."

"There's something queer i' his motives. The black-guard will try to marry you for your money."

"Look at who is calling who a blackguard!" she exclaimed.

"I go about stealing the honest way," the Brute said, employing a perverse logic. "That man lies every time he opens his mouth."

"My!" she taunted. "You're full of suspicions, like a jealous lover!"

"What man isn't jealous when there is something he treasures that other men want?"

He treasured her? If so, he was the first! All her life she had wanted to be cherished. Just her luck that such romantic words had to be spoken to her in a dreadful Cornish accent by a brigand, smuggler, and cutthroat!

"If you intend to abduct me," she said, swallowing, "or kill me, you might as well go ahead and do so now. It will save me having to do any more work on the house, at least."

He grasped her chin between his thumb and fore-finger and forced her gaze to meet his. Her heart leapt to her throat. "What's this about killin'?" Through the mask, his eyes narrowed at her. "I'm at yer service, Highness."

She blinked at him. "Thank you, but I have no need for a smuggler's service at the moment."

"Aye?" he asked doubtfully. "You wouldn't like a ride to the continent, or an errand run for you there?"

What an odd question. "Is that a reference to the fact that I drank your smuggled brandy once?"

He smiled and ran his thumb along the line of her jaw. "It's an invitation, Highness. Would you like to go with me and live in caves and hideouts and be free as the wind?"

Violet shivered. She could hardly swallow or find words at all. She felt as if her legs would not hold her. And yet, though a part of her dreamed of being swept away by this mysterious stranger as in a gothic tale, her practical side would not be denied. "I could never live in a cave. I can barely stand this drafty old house. And I wouldn't survive a day without Peabody."

"Pea-who?"

"My butler."

"Ah, yes, the fellow in the carriage."

She tore herself away from him. It was so hard to speak with those dark eyes drilling through her. That is, it was so hard to say what she needed to say, rather than the romantic nonsense that—surprisingly—she wanted to say. And yet how could that be? She had always been so levelheaded. Yet here she was, longing to throw herself at the most disgustingly inappropriate man ever likely to cross a lady's path!

Clasping her hands together, she turned her back on him and looked wonderingly at her house. "I cannot deny what I am. I am spoiled and I like my comfort, but I am willing to work for what I want. I learned that here at Trembledown, believe it or not. Perhaps restoring this house does not seem much to you, but I have never done anything like that before. And now I feel like I am actually contributing something to the world—oh, perhaps not anything important, but something that will be lasting. I feel like I belong to this place, in an odd way. I—"

The wind gusted, and when her words cut off, she had a queer feeling that she was all alone. "Robert?" It was the first time she had ever called him by his given name—if it actually was his true name—and she wondered later if she would have dared do so if she had thought he was really still standing next to her. But he was not there. She was by herself on the overgrown terrace.

Yet she sensed *someone* watching her.

She whirled in a circle, her gaze coming to rest on the doors she had been yanked through mere minutes earlier. A ghostly apparition in white stared wide-eyed at her through the door's glass panes.

Violet shrieked in terror, causing the face at the window to scream in response. For a few moments the two of them pierced the night with their cries of fright. And then Violet finally realized who it was.

With her heart finally slowing its frantic beating, she slipped back inside. "Peabody! What on earth were you doing?"

And—oh, Lord! —what had he seen?

His voluminous nightshirt fluttering behind him, the butler staggered over to a chair in a state of near apoplexy and collapsed in it. His chest rose and fell in shallow gulps. "I thought I heard a noise," he gasped.

"So did I," she said quickly. "That's why I was outside. Checking. On the noise."

His long nightcap seemed to sag in relief. "What a fright you gave me!"

She tilted her head at him. "You didn't see anyone, did you? Anyone besides me, that is?"

"No." His eyes watched her anxiously. "But you were talking . . ."

"To myself." She tried to think of some excuse for this but finally was forced to toss up her hands. "This place is driving me out of my senses, obviously."

"It will drive us all mad," Peabody rasped, his expression haunted.

Poor man. Violet patted his shoulder absently. She really would have to give him a little something extra when she sold the house. If she could force herself to part with Trembledown at all.

She frowned. Now where had that thought come from?

Damn and blast!

Stumbling about the cottage in the dark, the man nearly knocked over a figurine on a shelf. He bit back an exclamation and cursed the gewgaw, the clutter, the house. Junk everywhere, but the item he sought was nowhere in evidence.

What had happened to it? And what would happen if it could not be found?

He was sure it was here. It had to be.

What a fiasco. It had all seemed so simple. In times like these, a little information divulged to the correct party could make a man rich, and yet every time he turned around, there were obstacles in his way. Hysterical aunts and stubborn servants and accomplices who looked as if they might cut his throat as likely as not.

And what would happen to him if he did not produce what he had promised?

He became more reckless in his searching. The bedrooms would have to be attempted as well; there was no hope for it. The book must be found.

And if it was not found, more desperate measures still would have to be taken.

"Ouch!"

Violet let loose a curse that would have done her father's colorful vocabulary proud. The needle prick had not, in truth, hurt so terribly much. And yet she was already so tightly wound that anything might have set her off. Her volatile mood had nothing to do with the needle at all, or even the shabby job she was performing on the curtains destined for a guest bedroom. It had everything to do with Robert the Brute and the fact that she had barely slept a wink for thinking of her encounter with him.

She glanced over at Hennie, bracing herself to receive one of those reproving looks her cousin always aimed at her when she uttered a word of the King's less-than-acceptable English. But Hennie had her gaze trained on the window. Her eyes were glazed over in a blissful fog, and her lips turned up in a mysterious smile.

Violet couldn't help feeling a bit aggrieved. For all Hennie knew or cared, that needle might have hit a vein. She could be dead on the carpet and Hennie would still be sighing dreamily over John Cuthbert.

She looked down at her sewing. Making curtains—so dull—was not one of her accomplishments, alas, but she was trying to dress up the guest rooms before Sophy and her Aunt Augusta arrived. She should probably be grateful that Abigail's delicate condition precluded her making the trip from Yorkshire so that she was not put to more effort on linens. But the truth was she was disappointed that Abigail couldn't visit. She longed to show off her new home, and she had no doubt there would be much that they could discuss regarding Sophy's antics in London. Odd that she hadn't heard from Sophy or her aunt in a while—she worried that such a silence could be ominous.

Well, they would be here in person on Friday. She must persevere with this curtain.

She shot a competitive glance to view Hennie's progress and felt her eyes bulge in their sockets. In Hennie's lap—in plain view—was a snowy white length of material. None of the curtains were white. What on earth was Hennie up to . . . and how had it escaped her notice?

Because she had been mooning over the Brute, no doubt!

"What is that you're working on?" she asked Hennie. "I don't recognize the cloth."

Her cousin's face pinked. "I'm sorry, Violet. I've left off the curtains temporarily. I know you're in a hurry to get them done . . ."

"No matter," Violet said quickly. "They just need to be done in the next few days before the ball, since Aunt Augusta and Sophy are coming . . ." She allowed the words to trail off, not liking to think in too much detail about the ball. The dreaded event was too near for her liking; there was so much to be done that merely thinking of the word *ball* gave her heart palpitations. She'd already had enough of those for one morning.

"Is that for your bureau?" Violet asked.

Hennie, always sloppy with candles, had dripped wax all over her table.

"Oh no!" Hennie exclaimed. "It is my costume for the ball."

Violet paused. The fabric was white. Snowy, virginal white. Could it be that Hennie was actually going to cast

off her blacks because of two meetings with the marquess's rather drab visitor?

"It is only for the ball," Hennie hurriedly explained, as if
she had read Violet's thoughts. "I am sure Aunt Matilda—
dear, unselfish woman!—would not have wanted me to
bury myself in black for her sake."

Violet wasn't so sure about that. Aunt Matilda had
always struck her as the type who would very much enjoy
holding her loved ones in a chokehold from beyond the
grave.

"Do you think it too improper of me?" Hennie asked
nervously.

"Nonsense! You cannot mourn forever, and after six
months, there can be no harm in attending a party in
costume."

"Those were my very thoughts," Hennie agreed. "And
after all, there are so few costumes requiring all black,
unless one is to attend disguised as a person in mourning. But if the whole point of the party is to masquerade,
what purpose would my appearing in black serve? There
would be no sport in that!"

"So what is your costume to be?"

"Athena."

Violet nearly fell out of her chair. "The goddess?" She
couldn't have imagined a more un-Hennie-like character.

"Do you think I will surprise people?"

"You've surprised me."

Hennie looked pleased. "Good! I did feel that since
you were going to such trouble, Violet, that I should get
into the spirit of the occasion."

"I see," Violet said, smiling knowingly. "The change
was for my benefit, and had nothing whatsoever to do
with the appearance of Mr. John Cuthbert."

Now it was Hennie's turn to nearly plunge a needle

through her flesh. She hopped up, flapping her finger, as Peabody entered the room.

He looked at the two of them dubiously. Ever since he had seen Violet talking to herself on the terrace in the middle of the night, he had treated Violet as thought she were in a fragile mental state. Now he stared at Hennie hopping about the room with the same careful distance.

"Mr. Jacobs is here," he announced.

"Show him in."

Peabody hesitated. "I might add that he seems rather agitated."

Violet couldn't help smiling. "Then we should not keep him waiting, or he might turn raving mad and do damage to our foyer."

At her teasing, Peabody's lips turned down.

Moments later, Binkley was before them, but his usual winning smile was absent for once. In fact, he looked rather distressed.

"Mr. Jacobs, is there something wrong?"

"I thought perhaps you had heard—or that Constable Farkas had been by. There was a burglary at my aunt's last night."

"A burglary!"

"Someone came into the house during the night and ransacked the cottage while we were in our beds."

"Was anything taken?" Hennie asked.

"Some very valuable jewels of my aunt's have gone missing."

Violet and Hennie exclaimed in outraged sympathy. "How horrible for Mrs. Blatchford! She must be beside herself."

"It is not the loss of the jewels that upsets her, she says, so much as the sense of violation."

"Of course."

"Except that there were some very valuable pieces taken—things my uncle had given her, which makes it harder as they had additional sentimental value." Binkley shook his head. "Neither she nor I could imagine who would do such a thing."

Violet frowned. She could imagine all too well who could have done it, and more than likely who did. It was too much of a coincidence that Robert the Brute was out and about last night. Had he gone straight from her arms to his errand of thievery?

And what was he doing burgling houses anyway—did not smuggling provide him with an adequate income?

"I am so sorry," she said. "And you say you were in the house as it happened?"

Binkley wrang his hands. "Actually, I misspoke before. My aunt and the servants were all at home. I had gone to town."

"And you noticed no one, either on the road or when you arrived home?"

"Indeed no," he answered. "If only I had—I might have captured the brigand myself!"

Violet could well imagine what would happen in the battle of Binkley versus the Brute, and decided Binkley should be glad that no such contest had come about.

"How terrible this all seems!" Hennie said, a funereal tone in her voice.

Binkley allowed the somber moment to draw out a bit longer, then shook his head. "Well! I am not only the bearer of bad news this morning. I have happier tidings as well."

His former sunny smile was back in an instant, which Violet found odd, given what he had just told them. "Oh?"

"Yes, my aunt sent me over to invite you to join us for dinner tomorrow."

"But how could she?" Hennie asked. "She must be beside herself!"

Binkley bit his lip. "Indeed she was, but you know my aunt Blatchford. She enjoys having people around her, and it was distressing in the extreme to see her so unhappy over the robbery. In the end, I was able to convince her that having company would do her a world of good."

Violet and Hennie exchanged uncertain glances. "I would not like to intrude on her if she is feeling distraught."

"No indeed—your presence would go a long way in cheering her, I am certain of it." Binkley looked at Hennie almost as an afterthought. "As would yours, Miss Halsop."

"Then we shall be happy to attend, and thank your aunt for thinking of us."

"It will just be a small party," Binkley assured them.

Hennie blurted out, "Will your aunt invite the marquess?"

Binkley's enthusiasm dimmed. "I do not know."

"And the marquess's guest?"

Binkley looked confused. "What guest?"

"Mr. Cuthbert." Hennie said the name as if it required no further explanation.

"He is a friend recently arrived from London," Violet supplied.

Binkley's brow pinched. "This is the first I have heard of him."

"He was here last night."

"You mean the marquess was here?" Binkley's voice sounded almost as if he considered her having company in his absence a betrayal.

"The marquess has graced us with his presence many

times," Hennie said, darting a quick look at Violet and then swallowing back a smile.

What was that about?

"Indeed, he seems to make himself quite at home here," Hennie finished.

"So I have noticed." Binkley set his mouth in a smile before temper could get the best of him. "Well! I suppose we can all survive one night without his lordship."

"But I am sure your Mrs. Blatchford would like to make the acquaintance of Mr. John Cuthbert," Hennie said.

Binkley shook his head distractedly. "Who?"

"St. Just's guest. Such a pleasant man!"

"Oh." Binkley appeared less than thrilled at the prospect of another male guest. "Yes, she might, but this was just to be a small party."

Poor Binkley! He seemed almost dejected. Violet took pity on him. "You must tell your aunt how kind she is to want to have us when I am sure she must be very much distressed. I shall look forward to it very much."

He brightened. "Will you?"

"Of course." Perhaps the prospect of the little party would get her mind off all the troubles plaguing her—the ball, the Brute . . . "It seems we have not had a chance for a real conversation in an age."

"That is just what I was thinking!"

"But can't you talk right now?" Hennie interjected. When they both stared at her, uncomprehending, she explained, "I mean, isn't *this* an opportunity for conversation? It is not something two people need to make appointments to do, is it?"

Binkley chuckled mirthlessly. "A very astute observation."

Hennie smiled in satisfaction.

And yet, after they all had agreed that this indeed was an opportunity for talk, conversation fled them. They sat awkwardly for a few moments longer, speaking of the weather, and what a shame and outrage the robbery had been, and how much they would look forward to Mrs. Blatchford's dinner party.

After Binkley had made his bows and left them, Hennie clucked her tongue at Violet. "Far be it from me to advise you, but I do think it most unfair of you to encourage Mr. Jacobs as you do. Especially now."

Now? Violet was curious what that meant, but the very accusation that she was leading Binkley on distracted her. "I did not encourage him, did I?"

"I'm sure you smiled at him more than you should have. And then you told him that you would like to have a tête-à-tête!"

"Really, Hennie, I think you're reading more into my comments than Binkley did."

Hennie shook her head gravely. After her recent success with Mr. Cuthbert, she evidently considered herself an expert in male-female relations. "I don't know what to think. Just last night you were quite openly flirting with the marquess!"

Violet nearly jumped at the accusation. "When?"

"At dinner last night." Hennie's eyes turned down. "My dear . . . you let him *feed* you. I'm sure Mr. Cuthbert and I were both rather embarrassed by that spectacle."

"I allowed nothing! Is it my fault the impossible man shoved asparagus into my mouth?"

"And then by the double doors." Hennie clucked again.

"He kissed my hand," Violet explained in a huff. Indeed, she could hardly stay in a stable frame of mind any time she recalled the incident. "Then he had the impertinence to suggest that I should welcome his kisses because he is a marquess!"

"And yet did you not welcome his kisses later?"

Violet froze. *Later?* "What do you mean?"

Not that there was anyone nearby to hear them, but Hennie lowered her voice. "You needn't fear that I will reveal your secret."

Icy dread ran up Violet's spine. "Secret?"

"You see, I heard a noise last night and happened to look out my window . . ."

Violet felt all the blood drain out of her face. Hennie had seen the Brute kissing her! For a moment she felt as if her spine would buckle. Her shame was complete.

And yet . . . Hennie thought she had seen the marquess.

The marquess? It must have been very dark indeed for Hennie to confuse those two men!

"The night can play tricks on the eyes . . . or perhaps you were dreaming."

"There was no mistaking what I saw," Hennie insisted.

No mistaking it, except that she had wrongly identified the man in this case!

Violet did not know what to do. She could not own up to kissing the Brute. But if she admitted allowing the marquess to take liberties, it would appear that she had developed a fondness for the man.

What an impossible coil!

"You didn't actually see the marquess, you say?" Violet asked.

"Well, my dear, I did not stare at length. I was all astonishment. But I asked myself, who else could it have been but the marquess?"

Violet swallowed. "Who else indeed."

Hennie sprang next to Violet in one excited motion. "Oh, Violet! I am so happy for you!"

"There is no cause for celebration. We are not betrothed."

"But he must care for you a great deal. To have come

back to see you after they had left was so clandestine, so romantic!" She leaned back and sighed.

Violet was not sure how to present her secret lover. "Actually, I simply thought I heard an intruder . . ."

"And so you had," Hennie said. "A love bandit come to steal away your heart!"

Violet feared she would be ill. "That is not quite how I would characterize him."

Hennie gasped. "What a strange coincidence that the marquess should be running about on the same night Mrs. Blatchford's cottage was robbed!"

Violet swallowed. "Yes, it is rather."

"Well! It's lucky that Sebastian wasn't also robbed." Hennie squeezed her leg. "You needn't worry that I will go gossiping about this, Violet. Did I mention that I didn't even tell Peabody?"

"You are the soul of discretion, Hen."

"And don't think I wasn't tempted." Hennie giggled. "The poor man thinks you were outside talking to yourself. He was quite concerned, but I did not divulge the truth, even though it would have put his mind at ease."

Violet laughed halfheartedly. Now half the household thought she was crazy, and the other thought she was a fast creature who met men clandestinely in her garden.

"And Peabody would be so happy if he thought he was soon to be the butler to a marquess!" Hennie bit her lip. "Though I suppose the marquess already has his own butler. That will be a tangle."

"Domestic staff arrangements are the least of my worries," Violet said dully. For some reason, thinking of the Brute robbing Mrs. Blatchford depressed her. Naturally she knew the man was worse than a thief . . . but she had not known one of his victims before.

"Well!" Hennie said, patting her on the leg to bolster

her spirits. "You can count on me to keep a secret. Though naturally if you would like me to put in a word to Mr. Jacobs so he will not be quite so forward . . ."

"No!" Violet shuddered. "Tell no one."

"Of course," Hennie agreed. "Absolutely no one. My lips are sealed."

As Violet tottered off to her room, she wondered why her cousin's assurances failed to comfort her.

Chapter Twelve

"Ha! I understand that we can call you the kissing bandit, Sebastian," Cuthbert said as he strolled in from what was supposed to have been a short walk, but which seemed to have lasted most of the morning.

Sebastian, who had just returned from Mrs. Blatchford's, nearly jumped out of his boots. "The what?"

"Kissing bandit." Cuthbert rolled back on his heels and regarded him with undisguised mirth. Sebastian had never seen the man enjoying himself so. "And to think you made out that you were off on a government mission last night when you left the carriage. A mission of the heart, it was!"

"Where did you hear this?"

"I happened to pass near Trembledown on my walk this morning and saw Henrietta."

Sebastian's brows rose. "Henrietta, is it? Already she is no longer Miss Halsop?"

"Don't change the subject."

Sebastian tapped the letter he had just received from Minerva lightly against his palm. News of Napoleon's escape was raging through London, along with an interesting story about a young woman who was just coming out this Season. A young lady by the name of Sophy Wingate.

Cuthbert wagged a finger at him. "And don't bother with denials, either. Henrietta had the entire sordid tale from Violet herself."

Sebastian felt his jaw go slack. "From Violet?"

"She admitted all."

"I see."

But he didn't see at all. What misunderstanding had resulted in Violet having to confess to an assignation with her bitter enemy? How he would have loved to have been there when she was concocting this preposterous tale!

Except, of course, that it wasn't preposterous at all. It was the truth . . . but Violet had no way of knowing that.

"What did you hear at Mrs. Blatchford's?" Cuthbert asked. He had been at breakfast when the constable had come to tell Sebastian of the robbery. "Did the constable locate the stolen diamonds?"

"No, and I doubt he is likely to do so, for the express reason that I believe they are still in the house."

"What?" Cuthbert's brows rose. "But they searched the house and questioned all the servants, surely."

"Oh, yes. But they did not search Binkley Jacobs," Sebastian said grimly.

"I say now, St. Just! Do you think a man would steal his own aunt's jewels? Jewels he probably stands to inherit himself?"

"It would not be the first time something of the sort happened," Sebastian replied. "And Mr. Jacobs was out of the house when the robbery took place."

"Where was he?"

"He says he was at the Pied Hare, but when I met with

Jem, he said he hadn't seen Jacobs at the Hare while he was there."

"Perhaps they missed each other."

"It's possible." Sebastian shrugged. "Naturally, we cannot know for sure."

"No indeed!" Cuthbert said. "For that matter, your movements of last night look more suspicious than Binkley Jacobs's!"

Sebastian laughed. "I suppose they do. But I believe I found out something more precious than diamonds."

"What is that?"

"Mrs. Treacher is not our Nero. I all but offered to paddle her over to see Napoleon personally, and she seemed not the least bit interested." Would that she had shown no interest in the Brute at all. To Sebastian's woe, he had also discovered that Violet's weakness for the Brute was more pronounced than she had let on, and that his own vulnerability to Violet's lips was absolute. If he had stayed another five seconds, it would have been the cave all over again.

Would he ever be able to convince Violet that kissing a marquess was as satisfying as kissing a counterfeit smuggler?

Cuthbert was deep in thought. "That is something, I suppose."

"Something?" Sebastian asked. "I would call it a complete exoneration."

"But perhaps she simply did not need your services because she has another more trustworthy accomplice."

Annoyed, Sebastian scratched his jaw. Damn! Cuthbert was like a dog with a bone in this matter. "She did not seem to have any underhanded motives."

"Well, St. Just, you are probably right about the lady. I will agree that Mr. Jacobs is a more suspicious fellow."

"And let us not forget our vicar!" Sebastian said.

Cuthbert shook his head. "I saw Miss Cheswyn this morning, near Widgelyn Cross."

"Miss Cheswyn, too?" Sebastian asked. "Why, John—you're the Casanova of the sea path."

Cuthbert did not laugh. "Miss Cheswyn's brother is in Portsmouth, visiting a cousin who is ill."

"Oh." Sebastian twisted his lips. "So much for fine boots and spyglasses."

"Yes, he appears to be guilty of small extravagances, but not treason."

"It is a good thing, then, that we shall soon have the opportunity to watch Mr. Jacobs more closely," Sebastian said. "While I was at Mrs. Blatchford's, a note came from Trembledown, accepting a dinner invitation for tomorrow."

"A dinner party at Mrs. Blatchford's, so soon after the unhappy event of the robbery? I call that an odd situation."

"Mrs. B. is a social creature—I believe she would have sent out invitations this morning if she had had enough warning. She created quite a dramatic sight stretched out on her sofa in her maroon satin spencer and garish headgear to match. For a woman living a retiring life in Cornwall, she has a wardrobe well suited to drama."

"Then perhaps her dinner party tomorrow is to showcase her travails," Cuthbert said. "But we have received no invitation, have we?"

Sebastian smiled. "We have now. Naturally, Mrs. Blatchford did not want to let me know at first that she was having Violet over—I believe she is still trying to strike an alliance through marriage between the cottage and Trembledown. I pushed to find out what was afoot in Violet's note, however, and knowing the lady's weakness for partridges, I then promised to send some over for the occasion. Naturally, Mrs. Blatchford could not take my partridges without taking me as well."

His friend looked most gratified by this news. "Then Mrs. Treacher and Miss Halsop will be there?"

"Of course."

"Then you have performed an excellent morning's work, St. Just." Cuthbert lowered himself into a chair and folded his arms in contentment. "Had I realized the country afforded such excitements and pleasures, I should have inflicted myself on your hospitality much sooner."

"You do seem to have entered into the spirit of country living quite well."

All at once, the unfamiliar smile left his friend's face. "I shall miss it here."

"Are you leaving?"

"I must, of course."

"But not before the dinner party."

Cuthbert steepled his fingers. "No—I think it would be beneficial for me to make the acquaintance of this fellow Jacobs. Naturally, that must be weighed against my prolonged absence from London."

Spoken like a man had never been a week away from his desk before. Sebastian smiled. "But of course, your postponing your trip back to London would have *nothing whatsoever* to do with Miss Halsop."

Cuthbert frowned. "St. Just, please. I am a professional man."

"Duty before pleasure, eh, Cuthbert?"

A hint of a smile touched the older man's lips again.

* * *

Due to a mishap with the carriage door and Hennie's skirts, Violet and Hennie were the last to arrive at Mrs. Blatchford's, but as far as Violet was concerned that was just fine.

She might have been looking forward to this gathering once, but no more. Her spirits were very uncertain these days. Since the night when Sebastian and Cuthbert had come to dinner, she had not heard from the Brute. She had expected him to impale another note for her on a wall somewhere. But no. The man had apparently taken her at her word when she told him that she could not be part of his smuggler world. *One rebuff and he stomps off in the dark, never to be heard of again*, she thought. Just like a man, really.

And then she had heard that the marquess was to be present at Mrs. Blatchford's. The news had pleased Hennie for several reasons. First, she was able to tease Violet about being reunited with her lover (to this, Violet could only grit her teeth), and second, because whither goeth the marquess, so goeth Mr. John Cuthbert. Hennie had spent that afternoon bathing, powdering, and perfuming herself until she was a veritable rose in black.

Hennie practically had to pry her from the carriage when it arrived at the cottage. "Is something wrong, Violet?"

Violet sighed. "No—I will be fine."

As she exited the carriage she looked up in time to see Binkley's head pop through the door. Her host smiled with impish grace and rushed out to act as footman for them. "At last the evening begins! You will add the sparkle to my aunt's party that is at the moment sadly lifeless."

"Oh, is the marquess here already?" Violet quipped.

"Violet!" Hennie said, overhearing them.

Binkley laughed, and in that instant, Violet caught a blast of alcohol from his breath. He had obviously been at the wine decanter already. "Do not scold us, Miss Halsop. We are only having a bit of fun."

Violet accepted both Binkley's arm and more outrageous compliments about how their beauty would add to the atmosphere as well. His flattering comments nearly put the Brute's warnings out of her mind. Why should such a good-looking young man of leisure bother to chase her for her fortune? Why come all this way? He could do much better in London, surely.

Despite Binkley's words to the contrary, inside the cottage everyone seemed to be in high spirits. Mrs. Blatchford was seeing that everyone's comfort was attended to, and Hennie wasted no time at all in making her way to Mr. Cuthbert's side.

And then there was Sebastian. A blush rose to Violet's cheeks when she saw him standing by the fireplace— almost as if she actually *had* kissed him on the terrace instead of the Brute. And there was a wicked sparkle in those brown eyes of his that made her wonder if he had perhaps heard something . . .

But Hennie had promised to tell no one!

"Good evening," he said with a deep bow.

She dropped a quick curtsy and attempted to turn away.

"I trust your fears turned out to be for naught the other night?"

"Fears?" Violet asked, her voice shrill even to her own ears. "What fears?"

"Of the Brute."

She blurted out a nervous laugh. "He continues to make himself scarce. I had quite forgotten him."

"If only I could!" Mrs. Blatchford exclaimed. "Why, Robert the Brute's name was the first I thought of when I discovered my missing jewels. Many a night after your ordeal, Violet, I lay awake at night trembling at the thought of having such a one roaming our countryside—and now who knows but that he wasn't inside this very house just two nights ago!"

Violet bit her lip. "Surely not, Mrs. Blatchford. After all, why would a smuggler take to thieving?"

"I'm sure I don't know who else it could have been. Who can know how a criminal mind works—perhaps he has decided to expand his business. One doesn't like to contemplate the possibility that there are multiple thieves plying their trade in our area."

Violet felt the marquess's sharp, monocled gaze on her and realized she might have made an error in trying to eliminate the Brute as a suspect, so she felt compelled to agree with her hostess. "Of course it could have been the Brute."

"Most likely!" Binkley said, downing a glass of what looked like port in one swallow. "Who else could it have been?"

Hennie gasped. "Then he really is still in the area."

"And yet Violet does not tremble," the marquess said, eyeing Violet with a look that bordered on skepticism and amusement. "Thoughts of rhododendron beds and unfinished ballrooms have completely displaced thoughts of the Brute in her mind. Isn't that right?"

She gritted her teeth. "I try to set my mind on matters I have some control over."

"Very admirable!" the marquess exclaimed. "Don't you think so, Jacobs?"

Binkley was looking at her with calf eyes. "If you ask me, everything about Mrs. Treacher is admirable."

Sebastian secured his monocle and let out a sigh. "Unfortunately, I received a letter yesterday that contained news that may yet give Mrs. Treacher reason to tremble."

Violet and everyone else turned to him with interest. "What?"

"Napoleon escaped from Elba and has not been recaptured."

"Oh heavens!" Mrs. Blatchford exclaimed. "What a horror!"

Violet felt sick. The war had dragged on so long—most of her life, it sometimes seemed. She dreaded the idea of another. And what must Sebastian, who had lost a brother in the war, feel? He was probably sick at the news, too.

"But surely they *will* recapture him," Hennie said.

Cuthbert smiled at her. "Let us hope so, Miss Halsop."

Violet noticed Sebastian staring at Binkley. "You don't seem too startled, Mr. Jacobs," he said.

Because he is numb with wine, Violet thought disapprovingly.

"Oh . . . I had heard someone muttering about Napoleon at the Pied Hare last night," he admitted.

"You didn't mention it to me, Binkley," his aunt said.

He scratched his ear. "Why should I worry you about *that* when you had the robbery on your mind, Aunt? I didn't want to add to your troubles. Besides, they'll catch him."

At that moment the butler interrupted, announcing that dinner was served.

The marquess graciously led Mrs. Blatchford into the

dining room, and Cuthbert naturally took Hennie's arm. This left Binkley for Violet, and he purposefully seemed to drag his feet, lagging behind the others. Violet also suspected that a little too much wine on an empty stomach had gone to the young man's head.

"I was hoping to talk to you after dinner," he said.

"Why wait?" she asked, attempting to tug him forward. "I give you leave to speak to me during dinner. I dislike silence at a table."

"You misundershtood—or you are humming me." Binkley looked displeased with her bantering tone. "I thought perhaps we might . . . after all, you did mention our having a coze."

"Of course!" Violet promised. Anything to get the man to move. Not only was she aware of the others waiting on them, but she was quite hungry. "I am sure there will be ample opportunity."

"Splendid!"

During dinner, talk was divided equally among the terrible ordeal of the robbery, Napoleon speculation, and Violet and Hennie's ball. Even for Violet, who felt nervous about the upcoming event, the last was by far the preferable topic of the three.

"I swear, we have never had such a social whirl before this year," Mrs. Blatchford said. "I thought I would escape the Season in London this year, but instead I seem to have stepped into another hive of activity."

"We have Violet to thank for that," Binkley said, hoisting his newly refreshed wineglass her way. "Cornwall's always been deadly dull the other times I have visited."

"Then what brought you here?" Sebastian asked.

The table fell silent, and Violet felt her cheeks redden. *What impertinence!* Insulting a man at his own family table. "I am sure Mr. Jacobs is here to visit his aunt," Violet said, leveling a cool stare on Sebastian. "I've always said that there is no better excuse to socialize than visiting with family."

"Would you visit your relatives if they lived in the wilds of Cornwall?" the marquess asked her.

"Of course," she said.

"Despite the lack of entertainments and the wind and the salt air . . . and the smugglers?"

"I'm not sure that smugglers aren't part of the area's allure. When the time comes I might even use the local lore to sell my house . . . at an impressive profit."

"Didn't you inherit the property?" the marquess asked.

"Yes, I did."

"Then it is all profit, since there was no initial price to you."

"You obviously have never met my in-laws. Nothing is free in this world, my lord."

To her surprise, a hearty laugh burst out of Sebastian, and his mouth drew back in a very disarming smile. When their eyes met, she felt a strange frisson down her spine.

Once or twice before, she had noted that the marquess, for all his irritating manner, was not an altogether unattractive man. She felt it again now and had to look down at her potatoes to keep a blush from rising in her cheeks. What was the matter with her? It seemed that all she did these days was dream and blush about men!

She hoped Hennie hadn't been watching her.

Binkley, who she noticed was past his fourth glass of wine, shook his head. "I don't think we should emphasize the existence of local smugglers when it comes time to sell Trembledown."

The table went silent, and Violet felt for a moment that

her face might be turning purple. Had he actually said *we?* Wine or no wine, that was going a bit too far!

"Why ever would you be selling Mrs. Treacher's house?" the marquess asked.

Belatedly, Binkley realized his mistake. "Naturally, I merely meant to advise Mrs. Treacher, who is a woman alone and doesn't know about the value of property in this area." The young man glared at Sebastian and Mr. Cuthbert. "If the government was worth a damn it would rid this country of riffraff so decent people could travel about unmolested and we wouldn't have to worry about their affecting the price of land."

"So I take it that you are not a devotee of the Brute," Violet said lightly.

"I am not," Binkley declared. "Most emph . . . emphatically I am not. Why, if I were ever to run across that villain, you could be sure I would take care of him once and for all. You wouldn't have to worry about that pesky fellow again!"

He ended his speech with an imperfectly concealed belch.

Violet felt herself shrinking in embarrassment for the man, and darted a glance the marquess's way. Sebastian's brows were arched in distaste at Binkley's behavior, and she felt a knee-jerk annoyance at his condescending look. Could it be that he had never drunk too much at a dinner party when he was a young man?

Yes, Binkley was a bit too eager and unpolished— but wasn't he trying to overcome this? Why, from what Peabody said, his valet alone must be costing him most of his salary. All to sharpen a few of his rough edges. Sebastian's problem—well, one of them—was that he had *too much* polish. And no passion at all.

At the realization of where her thoughts were again

traveling, Violet wanted to weep at her own depravity. Passion! Was the only man alive who could make her happy in that regard Robert the Brute?

Surely that was impossible. If she blushed for Binkley's table manners, she shuddered to think what it would be like with the Brute at the dinner table!

Mrs. Blatchford wisely turned the subject back to the ball, asking after the visitors Violet would be having down from London. And while Violet trembled to think that her aunt and her sister would be here in a matter of days, she welcomed the change in conversation.

After dinner, the cards were brought out. Sebastian, John Cuthbert, Mrs. Blatchford, and Hennie made four, leaving Binkley and Violet as extras.

"Shall we stroll outside?" Binkley asked Violet quietly.

Violet hesitated. "It is so cozy here."

"But I am sure you would like to see my aunt's little fountain."

"In the dark?"

"The night is clear."

Apparently the man would never be satisfied until she had traipsed outside with him. And she had promised him a talk, after all. (Though she didn't understand why they couldn't talk before the warm fire just as well.) Wanting to avoid a scene in front of Sebastian, she allowed Binkley to escort her out to view the fountain, a very modest little pond with a stone frog spewing water from its mouth.

"It's very—"

Before she could pay Mrs. Blatchford's choice of statuary even the most modest of compliments, she found that Binkley had disappeared from eye level. She cast her gaze down and found herself staring down at the top of his head. He grasped her hands.

"Mr. Jacobs!" she exclaimed. "Get off your knees, do!"

"Dear Mrs. Treacher!" he said. "Violet! Would you think me impulsive if I tried to tell you how highly I regard you?"

"Impulsive, yes, and foolish!" She tugged at her hands, but he held them fast. "Do stand up, Mr. Jacobs. You will get moss all over your pants."

"Never mind my pants, dear Violet. I love you!"

"Nonsense!"

"Indeed, I do."

"But you hardly know me."

"What does it matter that we can only measure our acquaintance in days? From the moment I first met you, I sensed that we were meant to be together."

What drivel. Suddenly the Brute's warnings returned to her. Could it be that Binkley was trying to wheedle her into marriage for some kind of financial gain?

"Will you not be my wife?"

"Certainly not," she answered firmly. "I have no immediate intention of marrying again, and if you had taken the time to listen to me more closely on the subject before plowing forward you might have saved your knees some wear and tear."

"Confound my knees, Violet. Have you not heard me? I'm speaking of love."

She rolled her eyes. She was beginning to think she should never step out of doors at night. Doing so always seemed to result in her being set upon by some lunatic man. "And I am saying you are full of nonsense. You may not have realized this, but you are five years my junior, at least."

"It doesn't matter! I love you in spite of your age."

Those words gave her the strength necessary to push away from him. For a moment, without her support, he looked as if he might topple like a felled tree. "Mr. Jacobs, you are in your cups. I think it best that we both forget this encounter ever happened."

"Please, do not brush me off."

Violet felt as if she could have very easily . . . and yet she had to remember that she had very few acquaintances in the area. And she did like Mrs. Blatchford. "I am not brushing you off, Mr. Jacobs."

"I suppose now you shall try to avoid me."

"No, I shall not. I told you we should act as if this never happened, and I mean it. We are civilized people, after all." At least, she was.

"You mean it?"

"Of course!"

"Then will you go for a drive with me tomorrow?"

"Oh." She frowned. She had not meant to be *quite that* forgiving. "I don't think that would be a good idea."

His face crumpled. "There! You *do* hold a grudge."

"No, but . . ."

She had an idea. She could have Hennie come along on the drive. As long as she wasn't alone with Binkley, there could be no harm in indulging him and mending fences.

"Of course. If tomorrow is fine, I shall expect you."

"Bless you!" he cried, attempting to grasp her hands.

She tucked them safely behind her. "Now I really do think we should return to the others." Before he could contradict her, she scooted back inside to the relative safety of Mrs. Blatchford's parlor. Never had she felt so eager to join a card game.

* * *

A game ended as Violet came back inside, and Sebastian stood.

"Are you done playing, my lord?" Mrs. Blatchford asked.

"Yes, thank you."

"Come, St. Just," Cuthbert said. "We are only playing for imaginary stakes."

A good thing, too! Cuthbert was so much more focused on his lady love than his cards that he would have been bankrupt in no time had the stakes been real.

"It is not a matter of money, it is a matter of pride," he answered with a bow. "I try never to lose more than two games in succession."

"But your luck could change with the next hand." Mrs. Blatchford's lips turned upward in the smile of a seasoned card sharpie. This seemingly sweet little old lady could have made a fortune in the gambling hells of London.

"Alas, I am afraid if I sat through another hand, I would break my own rule." Especially with Cuthbert as a partner, since they were playing men against women. He and John were both so distracted, they were doomed.

"Perhaps I could persuade Mr. Jacobs to take my place," he said. "If he could tear himself away from Mrs. Treacher."

But Violet seemed to have torn herself away from him. Indeed, after Binkley followed her inside, the two were not even standing anywhere near each other in the salon. Violet had her back to them all and was very intently studying a china figurine of a shepherdess.

Binkley, wearing the distracted air and the mussed appearance of a man who had had too much wine, broke into a smile when he heard his name. But it was the glazed smile of one who had not been privy to what had been said before.

"Can I be of some service?" he asked.

"Dear Binkley! Mr. Cuthbert has lost his partner."

When Binkley saw that joining the gaming table would free up Sebastian to talk to Violet, his smile faded.

His aunt touched his sleeve. "You would not let me down, would you?"

He shook his head and once more settled a mantel of geniality over himself. "No, indeed, but I really do think we should play mixed teams, with you and me against Mr. Cuthbert and Miss Halsop. Would that suit?"

From the looks exchanged between John and Hennie, apparently that idea suited them very well.

"Are you interested in china, Mrs. Treacher?"

Violet, who had not heard him coming, jumped so violently that the statuette nearly slipped from her hands.

"Or is it the subject of the figurine that has enthralled you?" he asked. "I shall not be surprised to find you dressed as a shepherdess at our ball."

At his use of the plural possessive in regard to her gathering, Violet recovered herself and replaced the shepherdess to her table. "I should think you would be very surprised, since I have no intention of garbing myself as Little Bo Peep."

"A pity. The rustic garb would set off your charming figure to perfection."

She blinked at him and cocked her head expectantly.

"Is something wrong?" he asked.

"No . . . only I was waiting for the little barb that always seems to accompany your compliments."

He chuckled, and the sound brought stares from the gaming table. Cuthbert and Hennie sent him encouraging smiles. Binkley tossed him a hostile glare.

Sebastian offered his arm to Violet. "Mrs. Blatchford has a delightful little conservatory. Would you like to see it?"

Violet, also aware of the others watching her, hesitated. "Perhaps some other time."

"But you must go," Mrs. Blatchford, apparently so engrossed in the game that she forgot to try to discourage Violet from being alone with any other man save her nephew. "My lord, you must show her my orchids. I'll wager Mrs. Treacher has never seen such fine specimens."

"There," Sebastian said. "If Mrs. Blatchford is wagering, then it is certain that you must go. I have learned to my woe that she never wagers incorrectly."

The others—except Binkley—laughed, which made Violet relent. She slipped her hand through his arm and they strolled to a humid room enclosed on three sides with large windows.

"Very pretty," Violet said.

"Would you like to sit down?" he asked, gesturing to an ornate iron bench. "You look rather fagged."

One perfectly shaped brow arched at him. "Thank you very much." Nevertheless, she sat.

He waited just a moment before asking, "Would you think it impertinent of me if I asked you what your answer was?"

"Answer?"

"To Mr. Jacobs."

She scowled at him. "Were you eavesdropping, my lord?"

"Eaves-watching might be a more appropriate term," he said. "I was very fortunately situated at the card table, so that I had a clear view through the salon's picture window. And what a picture Mr. Jacobs made kneeling at your feet!" He winced for effect. "On pavestones, too. It quite makes my own knees ache just to think about it. Not to mention what it did to the state of his pants—his valet will be quite annoyed. I know my man would threaten me with resignation if I ever came home with those moss stains."

"Do not worry, my lord. I cannot imagine you ever being so overcome with emotion that you would kneel to any woman."

"I should hope not," he agreed heartily. "One must take care, you know. Such nonsense can lead to rheumatism. It is the night dampness that causes the damage."

He wasn't entirely sure—his monocle was a little cloudy—but he was fairly certain Violet rolled her eyes at him.

"But you did not answer my question," he said.

"What question?"

"Concerning your response to Mr. Jacobs."

Her chin jutted ceilingward. "My lord, I do not see how my conversation with Mr. Jacobs is any of your concern."

"You are absolutely right. I am being unforgivably inquisitive."

"Indeed!"

He sidled closer to her. "You answered no, didn't you?"

She let out a strangled cry.

"Say no more," he said, lifting his hands in a gesture of surrender. "I could tell by the man's whipped-puppy demeanor that you had responded to him in the negative."

"Binkley Jacobs is a fine man."

"Ah! Then you most definitely rejected him."

"How does that follow?"

"When a woman says she believes someone is a fine man, it generally means that she feels no passion for him. And am I wrong in guessing, Mrs. Treacher, that for you a marriage without passion would be unthinkable?"

Her mouth dropped open, and she looked at him with something between astonishment and horror. "I do not care to discuss this subject with you."

"And yet I feel sure that I am right. And I heartily agree with you, Mrs. Treacher. Too often we English treat our women as if they are bonds to be traded for wealth, then stored away safely in drafty country houses. I find that repellant."

"You do?"

"Does that surprise you?"

"Frankly, yes."

"That is why Mr. Jacobs's pursuit of you makes me ill at ease. He seems to have latched onto you as an advantageous match."

Red rose in her pale cheeks. No doubt she was remembering another man who had told her something along the same lines. "You make him seem so calculating. He is merely young."

"Mmm, poisonously young." He looked deep into her eyes. "You would do better with a mature man, one who could love you deeply."

Their gazes locked for a moment, and then she shook her head, breaking the invisible bond between them. "I fear I am going mad!"

"Why—?" He shut his mouth. He had almost called her "Highness."

"To be idly listening to this rubbish!" She glared at him. "Besides, the air is stuffy in here."

"Is it? I had not noticed." Seeing that she was determined to go, he kept close by her side. "At least you have put my mind at ease that you are not on the verge of making a grave, foolish mistake."

"My lord," she said, raising her head loftily, "I am

grateful to you for your interest. But I repeat, my life is none of your affair. And for your information, I still feel very kindly toward Binkley. He has promised to take me out driving tomorrow to see the priory ruins."

"You do not mean to go!" Sebastian said, aghast.

"Yes. Never fear, I shall have my cousin along with me to make sure that we do not get carried away."

She turned and led them out of the conservatory, back to the others. Binkley glared at the marquess the rest of the evening and made several barbed comments on the length of their absence from the room. Sebastian was only too happy to apologize for keeping Mrs. Treacher to himself for so long. "I confess she is so charming a companion I could have happily sat among the ferns and orchids until we both began to sprout!"

Comments like that did nothing to alleviate the young man's agitation or his increasingly belligerent attitude, but Sebastian enjoyed himself immensely.

On the ride home, Cuthbert smiled at him. "Living up to your reputation as the kissing bandit, St. Just?"

"Alas, no," he said with a sigh.

"Nevertheless, I feared young Jacobs would bean you on the head with your stick before the night was over."

Sebastian laughed. "You should stay for the ball, John. It should prove to be quite an event."

A shadow crossed the man's face. "I cannot."

"It is a few days from now. Surely that is not too long for you to stay."

"Too long? I have stayed away too long already." He sighed. "I promised Miss Halsop to take her out to sketch birds tomorrow. I should leave the day after that. It shall be our last visit together, most likely."

"Tomorrow?"

"Yes."

How very interesting—especially since Henrietta was supposed to be serving as chaperone to Binkley and Violet! Perhaps Violet did not know of her cousin's bird-sketching plans.

He rubbed his hands together gleefully. "You must pick up Miss Halsop early." Before Violet arose. As the party hadn't broken up until quite late, he hoped she would have a lie-in tomorrow morning.

His imagination was overcome for a moment, and he realized it was probably best not to think too much about Violet in bed.

"I'll have Cook pack a basket for you both. You can make a day of it."

Meanwhile, Sebastian had quite an eventful day planned for himself.

Chapter Thirteen

Because they did not arrive home from Mrs. Blatchford's until late, Violet stayed in bed longer than usual. Far longer than she should have. It took quite a bit of doing to be so sluggish under the circumstances; from the moment her eyes squinted open to the morning light and for the hours she attempted to ignore the intrusion of morning and get back to sleep, her ears were assaulted by the noise of workmen in the house.

On any other day, the sounds would have been comforting. The work needed to get done. And yet she felt such a desire for sleep! Just a few more blissful hours where she did not consider what a hobble her life had become since uprooting herself to Cornwall. Or even just a few more stolen minutes in which she could close her eyes and dream of dark eyes looking down into her face, glinting with humor. The Brute's eyes.

Or were they the marquess's?

Violet sat up. Upon her word, she was growing as addle-headed as Hennie!

And yet, she could not deny that the marquess, when he looked at her, had caused a small bump in the speed of her pulse. And she had enjoyed talking with him . . . to a point. He had been presumptuous, telling her not to go driving with Binkley. Not that she wanted to go driving with Binkley; on the contrary, she was dreading it. But she didn't want to be told what to do, either. She'd had quite enough taking orders from men in her life, thank you.

By the time she pried herself out from under the covers, dressed, and went downstairs, the breakfast room was empty. Peabody, sporting a new coat of blinding cardinal red, brought in a pot of tea for her with the post. Like the sun, he was almost too bright to look at; she was forced to squint. "Let me guess," she said to him as she opened a letter from her sister Abigail. "Quimby says red is all the crack."

"Just so, madam," Peabody responded.

His manner was a little standoffish, she thought. And his hair was still scaling up the summit of his bald dome in a greasy assault. Violet sighed, yearning for the old Peabody.

"Where is Hennie?" she asked him as she scanned the letter from Abigail, which cataloged her various stages of joy as she contemplated the small life she was about to bring into the world.

"I couldn't say."

Violet put the letter aside and set her teacup down. Something was wrong, and Peabody wasn't going to let her forget it until his grievance had been aired. It was disheartening how distant he was becoming. They used to have such rapport. "Is there a problem, Peabody?"

"I am sure I couldn't say, ma'am."

"There must be *something* afflicting you," she said. "Speak up, Peabody. I would hate to think of you bottling up your troubles. You know it makes you bilious."

He wrung his hands for a few undecided moments and then mustered the courage to announce, "If you must know . . . I intend to tender my resignation."

Violet felt her blood go cold. *Leave me?* She couldn't believe it! This was desertion, betrayal, and it cut her to the heart. "But why?"

An expression of agony wracked poor Peabody's face. "This situation is untenable! I am doing the work of five men!"

"I know—it's hard on all of us. Look at my hands: calluses!"

She held them out; he looked at them and shuddered. It occurred to her then, too late, that showing Peabody evidence of her own physical hardship was no way to make him want to stay. "But it is only temporary," she assured him.

"If you do not mind, ma'am, I will speak frankly. I do not believe this . . . situation . . . is temporary."

"What?"

He lifted a hand. "Far be it from me to judge you. Heavens, no. True, we have always been *of a mind,* one might say. I never thought that we should agree on every little matter for myself to remain most agreeably—nay, happily—in your employ."

"Oh, for heaven's sake, Peabody. Out with it."

"Well!" He lifted his nearly invisible chin a notch. "If you don't mind my being frank, madam, you are beginning to enjoy this rustic outpost more than I ever dreamed you would."

She laughed. Was *that* what had him in such a state? Would that all her problems were this easily resolved. "Utter nonsense," she said.

Her butler was not convinced, as was evidenced by his mournful eyes. "I see your expression when you look at the house. Something's changed, madam. Your gaze has the same possessive gleam you once trained on the Earl of Clatsop."

At yet another reminder of that unfortunate episode in her life, she managed, just barely, to suppress a shiver. "What a fool I was, Peabody! Remember how relieved we were not to be associated with the earl when we saw the shambles of an old castle he lived in?"

"Yes, greatly relieved."

"Think, then, how much better it is that I should have a gleam in my eye when I look upon this house. It also is a ruin, but we don't have to marry it. This is a solid investment!"

Her words did seem to have some ameliorative effect on Peabody, and yet still he remained planted, his hands stiff at his side. When she did not address him promptly—there was that worrisome bill catching her eye—he cleared his throat. "There is another matter."

"What?"

"The matter of the marquess."

She felt her heart dip in her chest. "What about him?"

"He possesses a butler already, ma'am. A very kind old gentleman by the name of Griggs."

"What of it?"

"If you were to marry the marquess—"

"Stop at once!" she cried, unable to let him finish. "That is rubbish."

Peabody's brows rose sharply. "Indeed? That is not what I have heard."

Violet sighed. "Tell me the worst, Peabody, and be done with it. What have you heard?"

"*Over*heard, ma'am, which in my opinion is more solid evidence."

She rolled her eyes at this reasoning. The eavesdropper's rationale. "Evidence of what?"

"Of a pending engagement between yourself and the Marquess of St. Just."

"That is false," she declared.

Peabody seemed unable to credit her words. "Naturally I would be very happy for you, madam. Indeed, I have hoped for such an occurrence. But now that I have learned about Griggs already installed at Montraffer—"

"The marquess has not proposed," she told Peabody in as emphatic a tone as she could muster. "Nor will he. He knows my feelings all too well."

As she said the words, something in her made her uneasy. Knew her feelings? At times it was as if Sebastian were speaking her deepest thoughts back to her, such as last evening when he had speculated on her desire for passion in her next marriage. The sensation had been shocking, disturbing. And yet she wondered, how did the man come by such an understanding of her inner workings? She had never met a person—male, female, or even Peabody—who seemed to read her mind like he could. It was almost more seductive than the sheer physical attraction she felt toward the Brute.

And just as dangerous, in its own way.

Her protestations did not appear to convince Peabody.

"I swear to you, Peabody. The marquess means nothing to me."

His eyes widened, and his hands clasped nervously. "Then, my lady, your reputation!"

She sat up straighter. "What of it?"

"You must be careful! There are whispers everywhere of midnight assignations and passionate meetings in conservatories."

Her blood felt chilled. "Who was saying these things?"

Peabody's chin shot up. "Please do not ask me to reveal my sources. I might be an eavesdropper, but I am not a tattle."

"Peabody."

"My lips are sealed."

"Oh! That phrase again. It always seems to presage someone going on a gossiping binge." She shook her head. Well. There was only one person who could be spreading these rumors. "Do you really have no idea where Hennie is?"

"She left," Peabody said. Then he added quickly, "Not that it was she and Mr. Cuthbert I overheard. I never said that."

"Mr. Cuthbert was here this morning?"

"Yes."

"And Hennie left with him?"

Peabody nodded.

As the implication of this news sank in—especially in regard to her own plans—Violet felt increasingly troubled. "When are they returning?"

"They did not say. As I said before, I have no idea where Miss Halsop might be. Mr. Cuthbert came for her in the marquess's carriage. Surely you heard it."

Violet could not remember. Maybe that was the sound that woke her, but if it was, it did not register.

This was most a most disturbing piece of news—one she had to absorb standing up. "But she cannot leave me today. She is supposed to be my chaperone!"

"A chaperone?" No doubt it seemed odd that his mistress, a widow in her twenty-eighth year, felt herself in need of a chaperone. Violet had chafed at having a chaperone even when she was a girl.

"Mr. Jacobs is taking me for a drive," she explained.

Peabody sniffed dismissively, but he did look relieved

that it was not the marquess coming to woo her into a marriage with one butler too many. "Oh. Only Mr. Jacobs."

Mr. Jacobs, who was more hotheaded than anyone but Violet seemed to realize. Or maybe she should not judge him by last night, when he was as drunk as a wheelbarrow.

Still, she did not relish being alone with the man. He might renew his ridiculous suit. "It was very bad of Hennie to have abandoned me without a word."

"I believe it is the last opportunity she will have to be with Mr. Cuthbert. He is returning to London." Peabody managed to inject a hearty note of envy into this last sentence.

Cuthbert leaving. Peabody threatening to give notice. Hennie abandoning her in her moment of need. Violet began to despair of what would become of her. She beseeched Peabody, "Please, let us hear no more of your leaving. I need you, Peabody."

The man did not appear unmoved by her words. "Oh, ma'am!"

Tears stood in her eyes. "I know I have landed us in a bit of a pickle here, but you must trust me to get us out of it. And I promise when I do, you will be better off and more respected among your peers than even Quimby. I will shower you with gold-liveried footmen and a positive dragon of a proper housekeeper. And should even a duke propose to me, if the man has a butler I shall simply have to refuse him."

Peabody nearly broke down, but managed to hold in his emotions with a quivering chin. "You are too good, mistress."

"I could not survive without you," she told him. "You must know that."

"Well . . . perhaps that is a bit of an exaggeration, madam."

"It is not," she declared. "Today, for instance. If you would agree to come with Mr. Jacobs and me."

He shook his head. "Oh no. Please do not ask that of me. I will serve you all my days, ma'am, but Mr. Jacobs's gig is not a conveyance I wish to ride in."

"I know it's a bit unusual asking you to accompany me, but it is only to the priory ruins."

"My skin is already red and wind burned enough. Any more exposure and I will look like a Tartar." He hitched his throat. "Also, if you would permit me, I would like to go to Widgelyn Cross today to see a man about my hair."

"Did Quimby recommend him?"

"No." Peabody ducked his head self-consciously. "I fear that Mr. Quimby's style of the Olympian and my scalp do not mesh with perfect felicity."

She laughed, pleased that they would be seeing the last of this unfortunate coiffure. "Take the rest of the morning and the afternoon, if you need. I suppose I shall be fine. And if you'll be so good as to gossip about my happiness in my single state, perhaps that would dilute the stories concerning the marquess."

"I'm sure I would never demean myself as to gossip," he vowed.

She laughed to herself as he left to fetch her toast. Peabody, not gossip? Perhaps roosters would stop crowing, too.

She was still hoping Hennie would return before Binkley arrived, but when she heard wheels drawing up before Trembledown, she looked out the window with a sinking heart. It was Binkley in his old gig. When he came through the door with his usual amiable demeanor, however, Violet decided she was being silly and overly judgmental of an incident that was in all probability an anomaly. No doubt Binkley had just gotten carried away by the moonlight and the burbling water of the frog fountain. One of those things that were bound to happen from time to time. Who hadn't lost his or her head in such a way once or twice in a lifetime? Especially a man under the influence of drink.

"What a fine day," she said after they were settled on the wagon and had set off.

"Now it seems so," he declared.

She decided to ignore this piece of unsubtle innuendo. "Oh? Was it cloudy earlier? I'm afraid I slept in frightfully late."

"The day was fair—it was my mood that was cloudy," Binkley admitted. "But now that you are here and I can see that we are truly friends again, I feel much better."

"You need not have doubted my friendship," she said.

He sighed. "I did not doubt. I only wish that there were more between us."

"Let's not go over that ground again," she pleaded.

He glanced over at her, and though he said nothing, the look in his eye made her uncomfortable.

Nevertheless, he said nothing more on the subject, and they passed a tolerable half hour driving across terrain that Violet was just beginning to appreciate. There really was a beauty to the raw wildness around her. She could understand Hennie's urge to wander around assaulting canvases with a paintbrush.

The old priory was nestled near the base of a steep hill, which made the sweeping stretch to its ruined gates all the more breathtaking. The stone walls of the edifice still stood, though the windows gaped open and the only roof was the sky.

Violet and Binkley got down from the carriage and walked around the outside, cutting a circle among the wildflowers and tall grass. An old graveyard stood to the side of the building, its few remaining headstones with their lettering erased by ravages of hundreds of years the only testament to the purpose of the sacred nature of the grounds around them.

"It's so quiet," Violet said. There were trees all around them, yet she heard no birdsong. Just the rustling of the breeze.

"Are you glad you came?"

Violet, so carried away with the scenery that an affirmation hovered on her lips, looked into Binkley's eyes and all at once felt doubt.

Sensing that she was about to pull away—as indeed she was—Binkley lunged forward and grasped her hands. "Oh, Violet! If you could know what your coming here with me today has meant."

She frowned. "What has it meant, Mr. Jacobs, except a pleasant way to pass the afternoon?"

"Shy creature! You need not pretend with me."

She yanked impatiently at her hands. "Shy, Mr. Jacobs, is one word that has rarely been applied to me. Please let me go."

He did not comply with her wishes. "Last night you made me the unhappiest of men, but I can say now that today has taught me to hope."

"You are forgetting yourself, Binkley."

"Ah, so coy—I know the tricks you ladies play before you make happy men of us."

"It will be no trick, I assure you, when I tell you that I have no intention of making you a happy man, now or ever."

"Naturally you are reluctant to again make the great leap that is marriage, but believe me; I have all of Cupid's artillery in my quiver to make you happy."

Violet sincerely wished for real artillery of her own

right now. What was the matter with him? Had he been drinking again? Was he mad?

"You are an impulsive pup!" she said, tugging more resolutely to free her hands.

"'Treat me but as your spaniel,' then, fair lady!"

The quote sounded vaguely Shakespearean, but there was no time to judge his literary acumen. To her horror, he lunged at her lips.

She turned away just in the nick of time, though his hot breath grazed her cheek. "I would not have a dog so ill mannered!" Violet yelled. *Or one so slobbery,* she thought, slapping at him. "I insist you take me home at once!"

"Don't pretend you don't want me," he said, breathing hard as he held the nape of her neck fast. "I know your game."

"It is no game!"

"You have been flirting with me since I first came here. I was happy to dance to your tune for a certain amount of time, but it grows late and I can't afford to waste any more time on wooing you. So don't pretend coldness now. Not when I need you."

He yanked her down onto a decaying log, which they both landed on with a teeth-jarring thud. She yelped in outrage. "How dare you!" Another carriage dress ruined!

"I only dare because I desire you so!" To her horror, he hovered over her, pinning her to the damp, molding matter beneath her.

She pressed her palms against his chest and gave him a futile shove that budged him not one inch. "Stop!"

"You're just playing the coquette—I've told you that I haven't time for that!"

"Time?" she was breathing heavily now, too, from the effort to escape.

His meaning was forever lost from her as he brought his lips down on hers. Her cry of outrage was lost to a shocked intake of breath. His mouth smelled of stale wine and desperation, and the choking urgency as he pulled her to him made her truly panic. She flailed against him, landing ineffective blows on his chest and shoulders. Then she felt a hand ruck her skirts up to her hips. She kicked her legs but could not stop the man from sliding his hands greedily along her calf. As he reached her knee, a muffled scream rent the air.

And then, in the next instant, her torment was over.

Violet heard a dull thunk and found herself suddenly freed as Binkley was yanked off her. She sat up and witnessed the astonishing sight of the marquess landing a blow to her attacker's jaw. Binkley was sent reeling. He fell to the dirt on his hands and knees, coughing.

Contempt twisted the marquess's mouth. "I believe the lady said no."

Binkley coughed. "Damnation, man!"

"Damn you, Jacobs! You ought to be horsewhipped!"

"You've bloodied my best cravat! It was Quimby's, too. Damme!" the man said, collapsing back into the grass. "He'll give notice for sure!"

At that, Violet nearly went and landed a blow on him herself. The animal had nearly forced his way on her—and now he whined about his clothes? He wasn't the one whose back had been ground into a pile of mildewed leaves!

The marquess took Violet's arm. "Come, I'll take you home."

Violet nodded, and as they walked away, they could hear Binkley still muttering and moaning.

But where had the marquess come from? She hadn't heard a thing. Of course, there was the wind, and she had

had Binkley's fetid breath in her ear, but she would have heard a carriage pull up, surely.

On the other side of the priory, some distance away, stood the marquess's horse. Perhaps that was why she had not heard him approach.

He mounted the horse and reached out his hand to her.

She shook her head in confusion. Was this good-bye, or an invitation to join him? She could not imagine managing to climb up on that huge beast.

As it turned out, no climbing was required of her. When she hesitated, the marquess bent down, grabbed her by the armpits, and pulled her up in one fluid movement. Her breath left her as she landed squarely on his lap.

"Hold on to me."

This was impossible. How could they possibly travel in this fashion? "But you can't—"

But he did. He kicked the horse he called Hannibal into a canter, giving her no choice but to throw her arms around his torso and hang on for dear life. After a moment, she put her head to his chest and shut her eyes as some of the tension flooded out of her.

If Sebastian hadn't come along, what might have happened to her?

Well, she knew what would have happened to her. The word *rape* hung in her mind like a threatening dagger. She couldn't understand why Binkley would have behaved like such a beast. What had he been muttering about?

Had she led him on? Binkley had said so . . . and so had Hennie.

Hennie! Oh, how was she going to explain her ruined condition to her cousin, to Peabody—and what reason could she possibly give for having the marquess bringing her home?

They passed a copse near an old well, and she moaned to the marquess to stop. He pulled up the reins and looked worriedly into her eyes. "Are you all right?"

She attempted to nod but then felt tears stand in her eyes.

He muttered a curse and pulled them both off the horse's back. Gently, he led her to the well and sat her on the soft grass beneath a tree. Then he pulled a flask from his vest pocket and offered it to her. "Here—drink."

She darted a questioning brow, meaning to come back with a quick retort on a man of his mild character carrying spirits on his person. Yet the words died on her lips. After seeing the man make mincemeat out of Binkley, she was no longer certain how mild mannered he was. She only knew that she was grateful. She brought the bottle to her lips and took a long, therapeutic draw.

A cough rose in her throat, and suddenly she wanted nothing more than to throw herself on the grass sobbing. Tears stood in her eyes, but the warmth of the liquor coursing through her veins bolstered her. She tried to swallow her coughing fit and ended up choking for some seconds. She only just saved herself from spitting up in front of the marquess. That would have been her final humiliation.

"You might as well leave me here," she said.

He sank down next to her. "Why?"

"I could not explain why you should have to bring me home to my cousin. I could not explain any of this day." To her horror, she felt moisture in her eyes again, and she dashed away a tear.

She half expected him to sneer at her. Maybe he thought she had been leading Binkley on, too. Hadn't he warned her last night not to go out to the priory with him?

"I should have listened to you!"

"Of course," he said.

She darted her chin up to glare at him, but he was not smirking at her. His eyes were dark with concern. The unfamiliar seriousness in his expression caught her off guard and made her confess, "I had no idea that Binkley was so unpredictable, so—"

"Vile," Sebastian said. "What did he say to you?"

She repeated their conversation as far as she could remember. It all seemed so inconsequential; yet Sebastian seemed absorbed by her words, as if he, too, wanted to parse them for insight into their neighbor's reprehensible behavior. "How shall I ever face his aunt again? How shall I—"

She gulped. How could she face anyone? She did not know how she could even talk to Sebastian.

And yet he was being so kind. Not at all judgmental or gleeful at what he would surely love to call her comeuppance. She would have expected him at least to wag a finger at her for having gone out with Binkley against his advice.

But he was not. He was treating her with such tender concern that it was almost her undoing. She wanted to throw her arms about him and let herself sink against all that strength again.

She heaved an uneven breath. "I have been a fool."

He produced a handkerchief and put it at her disposal. "You should not blame yourself for some blackguard's behavior."

"I cannot help it. I have made so many mistakes, misjudgments . . ." She thought of her weeks-long infatuation with the Brute and shuddered. "I have done nothing but made a cake of myself since coming to Cornwall."

He chuckled, and the comforting sound rumbled through her like the spirits had. He put his knuckle to her chin. "You are headstrong, stubborn, impossible to handle, and—"

She sniffed. "You make me sound like an ill-tempered horse."

"Sharp tongued," he added ruefully. "Yet one thing I would never call you, Violet, is a fool."

"You would not?" Just at this moment, it sounded as if he were paying the highest compliment.

"I would call you . . ." He looked deeply into her eyes as he cast about for words. A frisson of something shivered through her. Without the hated monocle, how distinguished his face was! "Beautiful."

There was something in that husky, gruff tone that caused her heart to skip a beat. These weren't mere words of flattery, or teasing. He meant them.

He bent down and brushed his lips against hers. Fleetingly. Far too fleetingly. They felt warm, firm. Commanding even in their reticence. When he pulled away from her, she felt a tightening in her chest that shocked her. The kiss had been too brief, a mere hint of a kiss. She wanted more.

"I am sorry," he said, his voice ragged.

"I am not," she declared.

"After what you have just been through!" he said. "I have shown as little restraint as that young fool we left in the dirt at the priory."

"No," she said, holding firm to his arms. "I gave him no encouragement."

He looked into her eyes as if some inner conflict were about to cause him to snap. "Violet! I should keep myself away from you."

"But why, Sebastian?"

"I always determined that I should be alone. I never wanted to be close to any woman. And yet you and your sharp tongue and your independence and foolish determination have done something to me I never would have expected. I find myself trying to think of ways to see you again and desiring you in a way I have not wanted any woman before."

Her own heart seemed in danger of racing out of control. Was he saying that he loved her? It was a shocking idea, yet strangely pleasurable.

He shook his head. "I am sorry. I should not have spoken. It was wrong of me."

She clasped her hands around his neck. "Surely if two feel the same way, there is nothing to fear."

"Do you mean that you . . . ?" He narrowed his eyes at her. "You would not shrink from an embrace after what you have just been through?"

She pulled herself closer to him. "Why not find out?"

"God help me," he said, before lowering his mouth to hers again.

Those lips—they were so masterful, so strong. She shivered slightly and wrapped her arms more tightly around him. The warmth of his mouth on hers thawed the last of her reluctance. The taste of brandy mixed with tobacco and the clean smell of him worked on her like a drug, and she sank against him, running her hands against his surprisingly broad chest. His whole body felt tightly coiled and barely restrained.

She had never experienced such a kiss . . . or had she? She hated to compare Sebastian with her illicit drunken passion with the Brute, but in his own way, Sebastian was every bit as thrilling.

"You're cold," he whispered. Then he stood away from her, shucking his great coat. "Put this around your shoulders."

She took the coat, and then, smiling, she spread it below her. She held out her hand to his. At the invitation, he hesitated only moments.

"You are a vixen," he said, dropping next to her.

He nibbled at her ear.

She laughed. She had never had a man kiss her so play-fully before. Her husband had been . . . well, not a loving man. To have the first man to woo her so coaxingly be the Marquess of St. Just, her nemesis, was as much a plea-sure as it was a shock. It was as if she were discovering a whole new person or was experiencing love at first sight with a man she had known for weeks and weeks.

He gently cupped a hand around her breast. "I suppose by tomorrow you will say you did not require rescuing at all."

She raised her chin. "I will say it now. I did not."

He smile broadened. "Liar!"

"I assure you that I would soon have had that pest of a man under control."

"You don't know what you are talking about."

"Of course I do. I was married, remember?"

A grumble rumbled in his chest. "You might have been married, but you know little of a woman's vulnerability, my lady." And as if to show her, he lowered his mouth to hers for a bruising kiss. Perhaps he was expecting her to fight, but instead she felt the need to sink her nails deep into the muscles of his vast shoulders. He pushed himself against her, yet she did not feel threatened, as she had with Binkley. Instead, she moved against him curiously, thrilling to the hard persistence of him against her thigh.

Her head was spinning. Breathless, she pulled away and raised a hand to his nape. Perhaps they could save themselves with words. "For that matter, how was it that you happened to be riding about the countryside playing knight errant?"

His gaze bore into hers, and she knew at that moment that he had been there specifically to look out for her. On another day, the thought of his spying on her might have made her defensive, but now she seemed to have no defenses. Not against him. Right now, in this moment, he seemed utterly wonderful.

He kissed her again, more gently this time. His lips coaxed hers as if to do all his wooing for him. And they were expert in the art of seduction. If she harbored any doubts about where this embrace was leading, they fell away beneath the gentle ministrations of his lips.

She anchored her hands on those broad shoulders and lay back against the silk lining of his coat. He hovered over her, contemplating her as if she were a delectable meal to feast on and he were the hungriest man in the world. And then his hands went to work—undoing buttons in an instant that had taken her long minutes to fasten. He untied the lacing on the shift beneath her dress with curious eagerness as if it were the wrapping on his only Christmas present.

"You are beautiful," he said. "More beautiful than I could have imagined."

Normally Violet would not have cut short anyone complimenting her. But she was desirous now for more than words. "I am also impatient."

"One should not be too impatient," he said, easing a hand beneath the skirts of her dress. "One misses so much that way."

His hand gently insinuated itself up her thigh, to the apex of her legs. Her body tensed in anticipation, and he bent down, kissing her again, relaxing her even as his hand ministered the most sensitive part of her body with frustratingly gentle concentration.

Her breath came in short gasps. She could not believe such tenderness could beget such fierce arousal. And yet she felt as if she were being consumed by heat swirling inside her. She feared she would begin to claw him like a tigress, but he did not seem to mind.

A cry of ecstasy escaped her lips, and he lowered himself on her, straddling her. He had shucked his breeches, and she could feel the heavy firmness of his arousal against her.

"Violet, I want you now. You are my every dream in one woman."

His every dream . . . it was almost as if he were speaking her own thoughts. She lifted her hips and welcomed him into her.

Violet closed her eyes and went still as he filled her, but in a few moments was meeting him thrust for thrust as they were carried off into a spiral of ecstasy she had heretofore only known once before. But before, it had seemed only like a dream . . .

Chapter Fourteen

With her long limbs still curled delectably about him, Violet released a long, pleasurable sigh. It sounded as if she were waking up from the sweetest dream imaginable. Indeed, her eyes, still dewy from the earth-shattering moments of their passion, had the look of someone being roused from a particularly satisfying slumber.

Sebastian understood perfectly how she felt. In his breast was a contentment he had not known for a long, long time. If ever. All the inner warnings he had always felt toward women like Violet had beaten a hasty retreat in the wake of those fevered moments of love. He had thought she would be a title huntress, a conniving woman. Yet he felt just the opposite now.

If anyone had been dishonest, it was him. And he wasn't sure what he would do about that.

Those beautiful blue eyes met his gaze. God, she was stunning. Sebastian reached out to tuck a loose strand of blond hair behind her ear. "How glad I am not to be in London this spring. I would not have missed seeing you thus for the entire world, my dear Violet."

She swallowed, and a becoming flush found its way into her cheeks.

"I have never been so fortunate in my neighbors before," he said, teasing her.

Though she was still looking at him, there was a subtle shift in her expression. The dreamy, love-dazed smile that had appeared when she first opened her eyes faded into something harder to read. She had not yet spoken, and the parade of emotions in her eyes told him that she was finding words difficult.

He wanted to reassure her—of what, he wasn't quite sure. He couldn't guess what she was thinking. "Violet," he said again, and then added, experimentally, "Darling . . ."

Her beautiful body stiffened, and she sat up, pulling her dress over her. "You mustn't call me that!"

"Should I go back to calling you Mrs. Treacher?" he asked, trying to finesse the awkwardness with a little humor.

She was not laughing. "Yes, please! Call me anything except darling!"

"Dumpling, then?"

She rolled her eyes as she hurriedly drew her shift up to cover her breasts. "We have made a terrible mistake, my lord."

"I would not call it that."

"But you must see that we have behaved rashly, that in a moment of high emotion, we were carried away by—"

"Our passions?" he asked, bending to touch his lips to hers once more.

She allowed only the briefest contact of their lips before she ducked away, shaking her long blond locks. "You must not, Sebastian."

He was a bit confused. "I know that relations between us have been somewhat complicated at times . . ." *She has no idea* how *complicated!* "But you must know that when I made love to you, I was sincere. And I had the distinct impression our desire was mutual."

"Oh yes!" She started attempting to right her clothes in earnest. "I lost my head completely. My wanton behavior was no act, I assure you. I am so ashamed, I can hardly find words."

He let out a low chuckle. "You needn't be."

"Yes, I should," she assured him. "You can count me as a conquest—but you must not think it is a conquest that will be repeated."

He frowned. "But why? You needn't worry that I think less of you. I believe that you are an extraordinary lady."

She snorted in what he had to admit was a very unladylike way, however. "Believe me, my lord, I am flattered. But there are things you do not know . . . things I cannot tell you." She hung her head as she punched a button through a buttonhole. The wrong buttonhole, as it happened, but he was afraid to point out that detail right at the moment. "I would mislead you to allow this to go on."

For a moment his heart stopped. Oh Lord. Had he been a fool after all, like that poor fellow Cuthbert was always going on about, the one with the opera singer?

He swallowed. "Tell me truthfully, Violet. Does this thing you cannot tell me about have anything to do with why you are in Cornwall?"

She blinked at him. "No . . . not exactly. Are you referring to Trembledown and my refusing to sell it to you?"

She looked so honestly befuddled that in that moment he knew once and for all that she could not be Nero. He felt a pang of guilt for even suspecting her again. But she seemed to agonize so over this secret . . .

"Would that it were!" she exclaimed, not waiting for

his answer. "I could not possibly tell you. You would never understand. I'm not sure I understand it myself."

He began to wonder if he knew her secret already. Good heavens! Could it be that she was in love with the Brute?

Was he his own rival?

He was attempting to fashion a reply when something in the distance caught his eye. Out on the sea. An innocent-looking boat with nothing distinctive about it except for the fact that it had a rather jaunty orange flag flying on it was headed toward shore. Toward the cove closest to Montraffer.

It had to be Jem's ketch; the orange flag had been decided upon as a signal to alert Sebastian in the event of an emergency. Sebastian jumped to his feet and started dressing.

Violet, who had been following his gaze, looked at him in wonder as he quickly hopped into his breeches. "Is something wrong?" she asked, standing herself now.

He snatched his coat off the ground and gave it a strong flap to clear the grass and dirt. His quick movement startled her.

"What are you doing?"

"I am preparing to depart, and I advise you to do the same. You might want to straighten your clothing some before we get back on the road."

She fastened a bemused expression on him. "What is wrong?"

"That boat," Sebastian said, trying to think quickly. What would make Violet most want to return home quickly? "It looks like a smuggler's ketch to me. I do not want you to become tangled up with smugglers again."

Her eyes widened and she again looked out to sea. "Is it the Brute?"

His rival again!

The barely concealed curiosity in her voice would have brought a smile to his face had he time to ruminate on such things. But he didn't. He needed to return Violet to Trembledown and head for his own place immediately.

"It very well could be the Brute, I fear," Sebastian said, biting his lip. He just hoped that Violet never got to wondering how he could possibly know such a thing.

"Good heavens!" Violet exclaimed. "We are still far from home, are we not?"

"Yes, which is why I must insist that we hurry, much as I would prefer to continue our previous discussion."

"Oh, it probably isn't a smuggler's boat at all. You're just trying to get rid of me as fast as you can. Just like all men, once you've had your way, you don't want to stay and discuss things."

As she looked at him frantically tugging on his boots, a little of the old sneering Violet returned. "You appear to be terribly afraid of smugglers, my lord. I thought you were only joking a while back when you spoke of trying to avoid them."

"It is no joke," he assured her. "Not that I am a coward, mind you, but . . . ." So saying, Sebastian picked Violet up and tossed her onto Hannibal before mounting behind her.

After giving out a squawk at being handled so efficiently, she turned to eye him, her mouth twisted in disgust. "No, indeed. I can see that."

He wanted to laugh. Expediency made it necessary to hide behind a coward's mask, but this charade would be hard to live down later. "What do you see, light of my life?"

Her mouth was set in a tight line. "That you are hightailing it as fast as you can to escape the menace of the Brute. I suppose I should be grateful that you have agreed to escort me home instead of bolting off to Montraffer, which is closer. You are most generous."

Sebastian tightened his hold on her, but he spoke carelessly. "That is not an outlandish plan. You have survived one of his escapades, but if I came upon him, I might be murdered!"

Her hands grabbed stiffly at the horse's mane. "You are quite right, my lord. A man like the Brute would probably make short work of you."

"Yes, yes. You don't mind if we move more quickly, do you, my love?"

Before Violet could protest his form of address, Sebastian kicked the horse into a gallop and it was all she could do to hold on. Hannibal's pace didn't slacken until they were about a half mile from Trembledown. There Sebastian reined in rather suddenly. The horse stopped abruptly and wheeled a little. His female passenger, however, kept moving. Before Sebastian could switch the reins to one hand and grab her, Violet pitched forward and slid down the horse's neck until she found herself unceremoniously on her behind in the middle of the road.

"Are you all right?" he called down to her.

She grimaced, but she appeared to be all in one piece.

Sebastian smiled innocently down at her. "If you don't mind, I believe I'll put you down a little ways from your place."

"Yes, you seem to have done that already." Violet made a production of picking herself off the ground and slapping at the dirt on her skirts.

"After all, you won't want to answer prying questions about why you are arriving back with a different escort than the one you left with."

"You are all graciousness, my lord."

"No need to thank me, it was my pleasure to escort you this far." He swept her a bow. "I bid you farewell. But I need not add, I hope, that I look forward to our next meeting!"

Not waiting for her reply, he spurred Hannibal and galloped toward Montraffer. He resisted the urge to turn around to see if she was watching him or was already stomping her way home. It mattered little either way; there would be a price to pay for his behavior since spotting Jem's boat. There were quite a few muddles between them that would have to be cleared up.

This was not what he had planned. Not even when he had been riding away from the priory, with Violet's shapely bottom pressing into his lap. He had been full of altruism then—well, altruism mixed with a little normal lust. Nothing more. A real Galahad.

Now he felt half Galahad, half cad.

But he had never guessed (never even in his wildest dreams, and he had experienced quite a few of those lately) that his damsel in distress would throw herself at him. He had been completely unprepared for his passionate reaction to her—and for her enthusiastic response.

His only answer had been to follow his instincts. His desires.

Now his better judgment was kicking in, and the complications were obvious. Yet, addlepated as making love to her had been, he could not regret it at all. Knowing now the depths of softness beneath the brittle veneer Violet showed the world, he could not imagine having walked away from her open arms this afternoon. She was exquisitely sensual, more giving and open than he would have dreamed. The memory of being with her would haunt him for years; perhaps it would sustain him, too. He had always been cynical when it came to all the claptrap people spouted about love. Now he would never question the poets whose lofty flights about love used to bring a sneer to his lips.

Lovewise, he was in the suds.

Meanwhile, what news could Jem possibly have to tell him? Nothing good, he was sure. And he couldn't help wondering whether his sudden appearance didn't have at least something to do with that thwarted lothario, Binkley Jacobs.

The walk was just what Violet needed to cool down before entering her house and facing Hennie and Peabody.

Mortification did not begin to describe her feelings. How could she! To have gone from Binkley's hideous advances into the arms of the marquess!

And the worst part—she had enjoyed it!

That was what truly frightened her. Was she turning into a strumpet? First the Brute . . . now Sebastian. And to think Percy had once complimented her for her lady-like sedate performances in the marital bed. If he could only see her now! He would be horror stricken.

She shuddered at this hideous thought. She even cringed a little, halfway expecting a bolt of lightning to strike her.

And yet it wouldn't be the first one to strike her this day. The first had been when the marquess had pulled her into his arms with such force. Reliving that riveting moment made her slow her pace. She had thought of many names for Sebastian in the past few weeks—master seducer was definitely not one of them.

Now it seemed almost as if he were sectioned off into several people. The popinjay, the amusing aristocrat who had made her laugh on more than one occasion these last weeks, the caring soul who had rescued her and who had made love to her so thoroughly and yet so tenderly . . . and then the coward who had darted away at the first sign of a smuggler's boat.

And yet she had melted in his embrace. Melted. He had stirred feelings in her that she thought only existed in the most lurid novels. His smoldering gaze and his kisses had made her want to give herself to him body and soul. And she had very nearly done just that. Percy had never moved her so during their lovemaking. She had never felt anything close to what she had in Sebastian's arms, except . . .

She shook her head, dismissing the thought before it could be completely formed.

And yet it niggled at her. The Brute! When she had opened her eyes next to Sebastian, she felt almost as if she had betrayed her erstwhile smuggler lover.

That was when she knew she had to let Sebastian go. It broke her heart, but given her past, it was impossible that she should in any way hold ambitions to be mistress of Montraffer. Imagine the lady of that great house leading a secret inner life as a cutthroat's moll! If only she could have explained to him her true feelings. If only she could understand them herself.

It was ridiculous, of course, yet she couldn't help thinking that if she could be with any man, it would be the Brute. Or a combination of Brute and Sebastian. If only the Brute were not a criminal! If he were a better conversationalist, and a trifle less untidy . . .

Oh, but what was the use of dreaming?

A shudder moved through her. She truly was a fallen woman now. Loose baggage, her father would have said. To think she had worried about how she would face the respectable world after what had happened with the

Brute! How on earth was she supposed to face anyone after her open-air tumble with Sebastian?

How would she even face Sebastian?

A frown tugged at her lips. For that matter, how would Sebastian face *her* after dumping her on the road so he could scamper back to the safety of Montraffer? He should be ashamed, really. She couldn't imagine a man being so terrified by a smuggler's boat. Especially a man who had just that afternoon clobbered Binkley as he had done.

In fact, it made less sense to her the more she thought of it.

What if his fear upon seeing the boat had just been an act? What if he was hurrying not to hide from the smugglers, but to turn them in? Perhaps the marquess was working to rid the county of the smugglers, which would be fine with her . . . except that he would also rid the area of the Brute. Would they actually capture him, and if they did, would they kill him?

Her heart beat fast at the thought. And yet she could not run to warn the smugglers. That would be a very ungenteel, not to mention illegal, thing to do.

She needed to put the matter out of her mind. Try as she might, though, she was still worrying over the afternoon's events as she approached Trembledown. As she was clearing the rosebush, Peabody burst out the front door as if he had been waiting for her.

He had that look on his face—agitation mixed with anger. She knew it well as of late.

"You might have warned me!" he exclaimed before she could reach him.

Violet stopped. Peabody usually had an eagle eye for details. Did he not notice that her dress was askew or that her hair had blades of grass in it? Did he not notice that she was walking home alone when she had left Trembledown in Binkley's carriage? Strange indeed! Something must have him truly upset.

"Warned you of what?"

"Your guests, ma'am," he said, his fingers drumming impatiently against his folded arms. "We are completely unprepared! I should never have spent half the day in Widgelyn Cross!"

For her part, Violet was glad he did. His hair was back to normal.

"What guests?" she asked, mystified.

"Your aunt, Miss Sophy, and Mr. Frederick Cantrell."

Sometimes she just didn't understand Peabody. "Really, Peabody, if you are going to start worrying about events that are days away yet, you will drive yourself mad. Remember: sufficient unto the day is the evil thereof."

His thin lips flattened so they practically disappeared. "This day's sufficiently evil, that is for sure. They have arrived."

"Who?"

"Your aunt, Miss Sophy, and Mr. Frederick Cantrell."

Violet's temples started to pound. "Aunt Augusta, Sophy and Freddy are *here*? *Now?*" she squeaked in disbelief. They weren't expected for two days!

Her heart sank. Today of all days! And look at her—she was a mess. And her mind was still in a flurry. How would she be able to stand before them all and make civil whiskers when her feelings were in an uproar?

Just as she was contemplating turning around and sneaking into the house by the servants' entrance, the door opened again and her youngest sister ran out, practically bouncing on her toes with excitement to see her.

"Yoo-hoo! Violet! Guess what? We're here!"

* * *

Sebastian tied his horse to a nearby branch before making his way into the cove where the ketch with the orange flag bobbed innocently in the water. It appeared that the men onboard had chosen this spot to cast their nets. But Sebastian would have been very surprised to see them make much of a haul fishing this time of the afternoon.

Sebastian made straight for the small cave where he knew Jem would be waiting. He stepped inside. "All right, Jem, this had better be good. You caught me at a most inconvenient time."

"I wasn't sure as how you would be in a position to see the boat, but I've news that I thought you might be interested in hearing."

"And that would be?"

"Well, it all happened on account of Hank's rib throwing him out of the house, see. So Hank went in search of a dram or two at the Old Spot."

"Good God, that's nothing but a thieves' den."

"Well, Hank hasn't the refined tastes that we have, me lord, so that I'm sorry to say they see much of his custom."

"Fascinating, but I am assuming there's a point to this story, Jem."

"Quite, quite, I was almost forgettin'. Seems that while Hank was havin' a bit of the wet at the bar, who should come in but an emissary of Robert the Brute!"

Sebastian drew back in surprise. "You begin to interest me."

"Aye, I thought I might. Seems that this here friend of the Brute's was looking to hire transport over the Channel sometime in the next sevennight."

"Ridiculous! The moon will be quite bright during that time."

"Yes, well, it seems the Brute is willing to make it worth the while of the ones as agrees to makin' the trip."

"And was anyone agreeable?"

"Aye, that they was. In fact, Hank was thinkin' that I would be interested and went ahead and volunteered my crew for the job."

"That was quite clear thinking for someone drinking the awful stuff they serve at the Old Spot."

"Aye, there's hardly a man alive with a harder head than Hank Hoblyn. So what should I do 'bout makin' arrangements, me lord?"

"By all means, agree to whatever plans are put forth. You want to be accommodating to the Brute. One would hate to get on the wrong side of such a notorious character, even if he is counterfeit."

Jem laughed. "Aye, that would be a shame. I'd be shakin' in me boots to face down such a desperado."

Sebastian smiled, but then went on soberly. "Did Hank say what this man looked like?"

"Nah, exceptin' that he'd light hair and looked like a gentleman dressin' down shabby-like. Well! A gentleman'd have to at the Old Spot, wouldn't he?"

"Mmm." Sebastian tugged at his chin. He had a passing suspicion this light-haired gentleman might be the increasingly erratic Binkley Jacobs. But why would Binkley think he could get away with impersonating the Brute? "It might be best if you were very careful at this meeting, until we know better what the man wants. Don't make the mistake of taking this too lightly. This could be quite dangerous, Jem."

The sailor spat, "You makes me blood turn quite cold. But don't worry, I'll take a care not to put the man's hackles up. We'll lull him proper."

As Sebastian rode away from his meeting with Jem, he pondered what this news could mean. It had to be that Binkley was planning on escaping to the continent in the next week with the stolen report of England's continental forces. These could be worth a small fortune with Boney on the loose. And no doubt Nero knew exactly who would pay him handsomely.

And it would seem that Binkley had decided to hijack the Brute's identity as the easiest way to make it over. Fortunate that he should stumble upon the Brute's actual gang. Since Jem was the only one who knew the Brute's true identity, it was also lucky that Hank had been thinking on his feet enough to play dumb and report back.

If anything, it all seemed too lucky. He didn't trust luck, and he couldn't imagine Nero would, either.

Sebastian was winding his way back to Montraffer, puzzling through all these new developments, when he noticed Hennie and Cuthbert in a meadow.

Although an easel with two chairs was set up, these had been abandoned and the two were on the ground under the shade of a two-hundred-year-old oak tree. Hennie was sitting rather straight with her back just leaning against the trunk. Cuthbert, Sebastian was amazed to note, was sprawled on his side and had a book open. Could his morose friend actually be reading to Hennie? If so, what did he consider appropriate literature for such a situation? The mind boggled to think of John Cuthbert poring over romantic literature, or poetry. Sebastian had never seen him read anything but government reports.

As he took one last look at the pair, they were so obviously and happily bound up in each other that he felt that he was spying on a moment of great intimacy—almost as intimate as the one he had just shared with Violet. But how quickly his moment with Violet had disintegrated. How would he ever make it up to her without revealing all?

It was a quandary.

Once Sebastian had enjoyed nothing more than playing Robert the Brute and dallying in espionage. He had embraced his double life as an escape from the rather dull routine of the *ton*. But now he began to wonder if, for the sake of romance, it wasn't time to hang up his mask.

Chapter Fifteen

As her sister tugged her inside the house, Violet felt as if she were being sucked into the eye of a storm.

"When did you get here?" she asked.

"Well over an hour ago!" her aunt Augusta exclaimed by way of greeting. "Exhausted and hungry from our journey. And not a soul about except for your servants, Violet—and Peabody was not even here! A very peculiar lot the rest of them are, I must say. Everyone seems to be afflicted with huge noses and that unfortunate shade of red hair. But then, I suppose they get a lot of inbreeding in an area like this."

"That's not inbreeding, aunt. They are related to each other."

"Well, isn't that what inbreeding means?" Augusta shook her head. "But that's neither here nor there. At least they seem industrious, some of them. They were all quite distracted with running up and down ladders in a salon that I assume is to be the ballroom."

"A very old grizzled fellow was finally persuaded to take our bags," Freddy explained.

"That would be Barnabas."

"Frightful man!" her aunt declared. "For a moment we feared he was that terrible Brute we've heard so much about."

The mention of the very man whose fate had been worrying her during her ride back to Trembledown made Violet's head snap up to attention.

Her aunt blanched. "Oh dear! I forgot that you were acquainted with . . ." Her words petered out. "That is, of course it was *not* he," she assured Violet.

Sophy laughed and turned to their traveling companion. "No, indeed—just an old retainer. He must be the ancestor to all those other servants, for his nose is the most bulbous of them all. Freddy felt so sorry for the man that he ended up hauling most of our trunks himself."

"How can you stand all this hammering, Violet? I'm sure it would drive me mad," Augusta said, tilting her head to the ceiling.

"It is just a little more frantic than usual for the ball, aunt. It's been a rush to get prepared."

Until she was able to settle them all in the salon, her aunt Augusta fluttered around her, exclaiming about the noises and asking if there was any food in the house. Meanwhile, Sophy talked a mile a minute about how terrible Violet looked and how awful Trembledown was. "Not nearly so nice as Peacock Hall!" she exclaimed, her nose wrinkling. Violet tensed reflexively to hear her work in progress maligned. "And why are you keeping all these cats?"

It was true, the population seemed to be reasserting itself again. They evidently no longer considered Dr. Loftus's Vermin Powder to be a deterrent to their happiness. Augusta's little spaniel, Lancelot, was a different matter, however. That little barking mop was in high dudgeon, furiously chasing every shadow and yapping at anything that moved. Outraged felines hissed at him from high perches on tables and bookcases.

"Quiet, Lancelot!" Augusta trilled. "He's probably hungry, poor thing. Of course we're all a little peckish," she hinted. "It was such a long trip."

Violet felt her lips flatten. "Perhaps we would have been better prepared if you had waited the extra two days and come when you were expected."

"Oh! But Freddy said we couldn't wait."

Violet turned her disapproval on that young man. Freddy Cantrell was the younger brother of their brother-in-law Nathan, the man their sister Abigail had married—a cloddish man whom Violet had never admired since he had ruined a pair of her dancing slippers at her come-out ball. (Although Violet had to admit that he appeared to have improved with age.) Freddy, at least, was not so rough around the edges as his brother Nathan. His fault lay in the opposite direction: he was a dandyish fellow, though she was glad to see that he had toned down his appearance since last they had met. Gone were the excessively high cravats and boots adorned with imported fur of his early university days. Today he was dressed in a well-cut traveling coat of bright green, with buff trousers and shining Hessians. The civilized look—but not overly civilized—took her aback. Only the ornate embroidery of a dragon on the purple silk of his vest made him stand out at all.

His expression was also satisfyingly apologetic for their premature arrival. "I am sorry, Violet. When you hear the circumstances, I am sure you will agree with me that it was necessary for us to leave London with all due haste."

Concern rapidly overcame irritation. "What happened?"

Her youngest sister bounded forward and took her

arm. She had been away from Sophy for so long, it took some adjusting to her energetic ways. "Just a little misunderstanding!" She laughed. "Don't listen to Freddy. You know how dramatic he tries to make everything seem. My goodness, I was only engaged to the man for a few weeks!"

"Engaged to *what* man?" Foreboding pressed at Violet's temples. She began to wonder if she might not need to resort to a tonic before this day was through.

"Count Orso." Aunt Augusta shook her head. "Or rather—" An over-the-shoulder glare from Sophy cut short the older lady's explanation. "Oh dear. I really must have some tea and refreshment," she said, fanning herself anxiously.

Violet dutifully sailed to the bell pull and ordered a pot of tea and whatever might be available in the larder for her aunt, who, even if two days early, *was* elderly. Then she turned back to Sophy. "Who is Count Orso?"

"My fiancé," Sophy said, rolling her eyes. "That is, my former fiancé." She flopped down in a chair. "And not even officially. Naturally since Father is out of the country, we could only have what you would call an understanding. It was all just a silly mix-up, really. And I am sure that people won't think a thing of it . . . in a few months . . ."

Violet tapped her foot impatiently. Not that she was one to start lecturing on romantic escapades, but she had a feeling her sister was just giving her a mere shadow of the real story. She turned to Freddy, her brows crooked questioningly.

The young man supplied, "Count Orso was not a count."

Sophy bolted up straight in her chair. "Well, what does that mean? You know those Europeans—especially the Italians—they hand titles around like sweets at a children's party."

Freddy sent Violet a long-suffering glance. "He wasn't Italian, either."

Sophy tossed up her hands. "Well, how was I to know that? He certainly *looked* Italian."

"That just shows what a goose you are," Freddy said.

"Don't you call me names, Master Frederick. He fooled you, too!" Sophy huffed. "Anyway, if Father had taken me with him to the continent as I begged and pleaded with him to do, I would have met scores of real Italians. Then I'm sure I would have known better how to spot a fake one."

"Travel is broadening," Aunt Augusta agreed.

Violent sank down on the sofa next to her aunt and leaned back. She was so exhausted that when Lancelot bounded into her arms, she did not raise a peep of protest. Besides, there was nothing that a dog with muddy paws could do to her dress that she had not achieved with her own activities that morning. She did draw the line, however, when the fat ball of fur started licking her chin.

"Down, Lancie!" her Aunt cooed. "Enough of that, now!"

"Yes," Violet agreed, setting the pooch resolutely between them. She had had enough of creatures lunging at her today. "Now tell me, if this Count Orso was not a count . . . and not Italian . . . who was he?"

Sophy clapped her hands together. "Oh, he was a magnificent specimen of a man, Violet. So handsome. Truly top of the trees! Everyone thought so."

"I didn't," Freddy put in. "I'll be hanged if I did."

Violet turned her skeptical gaze to her aunt, who piped up, "Oh, yes. Count Orso was quite the rage this Season. What a dashing figure he cut, Violet!"

"And you know how I always like those dashing, swarthy types," Sophy said.

Violet couldn't recall her sister ever being that discriminating. Her taste never seemed to rule out any type except the aged and infirm. "But you said he was not what he seemed to be."

"Well, he *was* swarthy," Freddy allowed wryly. "I thought him an oily, ugly customer. If you'll remember, I said so when we first met him. No genuine Italian count would have worn such inferior pomade on his hair."

"You're angry because he still owes you money from that boxing match," Sophy taunted.

The young man's red cheeks admitted this much was so. Yet he added, "But if I hadn't looked into his finances, you would have been more of a laughingstock in London than you are now."

"Why should you be a laughingstock?" Violet pressed, eager to know the worst and be done with it.

Sophy crossed her arms and sank in the chair. "Because Count Orso turned out to be, well, a humbug."

"His real name was Leonard Mole," Freddy announced. "Swarthy son of a Birmingham cheesemonger."

Violet gasped. "That's terrible!"

"Yes, he has been jailed for fraud . . . and debt."

"Good!" Violet declared.

"Not so good, actually," Freddy said. "While Leonard Mole was still at large, the papers had a field day. But once he was jailed, they turned their attention to Sophy."

"Wretched newspapers!" Sophy shook her head of thick dark hair in irritation. "Imagine, Violet. They are running dreadful cartoons of my likeness, calling me Countess Formaggio!"

"And Lady Cheddar," Freddy added miserably.

"How awful!"

"I never had any idea that the man had anything to do with cheese," Sophy declared hotly. "I never even saw him eat any."

"Three nights ago a mob of drunken men came to Grosvenor Square and sang until all hours," Augusta said, turning to Violet. "Oh, it was most upsetting!"

Sophy chuckled. "Though I did think it rather clever that they rhymed 'Your lovely brown hair' with 'Camembert.'"

"Yes, and really, they sang quite in tune, too," Augusta agreed. "But I was sure that Butterworth, who you must recall, Violet, has been with me donkey years, was ready to give notice."

Violet stared at the carpet. She had said there would be trouble when Sophy went to London, and now here it was. Though she was hardly in a position now to lecture her sister on the evils of falling in with low company. If it were known, Violet's recent behavior would overshadow Sophy's latest escapade by a mile.

Freddy leaned against the mantel. "So you see why I thought it best to bustle Sophy out of town *tout de suite*."

"Very wise," Violet admitted. "Thank you for looking after her so well, Freddy."

Naturally there would be some difficulties readying the rooms for them. And she had to send to town for more supplies as the kitchen was not yet prepared for so many. And she had no idea how she would handle having to hide all the turmoil going on in her own life with all these guests crawling about. Though maybe that would actually shield her from her troubles.

"What happened to you, Violet?" Sophy asked.

Violet blinked and pinned her eyes open, like a trapped rabbit. All of them were now staring at her curiously. "What do you mean?"

"Your dress. It's such a fright—you haven't even buttoned it properly. Is that how all people go about out in here in the country?"

"No, I was just—"

To her immense relief, Peabody came in bearing the tea tray. After he placed it on the table in front of her, Violet leaned forward to pour.

Augusta lunged forward like a hungry bird, tilting her head as she inspected the plate of food accompanying the teacups. She was apparently disappointed. "Cold meats," she said. "Have you no cake or scones with some fresh Cornish cream?"

"Unfortunately no, ma'am," Peabody said. "You find our kitchen in a state of woeful unpreparedness." He drew back, folded his hands, and added, "But that is often the case here."

Augusta pouted as she stabbed a piece of ham with her fork. "I suppose when one is two days early, one can't be too demanding." She looked up at Violet. "Do you have a bit of bread, perhaps?"

Violet bit back a smile. "See if Cook has some, please, Peabody."

The butler bent in a bow.

"What have you done with Hennie?" Sophy asked.

Good heavens! Violet had almost forgotten about her. She had been gone for hours and hours. Where *was* she?

Augusta nibbled a bit of ham and then shared with Lancelot, who gobbled the morsel with much more gusto than his mistress had demonstrated. "I was rather looking forward to being out from under the eagle eye of Butterworth. I should have asked the pastry cook to prepare a box for our journey—"

"You never answered my question," Sophy interrupted. When Violet looked confused—she found herself utterly unprepared for this onslaught of people—her sister gave her a verbal nudge. "About cousin Hen."

At least this turned the conversation away from her own bizarre appearance and the shortcomings of her kitchen. "I believe she is out sketching with Mr. Cuthbert."

Three pair of eyes blinked at her in astonishment.

"Hennie has a suitor?" Sophy asked.

Violet considered. "I would not go so far as to call him that, though he does seem to show a distinct interest in Hen. Unfortunately, I believe he is due to leave for London soon, so I expect you shall never meet the man."

Despite the novelty of Hennie's having a swain, Sophy's interest in the subject evaporated in an instant. In her own way, Sophy was a pragmatist. Her mania for men did not extend to those she could not see.

"I brought your costume for the masquerade," Sophy said, turning to more practical—for her—matters. "It is in my trunk. I hope it will suit."

Violet, who had been drifting off thinking about the marquess . . . and the Brute . . . tried to snap back to attention. "What?"

Her sister's brow pinched. "You look different. Very different!"

"I have been outside . . ."

"No, it is more than your frightfully mussed dress. Though I swear it's been an age since I've seen you looking so shabby, Violet. Not since Freddy's brother knocked you in the mud last year." She lifted a hand to her mouth to cover a laugh. "Do you remember?"

Violet's lips twisted. "It is kind of you to remind me. Perhaps I should change."

"But it's more than your clothes . . ." Sophy gasped. "I know! You are in love!"

Violet's insides leapt in alarm, but she glowered a warning at her little sister. "That is a bag of moonshine."

But Sophy would not be unconvinced. "Of course you are! I have been so wrapped up in my affair with Count Orso—" To the decided hitch of Freddy's throat, she corrected, "That is, Leonard Mole, that I completely forgot about your marquess."

To Violet's dismay, she felt a blush blooming in her cheeks. "He is not *my* marquess."

Sophy bent forward, laughing. "Ah, but I can see you desire him to be! And I'm sure he shall be. I have never seen you blush over a man!"

"I—"

Violet was saved. For once in her life, Hennie entered a room at an opportune moment. Her appearance at once drew attention away from the blush in Violet's cheeks, because Hennie was wearing the most bizarre headdress—a riot of wildflowers woven into a crown of twigs. It looked like someone had plopped a decorative bird's nest on her head. And standing next to her, as proudly as a laboring man escorting the Queen of the May, was Mr. Cuthbert, blushing as furiously as the woman next to him.

Sophy and everyone else in the room suddenly regained intense interest in Mr. Cuthbert.

And Violet couldn't help wondering—where had those two been all these hours, and were those grass stains on Hennie's gown?

Was there something in the air today?

By the following afternoon, Violet was finally able to devote her mind to the ball. She was sufficiently panicked, not to mention understaffed, to put her guests to work. They were, after all, just family. (Though the sight of Aunt Augusta in a mob cap and apron made her seem like a wholly strange person.)

Violet had to say, however, that Augusta was the most diligent worker of all of them. Freddy was an awkward hand at the odd jobs he was helping Barnabas with—or rather, the ones Barnabas was telling him to do. Sophy was inclined to stare out windows and daydream . . . no doubt wondering how different her life would be if she really had become the Countess Formaggio. Hennie and Cuthbert—whose return to London had been postponed yet again—made very little progress polishing silver. Compared to them all, Aunt Augusta was a veritable dervish with her feather duster.

By the end of the day, however, Violet had to admit that they had helped her out immensely. If Trembledown did not sparkle, exactly, it looked as well scrubbed as it probably ever had.

The workers sat down to a dinner that night that they felt they richly deserved. "I never knew what beastly things mops were!" Sophy said. "I hope I never have cause to be near one again!"

"At least you were not climbing up and down ladders all day, whacking at cobwebs and spiders," Freddy told her.

She laughed. "I'm sure it did you a world of good. You are always too idle!"

"Me? Did I not go riding with you just last Sunday?"

"Oh, were we riding? Judging from your performance I thought it was called falling!"

Freddy colored. "I only fell once, and wouldn't have if that beast you were riding hadn't become spooked at the sight of a squirrel and scared my horse!"

Sophy laughed. "You should have seen Freddy, Violet.

He was quite put out because he got mud on his new coat."

From the murderous look on Freddy's face, it was hard to believe that when he had first seen Sophy it had been love at first sight. They had even started to elope once, until they got into an argument that somehow seemed to have proceeded unabated now for a solid year. The two of them never stopped bickering, it sometimes seemed. And yet at times they appeared devoted to each other.

To Violet, who had never had a male friend, it was a very puzzling situation. A corner of her mind suspected that one or both of them still carried a torch for the other. And she heard in their verbal exchanges a little of the banter that she and Sebastian had sometimes taken pleasure in.

To his credit, Freddy took his anger over the riding incident out on the cutlet on his plate and not on Sophy.

"Are we going to have dessert?" Augusta asked. "Not that I especially care for any . . . but if the cook has gone to all the trouble . . ."

"Yes, I believe there is a mulberry tart."

Her aunt looked much relieved that the travails of the day would not end without some reward.

"I believe that you said you were inordinately fond of sweets, did you not, Mr. Cuthbert?" Hennie asked.

The man across the table smiled as if there were some shared secret between the two of them involving tarts. Indeed, the whole day it had seemed the two of them had been communicating in code. A lover's code. There was no other explanation for why a seemingly random word sent the two into smiling moonishly at each other, or a raised brow or tilt of the lips could cause blushes to fire their cheeks.

Violet shook her head. Far from losing Mr. Cuthbert,

she now wondered if they were ever going to be able to get rid of him.

Someone else must have wondered the same thing. At the end of the meal, Sebastian appeared, evidently wondering what had happened to his houseguest. His sudden appearance after a day's absence and just as Violet thought she was beginning to regain some sort of equilibrium concerning him nearly made her jump in her chair.

"Ah, here he is!" he said when he found Cuthbert installed at the table. "But I see he is safe and sound after all. I had thought I might have to send out a search party."

"I beg your pardon, St. Just," Cuthbert said, alarmed. "I was sure you would have received the note I sent over to Montraffer today."

"Note?" Sebastian asked. "Good heavens! It must have been misplaced. Well, well. All's well that ends well, isn't that right?"

Everyone agreed this was generally the case, but Violet had her suspicions. The too-innocent disavowal of receiving that note, for instance, made her wonder whether he had known the whereabouts of his friend all along. The other clue that the marquess was not being entirely truthful was the way he enthusiastically pulled a chair between her and Sophy and plopped himself down.

"I am ashamed of myself for imposing myself on you like this, Mrs. Treacher." His grin indicated just the opposite. "But did I hear we are having mulberry tart? I would not be averse to a slice."

Violet shot him a look but dutifully rang for Peabody and instructed him to include the marquess in the rest of the serving.

Sophy, who seemed to have grown a foot from sitting up taller ever since the marquess appeared, cleared her throat in a none-too-subtle bid for attention. "I don't believe we all know your new guest, Violet."

Her sister's dark eyelashes were batting madly, which surprised Violet by bringing a little sting to her breast. Not jealousy, surely. Or . . . perhaps just a little. Sophy had always had singular luck in captivating men, albeit not usually appropriate ones.

Violet made the introductions, though of course Sophy and everyone else knew perfectly well who the marquess was as soon as he had walked in the door. And his marked attentions to Violet did not go unnoticed. For all her protestations that Sebastian was not *her* marquess, Sebastian certainly was acting as if she were *his* Violet. She felt her pulse riot even as her face heated at his possessive smile. What gave him the right . . .

She suppressed a groan. *She* had given him the right, unfortunately. When she had fallen so willingly into his arms, what else was he to think?

But had she not also made it clear to him afterward that she would pursue no further relationship with him— indeed, that she could not? Overall, she found his behavior most cheeky for someone who had last been seen dumping her on the side of the road.

"I took the liberty of bringing you a few gifts from my cellar," he said, leaning close to her, yet speaking in a loud enough purr for all the table to hear of his generosity.

She squared her shoulders and leveled a chilling smile on him. "How nice. Tell me, what does the St. Just clan keep in its cellar? Potatoes? Skeletons? I'll have you know we've spent the day ridding Trembledown of cobwebs, so we've no need of any more spiders."

He indulged her sarcasm with a chuckle. "Only the finest wine and champagne this country . . . and perhaps a few across the drink . . . have to offer."

"Oh, spirits!" Violet feigned a relieved chuckle. "How kind you are—spreading inebriation to your neighbors."

He bowed from his waist. "Call it my contribution to our little party."

"We have been cleaning all day for *our* little party. A shame you couldn't have contributed to *that*."

He laughed. "Isn't it?" Before she could punish him with a glare, he turned with an affable smile to Sophy, who visibly melted under his gaze. Aunt Augusta, too, seemed to grow more animated, whereas before the marquess arrived she had seemed to be fading a little in the face of the long wait for the dessert course.

"I heard you arrived ahead of schedule, Miss Wingate."

Sophy chuckled. "Yes—Freddy insisted that we leave London so that—" She stopped herself, then blinked.

"So that . . .?" Sebastian asked.

Freddy jumped in. "We could help Violet prepare for the ball."

"Yes!" Violet agreed. Heaven knew she did not want the saga of Count Orso recounted for the marquess! He would think they were a family of gullible lunatics. First she fell into the hands of a smuggler, and then Binkley, and now her little sister had only just escaped a criminal fortune hunter.

Unfortunately, she feared he would hear about it soon enough. She tried to calculate how long the first posts from London to her various neighbors would take. The whole world and its wife would find out, she thought with dread.

"But wait!" Sebastian said to Sophy. "Do you mean that your sister put your small, delicate hands to manual labor?"

"Mopping!" Sophy said, glad to have her trauma recognized.

"What cruelty!" Sebastian exclaimed. "What a misuse of the notorious Lady Cheddar!"

Sophy's cheeks went bright pink, and Violet dropped her fork. She glared at Hennie and Cuthbert. She thought she could trust them not to go gossiping about *this*.

Although . . . those two also looked completely perplexed by the mention of Lady Cheddar. Violet recalled Hennie had not even been present when they were speaking of the matter.

"Where did you hear this?" Violet pressed Sebastian.

He chuckled. "A little bird from London told me. She even gave me a song to sing—a silly ditty that, if you do not mind my saying so, Miss Sophy, does not do you justice."

At the compliment, Sophy's spirits returned. "Thank you, my lord."

Sebastian warmed to the subject. "Though I did get quite a laugh from rhyming 'skin so fair' with 'old gruyere.' Or 'my lady cheddar' and 'who wouldn't want to bed—'"

"I think we've heard quite enough of that song!" Violet said, interrupting him. She wished she could have given the man a swift, sharp kick. How had he heard about this? Then she remembered that he was in regular correspondence with Minerva Plimpton, who would keep him current on all the *on dit*.

Sebastian feigned innocence, then looked at the abashed faces around the table. "Well! Of course it was a foolish rhyme—one of those utterly forgettable things mobs seize on one day and discard the next. Although now that I see the subject of the ditty in person, I must say that while the scandal may be forgotten, the lady in question will not be so easily forgotten by the *ton*."

While Violet sensed a double edge to this compliment, it won him a worshipper for life in Sophy. "You see?"

She turned to Freddy, beaming. "Everyone will have forgotten all about it by the time we return to London. They've probably forgotten about it already!"

Clearly, she did not understand that Sebastian's hearing the tale from such a long distance was evidence that it had *not* been forgotten.

"What does it matter?" Freddy replied. "You will only end up in some escapade that starts them talking all over again."

"Oh!" Aunt Augusta said, alarmed. "I doubt that very much. I am sure Sophy has learned a valuable lesson and knows she must be much more cautious in future."

The looks exchanged around the table revealed no such confidence, and the mischievous gleam in Sophy's eyes confirmed her own resolution to keep throwing caution to the wind. "Well, one doesn't want to be a stick. Besides, people *must* talk about something. Otherwise we should all die of boredom."

To Violet's dismay, Sebastian roared his approval. "Something tells me that our more disreputable presses shall always have copy while you are loose on the town, Miss Wingate."

Sophy preened as if she had just been paid the highest compliment.

After dinner, the group gathered in the salon. To everyone's sorrow, Cuthbert insisted that what he would love above all things would be to hear Hennie give a performance on her harp. No doubt because she was unnerved by his unwavering attention, Hennie's hands seemed to slip across the strings of that poor tortured instrument in even more slapdash fashion than usual. Not that she noticed. Nor did she seem to see the glazed eyes and drooping postures from the rest of her audience. She only had eyes for Cuthbert, who looked as if he heard nothing but heavenly music plucked by the fingers of an angel.

Violet seated herself as far from the harp as humanly possible; to her dismay she found the marquess drifting back to sit with her, even though he had to drag a chair halfway across the salon. She would never hear the end of this from Sophy!

During the performance, he leaned close to her. "I confess I could not stay away any longer, Violet," he whispered. "I had to see you."

She shushed him.

Obediently, he pinned his gaze on Hennie . . . for all of three bars of music. "Have you not thought about me at all?" he whispered through the corner of his mouth.

"Please, Sebastian," she said, as if her ears were offended by his whisperings. (As if her ears could be any more offended than they already were by that harp!) "My cousin is playing."

But as she said the words, Hennie finished her song. During the clapping that followed, everyone shifted in relief and pivoted in their chairs to begin their escapes.

"Oh, let us have another!" Cuthbert said, all enthusiasm. Apparently not hearing the groans from the other listeners, he suggested, "The Bach again. I believe that is my favorite!"

To the woe of all, Hennie was only too happy to oblige.

Violet, hoping to go unnoticed, stood and retreated to the hall. She could still hear, unfortunately, but she did not feel so trapped as she did in that chair with the waves of notes coming at her from one direction and the marquess's stage whisperings assaulting her from another.

But the marquess soon popped out of his chair, too,

and joined her. "I confess I have thought of you often," he told her. "You did not think of me at all?"

She took another step backward. It would be terrible if they were overheard. "I have thought of the inordinate hurry you were in to get away."

"You made it home, surely?"

"Yes, but now I wonder . . . did you make it home yourself, or did you go somewhere else?"

His eyes widened in surprise, then he turned and focused on Hennie. "Is that really Bach, do you think?"

A lame attempt to change the subject. "I am beginning to wonder if there is more to you than meets the eye, my lord."

"How so?"

"Could it be that you were in a hurry to report a sighting of a smuggler's boat?"

"What an odd idea!" he said. "Besides, upon closer inspection I found it was only a fisherman's ketch."

Sophy tossed a look toward them—an envious look, actually—and Violet lowered her voice. "I saw the labels on some of those bottles you brought over. They are French. I have half a notion that you have been receiving it . . . how shall we say. . . for services rendered to his majesty?"

"Turning in smugglers, you mean?" he said, amused. "You possess a more fanciful imagination than I would have guessed."

She frowned. He had not answered her question. But now that she had spoken her suspicion, it seemed rather foolish. Except . . . he did seem to ask so many questions.

He edged closer, so that their bodies were very nearly touching. "When I asked if you had thought of me, I had hoped your thoughts would have been of a more romantic nature."

She harrumphed.

"Ah—but perhaps that is too much to ask." His eyes narrowed. "Instead, you seem much more concerned about that Brute fellow. Were you afraid I would turn him in?"

She fanned herself energetically. "No, indeed! I never gave it a thought."

Blessedly, Bach finally drizzled arrhythmically to an end. More tepid applause followed; the audience had decided that a little encouragement could glue them in their seats till after midnight.

"Tell me, Violet," Sebastian said, able to speak in a more normal tone now. "Would it bother you if I said I was trying to capture the Brute?"

Her spine stiffened. "Why should it?"

"Why indeed? I wonder, what would you say if I told you that the Brute might be a traitor to England?"

"What do you mean?"

"A spy for France."

She found herself shaking her head, wanting to deny it. And yet why? She already knew he was a smuggler, a kidnapper, a thief. With all those things against him, the man had little honor to uphold.

But there was something curious about his question. "I suppose—*if* you were to tell me that—I would say, how did you come by this information?"

He smiled but said nothing, turning instead to Mr. Cuthbert, who was approaching them.

"Perhaps we should leave our lovely hostesses, John. Tomorrow night is the ball, and no doubt they will need their rest."

Violet was not sure whether to be relieved or disappointed that the marquess was leaving. In any event, she would see him soon.

After the two men said their good-byes to everyone, Sophy attached herself to Violet. "Oh, he's a dream! Much better than Hennie wrote about in her letters. He's handsomer than Count Orso, even!"

But was he more honest than Count Orso? That was the question that was beginning to puzzle Violet.

Chapter Sixteen

"Violet, you do look lovely!"

Violet turned before the mirror, pleased. The Anne Boleyn costume Sophy had brought for her fit perfectly, and she liked the way the Renaissance styling of the garment was in keeping with the age of Trembledown. She had always thought modern designs were quite daring, but the neck of this gown was tight and cut low, showing even more of her bosom than she was accustomed to. The velvet fabric was so sumptuous she felt like a queen, and in the spirit of the poor queen, fear of her ball not being a success even gave Violet the appropriate sense of doom.

"But how will anyone know who I am supposed to be?" she asked Sophy.

Her sister worried her lip. She was dressed in medieval garb that hugged her body like a second skin. Violet was about to lodge a protest against it, but given the show of bosom she was sporting, it would have been a little hypocritical of her. And since Freddy was supposed to be King Arthur to her Guinevere, she trusted that Sophy would have a suitable watchdog.

"Perhaps," Aunt Augusta suggested, looking majestic herself in her Boadicea garb, "you could have Peabody follow you about all evening with a block and an ax."

Violet laughed. As far as props were concerned, nothing could top Aunt Augusta's giant spear and Lancelot, who was wearing a tiny winged helmet fastened to his head to match his mistress's resplendent headgear.

"Even if people don't know who you are supposed to be," Sophy said, "I am sure you will be the rage of the ball, Violet. I was very right to pick out that blue color for you."

"Thank you. But I think you will outshine everyone."

Sophy delighted in the compliment. Then again, all day she had been vibrant with anticipation. In the most undignified way, she fell back against the bed and looped her hands behind her headdress. "I hope I meet some dashing, handsome stranger."

Uh-oh. Violet had been so consumed by getting the house prepared and seeing to food and drink and musicians, she had not looked ahead to what mischief her sister could get into under her own roof. "You must be careful at these masquerades, Sophy. All these men running around masked—they might feel more inclined to take liberties."

"Do you really think so?" she asked, eyes shining.

"Er . . ." Eagerness was not the reaction Violet had hoped for. "Never mind. Just be careful."

"And make sure you dance often with Freddy," Aunt Augusta counseled.

Sophy looked horrified. "Freddy!"

"You brought him all this way. You must make sure he has an enjoyable evening."

Sophy shrugged. "I suppose so—but he won't want to

dance with me anyway. He never has trouble finding partners."

Violet smiled at the petulant tone in her sister's voice . . . almost as if she were jealous of all these dancing partners.

"Not that I care, mind you," Sophy assured them. "But just so you know, he does not need me to pity him. Girls flock about him in London." She paused to consider this curious fact. "He does wear clothes well . . . and I suppose he dances very gracefully."

"I am going down," Aunt Augusta announced. "I might nip into the kitchen to make sure all is in order."

And to sample the cakes, no doubt.

As Violet put the finishing touch of a silver ribbon in her hair, she wondered about Sebastian. What would he be dressed as? Would she recognize him? Would he ask her to dance?

Not that she wanted him to. She just hoped he would be more civil than last night. In his own way, the marquess seemed to be as reluctant as Binkley Jacobs to take no for an answer. What could she do? She had told him they could have no future, and he disregarded her. Would she have to make a full confession about her night with the Brute to make him understand that she was not worthy of his affection?

As she worried about conveying her disinterest in him, she also wondered whether he would try to kiss her . . . and whether she would let him. As infuriating as he was, she could not help thinking about their lovemaking. God help her, a part of her still wanted him. If only she could banish both the Brute and the marquess from her mind forever!

There was a light rap at the door and Hennie scooted in. At the sight of their cousin, Violet and Sophy both sucked in their breaths. It wasn't only the fact that Hennie was appearing for the first time in months in anything but black. That was shocking enough. But her dress! The diaphanous white gown draped about her figure in a way that was almost . . . alluring. Violet couldn't say that she had ever seen quite so much of Hennie. One shoulder was bared, and silk-clad ankles peeked out of the bottom of her gown above golden sandals. It was shocking.

And her hair! After letting it be painstakingly curled by Lettie, Hennie was wearing it tied back loosely over one shoulder. Curled tendrils had already escaped their ribboned bond, creating a soft frame for her heart-shaped face.

To top off the Athena effect, Hennie had fashioned a brown owl out of feathers and attached it to her right shoulder.

"Hennie! You're magnificent!" Sophy exclaimed.

It was an astonishing proclamation—one Violet had never expected to hear from anyone's lips regarding their spinsterish cousin. And yet she could not help agreeing. Hennie did look wonderfully well.

"Oh, do you really think so?" she asked, her gray eyes bright. "I'm sure I shouldn't show myself like this at all."

"No—you must!"

"Mr. Cuthbert will probably be terribly shocked."

"He will not," Violet said. "In fact, behind your mask, he might not even recognize you." Violet wouldn't have.

This possibility startled Hennie more than anything. "But I shall die if he doesn't! How will he know to dance with me?"

Sophy laughed. "Don't worry. If you like I shall give him a hint."

"Thank you, that would be most kind. I don't want to

be a bother . . . but I was hoping . . ." Her cheeks went beet red and her words choked off.

"Hoping what?" Violet asked her.

"Well!" Hennie came forward and whispered conspiratorially, "I do not think it is too premature to say that I believe by the end of the evening Mr. Cuthbert and I may have an interesting announcement to make."

Sophy's brow furrowed. "A what?"

"She believes they will become engaged," Violet said. "I hope so, coz, though you've only known him a short time."

"Yes, but Mr. Cuthbert and I are so alike it often feels that we could count our friendship in years instead of mere days."

What a development! Violet had never thought when she brought Hennie to Cornwall with her that she would so soon be losing her companion to marriage. If anything, she had worried that she might decamp to Bath. Yet when Imogene had written to tell Hennie the sad news that she could not visit for the ball, Hennie had not seemed much upset. Indeed, the word *Bath* had not crossed Hennie's lips in many days.

In her excitement over an engagement—however speculative—Sophy rushed Hennie with a hug of joy. Hennie's owl toppled over and they had to pin him back into an upright position before they could go down.

"Don't move too abruptly, Hen, or you might end up punctured."

"Yes! I will be careful!" Hennie said, breathless with nerves.

Just before they left the room, Violet hesitated. They all had so many hopes. She couldn't help wondering if they all might need to take care this evening.

But no matter how much she girded herself, she could

not have prepared herself for the sight that met her when she went to greet her guests.

Robert the Brute was there.

And not just one—twenty of him.

Cuthbert, unaccustomed to masquerade balls (or large social affairs of any stripe), felt as if he had been cast adrift. Sebastian had been able to loan him a very serviceable jester costume, but it was not the type of thing he felt comfortable in. The leggings sagged a little on him. Altogether not the impression he had hoped to make this evening.

And now he felt doubly out of place, since most all of the other men had come as the smuggler Robert the Brute. Indeed, it seemed to be something of a joke among the locals. There were leather half-masks on everyone. The sight of so many swaggering masked men in tall boots made him feel that much more . . . well, a fool.

For the life of him, he could not find Henrietta. She was all he had thought about the whole day—in fact, the entire time he had been in Cornwall. All day long he had been ricocheting between anticipation and a torment of nerves over what he had to say to her. If he did not find her soon, his courage would fail him.

Stalking away from the punch bowl—she wasn't there, either—he bumped into a young King Arthur, who spilled cider down the front of his chain-mail tunic.

"Damme!" The king jumped back. "What the—oh! Is that you, Mr. Cuthbert?"

Cuthbert recognized the man behind the mask as Freddy Cantrell.

"I am sorry." He rattled his bells unhappily. "I am not accustomed to this getup."

"Never mind. Punch wipes right off the hauberk." Freddy dabbed at his mail. "This getup is deuced uncomfortable. I don't see how I shall dance without the sound of all this clanking metal drowning out the musicians."

"It's a very good costume," Cuthbert said a little enviously. He should have thought of a more dignified disguise for himself.

Of course, until a few days ago, he had not known that he would be going to a masquerade ball. Indeed, this was the first he had ever attended. And hopefully the last.

But since Cantrell was one of the few other men present not dressed as Robert the Brute, the two of them exchanged a look of camaraderie.

"You haven't seen Sophy, have you, Cuthbert?"

"I have not seen any lady that I know," he said gloomily.

Freddy laughed. "We can remedy that, I'm sure. Shall I hazard a guess as to whom you might be looking for?"

Cuthbert stammered for a moment before Freddy rescued him. "Never mind! I believe I spotted Miss Halsop not long ago. It's no surprise that you haven't picked her out yet—I almost didn't recognize her myself."

They snaked through the crowd along the dance floor of the ballroom a few paces before Freddy stopped, causing Cuthbert to walk right into him. "Here she is!" Freddy announced cheerily.

Cuthbert saw someone he recognized instantly as Sophy. She had only a hand mask and seemed to be using it as a fan more than a facial cover.

"Where have you been?" Freddy asked her.

"Dancing! Isn't this fun?"

"This costume is a damn nuisance," Freddy grumbled. "I haven't sweated so much since . . . well, since your sister sent me up those ladders!"

"Listen to him complain, Mr. Cuthbert!" Sophy

squinted through her mask as if it were a pair of spectacles. "That is Mr. Cuthbert, isn't it?"

Cuthbert nodded, causing his cap to jangle.

A ravishing woman in Greek garb standing next to Sophy gazed at him, making him more self-conscious. And more impatient to find Henrietta.

"If I had known this trip was going to be so strenuous, I would have stayed in London," Freddy declared.

"No, you wouldn't," Sophy said. "And I told you to be Robin Hood. That would have been so much easier on you, not to mention cooler. But you insisted on Arthur."

"Because you were Guinevere. But I have hardly seen you. Who have you been dancing with?"

"Brutes!" Sophy smiled as if she were in heaven.

They looked out at the dance floor, which was a sea of Brutes capering about. It made quite a spectacle, Cuthbert had to admit. It was quite a joke on Sebastian, too. He had thought Sebastian quite clever—not to mention daring—to think of coming as the Brute, but that disguise was the flavor of the night. Cuthbert didn't worry that anyone would recognize the real Brute in their midst. He could not pick Sebastian out of the crowd himself.

"Isn't it marvelous? All these dashing smugglers whisking one off in their arms," Sophy said on a sigh.

Behind his mask, Freddy rolled his eyes. "They are probably all cheesemongers."

She swatted him. "Don't start with that! Why don't you ask me to dance?"

"All right."

Belatedly, she looked back at Cuthbert. "Aren't you dancing, Mr. C.?"

Cuthbert stammered, "I-I was searching for Miss Halsop."

Sophy laughed. "Well, good heavens! Look to your right."

And then she and Freddy disappeared into the line of dancers preparing for a country dance.

Cuthbert cautiously turned. The ravishing goddess with the owl perched on her shoulder dropped an awkward curtsey. "Mr. Cuthbert."

At the dulcet sound of that voice, Cuthbert's legs went noodly beneath him. "*Miss Halsop*?"

She nodded so vigorously that the owl seemed to be seconding the affirmation.

"Good heavens!"

She smiled tentatively, though as he continued to gape at her in wonder, the lips beneath her gold mask went slack.

"You are the most ravishing Athena!" he exclaimed at last.

The smile was back, as was a very becoming blush. "Thank you. You are . . ."

He felt like kicking himself with his curly-toed boots. "A fool," he said.

"It is a very amusing sort of costume."

Now that their initial meeting was done, they both stared speechlessly at each other, then out at the dancers. In fact, an entire set went by before they spoke again, and then both spoke at once.

"Miss Has—"

"I have not danced all evening."

Her words brought him up short. Of course. He should ask her to dance. It was probably the correct thing to do anyway. He held out his hand. "Will you do me the honor?"

She put her gloved hand in his and he led her out. He was starting to perspire. It had been many years since he had tripped around on a dance floor. To his dismay, when the players began, they played a waltz. A waltz! How was this done?

Rather than admitting his ignorance, he looked at what the Brute next to him was doing and attempted to copy the movements. It was very distracting holding Henrietta so close. Having her body wedged in such proximity to his own made it exceedingly difficult to concentrate on what his feet should be doing. Not to mention, he was jangling so.

"Mr. Cuthbert?"

He looked down into those lovely eyes, which were gazing at him in puzzlement. "Oh—yes?"

"Are you quite all right?"

"Fine," he said, attempting to steer them in a turn. This floor was much too small for the number of dancers.

When next he looked at her, Hennie's cheeks seemed very red.

"Are you tired?" he asked, hopefully.

She shook her head wordlessly.

Withholding a sigh, he kept up the pace with diligence. What strange creatures women were! The dance was her idea, yet she did not seem to be enjoying it in the least.

Quite by accident, he mashed down on her foot. Hennie winced.

"I am sorry!" he exclaimed.

"It is all right, Mr. Cuthbert."

"Would you like some punch?"

She nodded.

Thank heavens! He whisked her off the dance floor as quickly as he could, all the while questioning her on the state of her toes.

"They are quite well," she insisted.

He deposited her in a chair and hurried to get her

some punch, then nervously spilled half a cup's contents on his way to her.

"Thank you so much," she said.

He nodded. "My dear Henrietta . . ."

She gazed at him over her cup. "Yes?"

"I . . . er . . ." This was hardly the place for the kind of declaration he intended to make. "I have never seen the terrace."

"Oh!" She jumped up, spilling punch down her front. "Oh dear!"

Cuthbert had to hurry to find a cloth to clean her dress. By the time they finally reached the terrace, he was quite fatigued. He hardly allowed Hennie's seat to hit the iron bench before he collapsed next to her and mopped his brow with his handkerchief. Who knew romance was so exhausting?

"It is a lovely evening," Hennie said.

"Is it?" Cuthbert looked up. Stars hung heavily against the ink-dark sky, holding court about the large yellow moon. "Oh yes—all the stars and whatnot."

She cleared her throat. "Such nights make me think of poetry."

"Do they?" How odd! If anything, he thought of Ptolemy. But women were such different creatures.

He really had very little experience of women, now that he thought about it. His own mother had died in childbirth when he was only four, and his father had not seen the need to remarry.

"Excuse me, Mr. Cuthbert," Hennie said, watching him expectantly, "but there was something you wanted to say to me?"

"Yes, yes, there was."

She blinked at him, and he felt his heart start to pound in panic. A few afternoons ago, everything had been easy between them. He had taken her into his arms as if he had every right to—as if she belonged to him.

But now that he was at the point of asking her to be his, he felt as if there were a stone wall between them.

"I . . . that is . . ." Dash it! He had never felt so ridiculous. "Would you mind if I removed my mask?"

"No, indeed," she answered hastily. "I shall take off mine, too."

"A very good idea."

They unmasked themselves. But instead of causing a more easy feeling in him, seeing her beautiful face so close, so trusting, so eager, made his stomach feel as if a large bird were flapping around in it.

Such a beautiful woman—and yet he did not even know how to dance properly. Nor, evidenced by their experience tonight, could they even converse consistently. What would happen if he married her and they ran out of things to talk about? That would be damn awkward.

And there was another problem. He had thought only of possessing her, of having her with him in his bed and at his table. But was it that simple? She was not a pillow or a salt shaker. She would take up quite a bit of room with her clothes, et cetera. Where would he put her? He only had a few furnished rooms. Most of his time was spent at the office.

It occurred to him suddenly that he had simply been overcome with first love. He was rushing things. He was a bachelor. Marriage was . . .

He swallowed. Well, marriage was not for him, obviously. This was the best of women, and if he had doubts about her, he was obviously not a marrying man.

But now he was in the basket. He had maneuvered them out here, in the moonlight, and he had to say something.

"I wanted to ask your permission to"—he swallowed—"to write to you when I return to London."

She blinked. "*Write* to me, Mr. Cuthbert?"

He nodded. "I hoped we might be able to continue our discussions concerning art and literature."

"Oh, I see." Her shoulders rounded.

"May I?"

She nodded. "Oh yes!" she said tightly. "Please do."

There was a pause.

"And will you answer?"

"Of course."

"Splendid."

Another long minute crawled by in silence before Henrietta cleared her throat and abruptly stood. "Is that all, Mr. Cuthbert?"

He jumped to his feet. His face felt hot—but it was probably just the temperature. Hennie's face was flushed, too.

"I think I shall go in now," she said, her voice looping up. "I should like to dance again, and no one will ever ask me out here."

He started to offer his arm, but she shook her head quickly and scampered ahead of him.

Cuthbert watched her scud away with a sinking heart. When she disappeared through the doorway, he felt a heaviness in his chest. He had made a mull of things. And now he was just as he was before. Alone.

That was not the comfort it once was, though.

Brandy had never tasted so good. Even if it reminded her exactly of the stuff the Brute had given her in the cave, it burned down her throat, leaving behind a pleasant, warm feeling. It almost gave her the courage to go back and face a roomful of Brutes.

What a nightmare!

There was a knock on the door and Violet quickly pushed the bottle behind a sack of sugar.

"Yes?"

The door squeezed open, and her aunt's head poked into the dark pantry. The whites of her eyes seemed huge. "My dear, what are you doing? Is everything quite all right?"

Oh yes, she thought sarcastically. *Don't all hostesses seek dark closets in which to hide from their guests?*

Instead, she smiled. "Of course."

"Your sister was asking where you were. Indeed, quite a few people were wondering." Her aunt frowned as she peered at the shelves behind Violet. "Are there any stray tarts in here, by any chance?"

"No."

"A pity. We are running out of sweets." She shook her head. "But you should go back to your guests, Violet. The ballroom is abuzz!"

"About me?"

"No—Napoleon!"

"Is one of the guests dressed as Napoleon?" She called that in questionable taste, considering the fact that the man was at large.

"No—the *real* Napoleon has reached Paris! One of the guests heard on the road from London. He must be about to raise an army—in which case it will be war for certain!"

Violet felt the blood drain out of her face. Perhaps that was why Sebastian had mentioned that the Brute was a spy—and why he was so agitated at the sight of that little smuggler's boat. But what did Sebastian have to do with any of this?

The brandy in her stomach began to churn.

"I should get back, too, dear. I left Lancelot with

Freddy, but I forgot to tell him to keep him away from the punch glasses. Lancie is liable to forget his manners when he gets tipsy, and we wouldn't want any doggy puddles."

When Violet finally forced herself to leave the safety of the pantry, Peabody was waiting for her. "I have some lemon water flavored with peppermint." He hitched his throat delicately. "Some say it quite ably disguises the odor of alcohol."

"Why should—" She blushed. He was the one man she could never lie to. "Thank you, Peabody. I believe I am rather thirsty."

She downed a glass of the tart, minty beverage and then gathered her courage to go back to the ballroom.

Peabody tagged after her. "Should we make plans to move inland, madam?"

She turned, confused.

"Trembledown would be most vulnerable should Napoleon launch an attack by sea," Peabody explained. "Like the Vikings!"

She had not considered that. It was a disturbing thought, but she managed to laugh. "We shall have to think of something. Perhaps we should tell the Monks to arm themselves and start drilling. We can have our own private militia."

She mounted the stairs, wondering what this news would mean for them all, when out of the corner of her eye she saw a Brute ducking into the library. She rolled her eyes. They were simply everywhere. She thought she heard another one running up behind her, but when she turned, she discovered it was Hennie creating the din. Her dress fluttered around her and her owl flopped over on her shoulder as she ran up the stairs. There were tears in her eyes.

"What is it?" Violet asked, worrying that the owl's pins had slipped, just as she had feared.

"Nothing!"

The keening wail in her voice belied the protestation, however.

Violet caught her arm. "Did you argue with Mr. Cuthbert?"

"Oh no!" Hennie cried. "He is going to . . . to *write* to me!" She flung her arm away from Violet and tore up the stairs. Instead of heading toward the ballroom, however, Hennie veered in the opposite direction and ran to her own room.

Poor Hennie! Violet shook her head. Why had that dolt Cuthbert developed cold feet? He had seemed so devoted to her.

Thinking of Hennie's problems took her mind off her own and made her all that much more shocked to find herself back in the ballroom full of Brutes. They came in all shapes and sizes, and aside from the oversized leather masks that they all appeared to have copied from the same source, most of them did not look authentic. A few came close, though.

Because Violet was so new to Widgelyn Cross, at least half of the guests she wouldn't have recognized even if they hadn't been wearing masks. Some, especially the women, were instantly recognizable even in their costumes. Miss Cheswyn, garbed as Joan of Arc, was dancing with one Brute, and Mrs. Blatchford as Salome—dripping dramatically in veils—was sharing a cup of punch with yet another.

Where was Sebastian? He had to be here. Violet had seen Cuthbert briefly when she had made her first pass through the ballroom. But so far, she had not seen the marquess.

Perhaps he had not come. But she couldn't imagine that.

Perhaps he had decided to heed her advice and pursue no further relationship with her.

She couldn't quite imagine that, either.

When she spotted her, Mrs. Blatchford beckoned Violet over with a waving veil. She didn't wait for Violet to arrive at her side to actually start talking, however. "Oh my dear, what a success. *Quel succes!* Have you danced with Binkley?"

Violet drew back in surprise. She had not expected that he of all people would come! "No."

"But you must! He does like you so—I can tell!"

Violet attempted to smile politely.

"And have you heard about Bonaparte? Such a shame they couldn't have caught him before he reached Paris! Now he will start stirring things up and no one will be able to travel to Paris!"

"Let us hope not."

"Anyway, Binkley will have to return to his post in London, I'm sure. Such a shame you two will have to cut short your little idyll."

Happily, Violet was saved from more of this awkward exchange when a short Brute came up to her and doffed his hat, revealing a bald head. "May I have the honor, madam?"

Violet nodded and gladly let him take her arm.

The ridiculousness of this fellow—who was actually the local doctor—in a Brute costume made Violet feel a little silly for coming so unstrung. The Brutes were only men in costume. She managed to smile pleasantly as she danced, and make the correct responses to the exclamations about that damned French devil.

Soon there was a line of Brutes asking her for dances,

and fortified by the earlier brandy, she agreed to them all. Then, during a waltz, she realized that perhaps she had become too relaxed.

"You don't recognize me, do you?" asked her partner, a Brute in a rather dandyish embroidered vest beneath his black coat. The real Brute wouldn't be caught dead in it.

Yet the voice was familiar. Violet gasped. "You!"

It was Binkley! It took an enormous amount of gall to show his face here, she thought angrily. (But of course he was not, in actuality, showing it.)

"Please do not look at me like that," he said. "Believe me, Mrs. Treacher, I was almost too ashamed to come here tonight."

Almost.

"I should think so!" And she wished he hadn't chosen her for a waltz! There was no getting away from him without creating a scene.

"I only came because I wanted to apologize. To beg your forgiveness—though of course I don't deserve it."

She glowered at him. "Have you been drinking?"

"Of course. I have been drinking for weeks," he confessed. "I don't know what else to do. I am a lost man!"

As if she should waste her sympathy on *him*! "You cannot feel that way because I refused you, Mr. Jacobs. We have only known each other a short time."

"Yes, but I had such hopes!"

"Hopes for matrimony? With me?"

"Hopes for money, from any quarter!" With tears in his eyes, he confessed, "I have debts, Mrs. Treacher."

"So do we all!"

He shook his head. "Not like mine. You don't know how hard it is to keep up appearances in London. There's the clubs and gambling—not to mention the expense of rooms and your wardrobe. Why, my valet alone takes up more than half of my money. I was jolly glad to leave London when I did; the problem had been building for months. Years, actually. And then I started being threatened with legal action. If I don't come up with some money soon it will mean jail! When my auntie—that dear old doting matchmaker—told me of your arrival, I seized on the idea . . ."

"You did not act like a man consumed with worry."

"It was a sham—I barely made it out of town. I went to the last carriage shop I could find that did not know of me and rented a conveyance so I would not have to arrive on the common stage. And when we met, I was most agreeably impressed with you. It was not only a matter of money, you are very beautiful. I may have been foolish in the extreme, but I meant no malice, I assure you."

"Your intentions were merely dishonest, Mr. Jacobs, but your actions were deplorable."

"Yes, I am so ashamed now of that day at the priory— I don't know what demon took hold of me. Desperation, I suppose. I felt I was losing your affections to the marquess, and I hoped that I could make you love me."

She was about to deny ever having affections for either him or the marquess, but she stopped herself. "Let us not speak of it. Of any of it."

"But I must, if only to beg your forgiveness. I am glad St. Just landed me a facer, I swear I am. In truth, I wish he had finished me off!"

"Really, Mr. Jacobs, there's no need for histrionics! Please lower your voice, at least."

He did, continuing, "Now I shall have to go into hiding, I suppose. Maybe I'll make for the continent. Perhaps I could find some occupation there . . ."

"Does your aunt know of your distress?"

Beneath his mask, his eyes looked panicked. "No, she must not know. She would be so disappointed in me, and I doubt that she has the means to help me."

To her surprise, Violet felt pity growing where moments before there had been only loathing. To speak so, he could not be entirely bad. There had to be a germ of honor buried in him somewhere. "You must tell her. You cannot face such distress alone."

"But shouldn't I? Haven't I made my own misery? I wish I had never been born!"

"You're beginning to worry me, Mr. Binkley. There's no need to do anything rash."

He shook his head sadly. "Do not fear—I am too much the coward to do anything truly desperate."

"Perhaps Mrs. Blatchford could help you a little, at least to get started, and then you will not be disgraced. You are young—you may yet redeem yourself."

For a moment he looked hopeful. "If I could only know that you will forgive me, that would be a small first step toward redemption."

She nodded as the music drew to a close. "Then I forgive you."

"And you will never speak of what happened?" he asked, as they bowed and curtsied politely to mimic the other couples around them. But the expression on his face showed her that it was important to him that she keep his confidence.

She nodded. "You have my word on that."

"Thank you, Mrs. Treacher! I shall always remember this."

Binkley went off then toward the punchbowl—he seemed to be very depressed still. Despite everything, Violet did feel some pity for him.

Another dance began and, distracted by thoughts of

Binkley, Violet went rather unthinkingly into the arms of yet another Brute.

"Having fun, Highness?"

Violet gasped. She stared at the man clasping her hand and sucked in her breath in shock. It was he! She froze.

He grinned at her beneath his mask. "You didn't think I would miss your big party, did ye?"

She stumbled forward again, though she doubted she was moving in time to the music. Was it a minuet? Her senses were dulled to everything but the man in front of her.

"How did you get in here?" she asked. Stupidly, she realized. For what was to stop him?

He clucked at her mockingly. "I admit to being a little hurt when you forgot to send me an invitation, Highness. But that was just an oversight, I 'spect."

As if she could just post him a proper invitation. What did he expect her to do, put a knife through one of her gilt invitations and hang it on the wall of her potting shed in the hopes that he would find it? Then she felt a horror creep through her. What if someone saw her with the Brute?

She looked around and thought how foolish she was to worry—no one would notice him at all. She had been dancing with Brutes for over half an hour. It was impossible to tell the identities of half the people present. Why, she had not yet seen Sebastian.

She gasped.

"What's wrong wi' ye?"

She looked up into his dark eyes. "You must go. Now."

"Why? I'm just beginning to enjoy myself."

Too much, it seemed to her.

"No, you must. There is a man here . . . he might be looking for you . . . you could be in danger."

He laughed gruffly. "Aye—and so might be he."

A shiver went through her as she imagined all sorts of horrors that might result from the presence of this man in her ballroom if he were discovered. *"Please,"* she entreated as the music ended. She made a show of clapping politely. "You must go."

The Brute clapped, too, and swept her a bow with all the proper form of a London dandy. "Only if you will meet me."

She searched his masked face. "Meet you where?"

"Outside. Now."

"But I am the hostess!" she said, too loudly. A few of her guests looked over.

"Aye, but you had time to sneak out for a nip, I noticed."

Her hand flew to her mouth. So much for Peabody's lemon and mint! "Please—I will do as you say. Only go."

He bent over her hand. "The terrace, then. You remember our terrace?"

Oh, Lord. As if she could ever forget!

"I will be there in five minutes. Mind you, if you do not come down, I will return and carry you bodily away— it would be quite like old times!"

"Yes, yes."

Smiling, he turned and took his leave.

Her legs quivered beneath her. Freddy came up to her. "Would you care to dance with a king for a change?"

She had to jolt herself to focus on him. "Have you seen the marquess?"

He laughed. "I take it that's a no."

Her lips trembled into a smile. "I'm sorry, Freddy. I need to talk to Sebastian." She had to make sure that under no circumstances did he appear on the terrace while she was there with the Brute. She could only imagine what would ensue if the two men met.

Freddy frowned. "I'm not sure . . . I think I just saw him leave the ballroom."

She bleated in alarm. "Good heavens! Excuse me."

She scurried out as fast as she could without causing a scene, then flew down the stairs. There was no sign of the marquess, thank heavens. She hurried out to the terrace, heart pounding.

From behind a shrub, a hand reached out and grabbed her, pulling her into the shadows with him. She found herself against that broad chest again, surrounded by the smell of liquor and tobacco and leather. Her heart sped, though she fought to loosen his grip on her.

"I am here, as promised. Now you must go."

"Oh, excuse me!" a voice announced. Violet and the Brute turned to see the figure that had just emerged onto the terrace from strolling about the grounds. It was Cuthbert.

Violet squeaked in surprise.

The sound made him come out of whatever daze he had been in. "Take no heed, I was just going in."

The Brute squeezed her arm and she bleated, "Fine!"

Cuthbert waved dismissively. "See you inside, then."

The Brute grunted.

When Cuthbert was gone, Violet collapsed against the man who was practically holding her up already. For a moment she had thought that Cuthbert would see she was with the Brute and challenge him. Ha! She should have known better. The man seemed to think nothing of seeing his hostesses manhandled.

But perhaps he did not know it was she.

Or perhaps he had become as immune to all the Brutes running around the place as she had during the course of the evening. To her woe!

"You must go!"

"Is that the man you were warning me about?"

"No—but he knows the Marquess of St. Just very well." She realized what she had done and clapped her hand over her mouth. She shouldn't have named him!

The dark eyes narrowed. "The marquess, is it?"

"He thinks you are a traitor."

"Ha!"

She searched his face. "Are you?"

"Would it matter, Highness?"

She attempted to wrench free. "Of course."

"Ah, then he's won you over."

"Who?"

"St. Just."

"That doesn't signify now."

"Then you care for him?"

It appeared he did not intend to budge until he had his answer. "Yes," she whispered. "But that does not mean I want to see you ki—" She couldn't finish the sentence. She felt so confused, and he just kept smiling at her. "Please—I don't want to know what you are. Just leave Trembledown and never return."

"Not before one last kiss."

"I will not willingly kiss a cad, a thief, and a French spy."

"No?"

"No."

"Then let me taste your lips again, Highness. You won't be compromised."

Before she could lodge another protest, his lips pressed against hers, and though she girded herself to fight him, she found herself responding to their warmth. It was a hopeless battle. The man stirred something in her blood that no one else could. No one except Sebastian.

That realization scratched at the back of her mind as she melted against that familiar chest and lifted her hands to loop around his broad shoulders. Her insides seemed to liquefy, turning her boneless in his embrace.

Violet moaned and pressed closer. He felt so familiar, and his taste was just as she remembered.

Just as she remembered from two days ago.

Her body went still.

He whispered in her ear, "Oh, Violet. Do not say you haven't longed for me as I have for you."

As if overtaken by fever, she stepped back woozily and looked into his face. Those eyes! She could see it now. They were Sebastian's eyes.

"Sebastian!"

She stood stock still, trying to make sense of it. He had tricked her! But how would Sebastian have known the Brute called her Highness?

The answer came swiftly. He would not. He could not.

"I don't understand," she said.

But just that quickly, she did. There was only one answer. In an instant she could see that Sebastian and the Brute were one and the same. It was laughably obvious now, in fact. A mask, a costume, an uneven Cornish accent. And add to that the fact that the Brute was so unlike the marquess!

All these weeks . . . from the very beginning . . .

Blood drained out of her face as images flashed through her mind. Of the Brute pulling her through the night and taking her in his arms in the cave. Of the marquess popping in his monocle and sneering at her during that first visit to Trembledown—why, he had probably barely had time to dash home and clean up before running over for a visit! And then he had kept up the charade, even beyond the afternoon at the priory, when they had made love . . .

Violet started to see spots.

"Violet!" The Brute—Sebastian—whoever the hell he was—reached forward to grab her shoulders and steady her. "Violet, speak."

When she finally did speak, it was a word that never should issue from a lady's lips. And it was accompanied by a gesture completely foreign to Violet, yet which seemed at this moment completely natural and very fitting.

A swift, sharp punch to the gut.

Chapter Seventeen

The blow took Sebastian unawares and sent him staggering backward. All things considered, he would not say that his unmasking was going well. Who would have guessed Violet was so adept at throwing punches?

"Let me guess . . . you are angry," he choked out, attempting both to recover balance and inject a little levity into the situation. At the same time, he was careful to keep a safe distance from her fists, which were now planted on her hips.

"Angry, my lord? Let us say furious! How did you expect me to react when I discovered that you had paraded around as a smuggler to make a May game of me?"

"It had nothing to do with you."

That, perhaps, was the wrong thing to say. She brayed in outrage.

"In the beginning, it had nothing to do with you," he explained more correctly. "If you would just let me—"

She lifted a hand to stop him. "I do not care to know why a nobleman dons odd getups and gallivants around the countryside kidnapping innocent women from their carriages. No doubt you think you have good reason. But then to keep up the charade! Why, from the moment you walked into this house you knew . . . and yet you pretended . . ." The words stopped, as if stuck in her throat like nettles.

"I had to."

"Ah, I see! This was all done against your will. Did you also have to send me notes? Come to my house? Did you have to follow me to the priory and then—" She shook her head. Indeed, her whole body seemed to be quaking. "Oh! You are a villain of the first rank!"

He stepped forward, causing her to take one step backward in a dance of avoidance. "Violet, surely you know that I did not mean you harm."

"I know no such thing! You are two entirely different people—and as far as I am concerned, one is just as dishonest as the other."

"I own that at first I was playing a game with you. Perhaps it went on too long. But you must admit in the beginning you were very antagonistic."

"Yes, because of the way you swaggered into Trembledown with that smirk of yours!" She released a guttural cry of frustration. "Now I know why you were smirking! No doubt you could hardly contain your mirth."

Guilt nibbled at him. What she said was true. He had behaved abominably. "I am sorry. I should have told you sooner, but I could not."

"You could have, but you chose not to! You kept up the charade. You have done nothing but trick me."

"And love you."

Far from making her melt, his words seemed to send her aquiver with anger all over again. "Do not mention that word in my presence!"

"My feelings were not false, Violet."

"But mine were—what I thought was real was not!

Could you not at least have told me the truth that day after"—she gulped—"after the priory? Why, I thought I was not worthy of you because of the night I had spent in the cave with"—her face, already red, darkened to a purple rage—"*with you!*"

He winced. "I am sorry."

"I am not," she declared, tossing back her head. "I am glad, finally, to know who you are and to realize how false you have played me from the beginning. Were you so angry that I would not sell Trembledown to you that you decided to seek revenge?"

"No." Then, remembering that the entire escapade had started out as a prank, he added, "That is, not exactly."

"You are not even very forthcoming in your confession!" She huffed out a breath. "Tell me, discounting the score of men prancing about in masks in my ballroom, does Robert the Brute exist?"

He shook his head slowly. "During the war, the government wanted to keep a sharp eye on the coast to confiscate contraband and make sure no secret information was crossing the Channel. Because it was useful to have a man on the inside, Cuthbert and I invented a smuggler named Robert the Brute and spread rumors about him to boost his reputation . . . or lower it, as the case may be. When necessary I donned his identity and accompanied the smugglers."

"And that was why you wanted Trembledown, so you could continue to monitor the coastline freely?"

"Yes," he confessed. "You see, there is more at stake than you and me."

She clasped her hands in front of her. "Oh, that *is* noble! And I suppose you donned that ridiculous getup, kidnapped me, and got me drunk in a cave for good King George?"

"You drank the brandy all on your own," he pointed out.

"And grappling with women on terraces?" she asked, ignoring his statement. "Was that for the benefit of King and country?"

He did not know what to say. He had gotten carried too far away on that occasion. If he told her that he had suspected she was a spy herself, he had no doubt that she would explode like a lit cannon.

At his silence, she huffed in scorn. "What sacrifice! Were you *ever* going to tell me the truth, Sebastian?"

"Tonight," he said. "That is why I asked you to join me out on the terrace."

She glared at him, giving him no credit for this belated urge to own up to his duplicity. "Tonight was too late." Her voice was a tired rasp. "Good night, Sebastian. And good-bye. I will not expect to see you at Trembledown anymore."

She turned and marched back in the house.

Too late. The stubborn set of her shoulders told him that it always would have been too late. Violet was too proud to stand for having someone trick her.

What had started out in fun many weeks ago now felt like a sad joke on himself. How could he have been such an ass? Events that had seemed amusing and exciting in retrospect now took on a more sinister character. And for the first time since the moment he had kidnapped her from her carriage, a question occurred to him that he should have thought of the moment before he dragged her from her carriage: How would he have felt in her shoes?

A pall had settled over Trembledown. As the servants swept away the party detritus from the previous night, a few of the more fortunate residents of the house lingered gloomily over teacups and plates of toast. Sophy was still asleep, and Aunt Augusta—who claimed a woman of her years should never be required to appear anywhere before noon—was taking a tray in her room with Lancelot.

The only reason Violet had not followed Aunt Augusta's example was that she could not bear to remain another moment in her bedchamber, where she had endured a sleepless night. In fact she had watched the dawn come up, eager for the moment when she could justify leaving her room. Unfortunately, she now found herself in the position of presiding over a table of doom.

Freddy seemed put out, but he would not say what had him so annoyed. Violet guessed it had to do with Sophy, but of course, Sophy was still slumbering blissfully upstairs.

Of the three of them, Hennie was in the worst shape by far. Poor Hennie! Apparently Mr. Cuthbert had given her a chilly indication of a permanent break. Her eyes were scarlet rimmed from crying. She moaned, sniffled, and generally did everything likely to get on Violet's nerves, including chattering on and on in the brittle tone of one who was about to shatter from the inside out.

Right now, she was nattering on about some book that Mrs. Blatchford had lent her that she now could not find. "I was going to return it to her today. I am sure that would have been a useful thing to do." *Sniff.* "But it is missing. And yet I know I had it yesterday, because—" *Sniff, sniff*! "Because I got it out to show Jo . . . Mr. Cuthbert!"

She blew her nose into her napkin.

Violet took some comfort from the fact that while she herself had been betrayed, she was not heartbroken. Not in the least. She was astute enough to know that she was well shot of a villain like Sebastian. She was angry, while Hennie was just a pitiful, wretched thing.

With a trembling hand, Hennie poured herself more tea from the cold pot, even though her cup was almost full already. "I am quite relieved, actually." The cracking of her throat belied her words. "Everything now is just as it ever was. I will just continue on as I always have, trying to be useful in whatever little ways I can."

Violet wondered, *do ants simply continue on when a big foot comes along and smashes their hill*? Because she felt like something similar had happened to her and Hennie. Two men, one bumbling and one malicious, had smashed up their lives.

Perhaps she should have heeded Hennie's entreaties and sold the house on first sight. They should have gone to Bath.

"You could go visit Imogene now," Violet suggested, thinking it might be a nice diversion for her cousin.

Instead, Hennie looked wounded. "You want to get rid of me?"

"No—of course not. I just thought you had always planned to go."

Hennie's chin quivered. "Yes! I shall enjoy visiting Imogene . . . and whoever else I can find shelter with, now that I have been turned out of Aunt Matilda's."

"You can always stay here," Violet assured her.

"Oh, you are so generous—and so kind to listen to my little troubles." Hennie hitched her throat and continued, "After all, I only knew Joh—Mr. Cuthbert—a very short while. Just a few days!"

Violet translated that sentiment to her own situation. For herself it had been mere weeks. Yet it seemed to her sometimes as if she had been here for years already. What had happened since she reached Trembledown could not be measured neatly by time alone.

"It is fortunate I have a character that is accustomed to

solitude," Hennie went on. "Or at least to facing life's slings and arrows by myself. Now, Violet, of course, *you* have been married, but I put away thoughts of marital bliss long ago. Indeed I did. I've said that many times, haven't I?"

The anguish in her voice took Violet out of her own misery. *Oh, Hen*, she wanted to shout, *please shut up*! If she didn't stop soon, Violet feared she herself was going to break down.

Hennie leaned back in her chair, looking very small. "I am a spinster. I have known that forever. I am sure there's nothing wrong with that."

"No," Freddy agreed glumly.

"No." Hennie chimed. "One might even say that as a woman of advancing years and independent means, I am . . ." Here her voice could remain steady no longer, and tears spilled down her eyes. "I am lucky!" she wailed before cutting off her words by biting into a piece of toast.

Violet sniffled along with her.

Freddy, looking from one to the other, tried to inject some cheer into the maudlin scene. "Well, Violet. Your ball came off splendidly."

Violet didn't know how to respond. *Splendidly*? Did that word have a new meaning this spring? To her, the event had seemed a disaster from beginning to end. The idea that someone could call it a success made her laugh—a sound that came out, unfortunately, as a demented cackle.

"Are you feeling quite well?" Freddy asked, leaning forward. "Perhaps we should send for a physician."

The prospect of a physician coming to examine her—maybe the very one she had danced with last night—and having to explain to him that her true malady was a disastrous evening at a masquerade ball made Violet collapse into whoops.

"Oh dear!" Freddy said. "If there is a doctor, I would be glad to ride for him."

Violet tried to contain herself. "Oh, yes. Tell him I am suffering from a terrible case of *mal de soirée*."

"What?"

Violet looked over at Hennie, who began to laugh, too.

At that moment, as Violet was convulsing and Hennie was blowing her nose, Sophy came bounding in. "Oh good—everyone is jolly! And food! I am famished."

She plopped into a chair before noticing that Hennie and Violet were laughing through tears and that Freddy was looking very, very anxious.

"What were you discussing?"

"We were just talking about the party," Violet said, still chuckling.

"And my being a hopeless spinster," Hennie added ruefully.

Violet smiled. "And me the eternal widow."

"I confess *I* had a wonderful time at the masquerade." Sophy leaned back and sighed. "Did you see him, Violet?"

"Who?"

"The dream of a man I met at the ball."

Freddy groaned.

Violet began to understand the source of his gloom. "Who was he dressed as?"

"Robert the Brute."

"How original!" Freddy sneered.

Sophy reveled in her own paradise of memory. "This one was different from all the others. He was magnificently built, and he had eyes that were a beautiful shade of green."

"Did you dance with him?" Violet sent up a silent prayer. *Please let her have danced . . . and nothing more.* With all her troubles the night before, she had paid scant attention to her little sister.

"He did not dance. He was elusive."

"What you mean is, you spent the entire evening chasing the man," Freddy said.

"I did not!"

"Every time I looked you were running after him."

"I was merely *pursuing* him," Sophy said, making a distinction significant only to her own rattled brain.

Violet frowned. "I might have seen this fellow entering the library."

"If he had a hunted expression, that was undoubtedly he," Freddy said. "A Brute of middle age, with green eyes, light hair, and medium build—not at all what *I* would call magnificent. From what I saw, he was a rather standoffish, preening fellow. The queer thing was I could have sworn I had seen him before."

"You had not," Sophy said, rolling her eyes chandelier-ward. "And as for his being standoffish and preening instead of elusive and heavenly, you are obviously trying to convince me there was something wrong with him by casting nasty slurs. You never want me to have any fun."

"I don't want you to make a scandal out of yourself like you did with that oily faux count."

Sophy's eyes flashed, and she held her head loftily. "I wasn't doing anything the least bit scandalous. My behavior was entirely unimpenetrable."

Freddy snorted. "If you mean *unimpeachable*, I saw you flirting with him outrageously behind a column."

"Snoop!" Sophy said, chucking her napkin across the table.

Freddy looked like he would lob it right back at her,

but to his credit he folded and put it back on the table. "Someone needs to look after you."

"And I suppose that someone is you?"

"You are my brother's wife's sister."

"And you are a killjoy and a damnable nuisance!"

"Sophy!" Violet chided. "Compose yourself. You should be ashamed for speaking to a guest in my house that way."

Sophy's face fell into a perplexed frown. "He's not a guest. He's Freddy."

Peabody came in from the kitchen bearing a bowl of berries for Sophy.

"Thank you, Peabody!" she said.

Now here was someone who could clear up the question of this mysterious gentleman. "Peabody," Violet asked, "did you notice a guest last night dressed as the Brute?"

Peabody looked at her as if she had taken leave of her senses.

"A specific one," she clarified.

"With heavenly green eyes," Sophy said.

"And Sophy chasing him," Freddy added.

Peabody tilted his head, and if Violet wasn't mistaken, a troubled look appeared in his eyes. "Could your inquiries possibly pertain to the man Miss Sophy was conversing with behind the pillar?"

Sophy went pink.

They must have spent a great deal of time behind that pillar!

"Oh dear." Wringing his hands, Peabody turned to Violet. "This is a subject that aggrieves me particularly, madam. I was hoping that nothing would come of the irregularity, but now I see I should have informed you earlier."

"Zounds, man!" Freddy said. "Tell us what you know."

"That particular Brute was not an invited guest," Peabody said, his tone growing irritable. "That was Mr. Quimby."

"Quimby!" Violet said, startled. "Mr. Jacobs's valet?"

"Just so," Peabody said.

"Good heavens!"

"As soon as I spied him, madam, I pulled the man aside and demanded to know why one of his station should be masquerading among the Trembledown guests. Quimby told me he had been sent to retrieve a book for Mrs. Blatchford. He said he came in costume on a lark." Peabody's sniff expressed his outrage that a member of his own professional club should so demean himself.

"Dear me, was it *A Short History of the Lands and Edifices of Cornwall*?" Hennie asked.

"I believe it was one and the same."

"I thought I had misplaced it!"

"No, ma'am. Mr. Quimby took it with him back to the cottage."

"The man must have been in his cups!" Freddy said.

Peabody looked stricken. "Such an indiscretion from one of my profession shocked me as well—especially since I have spoken of him before admiringly. He has deteriorated shockingly from the man once famed among members at the Dromio Club. The only excuse for his behavior I can produce is that too many nights at the Pied Hare have impaired his reason."

Sophy collapsed back in her chair, looking depressed. "A valet! But he was so mysterious. And those eyes!"

Freddy slapped a hand on the table, making them all jump. "Now I remember—I *have* seen him before! Quimby—yes, that was the fellow's name! He used to be the valet to the brother of my old school friend, Bertram

Humphreys." He laughed. "You know, Viscount Waring—he was renowned for his wardrobe. I thought I recognized that neckcloth—it was tied in quite an unusual way."

Peabody nodded. "Waring's Variation on the Mathematical."

"Exactly! I've tried it myself and it's deuced hard."

"It takes a skilled hand, sir."

Freddy shook his head in wonder. "Upon my word! To think that fellow last night was Quimby. Why, the Beau himself once said that no one had snowier linen than Viscount Waring, and as for boots, the viscount's couldn't be matched for their shine. The man has indeed come down in the world if he has moved from Viscount Waring to Binkley Jacobs."

Violet could only hope that Sophy hadn't been noticed fraternizing with a servant by too many people. Of course with the plethora of Brutes around last night, how was one to know it was an unsuitable Brute?

Again her conscious smote her. She had some nerve worrying about Sophy when her own behavior hadn't been anything to brag about.

When Peabody retreated, Sophy's good humor was completely gone, and the rest of the table sank back into muted gloom.

"But if he weren't a valet," Sophy lamented, "I think he would have made quite a dashing gentleman."

Hennie let out a ragged breath. "I am so sorry for you, Sophy. It is fortunate in many ways that I am so accustomed to disappointment."

"Oh, Hennie," Violet said on an exhale. She had meant to offer some sort of solace, but before she could utter another word, the door from the hallway burst open and John Cuthbert rushed in, breathless.

The man looked a fright. His clothes were wrinkled,

his hair uncombed. His bloodshot eyes provided evidence that he had not slept a wink since Violet had last seen him leaving the terrace.

"I am a damnable fool!" he announced to one and all.

As a greeting, it lacked élan, but he certainly had everyone's attention. Violet glanced around her. Freddy was sitting ramrod straight, and Sophy's eyes were wide as saucers. Naturally Hennie was the most stunned of all. As soon as she recovered from the sight of the man whose rejection of her she had been mourning for twelve straight hours, she jumped out of her chair, nearly overturning the entire breakfast table in the bargain.

"No!" Cuthbert cried out. "Do not run away, Miss Halsop, I beg you!"

Henrietta went still except for her trembling hands, which she sought to steady by placing them on the table. (And, Violet noticed, in the butter dish.)

Cuthbert rushed around to clasp those trembling greased hands in his. "Oh, Miss Halsop, forgive me for my boorish behavior last night! I was just too overwhelmed. You were so lovely! Costumed as Athena you may have been, but you were Diana to me. You have shot an arrow through my heart. I am captured, felled!" The man collapsed to his knees with an audible crack that brought sympathetic gasps from the others. "I am yours, dearest lady, if you will do me the greatest honor of agreeing to be my wife!"

The trembling in Hennie's hands spread to her entire body. Fat tears wobbled in her eyes, and for an agonizing moment Violet feared that she would not be able to find her voice to answer the poor man. But finally she was able to blurt out, "Oh yes! Oh yes!" Tears burst forth from her eyes along with the exclamation. "Oh, John!"

The man sprang to his feet and enfolded her in his arms. "Oh, Henrietta!"

"Dearest, dearest John!"

"My Hen, my dove, my sweet little partridge!"

Their lips came together in an exuberant kiss.

A lump settled in Violet's throat as she, Sophy, and Freddy all marveled at the reunion. They smiled furtively at each other and waited for the opportunity to congratulate the happy pair.

And waited.

The kiss did not end, and after a few moments it became rather obvious that they should leave the couple alone. Sophy and Freddy fled for the nearest door—the kitchen— while Violet quickly sneaked out the door to the hallway that Cuthbert had burst through only moments before.

It was hard not to be swept away in the emotion of the two lovers, despite the shock of hearing Cuthbert calling Hennie his partridge. Incredible!

But at least *someone* was having a happy ending.

Violet tried not to acknowledge the pang of frustration she felt. To think that she should be jealous of Hennie! Poor cousin Hennie, who had always been so hopeless. And of course, Violet was not jealous. Not really. She wanted Hennie to be happy, and she certainly did not covet Mr. Cuthbert.

But would she ever have a man love her so thoroughly, so exuberantly, that he would forget to comb his hair in the morning?

Still unable to face going up to her room—the chamber of sleepless torment—she turned into the salon. At least there would be a cat there to keep her company.

Instead of finding the feline Sebastian in the salon, however, she discovered the real Sebastian warming himself before the small fire lit there each day against the morning chill.

For a second he looked as startled as she was. "I did not expect to see you!" he exclaimed.

At that bizarre statement, she crossed her arms. "This is my house, is it not?"

"Yes, and I know I have been banished, but . . ." He raked his hands through his hair (which had been quite neatly combed, she could not help noticing). "I came with Cuthbert."

"We have seen Mr. Cuthbert."

Sebastian's dark eyes lit with interest. "Then he was successful."

"Quite. I believe he has won his little partridge."

Sebastian looked satisfied. "I am glad. I brought him—that is why I am here. He was in too much of a hurry to walk over this morning, and since he has never driven I was afraid he might run himself off a cliff before Miss Halsop could make him a happy man."

"I hope they will have a good life together."

"He is the best of men."

She felt compelled to testify to her cousin's superior character. "Hennie is like no other."

"Of course."

Their gazes locked. In her mind—her traitorous mind—Violet relived the moment just before he had taken her into his arms to make love to her. His eyes today had that same intensity, that same heat.

Blushing, she looked away.

"Well!" he said. "I am sorry to disturb you. I was told you were breakfasting."

"I was. Breakfast was interrupted for love."

"Ah."

She waited for him to make his excuses and go. Surely

that would have been the gentlemanly thing to do, since she had made it clear last night that she desired no further contact between them.

But he remained firmly, stubbornly planted in front of her fire. Violet supposed it was up to her to make an exit.

"Well . . . as you might guess, my lord, there is quite a bit to do here today. If you will excuse me . . ."

He stopped her before she could leave the room.

"Wait!"

She turned, and he was standing before her, having crossed the room in a few swift strides. He reached for her hand. "Violet! I am a fool!"

She laughed.

"What is so funny?" he asked, a hint of anger in his tone.

"That is how Cuthbert announced himself. Don't tell me you intend to propose, too!"

"And if I did?"

Her mouth clamped shut. "You can't be serious?"

He lifted both her hands, bringing her closer. "Can't I? Violet, if you would do me the honor—"

"*Oh*!"

Surprised by the exclamation, they both turned to see Freddy and Sophy standing behind them in the open doorway. Their eyes were wide, as if they could not quite comprehend being witness to two proposals of marriage in such a short span of time.

"Excuse us!" Freddy said, dragging a reluctant Sophy away.

Violet turned back to Sebastian in a fury. "Now look what you have done! Tongues will be wagging about this."

"Let them," Sebastian said. "Do not say you will refuse me. You cannot. It is a matter of honor."

She could hardly believe her ears. "Honor?"

"Of course. Have you forgotten?" he asked. "That day in the copse . . . There might be consequences."

Consequences.

He spoke nothing of his affection of her. Nothing of love.

Even Mr. Cuthbert had managed to do that!

She jerked her hands back, spitting with anger. "Is that what has you in such an uproar? You would marry me because I might be . . ." She gulped back a lump in her throat. "With child?"

His cheeks mottled with red. "I was trying to appeal to your good sense. Do not let our misunderstandings of the past jeopardize the future. You are a practical woman, Violet."

"Oh, I am!" she said, almost laughing. *Misunderstandings?* Is that what he was now calling the vicious farce he had been playing? "I am so practical, my lord, that I see no reason for a hasty wedding until we are absolutely sure a bouncing baby marquess is on the way. Indeed I don't." She grabbed Sebastian by the arm and started dragging him toward the door. "So just go back home, sit tight, and I will let you know if you should post the banns or not. You might have a bit of luck and be able to avoid matrimony altogether."

He planted his feet before she could push him out the door. His expression was almost angry. "You know that is not what I meant."

"What did you mean?"

"I want you to be my wife."

"But I do not want to be your wife. I intend to sell this house—perhaps even to yourself!—and then leave Cornwall forever. It has bitter memories for me."

"Bitter, because you feel I deceived you. If you would just let me explain."

She let out a ragged sigh. "You have explained, Sebastian. Your deceit was entirely honorable—you were thinking of England only. That is a stretch, though I suppose I have to take you at your very wobbly word. But what you have not explained to my satisfaction is why the game went on and on. Why could you never take me into your confidence?"

He cleared his throat. "I had a very good reason to want to speak to you in the guise of the Brute."

She tapped her fingers impatiently. "Which was?"

His eyes beseeched her. "What good does it do to go over this now? It is past us."

"Sebastian, just *tell me*."

"All right," he said reluctantly. Taking a breath, he announced, "I feared you were a spy."

Her body went still. She had to sift through that sentence three times before she could believe that she had actually heard him correctly. "A *spy*?"

Had he gone mad?

He lifted his hands. "It was just the timing of your arrival, you see—"

She cut him off with a shout of outrage. "Enough! I cannot believe you have the audacity to come here and accuse me—"

"I am not accusing you," he corrected quickly. "Naturally I do not think you are a spy *now*. I never would have proposed matrimony in that case. Isn't that proof that I have trust in you?"

"Am I to be relieved that you have exonerated me of something that I was never guilty of to begin with? That I never even guessed you suspected me of?"

He stepped forward. "Please, Violet. Trust me when I tell you that I had motives which I cannot fully explain."

"I *will not* trust you. I have no reason on earth to. You toss the word *trust* about like a child with a new ball."

He bowed his head. "If I only knew the words that would make you forgive me. But I do not."

"I do not know them, either," she replied. "I only know that they must be spoken with sincerity. I am not unforgiving, my lord. Why, I even forgave Binkley Jacobs."

Sebastian's head snapped up. "Jacobs sought you out? When?"

"He was at the ball last night." She added, "He was a Brute, too—at least he was dressed as one. His behavior was quite exemplary on this occasion."

"And he spoke to you?"

She did not like the avid look in his eye. "Of course. He said he was sorry. The man is a bit under the hatches and got carried away with fear of being sent to debtor's prison. That's why he was so desperate to marry me—it was just my money."

"Is that all?"

"Is that *all*?" A brittle laugh escaped her lips. "Isn't it enough that in one evening one man confessed he only wanted me for my fortune and another confessed he had been lying to me about his very identity? I call that a very notable amount of information to absorb. It was certainly sufficient for me."

"Violet, this is serious. Tell me what he said."

"The details of my conversation with Binkley are none of your affair."

"They may be, actually," he said.

"Why?"

Sebastian hesitated only momentarily. "Binkley Jacobs might very well be a spy."

This was inconceivable! "*I* am a spy, Binkley is a spy . . . Is there anyone in Widgelyn Cross you do *not* suspect? The vicar, perhaps?"

His cheeks reddened in such an incriminating fashion that Violet let out a bitter laugh. "Oh no! What, do you think Mr. Cheswyn is smuggling messages to Napoleon about the lamentable state of Britain's walking boots?"

His teeth were clenched so hard a muscle along his jaw popped. "If Jacobs said anything that might make you feel he would do something desperate again, you should tell me."

Binkley had seemed distraught, but not in the way that would make Violet think he would turn traitor. His thoughts had all seemed centered on avoiding bringing shame to his aunt. Violet had more of a sense that he might do himself some harm. And in any case, she had given Binkley her word that she would not speak of it.

"Do not worry, my lord. There will be no more trouble from that quarter. Perhaps you should follow your other hunch and waste no time getting over to the vicarage before Mr. Cheswyn brings catastrophe raining down on us all."

Sebastian shook his head but seemed ready at last to make a strategic retreat. At least temporarily.

"Good-bye, my lord."

He touched her hand, and then drew it up to her lips. "If you are ever in trouble . . ."

She covered a shiver of desire with a laugh and withdrew her hand. "Oh! Do you have other disguises, my lord? Do you occasionally appear as a knight in shining armor?"

He shook his head. "This is not the end of this, Violet. I will see you again," he said, and then he reached for his hat from the table and strode away.

When he left, Violet's legs went weak beneath her. It was a moment before she could recover. *Good heavens!* He had proposed. A marquess. The man who had occupied so many of her thoughts and dreams, so much of her heart.

And yet . . . what a proposal! Spoken with all the dread and reluctance of the condemned on his way to meet the hangman. Could she have done anything but refuse?

Sophy bounded into the room and whirled her around twice. "Oh, Violet! What heaven! I am so happy for you!"

"Why?"

"Because I am sure you will be so very happy! It is what you always wanted, and Sebastian is simply top of the trees!"

"If you are referring the Marquess of St. Just's very obliging offer, you may save your felicitations. We are not to be married."

Sophy went still, and her joyous expression collapsed. "You're not? But he was proposing."

"And I refused him."

Sophy gaped at her, dumbfounded. "B-but . . ."

Violet raised her hands. "Please Sophy, I cannot explain it all now. I—"

Words failed her, and she turned and hurried upstairs to her room.

"Congratulations, my lord!"

Sebastian met Freddy as he was heading for his horse. He had meant to wait for Cuthbert, but that man obviously was detained. Really, Sebastian supposed, he shouldn't have even come. That excuse about needing to save Cuthbert from driving off a cliff had been a sham. Probably it wouldn't have fooled even Cuthbert, if Cuthbert had given it a thought. That man had had other things on his mind this morning, obviously.

So had Sebastian. He was thinking too much about Violet instead of more important matters. At breakfast he had received a message from Jem that the faux Robert the Brute, as it were, was anxious to make a run soon. Now was not the time to be distracted by matters of the heart.

He shook his head. And he had not even noticed Binkley at the ball last night, even after he had spent a good deal of time trying to discern the identities of the Brute-masked guests. No doubt about it, he was slipping.

"There is no reason to congratulate me, Freddy," he said.

The young man's jubilant expression crumpled into a puzzled frown. "But I thought—"

"There is no reason to congratulate me," Sebastian repeated.

Understanding dawned. "Oh! I see . . . that is, I don't see . . ." Freddy struggled to say something comforting, or at least something not likely to cause offense. But in the end he could only exclaim, "Blast women!"

Sebastian managed a congenial chuckle. "Are you having problems along those lines yourself, at your age?"

"Me propose to a lady? I should say not—I'll be hanged if I'm *that* foolish." He winced as he realized how that statement might be taken. "Not that there is anything wrong in a proposal . . . to the right woman . . ."

" 'Right' is a difficult qualifier."

Freddy chortled. "Indeed! And the right woman for me is definitely not one who flirts with valets!"

That last statement could not help but capture Sebastian's

attention. The only person resembling a valet at Tremble-down was Peabody, and Sebastian could not imagine him being the subject of any young lady's fancy. "Who are you speaking of?"

Freddy stubbed his toe on the gravel. "Sophy! She flirted with that Binkley Jacobs's valet last night. A chap named Quimby."

That was odd and rather interesting. "Mr. Jacobs's valet attended the masquerade ball?"

"Peabody said Jacobs sent Quimby there to fetch a book or something," Freddy explained, looking preoccupied. "I must say, though, I still can't believe this man Quimby can be the same valet I was thinking of. You remember Viscount Waring's man? I mean, think of the viscount's appearance, and then consider this Jacobs character and his scorchy collars. He couldn't possibly be the product of the same valet who put such a shine on Waring's boots that had all the young bucks trying champagne and all sorts of outlandish things to imitate it."

"When you put it like that," Sebastian said, eyeing Freddy with interest, "it is a bit of a puzzle."

"Not to mention, a valet like Quimby would be more expensive to keep than an actress. I never heard that Jacobs was that plump in the pocket. Of course, after Viscount Waring put a pistol through himself, Quimby still had to make a living, but there are plenty of peers he could have worked for. Why accept a comedown like Jacobs?"

"I suppose the aunt could be paying him," Sebastian speculated.

"Perhaps." Freddy looked skeptical—in his experience aunts didn't come over with the goods for personal servants—but then he continued. "I was dancing with the vicar's sister last night, who was saying that Mrs. Blatchford is planning on making for the continent now that the war is over. It seems to be everyone's opinion that Binkley will be acting as her escort."

Sebastian looked with new respect at Freddy. "You seem to be remarkably up on the local gossip for having arrived so recently."

Freddy looked uncertain as to whether this comment was a criticism or not. "Well, one must talk about something when dancing and such at these affairs. You know how women like to dissect other people's lives. And of course, Binkley's devotion to his aunt is unusual. One would have thought he would prefer to be in London this time of the year, so people are interested. Something a bit havey-cavey about the whole crew of them at the Blatchfords', I think."

Sebastian shook his head. Freddy's gossip from last night filled in the last pieces of the puzzle and confirmed his and Cuthbert's latest conclusion regarding Nero's identity—they were fools not to have seen it at once! "I must go now." He tipped his hat curtly, in a hurry now to be off. "Good day to you. Tell Cuthbert I had to leave, but I will see him again this evening as we planned." He frowned. "And could you pass along another message?"

"Of course!"

"Tell him to remember that if I run into trouble, I'll send up the orange flag."

A look of curiosity passed across Freddy's face. "Orange flag?"

"It's a bit of cant between Cuthbert and me."

"Oh, I see!" Freddy smiled and nodded. "Yes of course, I'll tell him. Good day to you."

"Good-bye!"

Sebastian mounted his horse and galloped off in haste for Montraffer.

* * *

That afternoon the walls of Trembledown seemed to close in on Violet. She did not want to speak to anyone, and the thought of sitting down to a late luncheon of savory pie held no appeal for her. Quietly, so that her departure would not be noticed, she hurried out of the house and started walking at breakneck speed. For a short stretch, she even ran, and she had not run since she was ten. (Until the night she was captured by the Brute, that is, she thought darkly.)

But how good it felt! She wanted to keep going until she had left everything behind.

She continued on for quite some time, mulling over the past twenty-four hours. It was horrible to admit, but a part of her felt bereft. In the space of one day, she had lost not only Sebastian through his lying, but she had lost someone else, too. The Brute was gone. He had only been a figment of her dreams, after all. A character someone was playing—and she had fallen for the impersonation like a girl developing a crush on an actor in a play. She felt foolish, but she also felt sad. Her illicit love affair with a smuggler had made her feel more alive to the possibilities of romance than her cold marriage to Percy ever had. It had made her feel human.

She crested a hill and stopped to look down at the sea as she had done so often when she had wondered if she would ever catch a glimpse of the Brute or his boat. It was silly to remember that now. Still, she would miss this view when she left Trembledown. She would have to—

Violet's thoughts slammed to a halt as she saw a figure hurrying along below. She couldn't believe her eyes. It was Sebastian!

Or, rather, it was the Brute.

She pursed her lips and kept walking to bring him closer in view. What was he up to now? He scuttled uneasily across the uneven terrain, looking around him several times to see if he was followed. Violet ducked so he would not spot her, though she had half a mind to march down the hill and give him a piece of her mind. Some people did not know when to quit.

But just as she was considering busting in on Sebastian's afternoon pranks, something about the Brute's appearance jarred her. From this distance, the mask looked right, as did the long coat and large holstered pistol at his waist. But the man was wearing a bright red vest that struck a chord in her memory. Binkley had worn such a vest at the ball.

She frowned as she watched him reach the seashore and hurry toward the caves. Why would the Brute—even a fictitious one—go to a cave during the daytime? Smugglers did not operate until dark. Even she knew that.

Her lips parted as the answer occurred to her.

Binkley should not be left alone in a cave with a pistol. His mental state was too fragile. Perhaps he had been unable to tell his aunt of his predicament and was going to the cave to do violence against himself.

She hesitated only a moment before scrambling down the hill. At this point, the incline was sharp, and in her hurry she slipped and skidded as much as walked. Her heart pounded; her only thought was that she needed to hurry or all her efforts would be in vain.

She rushed to the mouth of the cave where she had seen Binkley disappear. There was no light as she stepped inside. "Mr. Jacobs?"

She called his name several more times as she began to creep along inside the cave. Each repetition sounded a little more desperate.

In reply, there was only sound of wind whispering through the dark tunnel, until a large hand caught her arm.

Violet tried to cry out, but another hand clamped down on her mouth, muting her scream.

Chapter Eighteen

The second after the hand let go of her arm, a pistol poked her in the ribs. His other hand released her mouth, but her captor crooked his arm about her neck in a punishing, choking hold. She could not see his face; she could only feel his hot breath on her neck.

"What are you doing here?" he growled at her.

This was definitely not Binkley.

She shook her head and felt beads of sweat fly off her forehead. She had never been so scared.

"Speak!" he bellowed. He squeezed her neck so tightly her knees began to buckle. She struggled frantically but could not free herself. It was as if she were being clamped in a vise.

"You were calling for Mr. Jacobs. Why?"

Her mind whirred. She had been calling for Binkley because she thought *he* was Binkley and that she was going to save him. She was going to be a savior, rescuing Binkley Jacobs from a moment of manic despair. So much for her one stab at heroism!

The pistol jabbing into her side spurred her to reply. "I thought you were someone else!"

He cursed at her. "Why were you following me?"

"I wasn't! I only saw you by chance, I swear it."

He laughed snidely and mimicked her. "Like hell!"

"It's true! I don't know what you are doing here—and why should I care? If you would just let me go, I won't tell anyone I saw you. I swear it!"

"Too right, you won't tell!" he growled back. "Come on, then!"

He shoved her ahead of him so hard that she stumbled almost out of his grasp and then was yanked back so hard he nearly pulled her arm out of its socket. She could not see her feet, but he prodded her onward and then wrenched her to the right. From behind she heard him strike a match against his bootheel and bend to light a candle.

The bare flame lit a small chamber that was not unlike the one where she had spent the night with the Brute. The real Brute. But this little room was entirely bare except for a filled canvas bag in the corner. There would be no blanket, no brandy. No Sebastian.

Oh God, she thought, her mind growing hysterical from tension. This man could kill her and leave her here. She wouldn't be found for weeks—if ever. This cave might be her tomb.

He threw her to the ground, and she cried out as the stone floor scraped her hands as she tried to catch herself. On her hands and knees, she felt miserable, helpless. She tried to breathe evenly to hold back tears.

She wanted to run, but where? Her captor was blocking the entrance. Also, there was still the matter of the pistol trained on her.

Gathering her courage, she looked up into her captor's face. His leather mask covered his eyes and nose, but there was something about that mouth. It had a cruel slant to it.

She had the disturbing feeling that she had seen this man before. "Who are you?" she asked.

He laughed. "My dear lady, you wound me. Do you not recognize Robert the Brute? I believe we share a previous acquaintance!"

She almost retorted that she knew there was no such person, and even if there were he wouldn't wear a bright red vest or speak in a cultured voice, but she stopped herself. Should she let on that she knew he was a fraud? She had been kidnapped once before—but that had been a sham. A game Sebastian had been playing with her. This man's demeanor was very different, and truly threatening. She feared he would kill her if she made a wrong move or said the wrong word.

He might just kill her anyway.

"Don't worry, Mrs. Treacher—we shan't stay here long."

He knew *her* name. So she had seen him before . . . *where*?

"We have a long trip ahead of us," he said, moving to bring the candle closer to him. "We are just waiting for our transportation."

Trip? That word panicked her. Where did he intend to take her?

Her panic was transparent. A grin spread across her captor's face—the smile of a man who enjoyed seeing panic in those over whom he held power. Violet shivered. It was the demented grin of a boy pulling wings off butterflies. "Do not look so frightened. Don't all women long to travel to France? Mrs. B. could never stop yapping about it, God knows!"

Mrs. Blatchford? How did he know Mrs. Blatchford?

She studied his face more closely. The eyes—she could barely see them in the dim light, through that mask. But they were undoubtedly green. Strikingly green. All the pieces fell into place. *The green eyes Sophy found so heavenly*! Violet certainly didn't find them so.

But he had to be Quimby—who else would have access to Binkley's red vest and have heard Mrs. Blatchford talking about France often, or have such a neatly tied cravat? More important, what was he doing here? Her mind raced frantically to remember what Peabody and the others had been saying about Quimby this morning, but she had been so distracted. Maybe his appearance at the ball had something to do with what he was doing now . . . or maybe he was simply a madman.

As if to confirm that last guess, a look of murderous disgust filled those green eyes. "Stop it! You'll get crow's feet squinting at a person like that!"

She gulped. Such a personal comment had to be the remark of a valet whose mind had run amok. Yes, undoubtedly Quimby.

Why would Quimby want to take her to France? She glanced furtively at the bundle in the corner, and memories of party guests gabbing about Napoleon and Sebastian seeing spies everywhere filled her head. Sebastian had seemed to think Binkley was a spy—his last words to her were a warning about him. But apparently he was wrong; it was Binkley's servant and not Binkley himself who was the danger.

She did not see how she would get out of this coil. She had no weapon, no leverage with the man at all unless she could get his sympathy. She cleared her throat and forced a pleasant and, she hoped, earnest expression. "You may leave me here. You have nothing to fear from me."

"Fear you!" He cackled. "I assure you, I do not."

"Then why risk taking me?"

"Because if I leave you, you might be found before it's convenient."

It seemed from his responses that she might actually be able to appeal to the man's reason. She sat up straighter. "But even if I am found, I won't say anything."

"No, you won't," he agreed flatly, "not when you're lying at the bottom of the Channel."

Her heart sank, but she could not give up. "But why have useless murder on your hands? I could not identify you. I don't know who you are!"

He sneered at her. "Lying wench!"

"I swear I don't!"

"I saw it in your eyes just minutes ago," he snapped. "You know, Mrs. Treacher. You know, and if you don't stop trying to play me for a fool I will put a hole through your head right now and bedamned the consequences."

That was one way to get an honest answer. "All right, yes. I do know you, Mr. Quimby, but only by reputation. My man Peabody speaks so highly of you."

Mentioning Peabody garnered her nothing but rolled eyes. "Dear God! How many gallons of wretched porter did I have to pour down that pompous jackanapes's gullet before I got a scrap of information about a book Mrs. B. loaned your cousin!"

Violet bridled for Peabody's sake. "Just because he shows a little discretion . . ."

Quimby roared with laughter. "Discretion! That's a laugh. I had to listen to every romantic escapade you have ever been involved in, madam, including a windy digression on the odds of your marrying the illustrious Marquess of St. Just." He snorted in derision. "A man who still wears buttons the size of goose eggs on his morning coat!"

Just the mention of Sebastian made her feel depressed.

She had ribbed him shamelessly about his suspicion of spies. If only she could turn back time . . .

No wonder Sebastian had been so suspicious of Binkley; he must have had reason to suspect him of the theft of government documents. Binkley was a minor clerk with the government. She wondered if Sebastian had ever considered Binkley's valet. Binkley had no doubt given the man access to government documents, and also had family on the coast.

But why was Quimby now disguised as the Brute?

Curiosity overcame fear. "Are you really Robert the Brute?" she asked him, putting a tremble in her voice that was actually very easy to feign.

One of Quimby's brows darted up. "Don't you know?"

"When I was kidnapped, everything happened so fast, and it was so dark." She lifted her hands in helpless confusion. "I cannot be sure!"

"No one can be sure!" He sneered. "Therein lies the beauty of the Brute—the man's terrified everyone, but no one knows him. Try to hire a boat to France, these swinish brigands will rob you blind and might just kill you for their trouble." His even white teeth broke into a self-satisfied smile at his own cleverness. "Ah, but say you're the Brute—the price goes down! The Brute makes even criminals shiver in their boots!"

"Then you took a chance," she said.

"A small gamble, perhaps, but it was worth the risk not to be bilked by smugglers who can smell desperation."

Perhaps Sebastian's imitation of an elusive cutthroat had put too much emphasis on elusive, she thought ruefully. Now a real villain was able to assume the Brute's identity because only she knew he was counterfeit.

"What is this?" she asked, nodding to a bag in the corner of the cave.

"Just all my worldly goods. Besides a wardrobe that Brummel would not turn his nose up at, there is in that bag a tidy amount of uncut diamonds. I had the foresight to liquidate my assets before leaving London into something portable and easily traded in other countries."

"Including the jewelry you stole from Mrs. Blatchford?"

"Stole?"

She arched her brows at him. "Well, didn't you?"

His eyes flashed with fury. "Miss High-and-Mighty! You think you are so deserving of all the good things you have. Do you know what it is like to slave for fools, for men of means but no taste who don't even know the proper angle to wear their own hats?" He lifted his head haughtily. "I do not steal. Your friend Mr. Jacobs owed me money, and sensing I would not be receiving it before I had to leave, I took what was owed me!"

"Am I to be impressed that you are no thief when you have vowed to murder me?"

His lips curled into an ugly sneer. "Perhaps if you are very good, I might leave you for the smugglers. A very agreeable pack of men, I assure you. I'm sure they would know how to treat a lady."

Oh God. Violet's stomach churned. She decided it might be best to cease conversation. The longer they spoke, the angrier she seemed to make him. Instead of winning him over, she seemed to have only made him imagine grislier ways of getting rid of her.

She slumped against the wall, dank though it was. Quimby, she noted, kept his back perfectly straight at all times. The only agitation he showed was in the constant nervous tapping of his perfectly polished boots.

After what might have been an hour or maybe more, a whistle reached them from somewhere outside the cave.

Quimby jumped up and dusted himself off. "Come!" he said, pulling her to her feet roughly. "It's time!"

He tossed the canvas bag to her, and she sagged beneath its weight. "You may have the honor of holding the treasure."

"Thank you so much!" she bit out sarcastically.

"And remember, there is a pistol trained on your back." With his other hand, he picked up the candle.

"I will try not to forget," she said.

He answered her with a well-polished boot in the small of her back. She stumbled toward the opening they had come in earlier.

"One foot in front of the other!" her captor growled, poking her in the shoulder blades with the pistol.

She minced a few steps before catching her footing again. The uneven stone beneath her feet was not easy to maneuver with the load she was carrying. She had to brace her free hand occasionally against the slimy walls to keep from falling.

After a moment, though, she realized she had a weapon at her disposal—and that weapon was surprise. Quimby was counting on the fact that he was armed to keep her from swinging his bag at him. That and the fact that she was afraid of him, as indeed she was. But there was one certainty that frightened her even more: if he got her on a smuggler's boat with him, she would be a dead woman. She would just as soon die by the gunshot as drowning in the deep.

Though of course, she would prefer not to die at all.

She did not wait. As soon as they reached a bend in the tunnel, she took a quick step ahead, rounded on Quimby, and smashed him against his face with the bag of loot.

Quimby reeled back and let loose a string of curses when he hit the wall. Violet sprang forward to grab the gun, but in that instant, the candle, which had fallen out of his hand, went out, plunging them into darkness. She grasped her hand out, hoping that it would make contact with the pistol.

Instead, Quimby's hand made contact with her arm. He wrestled it behind her, causing her to cry out in pain.

"I ought to kill you right here!"

He smashed her against the wall; she heard a crack as her skull hit jagged rock. Her legs collapsed beneath her, and for a moment he released her. But she was too rattled, too much in agony, to take advantage of the opportunity. In the time it took Quimby to feel about the ground for the bag and return it to her, she had barely been able to catch her breath and get back on her feet.

"Stupid woman!" he snarled, pushing her forward again. "I've ripped my coat!"

It was dark, but as she staggered along, she was seeing stars. Her head throbbed, her shoulder felt sore, and her heart pounded its dread with each heavy footfall as they came closer and closer to the mouth of the cave.

And then, suddenly, they were outside. The sun had almost disappeared since she had entered the cave. There was only the barest of light to see by.

A grizzled little fellow appeared before them. His eyes widened in surprise when he saw Violet. It did not appear to escape the ruffian's notice that Quimby had a pistol trained on her.

"You said naught 'bout a woman comin'," he protested to Quimby.

"I didn't know myself," he answered testily. "Where is this boat?"

The other man obviously decided not to argue with a gun. "'Round the rock here. Cap'n won't like carryin' a woman, sir."

"Confound him, then!"

The three of them had to scramble across stones and clamber over a large boulder jutting out into the water to get to the boat. The smuggler went first, followed by Violet, followed by Quimby and his gun.

The boat tied by the rock was a small ketch such as Sebastian and Violet had seen after their tryst. It bobbed so low in the water already with the crew on board that it seemed impossible any more people (not to mention Binkley's bag of goods) would be able to fit on it.

This was it, Violet thought dully. She tossed one last look up the cliff, in the direction of Trembledown. Just over that hill. It made her heart sore to think of all that had passed since she had arrived here.

Oh, Sebastian, she thought.

Quimby pushed her. "Climb in!"

Not seeing any alternative, she began to do as commanded.

"What's that?" a gruff voice sneered.

Violet's head snapped up. That voice! The man who had spoken was a man with a tobacco-stained beard overseeing the others. Clearly he was the captain of this motley crew. His black hat was nearly Napoleonic in fashion, but his coat and breeches were patched. He stood arms akimbo, at the stern. He looked thoroughly disreputable . . . and unfamiliar. She wavered in confusion. She could have sworn that voice was familiar.

Or was she merely slaphappy from Quimby's blow in the cave?

And yet, the longer she studied his face—those eyes!—the more convinced she was that she was right.

Sebastian!

Her heart leapt. He *did* have another disguise up his sleeve—and though it was not a knight in shining armor, at this moment she was just as happy to see him in his current guise of a grizzled smuggler captain.

"No woman!" he bellowed at Quimby.

Quimby glared back at him, all the while keeping the pistol trained on Violet. "She goes, Captain, or you get no diamonds."

The captain spat. "I'll take no women across the Channel— women be bad luck. This ain't a ferryboat, ye know!"

"Take her halfway, then, and toss her overboard for all I care."

The captain laughed evilly and looked away from her. Violet felt her brow knit in confusion. What was going on? If the captain was Sebastian—and she was sure he was—why did he not seize Quimby now?

"Well, if you're only going to feed her to the sharks, lad, welcome aboard!"

Several of the other men laughed with him.

"Maybe we can all have a little sport with her afore we toss her in the drink," the captain announced to his ragtag audience.

Violet's mouth dropped open as several of the captain's men howled enthusiastically and tugged her aboard by her armpits. She knew that Sebastian had to play along with Quimby, but that was getting rather too much in character for her taste.

"You traitors! You barbarians!" she screamed, feeling that some protest would be expected from her.

The men around her whooped with glee.

She folded her arms and sank to a crate to appear humiliated and depressed—conditions that required little pretending on her part. She had expected Sebastian to give her some sign that this was all an act. To meet her gaze and let her know that he saw the gash on her head, that everything would be all right. But he did not spare her another glance. Instead, he busied himself raising a small sail topped by an orange flag.

"Shove off!" Sebastian roared.

Men shoved the boat away from the rocks and then manned the oars as waves crashed over them and the bags piled high on the boat. The small vessel hit a wave and Violet was afraid she was going to be ill. They were bound for France?

She hadn't thought they would actually put out to sea! What was going on here?

"Do you have to fly that orange flag?" Quimby complained. "It's not only hideous, it's conspicuous."

"'S the flag of the *Highness*," Sebastian spat back. "If'n ye don't like it, ye can swim!"

The *Highness*? At last, a romantic gesture! Considering the condition of this tub, however, she didn't feel very choked up with emotion.

Boots strode to where she sat, setting her teeth on edge. They stopped, and she looked up into those familiar dark eyes. "Well, lass, can you swim?"

Was he mad? Surely he wasn't going to carry his charade so far as to throw her overboard at Quimby's bidding! Was she about to become one of those sacrifices that must be made now and again for king and country?

"I can," she said. And then to show Quimby that she wasn't beaten, she continued through gritted teeth, "And if I am able, I will swim back to England to see you hanged."

Sebastian threw his head back and laughed. Then, to her horror, he drew a pistol from his belt and cocked it. He yanked her to her feet, though she could only stand unsteadily against the motion of the boat. She fell against him. Then he lifted his pistol into the air and fired.

Violet closed her eyes against the noise. When she squeezed them open again, she wouldn't have been surprised to find the barrel of the gun in her face. But instead, an even more startling sight met her eyes.

Soldiers! The rocky beach was suddenly swarming with them. And from around a haystack rock jutting just off the shore, another boat appeared, as heavy with beautiful strapping soldiers as even Sophy could have wished for.

On the small vessel, Quimby realized a trap had been laid and let out a string of curses. Pandemonium broke loose. With Violet out of his reach, he collared the smuggler who had led them to the ship and held a pistol to his head.

The boat rocked furiously as men rushed Quimby, who ran with his hostage to the other side of the craft. A few panicked smugglers jumped ship just from instinct at seeing government men headed toward them. Quimby fired his pistol.

Violet suddenly found herself being encircled by a length of rope. Sebastian leaned in to her. "Stay close to the ship!" he whispered.

She blinked at him in confusion. Where else did he expect her to go?

Before she could voice a retort, she found out. He grabbed her up in his arms and unceremoniously tossed her overboard, plunging her into the deep. The cold, salty water was a shock, and for a moment she could do little more than sink like a stone until the line of rope about her waist jerked her up short. Then her protesting lungs made her fight her way toward the surface.

Violet came back up sputtering and choking and shivering with cold. Her skirts dragged at her, and it took her several attempts for her numb hands to grab a hook on the side of the boat. The vessel still swayed madly from the movements of the men on deck struggling. Meanwhile, gunfire roared above her head, which she kept down as low as she could, getting occasional facefuls of water in the process.

She could hear the sound of fighting above her and could only pray that Sebastian would win the day. Then again, there did not seem to be too much doubt that he would. Boats full of soldiers now were rowing toward them, picking up waterlogged smugglers from the sea as they progressed.

Sebastian peered down at her. "Give me your hand."

"C-c-can I trust you?" she said, teeth chattering.

He laughed. "You can, or you can spend the rest of your life as a barnacle on this vessel."

He reached his hand down, and she took it. The cold air made her shiver, and he took off his patched wool coat and put it over her shoulders.

She should have been thankful, relieved, overjoyed to be free. Instead, a wellspring of anger bubbled out of her. "Are you a madman? You could have killed me!"

"Highly unlikely." His lips were pulled into a smile, yet there was warmth in his expression. "I learned weeks ago that you are unstoppable."

On board, a smuggler was lolling against some boxes. Sebastian went to him.

"How is it, Jem?" Sebastian asked with more concern than she would have expected.

More than he had shown for her, certainly!

"Just a graze."

Sebastian gave him a handkerchief to stanch the wound.

The rest of the smugglers—the ones who had not gone overboard—were turning the boat around and rowing back toward the shore. Quimby, unmasked, had a blue lump the size of an egg on his temple and was lashed to a crate. Violet just refrained from going over to the man and kicking him.

She made do with trying out some of her father's more colorful epithets. Quimby sneered back at her until Sebastian stuffed a kerchief in the man's mouth.

When he turned back to Violet, he was smiling and pulling off his beard. "I never knew you had quite such a colorful vocabulary."

She planted her hands on her hips. "I have a few choice words for you, too!" she exclaimed. "Why did you let me think I was about to die?"

"I am sorry," he said. "You gave Jem and me quite a fright, you know. We were not expecting Quimby to have company. I had to send for reinforcements." He nodded to the orange flag. "I calculated that the sea would be safer than the deck once the fighting began—hence your drenching."

Her teeth chattered. "Oh th-thank you!" she quipped, burrowing in the big coat.

"By the way, what were you doing with that blaggard?"

"Quimby caught me when I followed him into a cave," she explained, shivering.

"Why would you do such a shatter-brained thing?"

This was difficult to admit. "I mistook him for Binkley, who I thought might be going to kill himself."

"What?"

"At the ball he had sounded so desperate . . ."

She shivered slightly, and he held her close. It was so comforting to lean against him, to soak up the warmth radiating from his chest, that she could not bring herself to pull away. Tears stood in her eyes—tears of relief. She never thought she would be so happy simply to be alive. To be safe in Sebastian's arms. But now that she was safe, he had some explaining to do.

"Were you as surprised as I was to discover it was Quimby who was the traitor, Sebastian? You never once mentioned *him* in your list of the local suspicious characters."

"Very witty, my dear. But actually, Cuthbert and I had started to suspect Quimby after the theft at Mrs. Blatchford's—we assumed that he had mislaid the plans he had stolen in London and was looking for them. We just never realized where exactly the plans were until this morning. Fortunately we were only just a little behind Quimby. We also weren't sure if he was acting alone or was in cahoots with Binkley. All was made clear this morning when I chanced to have a conversation with Freddy that revealed where the plans had gotten to— they were somehow tucked into a book that Mrs. B. loaned Hennie."

"But why did Quimby hide them to begin with?"

"I suspect that it had to do with that room search that took place the day after their arrival—you'll recall Binkley complaining that Quimby was in a temper at the prospect of having his room searched? He must have hidden them in the library and the book was loaned to Hennie before he had a chance to retrieve it."

"I can't believe Hennie of all people has had dangerous government secrets all this time! And it was Freddy who pointed this out to you?"

Sebastian nodded. "He also reminded me who Quimby's previous employer was—a man who we had always assumed was a spy himself. It now looks like we may have been wrong in that assumption and Lord Waring may have been murdered before he could turn his valet in to the authorities."

Violet opened her mouth to ask another question—for

she was still a bit at a loss—when the boat made land. At the water's edge, a few locals who had heard the gunfire or seen the many soldiers had gathered and helped pull the boat to a patch of sand. Freddy was among them. Violet thought his eyes might pop out when he saw her.

"Violet! Good heavens, what happened?" he asked. "We heard gunfire at Trembledown, and then Barnabas Monk said he had seen soldiers in town. We all thought the French had landed!"

Cuthbert, who had been watching the whole operation from the sea walk, looked concerned at this news. "I hope the ladies are all right!"

The ladies? Violet could not help thinking. *She* was wet, cold, and had nearly been frightened out of her wits, but Mr. Cuthbert was concerned for Hennie's welfare?

Freddie laughed. "Oh yes. Hennie and Aunt Augusta have barricaded themselves in the cellar, and I left Sophy changing into her best dress in case she is called on to care for the sick and wounded."

Violet laughed.

He looked at her again, taking in her wet hair and the patched coat. "What happened to you?"

"It is a long story, Freddy. It might take a while to explain, and I am still unclear on all the details of the adventure myself."

And before she could even begin, there was more important work to do. Quimby's bag was gone through. One of the first things they pulled out was *A Short History of the Lands and Edifices of Cornwall*; the book had several pages glued together in the back, inside of which was hidden the missing report containing enough information to see Quimby hanged for treason. Sebastian gave this to the authorities at the same time he handed over his prize prisoner.

"Mrs. Blatchford's jewels are in his bag, too," Violet said, "along with diamonds. I rather think that they belong to Mr. Jacobs." She improvised this last part; perhaps they would go some way into hauling Binkley out of debt.

She informed them all of what Quimby had told her in the cave, minus the insulting comments about goose-egg-sized buttons.

"That villain!" Freddy said, when he learned of all the evildoings of the valet he had previously held in such high esteem. "I don't suppose anyone will be wearing Waring's Variation on the Mathematical next season!"

Violet touched his arm. "Sebastian said if it weren't for you, they never would have caught Quimby. Which would have meant important England's secrets would have gone to France, and to Napoleon. You may have changed the course of history, Freddy."

The young man blinked in amazement. "By heaven! It's like that saying about for a want of a nail the horse was lost, for want of a horse the battle was lost, and then the war, and the kingdom. And I'm the nail!"

Violet laughed. And when she realized how wonderful it was to be alive, on solid ground, and actually laughing, she began to cry.

That night, after the tale of the day's excitement had been told again and again to the amazed ears of all the others at Trembledown, Violet felt the need to be alone. She walked outside. It seemed impossible that this day had yielded such high emotion, such intrigue and danger, and yet now all she was left with was a headache and a sore shoulder that didn't even require an interesting-looking sling.

She sank down on a bench near her newly planted lilacs and took a deep breath of the sea air.

"What now?" a familiar voice asked.

She jumped, not only because the words so mirrored her own, but because the voice was Sebastian's.

He had come over with Mr. Cuthbert. Her edict of this morning that she wished to see him no more seemed to have been ignored. Indeed, she could not say that she did not wish to see him. She just wished . . .

Well, it was difficult to know what she wanted. Her emotions were all a jumble.

"I don't know," she said, confused.

There was just a little room on the bench next to her, but naturally that did not keep Sebastian from sitting next to her. To be squeezed up against him, their thighs touching, was more intimacy than she was prepared for. And yet she couldn't bring herself to stand.

"I know what the wisest course of action is."

"I've no doubt you think you do." She shook her head at him. "You are always full of ideas."

His eyes shone in the moonlight, causing a tightening in her chest. "I would like to renew my offer to buy Trembledown from you."

"My asking price has gone up," she warned him.

"I will pay what you desire." He added quickly, "Within reason."

She laughed. "Ah, but sometimes I think we have very different ideas about what is reasonable."

"Do we? I hadn't noticed."

"Naturally!"

"You still believe I am arrogant and high-handed?"

"Without a doubt." She smiled. "But I admit there is more to you than I previously thought."

Encouraged, he reached for her hands and covered

them with his own. "Then I have another proposition for you. Let's consider Trembledown your dowry and have done with it."

She tilted her head. "Done with what?"

"All of this dancing about the main issue."

"What, exactly, are you suggesting?"

He looked thunderstruck. "Only that which I suggested before and you so foolishly rejected out of hand. That you marry me."

"Foolishly!" she exclaimed. "As if I should leap at the opportunity!"

He looked disturbed by her outburst. As if she were being stubborn beyond all reason. "Surely you must admit that you aren't indifferent to me!"

She tried to deny it but could not. He gave her hands a tighter squeeze. "Violet, if you knew how I felt when I saw you emerge from that cave. You must promise to be more careful after we are wed."

She sighed in disgust. "There you go again, my lord. Skipping a step."

"What step?"

"You are already dictating my behavior before you have successfully elicited an agreement to this marriage."

"But you must agree that it is not good for you to be chasing after criminals."

"I was not chasing him! I just happened upon him."

"Well! I would not want my wife to be kidnapped too often, you know."

She did not know whether to laugh or cry. "You are impossible!" she exclaimed. "You do not listen!"

He drew back in offense. "No more than you do, I expect."

"And there is our problem. I will not be bullied. I do

not want a husband who expects me to blindly obey his edicts. One such was enough for a lifetime."

"And I do not want a stubborn, headstrong wife."

She stood. "Then perhaps you have chosen wrongly and I am not the lady for you. And now, if you will excuse me, I have the headache and need to retire. Good night."

He stood and bowed, but she could not help noticing the thunderstruck expression on his face. As if he had never expected any woman to reject his proposal of marriage, much less have it happen twice in one day.

Violet sneaked up to her room without seeing the others. She could still hear Sophy's laughter floating above all the others', and she was not in a mood to join in the levity. In fact, it was hard to remember when her heart had felt so heavy.

Headstrong? Well, of course she was headstrong. What did he want? A weak-willed little fool?

What had happened to Sebastian? He once had said that marriage should not be without passion, but where was his passion now? As the Brute, he had swept her off her feet. As Sebastian he seemed now only to believe in a romantic variation of *noblesse oblige*. It was heartbreaking.

She was determined to be no one's passive wife ever again, no matter what title or position accompanied such an alliance. She'd already had one man marry her for her money. She would not consent to marry another who considered such a step merely expedient.

As her head hit the pillow she felt a tear trickle down her cheek. And yet, having had a taste of true love, how could she renounce that, either?

"I do not understand women," Sebastian announced. Cuthbert, who had pulled a chair close to the fire, leaned back with his feet propped up on a stool and his hands threaded in his lap. "I have come to the conclusion that they are wonderful creatures, if you find the right one."

"But what if the right one is simply maddening?"

Cuthbert chuckled, a sound that still took some getting used to. How very changed a man was John Cuthbert these days! Sebastian could still remember standing in his friend's office and discoursing on the unfathomability of females. Now he spoke as if he were an expert on relations with the opposite sex.

"The key, St. Just, is patience."

This was too much! "I don't recall your being overly patient this morning when you tore out of the house for Trembledown to blurt out your proposal."

Cuthbert was unmoved at being reminded of his earlier frenzied, uncombed state. "The other key is to know when to seize the moment."

"I see. So now you are an authority on romantic advice?"

The man shrugged modestly. "I believe there is a verbal gem about not arguing with him who achieves a successful result."

"No—you have had a great success, and I congratulate you. I, however, fear I must limp away from the dueling field in defeat."

"Nonsense!" Cuthbert exclaimed. "Come, St. Just. It is not like you to give up without a fight."

"But I have tried everything. I have flirted and wooed as I never have before. I brought her hams. I have made love to her until it is most improper that we do not marry, and I have asked her to marry me. Twice. And I have been refused both times for my trouble!"

"Ah, but remember, it is always darkest before the dawn."

Love seemed to have turned the man into a fount of

platitudes. "I expect she would have given a proposal from Robert the Brute more serious consideration than she gave to mine."

Cuthbert's lips turned up in amusement. "I expect you are sorry that you have had to hang up your Brute disguise."

Sebastian shrugged. It was true. He had felt a little bereft this afternoon, realizing his days hobnobbing with smugglers were at an end. Now that he had been seen by so many catching Nero, the Brute disguise would no longer be effective. Except, perhaps, at Minerva Plimpton's next masquerade ball.

"That mask was rather cursedly stuffy to wear, actually," he admitted.

"But it gave you a bit of dash."

Sebastian smiled. "I suppose it did at that."

"Women have a weakness for that particular quality, I've found."

Sebastian tried to remember when Cuthbert had shown dash, but gave up the attempt in short order. Instead, he thought of Violet and how enraptured she had seemed when she peered up into his mask.

"One good thing about all this," Cuthbert said. "I think we have found a valuable asset in young Freddy Cantrell."

Sebastian nodded.

"You say he is just out of university?"

"Finishes next term, I believe."

"We should see what we can do for the boy. The government needs all the sharp knives in its drawer that it can lay hands on."

"True."

The two men stared into the fire for a few moments longer.

"Yes," Cuthbert mused on a long, regretful sigh, "it is a shame you must have done with the Brute."

Sebastian stared down at the fire as a devilish idea occurred to him. It was foolhardy. Risky.

But would it work?

He pulled his gaze away from the embers and turned to Cuthbert. "Perhaps I am not ready to hang up my mask just yet."

Chapter Nineteen

The carriage trundled along at such a slow pace, Violet feared it would take forever to leave Cornwall behind them. They were going, at last, to Bath. But only for a brief holiday and to settle Violet somewhere suitable. Hennie was anxious to go to London to shop for her trousseau. Sophy was eager to return to London to attend more parties and create more mischief. Augusta wanted to return herself and Lancelot to their home off Grosvenor Square.

And Violet was simply anxious to go anywhere where she was unlikely to meet up with smugglers or marquesses. Hence, destination Bath.

The days at Trembledown since the capture of Quimby had been a misery. Of course she was happy for Hennie, and glad to have her sister with her. Everyone rejoiced that Freddy seemed to have found a patron in the Marquess of St. Just, who promised to use his connections to find Freddy a position in the government. It was a very propitious beginning for a youth who had previously seemed a hapless second son.

But to be so near Sebastian, to hear of him constantly

and yet see him not at all was a trial. Freddy had gone to Montraffer several times at Sebastian's invitation and was there now as a guest. Hennie and Cuthbert were back and forth between the two houses on a daily basis. But Violet had not seen the marquess since she had refused his second proposal of marriage.

Not that she regretted it.

Not too much.

But oh! If things had been different. What if there had been no Brute, no intrigue? What if they had met simply as neighbors?

She tried to imagine it . . . and yet found that she could not. Without the Brute, without the excitement of the past weeks, Sebastian would seem to her just like all the other noblemen she had met over the years. Full of a self-importance and condescension. To know the man capable of living a dual life—though he had done so at her expense—set him apart from the pack.

Sophy sighed. "It is too bad Freddy stayed behind with Cuthbert and the marquess. I think he would enjoy Bath."

Hennie scolded Sophy. "You should be glad that Mr. Cuthbert has taken such a particular interest in Freddy. He says the boy has a brilliant future ahead of him."

Sophy laughed. "I cannot imagine that fribble working for the government. Yet I suppose it is better than his joining the family woolen mill."

"I don't know about that!" exclaimed Aunt Augusta, who owned a large interest in that enterprise. "I find it a most stimulating business."

"Yes, because it makes money for you," Sophy pointed out.

Aunt Augusta roared in agreement. "Precisely so! There is nothing more stimulating than to have all one's dibs in tune."

Their laughter was interrupted by a gunshot. Violet's stomach flipped as the carriage jerked to a stop. The four women exchanged alarmed glances.

"Good heavens!" cried Hennie. "It is just like that other time."

Violet frowned. "Don't be ridiculous."

And yet, there was shouting outside, and she could swear that one of the voices sounded like . . .

But that was impossible.

Utterly impossible!

The door swung open, and when a long pistol shot through the door, Aunt Augusta pulled a growling Lancelot to her bosom.

It was, very clearly, the Brute. Violet's heart started pounding violently. What on earth was he doing?

Sophy sagged against her seat cushion in relief. "Good heavens! You nearly scared us to death."

The Brute growled at her. "Shut up, you!"

Sophy laughed. "All right. Just tell us what you want."

The Brute's dark gazed moved slowly from one to the other of them, until it finally alit on Violet. "You," he said. "I want you."

Oh, for heaven's sake. What kind of stunt was this? She opened her mouth to protest, but he grabbed her arm.

"C'mon with ye. We haven't got all day, Highness!"

She gasped for air. "Wait!"

But before she knew what was what, he was yanking her through the door.

She called after her sister. "Sophy! Hold the carriage!"

Sophy was leaning out the window and talking to their coachman. "I think we can dispense with Bath, Hal." Looking back at her captured sister, she smiled and waved. "We shall see you in London!"

Hennie stuck her head out a window and waved at her.

"Do not forget about his mask, Violet. To see his face is certain doom!"

She and the others in the coach laughed, and to Violet's horror, the women put their heads back in the carriage and it trundled on.

The Brute—*Sebastian*, she corrected herself in disgust—mounted his waiting horse and pulled her up onto his lap. She landed with a wince.

"This is outrageous!" she cried. "What do you think you're doing?"

"Kidnapping you."

That was apparently all the explanation he intended to provide her. He cantered the horse over the moors and down to the cliff overlooking the sea. When finally they were at an area far removed from anything she recognized, with just a cliff to one side of her and exposed rolling hills everywhere else, he stopped and dismounted and tugged her down, too.

"Now," he said. "Kiss me, Highness!"

She pressed her hands against his chest, but he was too fast for her. His lips descended on her mouth, warm and inviting. The kiss she had dreamed of so often! Angry as she was, she was powerless against it.

"What are you doing?" she protested when he pulled her down.

"I have been told there is something lucky about third times. So for the third time, I am asking you to be mine."

"And what makes this time different from the previous two?"

His gaze burned into hers. "Because this time I am a desperate man. You have humbled me. Love has knocked me off my self-styled pedestal. I love you, Violet."

Finally. Love. Why had he not said so before?

Probably for the same reason she had not. Too much pride.

"Oh, Sebastian!"

"And you know what else is humbling? I had to take a lesson in romance from John Cuthbert!"

She laughed, and he pulled her closer, so that their lips were tantalizingly close. "Dear Violet, do you remember what you said to me in the cave? You said you had never known passion."

"I have now," she admitted breathlessly. "With you."

"Together, you have passion and I have dash," he said. "What good are we apart?"

She shook her head. "No good at all."

He grinned, yet his expression still showed anxiety. "Will you be mine, Violet?"

She would have dearly loved to hold him in suspense, but she could not. She was too happy.

And yet, she did have one request yet. "Will you do me one favor?" she asked.

"Anything!"

"Take off your mask."

He squinted at her in bewilderment. But when she nodded at him that this was what she truly wanted, he complied with her request.

"There!" she exclaimed. "Hennie was right. She said it would be my doom."

He continued to look at her with a bemused expression.

"I am doomed to be yours," she vowed. "Forever, Sebastian."

A joyous smile lit his face, and his lips touched hers. The kiss—the first of many that day—lasted till they were both breathless. It seemed almost that fate had brought them together to save them from themselves.

From out of her sensual fog, Violet gasped.

Sebastian pulled back. "What is it?"

"We cannot marry after all!"

His joyous expression shattered. "Why ever not?"

"I promised Peabody that I would not marry a man who already had a butler, and you have Griggs."

Sebastian had one more trick up his sleeve. "Ah, but my London home is entirely butlerless at the moment. What do you think of that?"

"I think we must get back to Trembledown at once and tell Peabody that we are going to be a marchioness. He will be *so* pleased!"

Sebastian tossed his head back and roared his approval of that plan.